# DEADLY HOLIDAYS
## A COLLECTION OF MINDHUNTERS HOLIDAY NOVELLAS

## ANNE MARIE BECKER

ANNE MARIE BECKER

*Three stories for the other two of my "Three."*
*Kim Law and June Love,*
*I value your friendship, love, and support so much.*

# CHRISTMAS STALKING

## A MINDHUNTERS HOLIDAY NOVELLA

*For all who believe in the magic of the holidays.*

*And for Mom, Dad, Tod, Lorilee, and all of my loved ones who taught me the value of family.*

# CHAPTER 1

MATT HANEY LOVED HIS LITTLE SISTER, BUT HE WAS GOING TO KILL her. "Were you drunk when you came up with this idea?"

"She's nice," Becca insisted for the fourth time.

*Nice.* Matt cringed, his reflection distorted in the golden ball he was hanging on his parents' eight-foot Christmas tree. Fresh pine scent filled his nostrils every time he leaned in to decorate a branch.

"*Really* nice." In case he hadn't received the memo. "She's different. More…artsy. But I'm sure you'll have a lot in common."

"I'm sure." He'd prefer a little naughty over nice this Christmas. But only with the right woman.

His sister, also fluent in sarcasm, noted his lack of enthusiasm with a frown. "What? I thought you'd want someone outside of the usual lawyer scene."

Actually, he enjoyed the company of his fellow lawyers just fine. Which was good, since he spent most of his time building a reputation at the law firm where a sixty-hour workweek was typical. There was one lawyer in particular he liked way too much, and he wouldn't mind getting on Santa's naughty list with her. But he didn't dare share that tidbit with Becca, who was like a cat ready to pounce on its prey at the slightest sign of surrender.

He'd appeal to her common sense instead. "Let's be serious. A blind date on Christmas Eve here, surrounded by our family? No freaking way that's going to go well." Thirty-three years old, he'd settled in a small, remodeled, bungalow-style home within a minute's drive of his parents' Jefferson Park neighborhood northwest of Chicago. He wasn't too manly to admit he was a homebody at heart. And he didn't want to share his family time with a stranger.

"We all just want you to be happy."

He dropped a tangled ball of silver tinsel so that it landed in a glittery heap on top of her short blond hair, and grinned at the elfish image she presented. "There. Now I'm happy."

"No fair." She scooped up the glittery ball and tossed it back at him. It tumbled down his chest and clung to the ambitious pipe cleaner antlers of the reindeer on his ugly sweater—winner of last year's annual Haney Ugly Sweater Contest.

She scowled up at him, and he could hear her mentally cursing his towering height. She was a slender five and a half feet, whereas, on occasion, he had been compared to a Viking.

"Can't help it." His wide grin dispelled any indication he experienced remorse over their height difference. It was in his genes, as well as those of their three older brothers—who'd conveniently found excuses to duck out early on the decorating, the sneaky bastards. Apparently, the height portion of the twisted helix had skipped their sister. But Becca had made up for the difference, finding other ways to be mega-tough over the years. All five siblings, however, had various shades of blond hair and brown eyes in common.

Becca skillfully transferred the silver strands from his reindeer's antlers to the tree. The decorating was a Christmas gift to their parents, who'd be returning from a romantic Colorado ski getaway just in time to host the Haney Christmas Eve Extravaganza tomorrow evening. Matt pretended to grumble about the hours of decorating, but he loved every minute of it. Loved his family. Hell, he even loved the new, hideous, itchy sweater in his closet, ready to debut tomorrow night.

"So... The Date," Becca began again.

Matt plucked a candy cane from the tree and stuck it in her mouth. "No."

Becca transferred the candy cane to her husband, Diego Sandoval's, mouth as he returned from the kitchen with a tray of Christmas cookies and hot cocoa, God bless him. Diego accepted the peppermint treat and sucked on it with a wicked grin that was certainly solely for his wife. Matt snagged the tray before it was forgotten and dropped on the floor.

"You could use some feminine influence," Becca told Matt, not missing a beat as she handed Diego an ornament to hang on a higher branch. Over her head, Diego cast Matt a sympathetic glance. "I saw that." She jabbed Matt's arm.

Matt rubbed at the spot. "Hey, he's the one who rolled his eyes."

"You need to loosen up."

"You mean lower my expectations?"

"You lawyers always have to nail down the verbiage."

"Doesn't make it less true." Matt shook his head. "I'm not willing to settle for less than everything I want."

He'd dated before, though serious relationships had been few and far between. It wasn't that his expectations were unrealistic, but they were high—his parents' fault. Dolly and Donald Haney's solid, loving marriage had set the standard, and it would be a hard one to match. Still, Becca and Diego were doing a darn good job giving it a go and succeeding. Matt couldn't deny the evidence staring him in the face. True love did exist. But maybe it wasn't for him. Besides, with limited time to date as he worked his way up the ladder at Walters and Hammond, he wasn't sure he had the time to find his match, if she existed.

*She does exist, and you have found her.*

He shook off the image of the woman who was never far from his thoughts, irritated that his heart couldn't seem to accept what his brain knew—no matter how much heat they generated between them, he and Assistant State's Attorney Gwendolyn Pierce weren't right for each other. Gwen wasn't wife or family material. Sure, she checked off most of the boxes for his fantasy woman. Sharp wit and a sense of humor were keys. And the attraction was definitely there. The woman had legs for miles, expressive, almond-shaped hazel eyes, and silky chestnut hair that made him think of a stout beer, satisfying and rich.

But she was already married—to her work. Relationships required compromise and Gwen was incapable of bending, a fact he'd discovered when he'd attempted to date her a few months back.

"She's very sweet," Becca insisted. Matt had to rewind a moment to realize she wasn't talking about the woman in his thoughts, but some other woman who was dateless on Christmas Eve.

He grunted. "Sweet *and* nice? Tell me she loves cats and she's a triple-threat." But maybe soft and predictable was better than driven and sharp. Again, Gwen came to mind. Irritated, he spun back to the tree and resumed draping tinsel on its branches, one strand at a time, as his dad had taught them.

"I'm sure there'll be chemistry too." Becca's comment was punctuated by Diego's snort, followed by his *oomf* as her elbow connected with his ribs.

"No offense, Sis, but a family gathering isn't the place to discover whether I have chemistry with a woman. Especially when we're all wearing ugly sweaters."

"It's the best place to figure out if she'll fit in, and the best time to see if she has a sense of humor, which I know is important to you. No sense wasting time if she doesn't like our family, right? You could humor me for just an evening," Becca tried again when Matt didn't submit to her plan to shove him into the dating pool.

"What kind of woman doesn't have plans of her own on Christmas Eve? Why would she rather spend the day on a blind date with a stranger's family?" He shuddered at the thought. But then his stubborn mind drifted back to Gwen. She probably wouldn't have plans for Christmas unless it involved work. Would she even notice the holiday? Or maybe she'd see the snow and dream of their days together at the beach—and in the hotel room —while they'd attended a mutual friend's week-long destination wedding in Jamaica. They hadn't planned to hook up, but their attraction had been undeniable…until they'd returned to Chicago.

Becca snapped her fingers in front of his face. "Hey, where'd you go?" A light came into her eyes. "You already have a woman on your mind."

"Busted." Diego coughed the word into his hand.

Matt kept his expression carefully neutral. "Nope. Just letting my thoughts drift to protect myself from your unrelenting assault."

Becca eyed him and her voice took on a sly tone. "Fine. Keep your secrets. I'll find out soon enough." She handed them each an ornament. "Get back to work. Mom and Dad will be home in a couple hours, and this place needs to sing holiday season."

The Haney home already displayed enough Christmas spirit to choke a reindeer. He'd draped the boughs of holly over the mantel and wound them up the banister to the second floor, hung a ball of mistletoe in the front hall, and set up the tiny Dickensian village his mom collected. Sure, a few pieces had been broken and glued back together, but he could remember setting the thing up each year, and his father's good-natured grumbling about urban sprawl as the town grew. But this house was where Dolly and Donald had raised five children, and it had the normal scuffs and dents of a much-loved, well-used home. Matt wanted that for himself some-day. He'd even start a little holiday village, if the woman of his dreams desired it. Maybe it could be beach-themed.

The doorbell rang, saving him before his thoughts once more settled on Gwen.

"I'll get it," Becca said.

"She means well," Diego said when she was out of range.

Matt sighed. "She always does. But this time, she needs to stay out of it." He couldn't imagine the stress of entertaining a stranger during what should be family time. "I've been looking forward to a nice, normal few days off—except for wiping the floor with you and my brothers during the game, of course."

Diego laughed. "Don't expect that to happen again. I went easy on you last time, being the newbie and all."

Matt had to admit that Diego had fit right in when it came to their family festivities. And touch football, played in the neighborhood park right across the street, was one of the biggest, most competitive traditions at any Haney gathering. Diego had experienced his first game at Thanksgiving, and now he wanted his shot at redemption.

"Yeah, but have you factored in the snow?" Matt smirked as Diego glanced out the window. Sure enough, flakes were beginning to fall. By tomorrow, two or three inches were supposed to have accumulated.

Becca came back with a small package in her hand and a sly smile for Matt. "You really do have an admirer in your life. This was left on the doorstep, but it's got your name on it. Who's it from?"

He eyed the small red velvet box with the white satin ribbon tied in a bow. Sure enough, his name was on a tiny tag. "Unless there's a note, I don't have a clue."

"A mystery?" Becca, a security expert at SSAM—the Society for the Study of the Aberrant Mind—where she and Diego, an ex-NYPD detective, worked to hunt down violent criminals and protect the innocent, was both delighted and worried. She had reason to be concerned, as she'd had a secret admirer of the not-so-nice kind in her past.

He reached out and placed a comforting hand on her shoulder. "I'm sure it's harmless." At least, he hoped it was.

"But you have no idea who it could be from?"

He took the box from her. "I received another box, identical to this one, a couple days ago at my office."

Diego straightened, eyeing the gift. "A coworker?"

"Not sure. The first box contained a framed picture of me as a child." It had been a mystery Matt hadn't had time to explore. "I'd guessed some kind of practical joke or secret Santa thing from work. Whoever it is put some time into it if they dug out my third grade school picture. All I bought my secret Santa was a mono-gramed flask."

"And now that they've sent one to our parents' house?" Becca studied the box more carefully. All thought of decorating was gone as she honed her deductive skills on this new puzzle.

"It wouldn't be too hard for a coworker to get my address, or even my parents', I suppose."

Becca jerked her chin toward the box. "Open it."

The tiny thing suddenly felt like a hundred pounds. He pulled the ribbon loose and opened the lid. Inside was another two-by-three-inch picture frame. The shiny silver edges caught the lights from the tree and gleamed in multi-color. With one finger, he hooked the loop of red satin ribbon that made the frame an orna-ment and lifted it out of the box. "The picture inside is different, but otherwise this is exactly the same."

Diego examined the photo. "You, in court?"

"Appears to be." He was in pristine suit-and-tie, arguing a murder case to get the defendant acquitted. He could see his client from one of November's cases in the background.

"And the other picture you received was your third-grade school photo?" Becca asked. A frown tugged at her lips. "You didn't think that was odd?"

"Like I said, at the time, I figured it was some office joke, or maybe from one of you guys. Anyone could have gotten it from an old yearbook." His siblings often played practical jokes on each other. But in the three days since he'd received the first box, none of his family or his coworkers at Walters and Hammond had stepped forward to claim credit.

"As a semi-public figure who regularly defends criminals—" Becca began.

"They're not always guilty," he interrupted. As she was often on the side trying to put the guilty in prison, it was a recurring refrain.

"—you've got to be aware you could be a target."

He sighed. "Can we focus on the 'being merry' part of Christmas, please? I could use some normalcy." The recent case list had been demanding. Accused criminals didn't take a break for the holidays. And they each needed a defense lawyer.

"Do you remember this trial?" Becca pressed, pointing to the most recent framed picture.

Yeah, he remembered. Just as he remembered the prosecutor he'd gone up against that week.

Gwendolyn Pierce.

A whoop of laughter and the raucous notes of "Grandma Got Run Over by a Reindeer" drew Gwen's attention from the brief she'd been reviewing. She scowled at her closed office door. Beyond, the Cook County State's Attorney's Second Municipal District office holiday party rumbled on without her.

Another burst of laughter from beyond the thin door had her tucking her buds into her ears and dialing up the classical music that helped her focus. Part of her resented that she was enforcing a work lockdown on herself. But if she wanted to make a run at a promotion at one of the largest prosecutor's offices in the country, this was the price she had to pay.

Besides, Christmas was just another day in her life. Her parents, both circuit court judges in Indianapolis, hadn't held strong religious beliefs and hadn't believed in extravagant celebrations—or even non-extravagant ones. So birthdays and holidays had been sedate affairs.

Watching others celebrate always reminded her she was alone. She didn't begrudge her coworkers their bit of fun, but when it interfered with her work...

*Focus.*

She'd managed to return her attention to the document for at least ninety seconds before a knock on her door broke through Vivaldi. She released a strangled groan and yanked the ear buds from her ears. Immediately, "Baby It's Cold Outside" took over.

"Come in," she called. Her eyes widened as Matt Haney entered. A smile tugged at her lips as she caught sight of the sweater peeking out underneath his open jacket. Was that Rudolph's red nose and brown, pipe-cleaner antlers?

Beyond him, someone from the party shouted, "Good luck getting her to have any fun!"

Thankfully, Matt ignored them and shut the door, again muting the party. The air compressed in her throat as his great height and wide shoulders—he could have been a linebacker—filled her office. Dark blond hair was cut in a professional, short style that had a slight wave to it. His eyes were light brown, and always held a healthy dose of humor that charmed women, men, and juries alike. And he only got better as her gaze traveled downward. Firm lips, strong chin, wide shoulders, chiseled biceps. She liked to think she was an independent woman, but for a short while last September, in his arms she'd enjoyed feeling protected and cherished. It had been dangerously addictive. Three months later, she still craved his kisses.

She jerked her eyes away from him. "Didn't expect you." They hadn't spoken or seen each other in weeks, since the November trial when they'd faced each other in court.

"Since you're always working, I figured I'd have more luck pinning you down by just showing up rather than calling." His gaze moved from her to her computer and the open file next to it. "Looks like I was right."

"A master of deduction, as always." Damn, was that him that smelled like fresh mountain air, or had the pine scent come from the party?

"Did you forget it's a holiday?"

She rolled her eyes. "Hardly. The chaos outside that door reminds me every few minutes. Besides, it's the eve of Christmas Eve. Last I checked that's not a holiday."

"Bah, humbug."

"Excuse me?"

"How about having fun? Did you forget how to do that? Or how to relax?" The furrow above his eyebrows grew deeper. Was that anger or concern she sensed from him?

"Maybe," she conceded with a sigh.

That tugged a sly grin from him. "I could remind you."

Oh, she knew he could. He'd been a quite magnificent distraction until she'd nipped that in the bud. "No, thank you."

"Don't refuse, and don't thank me until I've at least tried." He wasn't even trying yet?

She shuffled the papers next to her into a neat stack, just to give her hands something to do. Her fingers twitched with the memory of raking through his thick blond hair as he smiled down at her, as he entered her. Her entire body tightened and quivered. The man was too charming and sexy for his own good—or hers.

"So polite, Gwen. I remember when you let that stuffy veneer slip. I liked it." His eyes glittered, his thoughts clearly back in Jamaica as well.

She'd liked it too. Too, too much.

But someone who planned to work her way up from one of Cook County's Assistant State's Attorney positions to a Bureau Chief had an example to set and something to prove. Especially since she wanted her next big promotion by age thirty-five, only a few years away. She had her whole career laid out, and so far, she'd reached each goal—with hard work and by avoiding distraction. Distraction only led to problems. Her parents had hammered that home time and again.

She was determined to ignore the holiday hoopla and Matt Haney, finish her work, and take a few hours off on Christmas to drink a bottle of wine and cozy up to a good book. That would be her holiday celebration. If Matt and her coworkers thought that made her a scrooge, so be it.

He pressed his hands into her desk and leaned down until his mouth was only inches from hers. "Say the word and I'll take you away from this."

God, he made her feel weak. Weak for him. Because damn it, she was scrambling to think of what magic word he wanted from her. She pushed back in her chair. "I'm good."

"Good enough that Santa will pay you a visit?"

Santa? She had no time for nonsensical, fictional heroes. Or real ones, for that matter. "Why are you here, Matt?"

"Nice to see you too." The sarcasm in his voice contained a hint of hurt that surprised her.

It was always too nice to see him, and that was the problem. "Sorry. I'm in work mode."

"Aren't you always?"

"Not always." She'd allowed him to steer her away from work for several magical days. But magic wasn't real and it certainly didn't last.

"Actually, I did have a reason for coming here. I need to ask a favor of Santa's grumpiest elf."

"One of your clients asking for a reprieve?" They'd run in similar circles for the past five years, but usually on opposite sides of the legal fence. If she were being honest with herself, it was part of the reason she was drawn to him. He could see shades of gray where she was usually a black-or-white kind of gal. And their differences, as well as their similarities, both challenged and intrigued her.

"It's not work-related. I wondered if you'd sent me something."

"Like what? A file?"

Again, he eyed her computer and piles of documents. "No. But I'm certain I'm wrong. You wouldn't have sent me a gift."

"A gift?"

"Clearly, you don't have the time or the desire to spread joy this season. Forget I asked."

"It was important enough to drag you here. What are you hoping I gave you?"

"Where did you get that?" His gaze was on a red velvet box with white ribbon sitting on a bookshelf behind her. "Is that for me?"

She frowned at the angry expression on his face. If she didn't know better, she'd think it was a mix of accusation and alarm. "I thought I made it clear I didn't have time to pursue a relationship."

"I thought so too."

She stiffened as her already heightened defenses went into overdrive. "What are you accusing me of?"

"That package is identical to two others that I received. What's in the third one, Gwen?" His tone was definitely dialed to attack mode. She'd heard it many times in the courtroom over the past few years. But there was enough concern underlying the steely words that she answered him.

"I have no idea. That box was on my desk a couple days ago when I got to the office. I assumed it was something from my boss, a keychain or something everyone received." She'd forgotten all about it, actually.

"You haven't opened it?" He studied her, his initial flare of anger defused.

She released an exasperated huff of air. "I've been busy. I must have dropped it there but had other things on my mind and forgot all about it. I'm guessing it isn't from you."

"It's not from me."

"Then why...?" *Then why do you care*, she'd been about to hurl at him.

"Open it." He scooped it up and set it in front of her.

She untied the white bow and neatly laid the ribbon on the table. The soft, blood-red velvet of the box felt rough against her fingertips and her heart accelerated. "It's not someone's ear, is it?"

"I doubt it's an ear. It'll be okay."

She grunted. "Like hell. There's something about this box that has you worried."

He gave her a grim smile. "I'll admit to that. I've been receiving similar gifts, and while they're not dangerous, I don't think they're meant to spread holiday cheer."

At his encouraging nod, she lifted the lid and went numb. This had to be a sick joke. It definitely wasn't meant to be cheerful.

# CHAPTER 2

MATT PEERED OVER HER SHOULDER AT THE CONTENTS. THE SILVER frame ornament, identical to the ones he had received, was different in one obvious way. It contained a picture of two little girls, their arms slung around each other as they beamed at the camera.

"Is that you?" Matt asked, his question nearly a whisper. Gwen had gone completely still. She wasn't even breathing.

She swallowed. "Yes."

Obviously, there was something more significant about the image than he was aware. He pushed for answers. "Who is that with you?"

"My sister."

"I didn't know you have a sister."

"I don't. Not anymore. She's dead." Gwen's forehead creased and despair clouded her eyes. He resisted the urge to pull her out of her chair and into his arms. "I don't understand why anyone would send me this."

He couldn't imagine losing Becca or one of his brothers. A

spark of anger burned in his belly that someone would hurt her this way. "Someone has a sick sense of humor."

She laid the frame back in its box but continued to stare at it. "I'm guessing you didn't receive the same picture in your boxes?"

"No, but there are similarities. The frames, for one thing. But the first had a photo from my elementary school yearbook."

"How many have you received?"

"Two. The other one arrived today." He looked around her office but didn't spy any other conspicuous gifts.

"Did you receive any others?" he asked. "Maybe at home?"

"Not that I know of." She picked up the frame and studied it. "Why my sister?"

"Could it have been sent by your parents? The similar packaging could be a coincidence." Though he doubted it, he had to consider the possibility.

"I don't think so."

"You should check."

She nodded, her gaze glued to the image. "I'll call them later."

He wanted to push, to urge her to call now while he could hear the answer and maybe help her through the rough memories that had suddenly etched lines on her beautiful face. What had her sister been to her, and what had happened? Seeing the pain shimmering in her eyes, he couldn't bring himself to ask. She swallowed, drawing his gaze to her slender neck.

"You're worried about these little gifts," she said. "Why?"

"There's nothing threatening about the gifts themselves." And yet, the picture in her frame was obviously distressing to her. "It wasn't until one of these boxes showed up at my parents' house this afternoon that I really began to worry. Whoever sent these things knows an awful lot about me. And about you, I'm guessing."

Her jaw dropped and some of the fire and fight returned to her expression. "You thought they were from me. That's why you showed up here out of the blue. It wasn't concern for me, but for yourself."

"No. I mean, yes, but not really."

She stood suddenly, forcing him back a step. "Oh. My. God. You did." Her heels put her at eye level with him. He liked that, liked that her lips were at mouth level, too. He wanted to both kiss her and throttle her in that moment, with the heat flaring gold in her hazel eyes.

"Is it such a stretch to think you might send me something?"

"We haven't exactly been nice to each other."

He stepped into her. "Except for that week we were exceptionally nice to each other."

"But gifts?" She took a small step back, her retreat hindered by her desk. She glanced down at the box. "This wasn't me."

"Obviously."

"Besides, if I have a problem with you, I tell you. I don't play games."

"Except in the courtroom." The sparkle returned to her eyes, and he definitely wanted to kiss her in that moment.

"Except in the courtroom," she agreed. "All's fair in love and war."

Their gazes locked for a long moment, some unspoken message moving on the undercurrent that flowed between them. There had always been this push-pull of desire, like the riptides of the ocean, and they could easily be swept away by it. The difference was he wouldn't mind drowning in her. She, on the other hand, didn't think he was worth the risk.

She looked away. "We should go to someone who can help. Maybe the police?"

"I told my sister."

"Isn't her husband a detective?"

"He's with SSAM now, like Becca. They specialize in the psychology of criminal behavior."

"Right. Well, the police should be involved if you think this is serious."

"We haven't received any direct threats. Besides, SSAM has resources, too."

"Absolutely, they do. But we need this on an official record, in case…" Her words trailed off.

"In case one of us gets hurt?"

The silky strands of her long brown hair shifted against her shoulders as she looked away and nodded, seemingly unable to speak the possibility aloud.

"Then let's go." He reached for her hand, but she pulled away.

"No." She still wouldn't meet his gaze. "I'm finishing up here and then I'll go to the station. You go on ahead and start a report. Text me the address and I'll be there when I can."

"We should go together."

But she wasn't listening. She put the lid on the box and handed it to him with two fingers, as if she couldn't bear to touch it. "Take this with you. I need to work."

"Of all the stubborn—" He cursed as the anger at her lack of concern for her own welfare bubbled up to the surface. Demanding she accompany him wouldn't work. Neither would taking her by the shoulders and dragging her out of here. Or kissing her until she was senseless and receptive to his suggestions, though he'd be willing to give that last one a try.

"I promise I'll be there within the hour. I just need to tie up a loose end or two."

He shoved a hand through his hair. "You're really going to work while the rest of the world is taking a break and you very likely received a threat? If there was ever a time you should put yourself first, should think of your own wellbeing, this is it."

She wouldn't meet his eyes. "I am. I just need a bit more time."

He froze. "You don't want to go with me."

"I need some space."

A mirthless laugh escaped as his chest squeezed. "I've heard that one before." Just a couple months ago, in fact. He'd returned from Jamaica on a high, thinking they would continue what they'd started. She'd shut him down quickly. "Fine. I'll go. Alone. But you're right behind me, right?"

"You bet. An hour at the most."

He stared at her another long moment, but she seemed engrossed in the document on her desk. "I never took you for a coward."

Her head shot up. "Excuse me?"

"In the courtroom, you're a she-wolf, a predator. But alone, with me..." He shook his head. "You're a chicken, scared." A smile curved his lips as her spine straightened. He doubted she knew it thrust her chest out in a way that nearly brought him to his knees.

"I am not."

"You are. You're scared of me." His voice dropped. "And of what we could have together." The truth of his words, while spoken to provoke her, rang true. The flash of guilt, heat, and regret in her eyes confirmed it, and it gave him immense satisfaction to discover that perhaps he wasn't the only one trapped in a confusing maelstrom of emotions.

He strode to the door but stopped to look back at her. "I'm pretty sure the best way to face your fear is head on. I'm ready when you are."

The noise of the office party swirled around him as he walked out, but all he heard was the curse she managed to squeak out before he closed the door behind him. His grin widened. Gwen Pierce wanted him as much as he wanted her. He only had to show her there was nothing to be afraid of.


An hour later, Gwen admitted defeat. Not only was the party outside her door growing increasingly loud, but Matt's parting comments had consumed her thoughts.

*You're scared of me. And of what we could have together.*

She wasn't scared. She was careful, which was why she'd given herself some space and sent Matt on ahead to the police station. If she let herself be tempted by him, what would be the cost? Because relationships always came with a cost—failure, pain, loss. She'd found that out when her sister had been murdered.

Her gaze slid to the spot on her shelf where the red velvet box had sat before Matt had forced her to open it. Some things were better left unopened. Her older sister Jenny had been dead for over a decade. What kind of sick person would force that box of memories open? Matt had suggested she call her parents to make sure they hadn't sent the frame, but she was certain they wouldn't have.

Disgusted by the distractions, something she'd usually over-come with hard work and fierce dedication, Gwen saved the docu-ment on her computer and shut it down. The trial wasn't until the new year, but that was only a week or so away. Besides, tomorrow would be a better day to work. The office would be quiet on Christmas Eve, as the staff had the day off. Hell, she had the day off, too, but there was nowhere she'd rather be. She wanted nothing more for Christmas than a successful trial and one more criminal off the street. That was what made her happy. At least, that's what she told herself.

She put her current file into her leather briefcase and donned her coat and scarf. After visiting the police station, maybe she could settle on her couch with a glass of wine and put these thoughts out of her head. Maybe even try to get a little work done.

A few co-workers called to her as she skirted the fringe of the cubicles the party inhabited, but she escaped their pull by calling back a few greetings and tossing them a smile. She kept her body pointed toward the elevator and her escape. Head down, party sounds fading into the background, her steps slowed at the empty reception desk. She hadn't checked her mailbox in the break room in days. Usually, their receptionist would have delivered anything important, but she'd taken the entire week off.

Suddenly, Gwen's heart beat loudly in her ears. Matt had received a second delivery, a second box. Was one waiting for her?

The break room loomed large down the hall off the reception area. Her feet wouldn't move.

*Oh, just do it.*

What was the worst she'd find? More boxes with more pretty frames? Not exactly life-threatening. Besides, it was more likely she'd find a pile of inter-office memos and another flyer announcing the nondenominational holiday party. "God Rest Ye Merry Gentleman" sounded from the iPod in the party area and someone booed. The song, with its somber, poignant notes had always seemed the downer of Christmas carols. Now, it sent a chill through her. The music abruptly halted and changed to Adam Sandler's "The Hanukkah Song."

She forced her feet forward. The break room was empty of people. The table was piled high with empty casserole dishes and store-bought boxes and bags of food, a staging area for the party. To her left, the rectangular cubbies that served as a mail system for items that didn't demand immediate attention filled the wall. Her eyes went to her cubby and the drumbeat in her head picked up tempo at the sight of a small box, looking like a red velvet cupcake with white silk icing, just like the other box she'd received. Would there be another frame, another reminder of Jenny?

"Secret admirer," a knowing voice said from behind her. She jumped a foot and maybe yelped a little. "Sorry." Gabriel, one of her fellow prosecutors, gestured with his red plastic cup toward the boxes. "It's been there since this morning."

"Why didn't someone tell me?"

"We were under strict orders not to bother you." Orders she'd reinforced with her closed door. Right. "Besides, we have an office pool going about when you'd discover it. And another pool about what's inside. And a third about who it's from." He winked. "Care to share?"

"Not really." She opened her briefcase and scooped the box inside before quickly latching it again.

The party was growing more boisterous and someone shouted, "Conga line," as some modern-day pop song began. The holiday music had apparently been abandoned in favor of something livelier.

"I think the natives are getting restless," she said.

"You don't know what you're missing." Gabriel grinned and saluted her with his cup before leaving.

True enough. She'd avoided the temptations of parties all her life, encouraged by her parents to bury herself in books rather than social obligations, unless those activities furthered her career. Both parents were judges in Indiana, and there had been no doubt that Gwen would follow in their footsteps—especially after Jenny's death. They'd transferred all of their expectations for excellence onto Gwen. Wanting nothing more than to restore her family, she'd accepted the burden. Not that it was all bad. After attending school at Northwestern, Gwen had fallen in love with Chicago. Here, she could build her own destiny.

Thoughts of her parents reminded her she'd promised Matt she'd call them to check if they'd sent the boxes, even though she knew it couldn't have been them. For one thing, they wouldn't have sent them to her place of business. For another, they didn't know about Matt, and had no reason to send him similar boxes. Once inside the elevator, she dug out her cell phone and hit *Dial* as the doors opened to the lobby.

"Hello, Gwendolyn," her mother answered, sounding stiff and formal. And normal.

As she crossed the marble floor to the employee exit, Gwen's scarf suddenly felt tighter and she cleared her throat as if it would help clear years of choked back emotion. "How are you?"

"We're well. The courts are closing for the rest of the week. It'll give us time to pack, which is good since our plane leaves at dawn tomorrow."

"So you are going to Europe, then." Hurrying outside, she hugged her coat tighter and held her bag closer as a burst of cold wind hit her. She hustled toward the parking garage across the street.

"Your dad insists." The sourness in her voice indicated Gayle Pierce would have been just as happy at home, not that they did big things for the holidays. Occasionally, they had a few friends over for a dinner where they could talk politics and debate the current headlines. "I assume you made other holiday plans?"

She could hear the tension in her mother's voice. She didn't want to have to entertain Gwen, which was fine, since Gwen didn't really want to have to sit through a formal dinner at her parents' impersonal dining room. But it felt like there was more to say, like Gwen had missed something. Had she handled something wrong, or not done enough? Not been enough? A familiar pang hit her in the breastbone.

"Did you need something?" her mother asked.

"I was wondering if you sent me a gift."

"No. I donated to a charity in our family's name, as usual." Gwen hadn't had received an actual, personal gift in a while. It supposedly built character.

"So you didn't send anything in a little red box? Anything at all?" She had to be sure before she headed to the station. Inside the parking garage now, she turned into the stairwell and started the climb to the third floor.

"What do you want from me, Gwendolyn?" Her mother's lips would be pressed together, lines forming in her forehead as she tried to figure Gwen out and still managed to give off a vibe of disappointment. Gwen could perfectly see the expression that had dominated her childhood. It hadn't been particularly shocking when Jenny had run away. Oh, Gwen had worried about her seventeen-year-old sister, but Jenny had never wanted to attend college or lead the life their parents had so neatly laid out for them. She'd never wanted to be Jennifer Louise Pierce.

It had only been after they'd learned Jenny had gotten involved in drugs, and when their parents had turned their backs on her, that fifteen-year-old Gwen had worried. Her worry hadn't been acceptable to her parents, so she'd buried it deep, soaking her pillow with tears instead.

"What is it you needed?" her mother continued, impatience heavy in her words. "I have a lot of packing left to do, and I want to catch a few hours of sleep."

Gwen caught her breath at the landing of the third floor and headed for her dark blue compact car halfway down the aisle. She also took a mental deep breath and plunged onward. Her sister had always been a taboo subject. "What happened to the pictures you had of Jenny?"

There was a pause. "Jennifer is dead."

"Yes, I'm aware." Gwen's patience was dead, too, as she stopped at the trunk of her car. "But what happened to the family albums and stuff like that? Did you give them to someone?" Gwen kept a shoebox of pictures and mementos at the small house she rented, but she'd left most of her past life behind when she'd moved to Chicago.

"They're in the attic."

"You're sure?"

Her mother heaved a sigh. "The last time I saw them was before we buried her. I haven't dug them out since. She's best left buried."

Hurt warred with anger. She'd never forget Jenny's sparkle and spirit. Ironically, she hadn't become a lawyer because of the pressure her parents put on her. She'd done it for Jenny.

"I have to go," her mother said, a new edge to her voice. "Have a good Christmas."

"Merry Christmas to you and Daddy." She hung up and stuffed her phone into her pocket.

And that's when she noticed something was wrong with her car. She circled the vehicle, her heart pounding as she saw the extent of the damage. All four tires had been slashed.

# CHAPTER 3

JUST MATT'S LUCK, ONE OF HIS BOSSES AT WALTERS AND HAMMOND, Richard Hammond, had retreated to the office to escape the holiday madness—Rich's phrasing—at his house. He cornered Matt, who had stopped in to grab the other gift box, the first one he'd received, which he'd left in his desk drawer, on his way to the police station. Nearly an hour had passed since Matt had reluctantly left Gwen to her own devices, and he was still trying to get to the police station. Had she gone on ahead of him? Would she wait for him or file a report and leave?

Or would she chicken out and not go at all?

He surreptitiously glanced at his phone, but there were no missed calls or texts from her. He had to hope that wasn't a bad sign, as his boss was still unloading on him.

"Three children, two of them married and with their own kids. Some of them are visiting from out of town, so they're staying with us. Makes for a lot of noise, especially with four grandchildren—all boys under the age of five." Richard shook his head, but his pride in his family shone through.

Matt knew all about the immediate branches of Rich's family

tree—had, in fact, grown up down the street from the Hammond children, who were near his own age—but he listened and made the appropriate sympathetic noises. He typed a quick text to Gwen when Rich wasn't looking. *You ok?*

"Deena's loving all of the company," Rich added, his fondness for his wife evident. "Nobody even noticed I snuck out. I needed a breather."

Matt held up a hand. "Really, no excuse necessary here. I understand completely."

"I imagine the Haney clan is the same when they get together."

"Definitely. None of us have kids yet, but gatherings are always noisy and busy and a heck of a lot of fun. Mom and Dad get home from their ski vacation tonight, and we're all planning to meet up tomorrow. Can't wait to hear how their trip went."

"You can bet Deena will be needling Dolly for details Christmas morning." Gathering at the Hammond house for a cup of coffee or a mimosa on Christmas morning had become an annual tradition. "I predict we'll be scheduling a trip of our own soon. You will be stopping by, right?"

"Looking forward to it."

"If you're not hiding from family, what case dragged you into the office today?"

"Actually, I'm about to head to the police station." Matt glanced at his phone, not bothering to hide it this time. Still no text from Gwen.

Rich frowned, probably mentally reviewing their current case list. "A client?"

"Nobody's in jail. It's me who might need some assistance from law enforcement."

Rich straightened and his gaze sharpened. "What's going on?"

"I've received a couple of strange packages. I didn't think much of the first one until the second one came to my parents' home today."

"What kind of packages?"

"Little boxes containing picture frames the size of ornaments, complete with personal pictures. I'm thinking some kind of stalker."

Rich's frown deepened. "Can't be too careful in today's world, especially in our business. Pipe bombs delivered to judges, anthrax to attorneys via their personal mail... Yes, go see the police. Trust your gut."

"That's not all. Gwendolyn Pierce received a similar gift."

"Pierce? The prosecutor you went up against in the Pritchett case? She's tough competition. What's she got to do with these gifts?"

"Not sure yet, sir." How could he explain that he and an assistant state's attorney had been close enough for him to think she might have sent him a gift? "I happened to stop by her office and saw she received an identical box. She hadn't even opened it yet."

Rich studied Matt. "Miss Pierce is a beautiful woman. Smart, too."

"She is," he replied cautiously.

"And I believe you both attended that wedding in September? Don't look so surprised. I keep my ear to the ground on all the noteworthy lawyers in this area. I suppose I don't have to tell you to be careful—not just with these random gifts."

"No, sir."

"But I'm going to tell you anyway." Rich grinned. "You two are often at odds on these cases."

"I am aware." So aware. The cases in which he'd gone up against Gwen were some of the most challenging and rewarding of his life. He'd enjoyed sparring with her.

He enjoyed her.

Especially when he won.

"What's she planning to do about this from her end?" Rich asked.

"I've told her I'm going to the police. She's supposed to join me." He pointedly looked at his phone again.

Rich pushed up out of his chair. "I should head home, anyway. Deena is expecting me soon. We'll see you in a couple days. Keep me posted on what comes of this, and watch your back."

"Always." With a grin, Matt added, "Good luck with the grand-sons." Rich waved him away with some muttered words about little terrors.

Matt's cell phone rang as he finally made his way down the hall to his office to get the first red box. The caller's number created a familiar pressure behind his breastbone. Gwen had only called him on his cell phone once, to break things off.

"Matt?" There was a tremor beneath her greeting that increased the pressure in his chest.

"What's wrong?" he asked, immediately on alert.

"Someone was here."

"Where? Where are you?"

"The employee parking garage. Someone slashed my tires. I also found another of those gifts in my office mailbox after you left."

He bit back a curse. He should have stayed with her. "I'll be right there. Don't hang up."

"But security's on its way—"

"You can talk to me while you wait, then." He didn't like that she was alone, or that she sounded a little shaky. In the years he'd known her, Gwen had never come across as anything but confident and prepared. With him, she'd only let down her guard once. This made twice. He looked into his work satchel, eyeing his two red velvet boxes and the one Gwen had thrust at him—the one with the picture of someone she'd obviously loved and lost. Whoever was messing with her was going to pay. He added his first gift box from his desk to the two boxes already in his bag. "I'm on my way."

"It's okay. Security will be here any time now. I just... I guess I needed to hear a friendly voice." That she'd thought to call him made Matt's heart swell with an unnamed emotion. "And I can call for a car or cab or something to get me to the police station. It'll be safe." Unless the person sending these strange gifts was watching and waiting for an opportunity to get her alone.

"Stay there. It'll only take me five minutes to get to you from my office." The village of Skokie, Illinois, where she worked was a northwestern suburb of Chicago, and just north of him. Using his shoulder to keep his phone at his ear, he zipped his coat, hitched his bag onto his shoulder, and fished his car keys from his pocket as he hit the parking lot at a run. The winter day brought night early, and it was full dark.

"You're not at the police station?"

"Hadn't made it that far yet. Is anyone with or around you?" he asked as he tossed his things into the back and slid into the driver's seat.

She gave a self-deprecating laugh. "No. I'm such an idiot. Everyone else is either gone or still inside partying. I should have asked someone to escort me out."

"I doubt you knew someone would be looking to slash your tires today." He pulled onto I-94 northbound and moved into the fast lane, grateful traffic was lighter than usual.

"Still, I should be prepared. I know what kind of people there are in the world."

The flicker of humor he'd felt a moment ago snuffed out. "Hang on. I'm nearly there. You still with me, babe?" The endearment slipped out, feeling natural on his lips but she didn't give him hell, which worried him even more.

"God, this is stupid. I can call triple A or something. I'm ruining your holiday. Security's here. I gotta go." Before he could stop her, she'd hung up.

The next few minutes were the longest of his life. He forced himself to breathe, but when she didn't answer when he called again, he cursed the distance between them. It wasn't until he entered the parking garage and found her on the third floor, standing with a uniformed security guard, hugging herself as the guard typed something into a mobile device, that he felt his chest loosen.

Matt quickly parked nearby and jumped out.

"I'll file the report and see if the security cameras caught anyone or anything unusual," the guard was saying as Matt approached. "The tow truck should be here soon. You have a ride home?"

Gwen accepted the business card the guard held out. "I can call a car."

"Or accept a ride from me," Matt said.

After the guard left, Matt circled the car with his phone's flashlight aimed out, eyeing the damage. The blue Volvo was sleek yet dependable, like its owner. There were puncture marks on each tire. No, not just puncture marks. Gouges, their jagged edges indicating the slashing had been done in anger. He returned to Gwen. "For the record, you're not ruining my holiday. And this definitely isn't your fault."

She stunned him by walking into his chest and wrapping her arms around his waist as if she'd never let go. She tucked her face against him and breathed deeply. "Thank you for coming."

He wrapped his arm around her, and her briefcase fell to the ground between them as she clung. A tremor ran through her. He bent his head to speak near her ear. "Hey, it'll be okay."

"I know. I'm just..." She released him and stepped back. The cold, which had permeated the open-air garage, immediately attacked him. Holding her had felt damn good, especially when he was feeling shaky himself. Adrenaline, probably, but also fear for the woman standing before him.

She huffed out a humorless laugh. "They were thorough, I'll give them that. Why would anyone hate me this much?" She bit her lip and looked away. "Forget I asked. There's a long list of criminals I've put away. We should start by looking at the cases in which you and I went up against each other."

He stepped up to her and touched her chin, nudging it upward until her gaze met his. "Nobody hates you, Gwen. They might hate what you did, but you were only doing your job. They don't know the real you." Not like he did.

A wave of possessiveness and protectiveness stunned him. He might not like the circumstances that had forced Gwen Pierce back into his life, but he sure appreciated the opportunity to win her back.

It was nearly nine o'clock when Gwen finally tossed her things to her couch on her way through the living room of the tiny house she rented in Edgebrook. The twin forces of anger hunger made her heels click more loudly than they should against her kitchen tiles. Behind her, the front door she'd left open for Matt closed and he followed her into the kitchen.

"I bet Officer Bates is laughing it up in the break room about now, and here we are starving to death." She peered into the fridge and willed an easy dinner option to appear.

Matt's hand landed on her waist as he leaned in and reached past her with his free hand to snag two beer bottles, hooking his long, strong fingers around their necks. He straightened and his hand was gone in the next moment. "I'm sure he's not laughing at us. Hell, I think he had a crush on you."

She snorted. "Either way, it's obvious he didn't take me seriously." The young officer had told her they probably had some kind of secret admirer on their hands and proceeded to ask Matt all kinds of questions about a possible love triangle with any of the females in his life. Matt had replied that the only females actively *in* his life were his mother and his sister. That had thawed Gwen's heart just a bit—until Bates had then turned to her to ask the same question about the women in her life.

When it was clear neither she nor Matt had received any direct threats—slashed tires apparently weren't high on the severity scale —the officer had given them the condescending "let us know when something more happens" dismissal.

Matt, on the other hand, was taking this seriously, and while Gwen had grumbled a little, she was grateful. He'd insisted on driving her home. Inviting him in had simply been the polite thing to do. Plus, he'd professed an interest in making sure her home was safe. And if she was being totally honest, she wanted him there if she were to discover any more little red boxes with pictures from her past. She still wondered how the stalker had found a decades-old family photo of her and Jenny. Suddenly, she turned and made a beeline for her bedroom.

"Where are you going?" Matt called after her.

"I have to check something." She slid open the door of her closet and reached for the top shelf, lifting the extra blanket that usually covered the box so that she didn't have to see it and be disturbed by memories unless she chose to.

"What are you looking for?" Matt asked from behind her.

"My parents have most of my childhood photos, but I have a shoebox of mementos, and a copy of the picture of me and Jenny that was in that frame was here." She sank onto her bed and stared glumly at the open closet. "It's gone."

The mattress dipped as Matt sat next to her. "When do you remember seeing it last?"

"A couple months ago, maybe?" She pressed her fingers to her forehead. "I can't be sure. I only pull it out occasionally." When she needed to remember why she was doing all of this, needed to remember Jenny. "Someone must have broken in." But again, they had no proof that would get the police involved, beyond filing another report.

"We'll get help." He took her hand. "We'll figure this out."

"We?"

"You're not alone. I'm in this with you."

The ice she'd packed around her heart thawed a little bit. "The police seem to think there is no 'this' to be concerned about. But that second picture…"

They'd opened her second mystery gift while at the police station, and it had been a framed picture of her in the courtroom, during the same case as Matt's second picture. The photos, taken as if an amateur had snapped them covertly while watching the trial, showed Gwen eyeing Matt as he'd picked apart a detective's testimony that had supported the State's case against his client. He'd been magnificent that day, and she'd eventually lost the case.

She stood, needing to pace. "I don't understand what this has to do with me and you. Is it about that case? Mrs. Pritchett was branded a golddigger and her dead husband was a major player in the Chicago business world, but your client was acquitted. Why would she come after us?"

"She wouldn't." Matt reached out to snag her hand and stop her pacing, then pulled her down to sit beside him on the bed. He traced a fingertip over a crease in her brow. "At least you're admitting now that there is an *us*."

"But there isn't. This is only a temporary situation."

"Only because you won't let it be something more."

The intimacy of the moment—reliving the past with him while he sat so close to her on the bed where she spent her nights dreaming about him—was suddenly too much. He'd gotten under her skin before, and she'd forced space between them again. She couldn't go back. Her career was her focus.

"So who seems to think there's something going on between us?" she asked. "Did you tell anyone about our week together?" That one glorious week had become her special secret, a treasure she pulled out and examined late at night, or when she needed a mood booster, or heck, any time it popped into her head.

"I never told anyone." He leaned back on his hands, deceptively relaxed when his eyes remained alert and on her. It was both irksome and comforting. The contradictions kept her on edge of the precipice, unsure whether to jump or run the other way. "But whoever this is seems to be focusing on my good parts and your..." His gaze traveled over her and he cleared his throat. "Well, they don't really know you, apparently, because you have some very good parts, and I have yet to see any bad ones."

She hardened herself against the compliment that had her body melting. "You just love that this person is highlighting your triumphs over me."

He scowled. "Actually, I hate it. It means someone is probably targeting you because of some ridiculous infatuation with me."

She sighed. "That's what I figure too. So, who's obsessed?"

His lips quirked. "I was hoping it was you."

"Well, it's not, so we need other suspects. Someone who thinks I'm a cold bitch trying to steal her man."

"I haven't dated since September."

Since her, he meant. She was still recovering from the shock of that when he paid her the best compliment she'd heard in a long time.

"Nobody who really knows you, who knows how much you care about this job, your clients, and the general public's safety, could ever accuse you of being cold. Your safety is my priority. I assure you I'm taking this seriously." His hand swept back the side of her hair and cupped the back of her neck. She leaned into the tender gesture before she could stop herself. The truth was, today had done a number on her nerves, and she needed the solace he offered.

His head lowered, his gaze holding hers captive. When their lips touched, the heat and shock nearly made her jump out of her skin. And then the familiar taste of him, the remembered pleasure of his mouth, had her jumping over that cliff. She sank into him and closed her eyes against a wave of longing so strong it threatened to suck her under.

He deepened the kiss, his lips opening against hers and coaxing a response. His tongue slid across hers, the wet heat setting off a tightening of her abdomen and a rush of warmth in the parts that wanted to touch him most. Swallowing a moan, she opened to him, letting him warm her from the inside. She breathed him in, taking comfort in his scent as she wound her arms around his neck and met him thrust for thrust, nibble for nibble.

The sound of a stomach growling—she wasn't sure whose— had him pulling back with a soft laugh. His thumbs stroked the sides of her neck and sent a wave of delicious shivers over her skin before he released her to stand and pull her to her feet. "Let's find a restaurant that delivers late. Full stomachs should help us figure out a plan."

She needed food and there was no way she'd sleep tonight without defusing her thoughts, so she agreed. "I suppose feeding me is the least you can do, since this is all your fault."

His deep, throaty laugh tugged at her abdomen. "I'm guessing you haven't eaten since lunch."

Or before. "I can't remember."

His laughter faded and he took her shoulders, turned her and marched her to the living room. "Do you have any takeout menus?"

She removed several menus from a drawer in a side table next to the couch. As he perused their contents, she paced her living room. It wasn't that she was scared, exactly. She wanted action, needed to figure this puzzle out and restore her orderly life. Needed to put Matt back into the little box she'd relegated his memories to before he wriggled his way back into her heart.

"Chinese okay?" he asked.

"Fine." She nibbled at a fingernail.

He eyed her as he dialed the number and gave their order. It didn't escape her notice that he'd selected her favorites. Either he had a good memory of their week together or he'd noted what she'd circled in the menu. Probably both. Why did he have to be so attentive, so damn perfect?

On one of her trips across the room, she stopped near the small

Christmas tree that sat on a corner table. It was adorned in minia-
ture candy canes, red ribbons, and a few sparse ornaments,
including the one Jenny had made for her—a thumbprint
snowman pressed into clay—when they'd been in elementary
school. She traced it with a fingertip before turning to pace again.

He hung up. "Would you sit down?"

"Not sure I can sit still. We should discuss the trial where those
pictures were taken. Maybe the stalker was there?"

"Or had someone take the pictures for him or her." He went to
the side table and tossed in the menus, then removed a legal pad
and pen.

Her briefcase lay on the couch beside her, where she'd flung it.
They'd put the boxes in there after meeting with Officer Bates. She
went to it and removed the frames and laid them side-by-side on
the coffee table. They'd been dusted for prints at the police station,
but their gift-giver had either worn gloves or wiped the frames
clean before sending them. She took the seat beside Matt studying
the pictures.

"These have to be from a woman," she said. "What male would
send such nicely wrapped gifts, take such care to make them
match, tie silk ribbons in pretty bows, and make sure to make me
look like a failure while you look like the success?"

"You could never be a failure." The vehemence in his tone had
her looking at him. The intensity in his eyes touched her.

"Thanks."

"Nothing to thank me for. The times I went up against you in
court were some of the most challenging defenses I ever
presented. Not because of the case matter, but because I knew I
was going up against *you*. You keep me on my toes." He reached
out to brush a piece of hair from her cheek. His thumb hesitated at
her jawline, stroking gently. "It's one of the things I love about
you."

He loved things about her? She opened her mouth to speak, but
no words would come. Tightness pooled in her belly and worked

its way into her chest. Her breath hitched, and she released it slowly as he leaned in and touched his lips briefly to hers. But that was all he did before pulling back again. She fought down a twinge of disappointment.

They spent the next twenty minutes talking about the State's prosecution of Louise Pritchett for the murder of her husband, and how the dead man's family might have motive for revenge against Gwen for failing to put the widow behind bars. Matt had been stunning in his closing speech. The defendant, once acquitted, had moved to Florida, from what Matt could recall.

Surprised at how quickly the time had flown while they'd been lost in memories of the trial, Gwen looked up when a knock sounded on the front door.

Matt immediately stood. "I'll get it." He looked through the peephole before opening the door to pay the deliveryman and accept the box of Chinese food. After the man left, Matt remained in the doorway, his gaze directed downward. When he glanced back at her, concern deeply etched into his brow, her stomach plummeted to her toes.

# CHAPTER 4

Matt's skin prickled with alarm. Their secret admirer had been within feet of them, just on the other side of Gwen's front door, no more than a half hour ago. The two red, white-ribbon-wrapped boxes on her doormat were proof of that. The stalker knew they were here, together. Was he or she watching him right now? Matt looked up and down the dark, quiet street. There were plenty of cars parked along the sidewalks, but no sign of life at this late hour. The stalker was certainly becoming more daring, coming so close while they were just inside. Would he or she also become more dangerous?

He withdrew his phone from his pocket to snap several pictures. The velvet material would make it impossible to lift prints and the police were reluctant to do much without a direct threat, so he scooped the boxes up and turned from the door with Chinese food in one hand and the boxes in his other.

Gwen's gaze roved over the red velvet and her puzzled look gave way to alarm. "Is that…?"

He set the food and boxes on the coffee table, went back to the door to lock and deadbolt it, glanced at the front windows to be sure the curtains remained tightly shut, and then took a seat next to her. "Shall I do the honors?"

She gave a tight nod and he began unwrapping the latest gifts. Each box held the expected silver frame ornament. The difference this time was that one was empty and the other contained a picture of a tombstone. He read the engraving and glanced at Gwen, who had gone white. Her name, birthday, and a death date were inscribed. The death date was simply the current year, no specific day indicated.

"It's not real." Matt stated the obvious because he didn't know how else to console her. "And I'm staying with you so that it will never become real."

"That's ridiculous. You can't stay with me twenty-four-seven."

"Then I'll hire a bodyguard." No way was he letting some crazy woman get to Gwen. With a frown, he glanced around the old, cottage-style house she was renting, noting the archaic windows and doors. "Hell, a security system would be a good idea, too." Matt took out his phone again.

"W-who are you calling, the police?" The slight stammer told him just how freaked out she was feeling.

"Not the police this time," he said. "SSAM."

"Manchester's group? But we're not dealing with a violent repeat offender."

They didn't know that for sure, but he didn't argue. SSAM was a private organization in Chicago headed by Damian Manchester. His daughter Samantha had been the victim of a serial killer. When the police failed to apprehend her killer, the experienced businessman had fought back the best way he could—by founding an agency dedicated to finding repeat violent offenders, including serial killers. Usually, they dealt with cold cases that had fallen through the cracks, like his daughter's.

"My sister works at SSAM. Becca will handle this faster than the police can." Besides, they'd seen what the police could do when there was no overt threat—nothing.

Gwen's eyes traveled over the framed pictures and lingered on the new ones. He moved to sit on the coffee table, at least partially blocking her view and caging her in with his knees. He gripped her hands within one of his as he speed-dialed his sister.

Becca answered within seconds. "Where are you? The gang's all here. The parental units are glowing. They're giving out gifts—just the ones from their trip." Laughter and conversation came from the background.

He closed his eyes and cursed.

"You forgot?" Becca's incredulity was clear. "You were here decorating just hours ago. How could you forget we were going to welcome them home?"

He opened his eyes and met Gwen's gaze. "Something came up."

"It had to have been something pretty damn important."

She was. "It is. That box I got earlier? I got another one, and so did a friend of mine." He squeezed Gwen's cold hands. "It appears we have a stalker."

"We? You and your...friend?" He could hear Becca's heels against tile, and the sounds of their family faded further into the background. "Okay, I found a quiet corner. Tell me about these boxes."

"Still don't know who my secret Santa is, but I'm not the only one getting little surprises." He ducked his head to meet Gwen's downcast gaze, wishing he could read her thoughts. The best he could do was let her know he was there for her, that she wasn't alone. He didn't ever want her to feel alone.

Her gaze lifted. Surprising him, she suddenly gripped his free hand tightly and brought it to her mouth to press it against her lips in a gesture of appreciation.

"Who's the friend? Someone special?" Becca's words pulled him back to their conversation.

"Yes." And that was all he was going to say at the moment. But his sister was in full-on investigation mode.

"Did you two go to the police?"

"Yeah. Just got back about an hour ago. They can't do much without a direct threat. And then we got another pair of gifts just now."

"I'm coming to you. I'll make an excuse and get away. Hell, I should probably bring Diego too."

"Don't. Can you stop by my house in the morning?"

"It's no trouble. Are you at the office?"

"Actually, I'm at Gwen's."

"Gwen? Wait. Gwendolyn Pierce? Your special friend is the ASA you went up against last month?" There was a beat of silence as his sister absorbed that. "And she's receiving pictures too?"

"Yeah, nearly identical gifts and frames. The only difference is the pictures inside. We'll be okay for the night. So far, this hasn't been dangerous, though Gwen's tires were slashed today." At Becca's sharp intake of breath, he hurried on. "I don't want to worry Mom and Dad when they've just returned, especially when we don't know if it's anything to worry about yet. You know how they get."

Becca blew out a breath. "They are looking pretty happy, and they'll be full of questions if I leave now. You sure you're both okay?"

"I'm okay, and I'm going to make sure Gwen's okay." His eyes refused to let Gwen look away, and he silently commanded her to obey the demands he was about to make of her, even though she'd be furious if she knew that's what he was thinking. But he couldn't think past keeping her safe. "Can you make an excuse for me? Something that won't worry them."

"Of course. I'll be at your place in the morning. Be prepared to answer some questions."

He got the message loud and clear. He'd be answering questions about Gwen as well as the packages. "Wouldn't expect anything less."

"And be careful, damn it. You're my favorite brother."

"Why wouldn't I be?" he said with a chuckle intended to put her at ease. After hanging up, he slipped his phone into his pocket and took both of Gwen's hands again. Still cold. He gently rubbed at them. "Becca will stop by to check things out in the morning."

"Here?"

"My place."

"But I should be there."

He nodded. "You will be. You're coming home with me tonight. You don't have any added security, so I'm keeping you within reach at all times to make sure you stay safe." She opened her mouth, and he waited for an objection. Instead, she closed her mouth, a look of resignation crossing her features.

"I don't want to be alone." She shuddered and he moved beside her to pull her into his arms. The soft scent of her hair filled his nostrils and took him right back to that hotel room in Jamaica and the nights he'd held her. "I won't let anything happen to you."

As they pulled up to the curb outside of an updated 1920s brick bungalow home in the Jefferson Park suburb five minutes south of her place, Gwen sat up straighter in the passenger seat, feeling exhaustion give way to curiosity. Matt's home. It was old, but obviously well-maintained. It was also charming, just like him. And dependable and secure and handsome... There seemed to be no end to the positive adjectives that described the man beside her. Not that it was any surprise to her. She'd already known he was perfect. She was the imperfect one, and the reason a relationship between them would ultimately fail. Still, despite the craziness of the day, being with him had put her in a surreal, dream-like state of mind.

As if on cue, fat snowflakes drifted from the sky, melting as they hit the windshield. The two-story house beyond became a shimmering wonderland. Despite the stress of the evening, she smiled. Something about being by Matt's side made her feel like she could face anything.

"What are you smiling about?" he asked, his gaze on her mouth.

"I feel like we're in a snow globe or something." If only that were true, they'd be locked away, safe from whoever might want to harm them. She turned to look back at the quiet street.

"I don't see anyone," Matt said.

"Doesn't mean she isn't there."

He frowned. "You're sure she's a she?"

"Like I said before, the delicate little gift boxes, color-coordinated and adorned with hand-tied ribbon? Silver picture frames? Not to mention the obsession with all of your good qualities to the exclusion of the negative."

He sent her the arched brow again. "What makes you think I have negative qualities?"

She snorted. He was trying to ease her worry with teasing, and something inside of her lightened at his efforts. So she responded in kind. "I spent a week with you, remember?"

"Yes, I definitely do." His brown eyes heated as he gazed at her.

She looked out the window again. "So this is your home?"

He nodded. "It might not look like much, but the interior has been rennovated."

"It's lovely."

"I always wanted to settle near family, but I do like my comforts. When this house came on the market, I snapped it up."

"How close is this to your family?"

He gestured to the left. "My parents live a couple of blocks that direction. In fact, one of my spare bedrooms is full of Christmas presents. Everyone wanted to leave them here because I live closest."

"Everyone?"

"You know about my sister, but I also have three older brothers. With the exception of Becca, who lives in an apartment with

Diego closer to downtown, we live within a ten-mile radius of each other."

Her eyes went wide with amazement that he'd want to be so close to his parents, and that he was so close both emotionally and physically to all of his siblings. A sharp pang of longing struck her. If Jenny had lived, would they have been that close? She liked to think so. But dreams weren't reality. Gwen was alone against the world.

"Let's get inside." Matt said, probably mistaking her shiver for a chill.

The snow had already formed a slick surface on the sidewalks. Colorful holiday lights created a rainbow that reflected on the wet surfaces. He reached into the backseat for the duffle bag she'd thrown together then led her up the walk to his front door. Once inside, he wiped his boots on the mat and told her to wait in the front room as he did a quick sweep of the house, including the upstairs and, apparently, a basement. Gwen kept her phone in her hand, ready to call the police at the slightest sign of trouble. She tried to calm her nerves by listening for his footsteps as they moved throughout the house. As long as he was moving, nobody had attacked him.

To her right, the living room was furnished with a leather couch and chairs and a large flat-screen television. Hardwood floors peeked out from beneath a soft area rug, a brick fireplace, and fleece throw blankets on each of the chairs added comfort and character. A medium-sized Christmas tree and a strand of lights along the fireplace's mantel made it homey. Looking past the living room, she caught a glimpse of a dining room and kitchen at the rear of the house. In front of her was a staircase that likely led to two or three bedrooms, judging by the size of the home. To her left was a small office that was homey but also utilitarian, as the bookshelf behind the desk was filled with law books.

"Can I get you something to drink?" Matt asked as he descended the stairs and took her coat. He acted as if he hadn't just been looking for a boogeyman. Apparently, he hadn't found any monsters.

"Sure." She followed him to the dining area where he sat the Chinese food, which they'd opted to bring with them rather than lingering at her place. Instead of a wall, a large quartz-covered island separated the kitchen from the dining room. Her eyes trailed Matt as he went to a cupboard to get plates. The kitchen was neat and recently remodeled.

"I can warm the food if you want. It might pair with a red wine?" she suggested hopefully. Following the upheaval of the past few hours and the thought of spending the night under the same roof as Matt after so many weeks of dreaming of him, she could use a little liquid courage. Besides that, her body burned for him. Perhaps imbibing would numb her desire.

He grinned. "You read my mind."

Over their warmed-up meals and glasses of pinot noir, Gwen was surprised to find herself relaxing. She sat back and looked over to find Matt studying her.

"What's different, do you think?" he asked.

"Different than what?"

"Than last time we sipped wine together? Or are you planning to run on me again?" There was a hint of hurt in his question that shocked her. She'd always assumed that after the week they'd spent together he'd moved on once they'd each gone their separate ways. It had only been a week, after all. An amazing, perfect week that had stuck with her no matter how she'd tried to forget it. But she'd never thought he'd taken her rejection hard.

She pretended to examine her glass, as if the answer lay in the vintage. "That was a tough week."

"Gee, thanks."

She looked up sharply and saw he was teasing her, but there was a gleam of curiosity in his eyes. "Not you, of course. That was...wonderful." One glorious week spent in Matt Haney's arms.

"Then why'd you back away? You didn't even want to try

dating. And no more lame excuse about a messy breakup. Who's to say we would have broken up?" He leaned forward, earnest in his desire to understand why she'd acted the way she had. They might indeed have been able to make it work...at least for a little while.

"I don't do relationships."

He pinned her with his searching gaze. "Why not?"

"They're distracting. I'm on a mission," she added when she saw that explanation wouldn't be enough to satisfy him. "And I can't lose sight of that."

"Your career, you mean. Does this have to do with Jenny?"

Surprised at his insight, she met his gaze again. "Yes. I vowed I would find justice for others like her. In that one week with you, I lost sight of that."

"But everyone needs down time. Family. Connections with other people."

She started to shake her head in denial, but couldn't. He was right, and his gaze held hers captive. "I've always been driven. It's hard to picture a future different than I always imagined it."

"It's scary to reach for the unknown. Relationships can be messy, but they're worth it. At least, one with me would be," he added with a boyish grin. "And if you decide you want to try, we'd find the right balance of focus and distraction together. After all, you're not the only one with a career to pursue. I understand the dedication and long hours it requires. But I also know how having my family there for me has been my refuge." He let go of her fingers and rose to clear the table.

She sat in thought as he moved around her, poured her the rest of the wine, and removed their empty plates. He'd suggested she was scared to imagine an alternate universe where she could balance a relationship and a career. Hell, she didn't want the kind of cold, quiet relationship her parents had, so maybe she'd just never wanted to fight for something like that. But, a refuge? She liked the sound of that, and something inside of her ached at the thought of having someone to lean on. Someone who understood the demands of her job. Someone who understood her.

She finished her wine, then stood and joined him in the kitchen where he was storing their leftovers in the refrigerator. When he closed the refrigerator door, her gaze landed on one of the many photos he'd stuck there with magnets. Most of the pictures were of his family, but one was familiar. She'd had an identical copy at her place. Matt and her at the hotel restaurant in Jamaica. A man had been going table-to-table, offering to take pictures. Matt had bought two copies, insisting they'd want a memento of their time there together. Though she'd mentally scoffed at the romantic notion at the time, she'd kept her copy, even if it had been shut away in a box—the shoebox that had somehow disappeared from her closet.

Matt followed her gaze and smiled. "That week was one of the best times of my life."

"Mine too."

"Then why did it have to end when we came back to Chicago? We had the start of something good."

She wiped her hands on her jeans, suddenly nervous. "The week we…connected…in the Caribbean was out of the norm for me. It was the anniversary of Jenny's murder. My normal guards were down."

He leaned against the counter. "You don't think we would have gotten together otherwise?"

"Maybe. I've always found you attractive." Heat flooded her cheeks but she ignored it. Some part of her felt she owed him a decent explanation. "I'm just telling you that was part of the reason I decided to go to the wedding. I needed to see if going somewhere far away from here would help. That anniversary has always been tough for me." She stopped and licked her dry lips. "So I was vulnerable. But after a few days, I was reminded that I had a job to return to, a career to fight for." In fact, she'd been doing well leaving real life behind until she'd called her parents to check in, foolishly thinking her call on Jenny's anniversary date would be taken as support. Instead, they'd again taken the opportunity to remind her she had a role to fill in the family.

Matt stepped forward and cupped her cheek, forcing her attention to the present. "I respect your amazing talent and dedication, but why can't you have both?"

"You're too much of a distraction."

"I'm certain you would be able to handle me."

"I just can't." But it was becoming increasingly difficult to remember why she had to dedicate all of her time and energy to one cause. Other people managed to juggle family and career. Why couldn't she?

He sobered. "Jenny will always be with you, whether it's an anniversary or not. There will always be reminders. And I will be here to help you through them if you'll let me, if you'll give us a chance." There were promises in his gaze, and a desire that echoed her own, a need she hadn't recognized before. He'd always been forthright with his feelings, telling her he wanted her, wanted to try for a relationship. She'd been the one who'd chosen not to believe it.

She decided in that moment to take a risk. Where it would lead, she had no idea, but she was tired of fighting her desires.

"I want to try." She stepped closer, closing the small gap, and tipped her mouth up to his.

The kiss was soft and warm, the taste of him familiar and comforting. His surprise gave way to a groan of desperation, and his arms wrapped around her to press her against him. He angled his head, his tongue invading as she threaded her fingers through his hair, tugging him closer, locking him in place so she could take her time exploring him. Her body remembered the scent and taste of him and tightened with a pleasurable ache that bordered on pain.

His fingers brushed the bare skin of her abdomen as they

moved beneath the edge of her shirt. Her stomach muscles contracted, adding to the coil of need.

She pulled away just long enough to whisper, "I don't believe I got the entire tour yet."

He studied her a moment, want and heat in his eyes. "Would you like to see the bedroom?"

"Yes, please."

He took her hand and led her to the staircase. But her lips tingled, wanting more of his kisses. On the stairs, she turned into his arms. Their mouths were level here and she took full advantage of the angle to capture his mouth beneath hers. Somewhere in the recesses of her mind, she realized he'd begun backing her slowly up the stairs. His lips never left hers as their feet reached the landing.

A few steps later, she pulled away to take a breath and realized they'd made it to the master bedroom. Matt nudged her back onto a king-sized sleigh bed. His mouth descended to attend to other parts of her body, moving clothing out of the way as he kissed every inch of skin he could uncover, leaving a hot trail in his wake. She scrambled to assist him, lifting her shirt and scooting out of her jeans before reaching for his shirt buttons.

"What happened to the ugly reindeer?" she asked.

He huffed out a laugh that tickled her cheek. "Changed when I went to the office. Just before I ran into my boss, thankfully."

She smiled and finished with the last button, then shoved the shirt off his shoulders.

"One advantage of the Caribbean was a lot less clothing to remove," he muttered, fumbling with the button on his pants.

She grinned. "And we kept it off most of the time. Of course, it wasn't cold there."

His brow arched and he crossed to a mantel she hadn't noticed. A gas fireplace, a bed, and Matt? God, she might never leave. The flames sprang to life with a press of a button on the remote he lifted from the mantel.

"Now you'll stay naked?" he asked hopefully.

"At least until daylight," she said, letting her gaze drift over him and his impressive arousal. She'd missed this playfulness between them, missed feeling connected to him.

"Then we'd better not waste any more time."

He shed the last of his clothing, pulled a condom from the bedside drawer, and after sheathing himself, returned to her. He crawled up her body, taking the leisurely route and kissing every sensitive part along the way. The arch of her foot, the back of her knee, the curve of her hipbone, the dip in her waist, the underside of her breasts, the tips of her nipples. Everywhere he licked or touched burned for more.

She was an inferno by the time he claimed her mouth again. Shifting her weight, she nudged him to his back and climbed on top of him. His ridge of desire pressed into the juncture of her thighs, making her throb and ache for him. She rubbed against him, nearly purring.

He moaned and gripped her hips. "You drive me crazy."

She nipped at his jaw, then kissed it, savoring the salt of his skin. "Ditto."

Interlacing her fingers with his, she lifted her hips to sink onto him slowly, feeling every delicious inch of him as he entered her. Her eyes locked onto his and held as they found their rhythm. She quickened the pace, wanting to watch him lose control. He freed one of his hands to reach between them and press against her sensitive nub in the exact way he knew would send her over the edge into oblivion. Within moments, they surrendered to each other and their passion.

He knew her body, and her mind, so well. Somehow, that didn't scare her as much as it used to.

# CHAPTER 5

MATT WOKE TO GWEN'S WARM WEIGHT AGAINST HIS SIDE, HER SILKY hair spread across his cheek and pillow. Through the windows he'd failed to cover the night before, when he'd only had thoughts of losing himself in Gwen, dawn's light was beginning to glimmer. He made a silent vow to keep her in his bed, warm and safe, as long as possible. He didn't want to see her worried again, but they only had a couple hours before Becca and Diego would invade their haven with questions and theories. A fierce wave of protectiveness broke over him, and he pressed his nose to Gwen's temple to breathe her in, comforted by the fact she'd remained by his side.

He stroked her hip gently and she stirred.

"Mmmm." She stretched against him, and her nipples brushed his ribs. He grew hard and turned toward her, aligning their bodies. His hand skimmed her thigh until he found the back of her knee, and he pulled it up until her leg lay on top of his. Her eyes fluttered open, and her hand drifted downward between them to stroke his hard shaft. He nearly came apart. Her soft lips curved into a wicked, sleepy smile, and she claimed another piece of his heart.

A half hour later, when they'd sated each other, showered together, dressed, and gone downstairs, he started the coffee pot as she looked in the fridge for the makings of a breakfast. She scrambled some eggs while he made toast. As he ate, she sat across from him, sipping her coffee silently, barely touching her food. Though he didn't like it, he could understand her retreat into silence. Their night of reprieve had ended. It was time to face the danger at hand.

Somehow, he was going to have to convince her to stay with him. Not only was she possibly in danger, as the picture of the tombstone had threatened she'd die this year and there were only seven days left, but it was Christmas Eve. He was sure if he didn't intervene, she'd be spending the day alone, locked away in her office again.

"Come with me to my parents' house this afternoon," he said.

Her eyes cleared and she seemed to refocus on him, as if her thoughts had taken her far away. "What?"

"The Christmas Eve bash starts around three. And I do mean bash. There's flag football for whoever wants to play, and a contest, complete with ugly sweaters."

She glanced down at the yoga pants and long-sleeved tee she wore. "I don't think I could."

"You can. And I'm not leaving you alone until we figure out who wants to hurt you."

"You don't have to babysit—"

He stopped her argument by leaning in for a kiss. Before the heat could build until he lost himself in her, he pulled away. He took pleasure in the slightly dazed, hooded look in her eyes. "I'm not your babysitter. But I will be standing by you. For one, I'm the reason someone's targeting you. And two, I *want* to, because I care about you."

The tiny furrow between her eyes deepened, but there was no time for her objection as the doorbell rang.

"I'll put a fresh pot of coffee on." Gwen moved to the kitchen as he went to the front door to greet Becca and Diego.

He swung it open, then frowned down at his sister. "You didn't bring Diego?" Not that he didn't trust his sister's abilities, but he wanted all hands on deck when it came to Gwen's safety.

"He's around back." Becca pushed past him and removed her coat. "Seems you had a late night visitor last night. Unless your friend was out walking alone after the snow fell. She is still here, isn't she?" Her head tipped, trying to peer around him to get a look at Gwen.

"She's making coffee."

"I like her already."

He led the way to the dining room and spied Diego through the back window. He seemed to be walking with extreme care as he intently studied the snow. Gwen watched Diego through the window above the sink, but she turned as they entered the kitchen.

"You must be Becca." Gwen extended her hand to his sister and smiled.

Becca shook her hand. "And you're Gwen. So nice to meet you. I wish it was under better circumstances."

Gwen hid a shudder and Matt wished he were close enough to put an arm around her.

"Matt has a few more eggs if you want me to scramble up some breakfast," she offered. "Won't take long."

"No, thank you. We already ate. But I wouldn't say no to a bit more caffeine." Becca moved with the experience of someone who'd been in Matt's kitchen many times, going to a cupboard and removing two mugs.

"What's going on outside?" Gwen asked.

"We saw footprints going from the sidewalk to Matt's car out on the street. The snow froze hard as the temperature dipped, so the prints are pretty well preserved."

"They also lead around to the backyard," Matt guessed.

Diego's gaze was on the ground as he stepped carefully toward the house, his boots crunching as he came up to the sliding glass door that was a rear entry into the informal dining area. Matt and Gwen had eaten dinner there last night and breakfast there this morning.

Matt cursed. "She came close." This time when Gwen shuddered, he moved to her side and put his arm around her shoulders.

Becca frowned as she watched Diego retrace his steps, his phone out to take pictures of the ground. "And they seem small. I'd guess women's boots, the kind with a low heel. Probably size six."

The front door opened and closed and a minute later, Diego appeared in his socks, having left his wet boots in the foyer. Matt greeted his brother-in-law and introduced him to Gwen. He didn't like the way she kept glancing warily toward the backyard, so once they had their coffee, he led them all to the living room.

"Prints go all the way around from the sidewalk," Diego said as he and Becca settled on the couch. Matt and Gwen took the two chairs near the fireplace. "Circled your car, then went through the gate to the back. Spent some time exploring or pacing back there."

"Right up to the dining room window?" Matt suppressed a surge of anger at the invasion of his privacy. With the interior lights on late last night, whoever it was would have been able to watch them eat and move about the kitchen.

"And to the rear fence line." Diego paused and cupped his warm mug. "From there, one can almost see into the upstairs bedrooms."

Gwen shot Matt a sharp glance, probably wondering the same thing he was—had their stalker seen them in the master bedroom together? But the light from the fireplace had been low, even if he'd left the curtains open. Still, if the stalker had been there at the right time, she would have seen them kiss and leave to head upstairs together. After that, only one room's lights would have turned on...and off again shortly after. Their stalker might have guessed what had happened next.

"No gifts this time," Gwen said. "She didn't leave any more boxes?"

Diego shook his head. "I didn't see any."

"Maybe we pissed her off and she left," Matt said hopefully. "She probably didn't intend for me to bring Gwen back to my place."

"More likely you pissed her off by staying together, and she won't leave you alone," Becca said, concern heavy in the look she sent Matt.

"Too bad the Johnsons are gone and took Waldo with them." At Gwen's questioning look, he explained. "The neighbors who share the rear fence have a Rottweiler. Waldo would have barked up a storm at the first sign of any trespasser." Unfortunately, they were in Texas for the holidays, visiting their kids and grandkids.

"We'd like to see the gifts you received," Becca said.

Gwen stood. "I'll get them." Matt hated the haunted look in her eyes, but she seemed to want space, so he stayed seated as she disappeared up the stairs.

Becca took the opportunity to corner him. "How well do you two know each other? More than just friends, right? Certainly enough to make a stalker jealous."

He rubbed a hand over his face. "Yeah. It's more."

"How long?"

"We had a one-week fling a few months back, and I tried to make it more, but she shut me down. We faced each other in court in November, but that was it until this happened. Ironically, the stalker is the reason we reconnected."

"You should have taken her somewhere safe."

"It's safe here," he insisted.

"The stalker obviously knows where you live. Hell, she knows where your parents live." The delivery of one of the little boxes yesterday was proof.

"Gwen was shaken up. I wasn't about to abandon her or hole up in some strange motel. It's the holidays. I doubt we could even find a bodyguard for hire on such short notice this week."

Becca blew out a breath, calming as Diego put a hand over hers. "Let's just keep everyone close," the cooler-headed man said. "They tried going to the police. Without a direct threat, it's up to us, and we're obviously equipped to handle this." He brought his wife's hand to his lips and kissed her fingers. "I know I wouldn't want to go up against you."

Becca finally relaxed. "You're damn right." She jabbed a finger toward Matt. "You'll be at the family gathering, and you'll bring Gwen. We'll go with your safety-in-numbers theory for now."

GWEN TOOK AN EXTRA MOMENT UPSTAIRS TO COLLECT HERSELF. THE stalker had come close again, so close she might have seen her and Matt kissing, if not more. Waking up in Matt's bed had been surreal, and wonderful, and now the beauty was tarnished. They'd had little time to enjoy being together before reality once again intruded.

She found the boxes in her bag, where she and Matt had put them while hastily packing a few things at her place last night. She carried them downstairs and into the living room and set them on the coffee table in front of Matt, letting him do the honors of opening them.

He laid out the two frames they'd received first. "Gwen and I each got pictures from our childhoods. Mine is a typical picture from elementary school."

"And mine is a picture of me with my sister," Gwen said.

"But there's a dark vibe to yours?" Becca asked, examining the smiling photo of the two young girls.

"My sister is dead." Her heart twisted like a wrung out wash-cloth. At least her voice didn't waver this time. "Murdered when she was eighteen."

"I'm sorry." Becca sent her a look of genuine empathy. "I have to ask if her murderer could be involved in any way."

Gwen couldn't hide her shock. "I don't think so. He was some drug-addicted guy she'd been living with. He should still be in jail."

"We can double-check that," Becca said matter-of-factly, but her sympathetic smile never wavered. "Sounds like he wouldn't be the type to send little gifts."

"No." Her mind flashed back to the mug shots she'd seen of the man who'd killed Jenny. He'd been disheveled and crashing after his latest drug high. She couldn't imagine the man tracking her down now, let alone sending her and Matt pretty little boxes. "But the only way someone could have gotten that photo is either from my parents' attic or my home. The box where I last saw the picture is missing."

"The stalker broke into Gwen's house," Matt said, "while my picture could have been taken from the yearbook if one knew where to look. Gwen's obviously in more danger than I am."

Becca looked doubtful but refrained from comment. "And the first gifts arrived at your places of business a few days ago?"

"Yes, but Gwen hadn't opened hers when I went to see her yesterday. It was still sitting on her shelf."

"And the second boxes?"

"You were there when mine arrived at Mom and Dad's house yesterday morning."

"Mine was in my inter-office mailbox, in our mailroom," Gwen said. "I probably wouldn't have found it until after the holiday if Matt hadn't warned me to watch for one."

Diego sat forward to examine the next two frames as Matt laid them out. Matt's showed him in all of his glory, a triumphant grin after his client was acquitted. "Gwen lost this case against you?" He looked from Matt to Gwen. "Was there anything significant about that case?"

Gwen gave a small smile. "Matt presented an excellent defense. Other than that, it was the most recent time we came up against each other, just a few weeks ago."

"And this was the only time you guys were near each other since your time together in Jamaica?" Becca asked.

Gwen stiffened. "You know about Jamaica?"

Matt sent her an apologetic glance. "I had to tell Becca a little about our history so that she knows what the stalker might know." Gwen supposed he was right, but it didn't make her feel any better that their special time together was no longer a secret.

"The third boxes," he continued, talking to Becca again, "arrived last night. Both of them were on Gwen's doormat when our food delivery arrived. They hadn't been there when we arrived at her house about an hour before that."

"And inside those?" Becca prompted.

"Mine was an empty frame, but Gwen's..." He stopped and glanced at her. "Hers was a picture of a tombstone with her name, birthday, and a death date on it."

"What was the date of her supposed death?"

"No day, just the year," Gwen said, anger swelling and mixing with fear as Matt removed that frame and handed it to Becca.

"This year," Diego noted, looking over his wife's shoulder. "That leaves about a week yet for the stalker to make her move if she's serious about her intent to harm you."

"Okay, so you were right about the safety in numbers system," Becca said. "Until we can catch this person, I think you two should stick together. At the very least, until the end of the year. I can maybe get a bodyguard from SSAM, but most are on cases or on vacation."

"I'll guard her with my life," Matt said. "At least until we can find someone else."

Gwen steeled herself against a wave of dizziness. The end of the year was a week away. Surely, Matt wouldn't want to stick by her for an entire week. He'd be sacrificing his family and work time for her. She couldn't accept that, couldn't meet his gaze. Looking down at the table, seeing the frames laid out, she gasped.

Matt turned to look at her. "What?"

"I just noticed the Dickensian pattern."

"The what?"

"Ghosts of past, present, and future, like in *A Christmas Carol.*

Becca leaned forward to look again. "You're right."

"Does that mean we won't be receiving any more boxes?" Matt's tone was hopeful. "All I have to do is donate a dinner to Tiny Tim's family or something?"

Becca shook her head. "I don't think this person's going away that easily. For one thing, if she did slash Gwen's tires, all four of them, that seems like overkill to me."

"There's a degree of emotion in this stalker that concerns me," Diego said in agreement. "And amateurish, too, which isn't a good thing. Sometimes, lack of experience is more dangerous."

"What I wonder is how this person linked you two together…in a romantic relationship, that is." The thoughtful look was back as Becca's gaze moved between them.

"There's no relation—" Gwen gave up her argument as Matt's hand reached over and squeezed hers.

"It doesn't matter what you think at this point," he said. "It's what the stalker thinks that's important."

She pulled her fingers from beneath his. "All the more reason for me to leave. This person could be watching our every move. Being here puts all of you in danger."

Matt shook his head. "You've got that backwards. I'm the one putting you in danger. But I refuse to run from this. We weren't even openly dating, and still this person latched on to you as a reason she can't have me. There's no way I'm letting you out of my sight until we catch her."

"What about people you saw that week you spent together?" Becca asked. "Could any of them have done this?"

"I doubt it. We were at a mutual lawyer friend's destination wedding in Jamaica, and there were only a couple dozen people. I can get you a list of who was there."

"That might be helpful," Diego said, standing. "I think I'll run this by the head mindhunter at SSAM. Lorena Castro's the best at profiling violent criminals."

"This person hasn't done anything directly threatening," Gwen protested, but it sounded weak even to her own ears. The woman's actions hinted at a dark obsession.

"She might have broken into your house at some point in recent weeks. And then recently, trespassing on private property, slashing tires, and approaching your doorstep while you're inside?" Diego rubbed a hand over his jaw and his gaze met Matt's. Some silent message passed between them. "I believe this woman is escalating, and I wouldn't underestimate her capacity for harming either one of you, especially Gwen."

Gwen sagged back into her chair. "I hate that I'm ruining your family's holiday plans."

Becca stood and came over to run a soothing hand down Gwen's arm. "I went through a stalker situation myself a few years back. I understand the fear and loneliness. I couldn't have handled it without my friends and coworkers at SSAM." She cast a smile toward Diego. "Or without my future husband. He was instrumental in saving me."

"Not that she let me at first," Diego said with a grin.

"My point is we won't let you, or Matt, go through this alone."

"You're not ruining our holidays," Matt said. "Heck, our mother would consider it the best gift ever if I brought a woman home. I've never done that before. I'll get all the special attention."

"He's right," Becca said, then stood beside her husband. "How are we going to top that, honey?"

Diego's grin widened. "My cooking, of course."

"Besides, I already told her Matt's bringing a guest, so if you don't show up, you'll have to answer to Mrs. Dolly Haney." Becca released a mock shudder. "In the meantime, Diego and I will dig into the list of people who attended that wedding just as soon as you can get that to me."

After Becca and Diego left, Matt and Gwen came up with the list of guests, including the bride and groom, who were lawyers in Chicago. Just thinking about that week and how she had lost herself in Matt, made Gwen long for that blissful escape from reality. Matt's phone made a whooshing sound as he sent the information to Becca.

"I just can't imagine any of those people stalking us months later." Gwen chewed on her bottom lip.

Matt sighed. "Me either, and especially the women on the list."

"You don't believe any of them could fall for you?" She snorted. "You're easy to fall for."

He ducked his head to catch her gaze. "Really?"

She shook her head, but her heated cheeks belied her true feelings. "I see you're going to take that as a compliment."

"Just a good sign that maybe you're falling for me." He leaned forward and caught her mouth with his in a searing kiss that was as brief as it was hot. "Before I get carried away, let's make sure you're prepared for later."

"Prepared?" Her heart dropped. "You don't think I can handle your family? Or maybe you don't feel I'm a good fit." She'd never felt like she fit in with a family…any family. Her gaze landed on her sister's picture, which still lay on the coffee table next to the others. Once, she'd felt like she'd had a close bond but that had been stolen from her.

His hand settled on her knee, and he waited until she swallowed and met his gaze before he spoke. "You're more than enough, and a perfect fit because you're perfect for me."

Her eyes grew moist, but she blinked back the emotions that flooded her. "Then what do I have to prepare for?"

"You'll need an ugly sweater for the contest. And I need help wrapping the gifts in the spare bedroom. We'll be moving them to Mom and Dad's tonight."

She glanced at her watch. Most of the morning had slipped away already. She thought about mentioning she should go to the office and get some work done, but didn't feel the inclination, which worried her. She'd broken things off with Matt before because she feared she'd lose focus. She had work to do, and he was a major distraction. Especially as she was, indeed, falling for him—hard.

# CHAPTER 6

THE HANEY HOUSEHOLD WAS AS NOISY AS EXPECTED, BUT IN THE most delightful way. A tall blond man, obviously one of Matt's brothers, greeted them at the door. Gwen had barely been introduced to Billy when Michael, also tall, broad-shouldered, and blond, swept in and relieved her of the pie plate she carried. He sniffed it appreciatively. The two men could have been twins, but Matt explained that, while they often shared a bond that rivaled twins, his two older brothers were a year apart. In the living room, she was introduced to the eldest brother, Seth, and Matt's father, Donald.

"Dolly's in the kitchen," Donald explained. He was a tree trunk of a man, and was evidently responsible for the height gene his sons had inherited. His brown eyes twinkled warmly. "She'll be thrilled to meet you."

"Told you," Becca said as she and Diego passed, their arms laden with wrapped gifts as they helped transfer them from Matt's trunk to the base of the Christmas tree.

Gwen was grateful that Matt let them handle the presents, preferring to stick by her side while his brothers asked her question after question, mostly derivations on the theme of how Matt had gotten so lucky. At least their ugly sweaters added levity to the event and helped her relax. Even Donald's sweater was comically hideous.

Matt took her coat and hung it on a nearby hook.

"You came prepared," Seth said with a grin, gesturing to the sweatshirt she wore. She and Matt had bedazzled it with twinkling lights connected to a portable battery pack.

"She wanted to fit in," Matt said, putting his arm around her waist. The warm weight of his hand on her hip was comforting.

"Eggnog?" Becca asked a few minutes later, using the excuse to pull her away from the inquisition. "Sorry. I know they can be a bit much."

"I'm not used to so many people," Gwen admitted.

"Your family isn't like this?" Becca had led Gwen into the kitchen where Diego and Dolly, the Haney matriarch, were slicing and assembling ingredients. The smell of herbs and spices scented the air.

"It's just me and my parents. Sometimes they invite colleagues over. They don't do much for the holidays." Even before Jenny's death, they hadn't been the type to engage in traditions, but after Jenny had run away, it had been like they'd shunned celebrations of any type. A flash of memory hit her in the sternum. Jenny waking her at midnight to creep downstairs. They swarmed over the presents, shaking and peeking and guessing whose was what, and picked through the stockings before putting everything back as it had been. And then before crawling back to bed, they nibbled at whatever cookie remnants Santa had left behind. She'd forgotten about those lighter days, when her family had still felt like a family.

"We're all glad you joined us," Dolly said, overhearing Gwen's comment and immediately wiping her hands before coming around the island to embrace her. Her hair, shoulder-length and a natural blend of white and blonde, smelled of the sugar cookies she'd baked earlier. Her face, round, happy, and glowing, was welcoming as she pulled back from Gwen. "I'm so pleased to meet you. Matt speaks highly of you, as do the others."

Surprised, Gwen looked from Becca to Diego, who smiled at her. She cleared her throat of a sudden emotion she couldn't place. She searched for a way to identify it and was stunned to realize it was a sense of belonging.

"Thank you for the pie, by the way," Dolly said. "Mixed berry is Don's favorite."

Gwen swallowed the chunk of emotions clogging her throat. "It's my pleasure. What can I do to help?"

Dolly made a shooing motion. "Just go and enjoy the afternoon. Diego and I did some prep work for tomorrow's dinner, but we're about done. You are coming tomorrow, right?"

"Um…" Their easy acceptance of her, a near stranger, was overwhelming, and she felt her throat tighten again. But she couldn't promise to be here. She didn't belong with their family, especially when she might be putting them in danger simply by hanging around Matt.

Becca wrapped an arm around Gwen's shoulders. "Of course she is, especially since she's probably going to win the ugly sweater contest. Winner is waited on by the rest of the family all day on Christmas," she explained.

Gwen looked down at her sweater, which was really one of Matt's old sweatshirts that had been repurposed. She and Matt had laughingly engorged it with assorted bling until she couldn't bear to look at it without blinking at the reflection of light and color. But it had the bonus of smelling like him, and she knew she'd keep it long after today's contest was over.

Gwen grinned. "Who knew Matt could wield a glue gun so well? Your brother is a man of many talents."

She surveyed their sweaters and realized they all had talent, as each sweater was more ugly than the last. Except Diego's, whose t-shirt said "this is my ugly Christmas sweater" and he'd duct-taped a couple pieces of tinsel to it. Becca's, on the other hand, looked like a snow globe had exploded all over her in some kind of wintery scene. She left a trail of fake snow in her wake.

Dolly started pushing Diego toward the door that led to the living room. "The pizza will be here in an hour. Go get that football game underway. We'll do the ugly sweater contest after dinner."

"I'd love to help clean up," Gwen said.

"If you change your mind, we'll be in the park across the street," Becca said easily. "I'll go get our change of clothes. Can't play very well in these." She did a spin on her way out and another dusting of fake snow fell to the floor. Dolly's sigh turned into a helpless chuckle.

Gwen went to the pantry in search of a broom. As she went to work sweeping up crumbs and the remnants of Becca's sweater, Dolly told stories about each of her kids. The crinkled laugh lines around the woman's eyes spoke of a happy life.

"You've raised a wonderful family," Gwen said, a bit wistful.

Dolly's eyebrows went up, but her smile didn't falter. "I appreciate the compliment. It's not always easy, but having them in my life is worth it. I couldn't help but overhear what you said to Becca…about it just being you and your parents."

Finished sweeping, Gwen set the broom back in its place and grabbed a dishcloth, wiping down counters as she spoke, thankful that she had an excuse not to meet the other woman's gaze. Dolly was easy to talk to, but that didn't mean the topic was an easy one.

"My parents loved us, but they were demanding," Gwen began. And fairly cold, she realized, now that she'd basked in the warmth of the Haney family. "They expected us to behave at all times. I had an older sister. Jenny rebelled against the pressure as a teen, ran away from home. She connected with the wrong kind of people and a few months later, she was murdered. Some kind of drug deal gone wrong, the cops said."

"I'm so sorry." The words weren't filled with pity, but with empathy.

Gwen turned away to hide the tears that sprang to her eyes. An arm came around her waist and, incredibly, Dolly hugged her. It was a sideways hug, but it was more than Gwen's mother typically gave her. Even in the good years, her parents hadn't been touchy-feely. And here was Matt's mom, offering comfort to a near-stranger.

Tears blurred her vision. Gwen sniffled and swiped at her nose. A napkin appeared in her view, and she took it gratefully from Dolly, but refused to let the tears fall.

When Dolly pulled away, she handed Gwen a storage container full of beautifully frosted cookies and a decorative platter. Gwen took the hint and started laying them out on the tray, thankful she wasn't being asked to dredge up difficult memories. She'd already been through that once today.

"You know," Dolly began tentatively, "Matt has mentioned you from time to time over the years."

"Years?" Gwen couldn't hide her surprise. "I can only imagine what he had to say about me."

"He noticed you as an up-and-comer when he first started defending cases. Sounds like you two climbed the respective ranks together. I confess, the first couple times he spoke of you, I thought you might be some kind of ogre out to make his life difficult."

Gwen laughed, not at all hurt by Dolly's description. Instead, the laughter seemed to break through something in her chest, making her feel lighter. "That sounds about right."

"But then, this past year, when he talked about you it seemed… softer. Less about his frustration at losing a case and more that he was impressed that someone had beaten him." Dolly grinned. "You've been good for him. I think he enjoys the challenge."

"Just between you and me, I enjoy it, too."

"I had hoped, when you two got together in the Caribbean… Well, it's none of my business."

"He told you about the wedding?" Gwen's cheeks burned like hot coals.

"Oh, not much. He mentioned the bride and groom were mutual friends and that you'd be there. He came back from that trip so happy. I had my guesses about what had happened. But then he was so down the next week."

That would have been after Gwen had told him with finality that they had no future. Her chest tightened at the memory of how she'd hurt him, though she hadn't thought she'd had that kind of power back then. Remembering how he'd been with her the past couple days, she knew now what they shared ran deeper than a one-week fling. She just didn't know what to do with that.

Dolly squeezed her hand. "As I said, he didn't tell me much about his trip, but I can guess. Besides, I know my children well. He cares deeply about you. Love is never easy, but it's worth the sacrifice."

"Love? We only had that week together." And the past twenty-four hours. She'd felt closer to him during that time than she ever had to anyone. How was that possible? "How did you know Don was the one?" The question was out of her mouth before she could doubt the wisdom of voicing her innermost thoughts.

A smile of memory tugged at Dolly's lips. "I imagined a future with him, and a future without him. And the first was so much more colorful and fun than the second. I never regretted choosing a life partner who challenged but also energized me. Life's been more rewarding with him at my side, supporting me in whatever I choose to do."

They were silent for a long moment as Gwen absorbed that, tried to imagine what a life with Matt would be like. How he'd support her in her career because he understood what challenges would face her. And she would support him too.

And without him, there was the career path she'd always envisioned—an endless stretch of productive days followed by achingly lonely nights.

. . .

MATT FUMBLED THE CATCH. AGAIN.

From the sidelines, his dad offered some helpful advice, cupping his hands around his mouth to shout, "Focus, Mattie!" A groan from his teammate Seth echoed down the field as he saw the result of Diego's pass. Diego simply smirked. The bastard knew Matt was distracted.

Matt called a timeout and jogged toward Seth and Diego for an impromptu team powwow at the line of scrimmage while Becca, Michael, and Billy took the merry-go-round for a spin. The field wasn't regulation length, boxed off as it was by the playground and sandbox—currently covered in two inches of snow—at one end and a small parking lot at the other. The snow made running a bit perilous anyway, so the shorter field was just fine.

"What's up?" Seth asked. "That should have been a guaranteed TD."

"Distracted." Matt brushed at his cheek as the soft kiss of a snowflake landed there. The snow would be falling more rapidly within the hour, but currently, the sun was still peeking out from between December's gray clouds.

Seth grunted. "Get undistracted."

"Yeah, okay." But his stubborn mind wanted to dwell on Gwen. He could still feel her creamy skin against his fingertips, hear her moan echo in his ears, see her hazel eyes lock on his just before she came—

"Break's over." Diego slapped Matt on the shoulder and grinned as if he knew where Matt's mind had just gone. Sure enough, the rest of the Haneys were jogging toward them.

"What's the holdup?" Billy asked.

Michael grinned. "It's the woman. Can't blame you for hiding her from us, by the way."

"He's afraid she'd ditch him." As if either of them could keep up with Gwen's wit and sarcasm.

Matt shook his head. "I am worried, but not about that."

As their father joined them in the middle of the field, he decided it was time everyone knew what was up. He exchanged a glance with Becca and launched into an explanation for why he was distracted—one that only hit the highlights about his apparent stalker and how Gwen might be a target because of someone's obsession with him.

"There were footprints in the snow outside his house this morning," Becca added. "So whoever she is—and we believe this is a woman—she's getting more reckless, and possibly dangerous." The group's mood turned serious, and everyone began tossing out advice on how to play it safe and where to direct the investigation, rallying around Matt and Gwen in support.

Seth grinned. "Gwen can stay with me if she wants. Might be safer anyway, if some crazy chick is trying to get to you."

"Stuff it," Matt replied without heat. He could see the concern beneath the teasing in his brother's words. Besides, no way was Gwen going to stay with anyone but him. She was his to protect, and he intended to keep it that way.

"You know we have your back," Diego said, and there were affirmations from the rest of his family that caused Matt's heart to swell with love and pride. One of Diego's arms was draped over Becca's shoulders, and the other hand palmed the football.

Becca snatched the ball from Diego. "That pizza will be here any minute. Are we finishing this game or what?"

Diego easily stole it back. "And I have to head to the airport soon, so let's do this." His mother, Estella Sandoval, was flying in from New York City to share the Christmas holiday with the Haneys. Raised in a large, tight-knit family, the bonds of siblings, parents, and extended family were just as important to Diego as they were to the Haneys.

Gwen apparently didn't have that same sense of family. He recalled the longing in her gaze when she looked at her sister's picture and his heart ached for her. Perhaps she didn't have those bonds because someone had taken them from her when they'd murdered her sister. And now, the stalker was opening old wounds. Renewed anger surged and Matt suddenly had extra adrenaline to burn.

He took the ball from Diego and thumped it between two palms. "Ready when you are."

A half hour later, the game abruptly ended in a tie as a pizza delivery car drove up to the Haney house across the street. Don was already waiting on the porch to pay the young deliveryman. The players raced each other to the house. Halfway up the walkway, Matt stopped to fish his cell phone out of his pocket as it rang. He frowned at the caller ID, which said Chicago Police Department.

"Mr. Haney? This is Officer Bates." The young officer they'd met with yesterday evening.

"Did you look into the information we gave you?" Though the police hadn't been able to make the situation a priority without a direct threat, Bates had agreed to find out if the man who'd murdered Gwen's sister was out of jail. It was a long shot, but worth pursuing.

"The man you asked me about died in prison a couple years ago." Quite literally, a dead end.

"Thank you for checking for us."

"I've got another reason for calling. We've arrested someone who could be connected to the stalking. Louise Pritchett. I believe you know her?"

Matt's nerves tingled. Given the subject of a couple of the pictures they'd received, this suspect didn't seem like such a long shot. "What happened?"

"A neighbor called to report a drunk and belligerent woman banging on Ms. Pierce's door a little while ago. Apparently, Mrs. Pritchett was trying to locate you there and was rather insistent. She wouldn't leave."

"I have no idea why she'd think I'd be there or why she was looking for me."

"Hopefully, we'll figure that out as we question her. She'll be spending the night in lockup until she sobers up. Actually, she's asking for you to represent her."

Matt hadn't heard from Louise in weeks, and while she'd been something of a flirt while he'd worked on her case, he hadn't taken it seriously. Was their stalker now behind bars? "Given the circumstances, I think you should refer her to someone else. Please keep us posted, especially if she's released."

As he hung up, the snow started to fall in earnest. Inside, he found his family gathered around the table, devouring pizza as they laughed and teased. Gwen sat in the middle of it all, looking relaxed and happy, as if she belonged there. He simply stared for a moment, drinking her in until she looked up and caught him watching. She smiled, a question in her gaze.

"Was that news?" his dad asked from the head of the dining room table.

"Actually, yes." He took the seat next to Gwen and saw that she'd loaded a paper plate with two slices of supreme pizza, which she handed to him. She'd remembered his favorite from their days in the hotel together. His heart warmed. His eyes held hers as he answered. "That was Officer Bates. The police arrested Louise Pritchett. One of your neighbors called because Louise was banging on your door, drunk and upset, apparently. She might be our stalker."

Gwen frowned. "We should get to the station."

He shook his head. "Tomorrow will be soon enough. We should enjoy our night. Besides, I know my ex-client well. Sweating it out in a jail cell might make her more eager to confess."

His gut told him this stalking business wasn't over yet. He'd grab onto this moment of peace with his family and worry about Louise tomorrow. For now, he'd enjoy every second he had with Gwen.

# CHAPTER 7

GWEN WOKE UP EARLY CHRISTMAS MORNING WITH A RADIATOR plastered against her. At least, that's what it felt like. One side of her face lay against Matt's broad chest. If she turned her head just a little bit, she could press her lips to one sculpted pec.

"Mornin'." His throat rasped with the rust of sleep, sending tingles throughout her body. His wide palm cupped her butt cheek possessively—and damn if she didn't like it.

"Good morning."

"What time is it?"

"Early." The sun was up, but just barely. They hadn't gone to bed until nearly two, after returning from Midnight Mass. Becca and Diego had come with them to do a sweep of his house, making sure it was safe and locked up tight before they said goodnight and left for their own bed.

"Sleep okay?" He craned his neck to study her through heavy-lidded eyes.

"My brain clicked on."

His fingers swept her hair back off of her face, then lingered to play with the strands. "What's on your beautiful mind?"

"I want to go to the police station to question Louise. Then maybe go over that wedding guest list with Becca and Diego. And then I should get some work done."

"Your big, beautiful brain definitely clicked on. It's Christmas. You're allowed to take a break."

"That's just it. I can't take a break. There's too much to do." And he was distracting her again.

She began to pull away, but his arm tightened around her and before she could come up with an excuse, his lips had captured hers in a languid, bone-melting kiss that had her body relaxing and stretching out over his. He cupped both bare butt cheeks, holding her close against his erection.

After a long, thorough kiss, he pulled away enough to search her face. "Better. You were way too far into your head for this early on a holiday. Had to stop that. Besides, Louise isn't going anywhere. I asked Officer Bates to notify me if she's released on bail."

Gwen shook her head. "But I have things to do—"

"And there you are, back in your head again." He heaved a long-suffering sigh and stroked a finger over her lips. "Merry Christmas."

"Merry Christmas." Her hands rested on his shoulders, as if they didn't know whether to push him away or pull him closer.

"We could wake up every morning like this. Every Christmas. Until the little ones came running in, that is."

Her heart pounded fast and hard. "Little whats?"

"Little Haneys. Or Pierce-Haneys, if you like."

She liked the image a little too much, actually, and her breath caught at the image he'd painted.

Laughter filled his eyes and rumbled out of his chest as he caught her in a stunned moment. "I like surprising you. It makes the gold in your eyes sparkle." His humor faded. "We don't have to have kids, of course. I just want you in my life. Everything else will fall into place as we progress." He shifted to look into her eyes. "Do you want kids? A family?"

"I don't know." But deep down, she thought she did know. "I might."

"Well, we have time to figure that out. In the meantime, just in case, we'd have to practice. A lot." His teasing tone had returned. "You do know that's where lawyers come from. And doctors and dentists and plumbers and—"

"Yeah, I get it." She pushed against his chest and rolled off of him.

"I don't think you do." His voice stroked her like a caress as, propped on one elbow, he watched her rise and gather clothes from her suitcase. "Haneys mate for life and I've found the partner I want. And I don't regret letting her know how much she matters to me."

She stumbled for words, overwhelmed by the thought of a different future than she'd imagined. In the end, she respected his honesty with some of her own. "I don't know what to say to your...proclamation."

"I wanted to lay all of my cards on the table."

"And those cards have kids on them?"

"If you want them. If you don't, I'd still love you just as much."

*Love.* Did he even realize what he'd just said?

Knees weak, she sank down onto the side of the bed. "You're so certain of what you want."

His hand reached out to take hers, his thumb stroking her wrist. "Not really. I just know that I want you. I know you can't picture our future yet, but we don't have to have it all mapped out. Whatever you decide you want, I'll make it happen." He kissed her hand. "I want you in my life. And yeah, maybe I've put some thought into what that life might look like, but that's only because I didn't have you here to give me your side of it all. The picture will be shaped by both of us."

Struck by emotions she couldn't name, except for fear—she

knew that one well—she gently tugged her hand away. "I should get moving."

She rose and walked to the bathroom with her clothes. She stopped as she came across her discarded ugly sweater, tossed to the floor last night in their haste to get each other naked. They'd had such fun creating it yesterday. Today, it was time to return to her reality.

Matt came up behind her and wrapped his arms around her waist. He placed a soft kiss on her bare shoulder. "I still scare you."

"Yes," she whispered. "No."

His huff of laughter against her ear sent shivers across her skin. "Which is it?"

"You don't scare me. The future you want does. It doesn't feel possible."

"We'll make it possible. Together."

"I have to go." She started toward the bathroom. She needed some distance, some perspective. Before she got far, however, he pulled her back around to face him.

"Go where? The office?" He frowned. "I thought you'd stick close for a few days. We have plans at my parents'."

She didn't want to share her holiday ritual. It was private, just for her and Jenny. "I have somewhere I need to be."

He crossed his arms over his chest and waited patiently for her to continue.

She sighed and, seeing the stubborn set of his jaw, relented. "On holidays, I try to spend a couple hours in a local soup kitchen. It's not much, but it makes me feel like I'm doing something for people like…"

"Like Jenny," he finished when her name caught in her throat. His eyes softened.

"Yeah. It's actually a shelter my sister went to from time to time. I got to know the people who run the place."

Suddenly, Matt was on the move, disappearing into his closet.

"Give me some time to shower and make coffee and I'll join you," he called back to her.

She nibbled her bottom lip, caught between wanting some space and wanting to be with Matt. "I thought you had some kind of brunch thing with your boss."

He reappeared holding cargo pants and a forest green Henley. "He'll understand. I'll call him. Go have your shower," Matt said, turning her toward the bathroom. He leaned down to speak in her ear, his chest brushing her shoulder blades and creating a wave of need in her belly. "In fact, I think I'll join you after my call. It'll save time."

In the end, it hadn't saved time, but they were both squeaky clean and caffeinated when they left Matt's house.

They reached the soup kitchen within the hour and were immediately put to work serving food. Chains of construction paper garland made by the local elementary school added a festive flair to the cafeteria. Holiday scents—roasted turkey and baked ham, gravy, sweet potatoes, and all the other trimmings of a full meal—filled the air. A seemingly endless stream of people moved through the line, but it was the first time Gwen had felt relaxed in days. Here, she knew exactly what was expected of her and was confident she could deliver.

Over an hour later, Matt straightened and stretched. "We need more mashed potatoes. I'll be right back." He cast a concerned look over the line of strangers.

"I'll be fine," she assured him, and he disappeared into the kitchen. "Turkey?" she asked a woman in line a few seconds later.

When Gwen reached out with the tongs that gripped the slices of turkey, the woman grabbed her forearm in a vise-like grip and yanked her forward. Gwen was so surprised by the move that she clutched onto the counter with her free hand to keep from falling into the turkey and gravy.

"Try to be high and mighty and you'll land in the mud." Beneath the thin skin of the older woman's bony hands, purple-blue veins bulged. "This is your life now and forever, Gwenny. Serving the wretched. It's where you belong."

"What did you say?" Gwen's question was a whisper, possibly because her lungs were pressed against the counter as the woman still held tight to her arm, but also because nobody had called her Gwenny in years.

The woman's breath smelled of onions and dill pickles as she spoke. "Don't think you're above me, Gwenny." There was that nickname again. Her chest squeezed painfully.

"I—I don't."

"Let go of her." Matt's quiet, firm voice came from over Gwen's shoulder just before a tub of mashed potatoes appeared on the serving bar. His hand covered the older woman's where it gripped Gwen. The woman's cataract-glazed eyes met his and then Gwen's. She let go.

Gwen yanked her hand back, hugging it to her chest. She could still feel the throbbing where the talon-like squeeze had likely bruised her forearm. The old woman seemed harmless again, her smile beatific as she turned on the charm for Matt. He stood rock solid and stiff with barely suppressed anger.

"Merry Christmas," the woman said with a cheerfulness that didn't match what had just happened. From the depths of her oversized coat's pocket, she withdrew a red velvet box that Gwen recognized all too well. "And Santa wouldn't forget you, sonny." She pulled out another box and tossed it to Matt. He caught it in the air easily and the woman cackled with delight.

"Where did you get these?" Gwen's gaze swept the room.

"Pretty young thing paid me to give them to you," the woman said. "Paid me real nice, too. In fact, I'm going to get me a turkey dinner *and* a slice of pie at the diner down the street."

Before she could turn away, Matt had come around the counter and blocked her exit. "Not until you give us a description of the woman."

The woman snorted. "You going to pay me too?"

He pulled her aside so that the serving line could continue and fished out his wallet, handing her a twenty. Gwen turned over serving duties to another volunteer so she could join them.

"A description," Matt demanded again.

The woman shrugged. "White lady. Snow hat, hair all tucked up under it so I couldn't see its color. Eyes were dark brown. Nice clothes and new shoes. Nails all done up in Christmas red. Real festive-like. Makeup perfect. You know the type."

"She didn't give a name?" Gwen asked.

"Nope. Paid me extra not to say anything too. But I figure a woman's gotta take every opportunity life hands her, right? Besides, I doubt she'll come around this neighborhood again. Didn't exactly look like she fit in. Made her real uncomfortable too." The woman released another loud crack of laughter that had people turning their heads her direction.

Matt's ignored them. "You said pretty *young* thing. How young?"

"Late twenties, early thirties, I'd say."

"What about the nickname? Did she tell you specifically to call me Gwenny?" She could feel Matt's sharp gaze on her, but she kept her focus on the woman. When she hesitated, Matt pulled out another twenty.

The woman grinned and answered. "Said to make sure I mentioned it at least twice."

"If we have any other questions, where can we find you?" Matt asked. "We'd pay for answers, of course."

At the mention of further possible income, the woman provided the cross streets where she often spent her days and the name of the shelter where she spent her nights.

"I don't want no trouble, though," she said, sobering. "I've had enough of that."

"No trouble," Matt readily agreed. After the woman left, he turned to Gwen. "You okay?" There was a hard edge to the words that spoke of his concern.

"I'll be okay." But the tiny red box felt heavy in her hands. "I don't want to open it."

Matt glanced at his box, equally reluctant. "We'll wait until we get somewhere private. What was that about the nickname?"

"It's what Jenny used to call me. We were Jenny and Gwenny." She squeezed her eyes against a sudden onslaught of tears. Her eyes shot open. "This means it wasn't Louise Pritchett who did this. They have the wrong woman in jail. Our stalker's still out there."

MATT WANTED NOTHING MORE THAN TO PULL GWEN INTO HIS ARMS and comfort her, but they were in a very public place where a curious, hungry crowd shifted around them in a meandering line. The stalker could even be among them. He had to get Gwen somewhere safe, and then he could hold her. And look inside the boxes. He didn't want to open them. Gwen's last one had been a tombstone. Given the escalation of their stalker's gifts, this one was sure to be worse.

"Give me a moment to grab our coats and tell the shift supervisor that we're leaving," he said. "Don't go anywhere." He left her leaning against the wall but within his line of vision as he hurried to say their goodbyes, taking a second to text Becca the latest development.

He returned to Gwen's side within two minutes. Concern gripped him as he surveyed her. Her arms were wrapped around her waist, her face drawn tight as she seemed to be thinking hard. Other than that, she hadn't moved.

He held out her coat. "Let's go home." His words seemed to snap her out of her reverie, and she slid her arms into the sleeves. Even through the layers, fear and anger vibrated through her and into his fingertips as he buttoned her up.

He drove them to her house, wanting to get her somewhere warm and familiar as soon as possible. She hadn't said a word since mentioning her sister's nickname for her, or that the stalker was still out there, aware of deeply personal things from her past. Where had she gone in her head? Her gaze was directed toward the passenger side window. The red velvet box was clutched tightly in one hand. He'd stuck his own inside his coat pocket.

Once inside her house, he dead-bolted the door and turned to take Gwen's coat. After, he no longer resisted the temptation to pull her against him. She went willingly into his arms and clutched him close as his hands moved over her back, his lips finding her temple.

"It'll be okay," he murmured against her hair. "I promise. We'll get through this, but you've got to talk to me."

She pulled away and looked up into his face, her eyes full of remembered pain. The pain gave way to fear as a knock sounded at her door.

"It's only my sister," he assured her. "I asked her to meet us here."

He opened the door to Becca, who moved to hug Gwen and cast him a worried glance over Gwen's shoulder. "Diego would have come, but we were in a meeting with Lorena at SSAM. He stayed to get the rest of the stalker's profile from her."

"We appreciate everything SSAM is doing, especially since it's a holiday," Matt said.

Gwen added her gratitude, then gestured toward the kitchen. "I think I'm going to make some tea. Would anybody else like some?"

Becca rubbed her hands together against the chill that had made her skin bright pink. "Yes, please."

In the small kitchen, Gwen removed the kettle from the stove and went to the sink to fill it. Becca's eyes moved to the scratch marks that were evident on Gwen's forearm. Her questioning gaze met Matt's. The homeless woman had hurt her, but Gwen didn't even seem aware of it.

As Gwen set the kettle on the stove, Becca wrapped an arm

around her shoulders and led her back to the sink. "How about we clean these before they get infected."

Gwen looked down and released a soft sound of dismay. "I didn't even see those."

"Let me," Matt said, needing to do something to help her. Restless anger bubbled inside him. He turned on the tap and let the water warm before gently tending to the wounds. "Would you mind looking for a first aid kit?" he asked Becca, who quickly disappeared in the direction of Gwen's bathroom.

"I can't believe I forgot about the scratches," Gwen said.

Matt gently washed the little half-moon scrapes. "You're in shock." He, on the other hand, was furious. This had gone far enough.

Becca returned with a box of bandages and a tube of antibacterial ointment. She handed them to Matt and then moved to the stove to pour three mugs of tea.

"I'll be right back," Gwen said. "I want to change my shirt. I spilled gravy on it when she grabbed me."

"Rough morning," Becca said, following Matt into the living room. He picked up the two latest boxes from where he'd left them on a table near the front door, and they settled on the couch. She examined him closely. "Merry Christmas, by the way."

Matt ran a hand across his forehead, rubbing at the tension coiled there. "Could be merrier. Hard to see her so shaken up." He resisted the urge to hurl the red gifts across the room. He could guess what was inside. More frames, but what would the messages be this time? With each successive gift, Gwen's confidence seemed a little more shaken. "I don't want to see her hurt anymore."

"Open them," Gwen said from behind them, her voice steely. "I won't let her hurt me anymore."

She came around the couch and sat next to him. Her gaze was steady, and he did as ordered, opening his first. It contained a silver frame, this one with a picture of two gold wedding bands.

He huffed out a humorless laugh. "No secret what this woman wants."

He opened the other box and held up a silver frame, identical to the others. Inside this one, however, was a picture of another tombstone, this one with Jennifer's name engraved. There was also a note, which was new.

*"You weren't good enough for your sister and you'll never be good enough for Matt. You'd be better off joining Jenny,"* he read from the paper. "I don't recognize the handwriting." He fought the urge to crumple it or rip it to shreds.

Gwen surprised him by laughing. "I think our stalker's run out of tricks. My sister's been gone for more than a decade. I'm not so fragile as to fall to pieces with a couple of vague threats and references to her. Jenny's issues weren't mine to solve. It took me years to understand that, but I got there. And I became a lawyer to help people. I know who I am. I'm comfortable with who I am. This bitch only wants to attack me to get to you. I'm not going to let her hurt either of us." She shoved to her feet and paced the living room.

In that moment, Matt wanted nothing more than to take Gwen into his arms and show her how much he loved her. Unfortunately, that would have to wait.

Becca smiled as she leaned toward him. "Protective and strong. I definitely approve of your taste in women."

"The stalker is after me," Gwen said as she wore a track in the carpet. "So let's use that to get her."

"No," Matt said firmly, getting to his feet and stepping in front of her. "Not going to happen. Besides, what the woman really wants is me."

"So let's shove our relationship in her face then. I'm done waiting for her little presents and attacks."

Matt's heart swelled. *Relationship.* Was she finally admitting that's what they had? He grinned. "I'm game."

Becca stood too, now, with a roll of her eyes. "Of course you are. But you're not doing this alone. This woman will be watching for her opportunity. She'll be watching when you bring Gwen to Mom and Dad's."

Gwen went completely still. "I don't want them in danger. They're wonderful people. I can't ask them to do that for me."

"You don't have to ask."

Her confused gaze met Matt's. "Why would any of them do this for me?"

"Because I care about you." He had no qualms, no uncertainties about their future. But he also had the benefit of a lifetime of unconditional family love to draw from. He knew a good thing when he saw it, and he saw it in Gwendolyn Pierce. "Besides, they know I'm in this for the long haul, so you'll likely be around for a while. If you'll get past your stubbornness, that is."

Her eyes flashed with a satisfying amount of heat, but it was chased away almost immediately by doubt.

"Trust me, Gwen. Lean on me. I won't let you down."

# CHAPTER 8

"I'm going to the office," Gwen said, heading for her briefcase. Definitely not the reaction he'd been hoping for when he'd asked her to lean on him.

"Wait, what?" Alarmed, Matt moved to stand in front of the door. "The hell you are."

"I'm not letting this woman derail my life, and I'm certainly not giving her a reason to target your family."

Matt exchanged a look with Becca who looked as concerned as he felt. "Why don't we go to the station together first?" he suggested. "The police will want to hear your side of the story, and we can talk to Louise." Perhaps Louise had been directly contacted and drawn into this by the stalker, as the homeless woman had.

"The police have said their hands are tied."

"We have evidence that you've been hurt. They can find the homeless woman and question her. And they haven't seen the latest frames, or the note."

Becca moved to stand at his side. "And I, for one, am not going to let this woman harm my brother. If you step aside, she'll think she has a clear path to him."

Gwen's shoulders sagged and she set down her briefcase in surrender. "I don't want her to win, but I don't want to put you in danger. Fine. Let's go to the police station."

Matt's relief was nearly palpable as he snatched up the note, frames, and boxes before she could change her mind. He didn't intend to let her out of his sight. No matter how much she wished she could return to her existence of two days ago, before he'd landed in her life again, he wasn't going to let that happen.

He drove the three of them to the police station where they showed Officer Bates the most recent of the little gifts they'd received, as well as Gwen's arm and the note. Finally, they had a more direct threat to work with.

"Can I speak with Louise Pritchett?" Matt asked.

Officer Bates looked away. "She's been released. Made bail before I even came on shift."

Beside Matt, Gwen went completely still. "Was that before ten this morning?" she asked.

"Yeah. About nine, I'd say."

Matt leaned forward, clasping his hands between his knees to keep from reaching for the officer's throat. "You agreed to notify me if there was movement on that case."

Bates shifted papers around his desk. "Yeah, well, crime in Chicago keeps us kind of busy."

In under three minutes, Matt had left a phone message for Louise asking her to call him, and had them all back in his car, headed downtown toward the Loop. A short while later, he pulled into the parking garage beneath the five-story building where SSAM was housed and rode the elevator to the top floor. There, Becca used her security access to get past the lobby.

Diego was waiting in the conference room and gestured to them to take seats around the large table. "Unfortunately, Lorena had to leave but she left the stalker's profile with me, and incorporated this morning's events too. She said we should call her if we have questions." He began reciting the pertinent facts. "Suspect is most likely a female between the ages of twenty-five and thirty-five, probably someone Matt knows more than just a casual acquaintance or has bumped into several times. She's not likely in a relationship, and her previous ones have been intense but brief, yet she'll profess a belief in the power of love that borders on delusional."

"That fits given the gifts she's delivered," Matt muttered.

"She comes from a middle class or higher socioeconomic background and was given everything she wanted. She'll seem stable in the rest of her life, probably hold down a job or even have a career, but that will deteriorate if her campaign for Matt's affection doesn't succeed."

"Meaning she'll become more dangerous." Matt reached for Gwen's hand. She threaded his fingers with hers, accepting his offer of comfort. "The age range would seem to rule out Louise Pritchett, but we already suspected that because of the homeless woman's description of a *pretty young thing*."

"But doesn't rule out some of the guests at the wedding," Gwen said.

"I don't recall any of them showing that kind of interest in me."

"Did Lorena say anything about the way the stalking has played out?" Gwen asked. "The perfect little packages, the frames, the pictures?"

Diego flipped to a page in the folder in front of him. "Lorena thinks those are related to the stalker's image of a perfect family. In fact, the use of frames indicates the picture-perfect images the stalker envisions."

"And the Dickens theme? The use of ghosts of my past, present, and future? I'd like to know why she's using my sister's memory as a weapon."

Diego scanned Lorena's report. "She reiterates that this woman might have had a past with Matt, and she wants a future with him. When Becca told me about the note with today's package, I ran it by Lorena. The stalker sees herself as better than you...a better partner for Matt, but probably a better sister too. So she probably has siblings. She's made you, Gwen, into a Scrooge, to justify what she's doing. She believes you're stealing Matt's affections, but that you're not worthy of him."

Matt snorted and glanced at Gwen. "She's got it backwards. I'm not worthy of you." Some of the anger in Gwen's expression faded.

"That's the gist of the report," Diego said, closing the folder and sliding it to Matt.

Becca glanced at her watch. "Mom and Dad will be expecting us for dinner soon. You are coming, right?" Her pointed look was directed at Gwen, and brooked no argument. "You're not putting us in any danger we're not already in, so save that argument."

Gwen sighed. "I wouldn't want to disappoint your parents."

"I'll take that as a yes," Matt said. "But I believe Gwen wanted to run by her office first."

Gwen looked at him in surprise. "You're okay with that?"

"Of course." He'd show her that she could balance a relationship with him and her career. He had faith she could handle anything.


TWO HOURS LATER, DOLLY'S embrace was as warm and homey as freshly baked bread. Gwen closed her eyes and basked in it. She was starting to get used to the family's easy affection.

After an extra squeeze, Dolly pulled away. "You're just in time. We were about to open presents. Then, dinner."

"And dessert." Matt lifted the portable pie dish and gave his mom a one-armed hug.

Dolly looked surprised. "You baked?"

Matt tipped his head toward Gwen. "It's courtesy of Gwen, so you don't have to worry about a trip to the ER."

After a round of greetings from the rest of the family, who were already assembled in the living room around the tree, Gwen was introduced to Diego's mother, Estella Sandoval, who was obviously considered another member of the family. Space was limited, but Matt sat in a big, comfortable chair and Gwen perched on the arm. His hand naturally moved to her waist and she enjoyed the small intimacy, surprised to find that it calmed her nerves.

This was the holiday she'd always envisioned. Family gathered around a beautiful tree or a home-cooked meal, happy to simply spend time with each other. She sent up a warm thought for her parents, whom she'd phoned earlier to wish a merry Christmas. They'd extended the same wish, and asked about her plans before ending the brief call. They loved her in their way, but were simply a different kind of family. Then, she sent up a prayer of thanks that she could share in this moment with Matt's family, even if she was an outsider.

*You're only an outsider because you're afraid you won't fit in.*

On the heels of it, a memory of Jenny, sharp and clear, settled in her mind. It had been her first day of high school. Jenny, age sixteen, was already a junior and had driven them to school.

*"You can't be afraid to make friends." Jenny grabbed their backpacks from the trunk and handed Gwen hers. "But it takes effort. You're so quiet, I worry about you sometimes."*

*Gwen was more focused on pleasing her teachers than making friends. Most of hers had gone to the public school, rather than the private high school her parents had selected. She hugged her backpack to her chest. "What if they don't like me?"*

*Jenny smiled at her as they approached the school. "What's not to like? Besides, nobody should be alone. You just have to find your place and everything will be fine."*

A year later, Jenny had run away to find her place. Gwen had never found hers.

Instead of letting the memory settle into sadness, she forced herself to examine it fully. What if she could open up her heart to these people? Matt had said they'd welcome her, and all of their actions had echoed that warmth. She'd been the one holding back. What if she'd finally found her place?

"This one's for you, dear," Don said, drawing her out of her thoughts. Matt's father held out a package—a silver gift bag, thankfully, and not the red velvet boxes Gwen had come to dread.

"What's this?" She turned to a grinning Matt.

He shrugged. "It was all them. I have no idea."

"Thank you," she said to the room. She blinked back the tears in her eyes and dug into the bag as if it were her first gift ever. Inside was a keychain with a small multi-gadget tool attached.

"We didn't know what you could use," Don said, "so we got you something useful in any scenario."

"Next year, we'll know you well enough to know exactly what you'd like," Dolly said.

"It's perfect." Gwen was touched that they'd think of her, but also that Dolly was so confident Gwen would be around next Christmas.

"It even has a wine key." Dolly winked.

"You really didn't have to," she said.

"Oh yes, she did." Don squeezed his wife's shoulder. "You see, her Christmas gift is seeing everyone around her happy. And my gift is seeing her happy." With his free hand, he pulled a long, slender gift box from behind his back and presented it to her. Dolly eagerly opened it and exclaimed her delight at finding a brightly colored silk scarf inside. "I saw you admiring that at that shop near the hotel where we stayed."

After Dolly had donned her gift, everyone received a present. They'd exchanged names, so that each person had one special item. Gwen enjoyed her front row seat to their excitement, ribbing, and gratitude and for once, didn't feel like the outsider. Peace settled over her. Her place was here, with them.

Matt's hand rubbed circles on her back. "You doing okay? I know we can be a bit much."

"Not at all. You're just right." She leaned down to kiss him and tasted his surprise. The kiss was akin to a public declaration of their relationship, but she was going with what she felt in the

moment. It was her new motto. In the past couple days, the exca-
vation of her past with Jenny had reminded her that life was short
and that she should appreciate what she had while she had it.

The dinner that followed was filled with delicious food, funny
stories, and much laughter.

Don stood when the doorbell rang just as they were finishing
their meal. "I forgot to mention the Hammonds might be dropping
by for dessert. Since Matt missed the traditional mimosas this
morning, I figured an invite was in order. Gotta keep in good
standing with the boss." With a wink for Matt, Don left to answer
the door.

"Marilyn was disappointed you weren't there," Dolly added.

Becca smirked. "Especially since you didn't agree to the blind
date."

Matt gave his sister an incredulous look. "The *nice* girl you
wanted me to bring home to holiday dinner was Marilyn? If I'd
been interested in her, I could have asked her out at any point over
the past dozen or so years."

Gwen glanced from Matt to Becca. "Who's Marilyn?"

"The boss's daughter," Billy said from Gwen's other side. "And
our neighbor for, like, ever."

"How about we have dessert in the living room?" Dolly
suggested. "There'll be more room, and I need to clear the table."

"Let us clear, Mom," Becca offered. "You go visit."

"You'd better go say hi," Gwen told Matt when he hesitated. "He
is your boss."

"I'd like you to meet him."

"I'll be along after I help."

Becca, Diego, Seth, and Gwen stayed behind to help clear while
Matt and his other brothers carried several pies, plates, and uten-
sils into the living room. Dolly took a moment to put coffee on
and then joined the others in the living room.

"Marilyn wanted to date Matt?" Gwen asked Becca as they
waited in the kitchen for the coffee to brew.

Becca shrugged. "I bumped into her recently and she asked how he was doing. I thought I'd suggest a date, but now I see why he was so reluctant to agree. He was holding out for something better."

"Was the blind date your idea or hers?"

Becca's expression turned thoughtful. "I'm not really sure how we came around to me deciding to ask Matt if he'd go on a date with her. I've never tried to set him up before." Perhaps Marilyn had learned enough lawyerly techniques from her father to know how to manipulate a conversation until she got what she wanted.

"Does she wear size six shoes?"

Becca's eyes widened. "Possibly. We should join the group and see how she acts around you and Matt." She put the filled coffee pot on the tray that already held cups, creamer, and sweeteners and led the way to the living room.

Matt was serving up slices of pie and sent Gwen a smile that soothed her nerves. A distinguished, silver-haired man in a pullover sweater sat sandwiched between a lovely older woman with perfectly styled hair and Dolly. There were no other guests. Matt introduced Gwen to the Hammonds.

"Marilyn didn't make it?" Becca asked.

"She sends her regrets," Deena, Richard Hammond's wife said. "She had a date."

Becca's eyebrows rose. "A date?" Perhaps Marilyn wasn't their stalker after all.

"She wished she could have caught up with you all this morning. Dolly said you had other plans?" Deena's question was directed toward Matt.

"Gwen and I volunteered at a soup kitchen downtown," Matt said. "It was an enlightening experience. I'm sorry I missed the brunch, but I didn't want her to go alone."

"Understandable. Rich mentioned you two might have a stalker." Deena's eyes went wide.

"How did things go at the police station?" Richard asked.

"They couldn't do much, unfortunately," Matt said. He gave a brief history of the events of the past couple days. Gwen understood he was downplaying his descriptions for his parents' sakes.

As conversation drifted to other things, Matt leaned toward Gwen so that only she could hear him. "I'm glad I didn't accept that blind date. I would rather be with you."

"Do you think Marilyn could be our stalker?" Gwen asked quietly, tentatively. After all, Matt had known the woman for most of his life and she could be wrong.

To his credit, Matt considered the question. "She fits the profile in some ways. She's known me for decades, was brought up in a stable home, and is employed. But I never got the sense she was so in love with me that she'd harm anyone in my life. I've seen her enough over the years that I'm sure I would have been aware of something like that."

"Still, be careful if you see her."

Matt placed a quick kiss on her lips. "I love that you're worried about me."

And she loved him. It came to her in a lightning strike of emotion that hit her in the chest. He'd slipped past her defenses and made himself at home in her heart. And if she lost him now, she didn't know if she'd survive. The risk was worth the reward, and she was ready to risk it all.

"Can we go home yet?" she asked.

He must have seen the heat and promise in her eyes because he grinned. "Let's say our goodbyes."

# CHAPTER 9

*HOME.* GWEN HAD CALLED HIS PLACE HOME. THE WORD, ON HER LIPS, had made Matt's heart sing. Though it was only eight o'clock, it was fully dark and the snow was heavy as they said their goodbyes and left his parents' house.

He pulled up to the curb and turned in his seat to face Gwen. "Are you okay?" She'd been quiet on the short drive, but something was different, as if whatever barrier there'd been between them had been demolished.

The smile that bloomed on her lips was brilliant. "Absolutely." She leaned forward to pull his mouth to hers for a hot kiss. Within seconds, they'd steamed up the car windows, giving the impression they were encased within a protective cocoon. Her lips were soft and open. Her body pressed as close to his as possible. Heat and desire rushed to his groin, and he ached to have her.

He pulled back an inch, smiling as they caught their breaths. "Not that I'm complaining, but something's different."

"Butterflies," Gwen said, another smile lighting her from the inside.

"What?"

"I feel butterflies in my stomach. You set them free. I realized tonight that I want that future you pictured. I'm ready to try."

Words had never knocked the wind out of him before, but he was suddenly breathless. "Best Christmas gift ever," he said when he'd finally found the air to form words. "How about you go inside and start the fireplace in the bedroom while I unpack the car?" He could leave his gifts in the car, but his mom had sent several containers of leftovers with them. It would be criminal to let them go to waste. Besides, he needed a moment to gather his wits. Gwen's words had scattered them to the four corners of the earth.

She accepted the key he held out to her. "Hurry. I'll be waiting." She gave him a hard and fast kiss before she got out of the car. He watched her until she disappeared safely through the front door.

He leaned his head back against the headrest for a moment after she'd gone. A future with Gwen. It was all he could have hoped for and more. *Please God, don't let me screw this up.* But he knew they'd be good together. And tonight would be just the beginning.

He grabbed the packages out of the backseat and picked his way up the slippery walkway. He went inside, smiling as he heard footsteps on the floor above—Gwen getting ready for him. He'd sensed a shift in her and he was going to take advantage of it. He'd give her everything she ever wanted. Together, they'd build a future.

He was inside the kitchen within a few long strides and set the containers on the counter. Deciding a bottle of wine might be a nice addition to their evening, he detoured to the pantry and cupboards to grab a bottle and two glasses, then set them on the counter. He opened the refrigerator door and bent to put the leftovers inside when something crashed against the back of his head and pain exploded up through his skull. Gravity pulled on him and everything went black as he collapsed to the floor.

. . .

"MATT, HONEY, ARE YOU OKAY?"

He blinked his eyes and tried to bring the woman's silhouette into focus. The lights behind her were too bright. He recognized the voice, though. "Marilyn?"

"Oh, thank God. I thought you might be dead." Marilyn Hammond shifted, blocking out the brightest of the light. He blinked until he could make out her porcelain-doll features. Blue eyes, pale skin, cheeks pink with the cold and expertly applied makeup.

"What happened?" He tried to sit but a wave of dizziness hit him and he lay back again. The back of his head protested as it connected with the floor with a sharp pain. It felt like there was a bump or bruise back there. Tile, cold and hard beneath him. So cold. Something wasn't right. He blinked again and saw his kitchen ceiling. The cold, he realized, was coming from his open refrigerator.

"Your front door opened as I walked up. A woman pushed past me on her way out. She was in a huge hurry. Said something about how she couldn't do it."

"Woman?" Matt frowned.

"Brown hair, a little taller than me. She was wearing a tan coat."

"Gwen." He closed his eyes again, trying to make sense of Marilyn's words, but his brain was foggy. No, it couldn't have been Gwen. She was upstairs in his bedroom and he was supposed to join her. *I'll be waiting.* Why would she leave? And in a hurry, no less? And why was he on the kitchen floor?

He pushed to his elbows and let the dizziness pass before he came to a sitting position. Marilyn shifted back to give him a little space. She smelled of vanilla and was impeccably dressed in suit pants and a silk blouse, her hair and nails perfect, as always. She beamed at him as she caught him looking at her.

"What are you doing here?" he asked.

Some of the brightness in her smile dimmed. "I'm here for our date. Becca told me she was going to set it up." Rich had mentioned that's why Marilyn hadn't come by the Haney house for dessert. She'd had a date.

"But I never agreed to the date." Alarm bells were starting to go off. Where was Gwen? Something was definitely wrong, and when he looked beyond Marilyn's smile, he caught a quiver of determination in the set of her lips, a glint of mania in her eyes.

He pushed to his feet, grabbing for the counter when the room began to swim. Near his hand, he spied the wine bottle he'd planned to enjoy with Gwen tonight, but it wasn't next to the glasses where he'd left it. Is that what someone had hit him with? The back of his head throbbed an affirmative answer.

Marilyn grabbed for his waist, wrapping an arm around it to steady him. "I assumed Becca had set everything up. But that's okay. It's not that late yet. We can have a drink at least, and talk about this."

"No. Gwen and I—" He clutched at his forehead where an ache began to slam repeatedly like a semi-trailer truck against the back of his eyeballs.

"Are over, apparently," Marilyn finished. "Why else would she hit you on the head and run away?"

"No. She loves me." And in his gut, he was absolutely certain it wasn't Gwen who'd hit him. Had it been Marilyn?

"Maybe she got some sense knocked into her," Marilyn said with a smirk, as if he were missing out on a private joke.

Where the hell was Gwen? The alarm bells in his head were clanging louder as his gaze searched the kitchen and dining room. Damn, he should have checked the house before he let her go in, but he'd let himself be distracted by the promise in her kiss. He hadn't been thinking straight, he'd only been thinking of their future. He shifted, intending to check the living room and then upstairs, where she should be waiting for him.

The arm gripping his waist tightened. "Take it easy. We've got all night."

"I need to sit."

"You poor thing. Let me help you." Marilyn led him into the living room and helped him to the couch. He was feeling stronger with every step, but instinct told him to act like he needed her support.

"How about I pour you some of that wine?" Marilyn suggested.

No, wine was too easy. He needed her gone for a few minutes. "I think something stronger is in order. I have brandy in the pantry." Somewhere on a high shelf, near the back, where she wouldn't find it so quickly. "Yeah, I'd really like a brandy."

"Anything you want, honey. Don't you move."

He closed his eyes and tried to appear compliant and weak. A moment later, he heard her boots clicking on the kitchen tile and the pantry door opening.

"Luckily, I remember where everything is from when Daddy brought me over to see your new place," Marilyn called out. "It was about a year ago and I remember every detail. Do you?"

"Yeah, I remember," he called back, though his memory of the time was vague. His gaze searched the area and he spied Gwen's purse near the front door. She certainly wouldn't have left without that.

"What about how we met? Do you remember that?"

"Grade school." He glanced toward the kitchen, but couldn't see Marilyn. It sounded like she might still be in the pantry. He'd been in third grade when her family had moved to the neighborhood. The same grade as the first picture he'd been sent.

Knowing now that some harm must have come to Gwen, he pushed to his feet, swayed, took a moment to find his balance, then swallowed down the nausea and forced his legs to move to the base of the stairs. He kept his gaze on the hall that led to the kitchen.

"That's right," Marilyn called, still deep in the pantry. "You didn't really notice me until we were in the school's production of *A Christmas Carol*. Of course, I was only a kindergartner, so you didn't have reason to notice me. But during play rehearsals, you finally paid attention to me. I was one of the Cratchitt kids, and you were one of the ghosts. I always liked that story. And you helped me learn my part."

He rubbed a hand down his face. Suddenly, the theme of the little gifts they'd been receiving made more sense—and Marilyn's obsession seemed even more chilling. Momentum, fear, and determination had him on the upstairs landing within seconds. His heart pounded as he moved to his bedroom door, but he froze as he spied a splash of red on the horizon. Not blood, but the scarf Gwen had been wearing.

Gwen *had* come up here. She hadn't had cold feet. He paused and looked down to the first floor from the landing but didn't see any sign of Marilyn.

"Got any crackers to go with that brandy?" he called down the stairs, hoping to stall her a little longer. "I'm feeling a little shaky." Not a complete lie, probably because of all of the adrenaline coursing through his system. While she was rummaging through cupboards, he'd call the police and figure this out. He reached for his cell phone but it wasn't in his pocket. Marilyn must have taken it after she'd knocked him out.

He pushed open the bedroom door and forced his shaky limbs to carry him over the threshold. It was dark except for the flickering of the fireplace, lit in warm invitation. But Gwen wasn't waiting in his bed. Her coat was draped over the end, though. His gaze became frantic as it swept the room. There. On the other side of the bed, on the floor, he saw a pair of feet. Gwen's boots. The nausea and dizziness dissipated as adrenaline surged again and shoved them out of the way. He ran to her, kneeling by her unmoving body. His hands ran over her, searching for injury. Her wrists had been tied behind her back with a thin rope—a cord from the tieback for his curtain, he realized. Blood trickled from her temple and a nasty bump had formed there.

"Baby, talk to me." He felt her neck for her pulse, the truck in his head still slamming repeatedly into his skull.

Gwen's answering moan and the feel of her steady heartbeat beneath his fingertips had him releasing a shaky breath of relief. But before he could untie her, scoop her into his arms, and carry her away from danger, another voice spoke to him from the doorway.

"Matt, you bad boy," Marilyn said in a singsong way.

A wave of chills traveled through his body. Another icy wave crashed over him as he poked his head up over the mattress and spied the gun in her hand, pointed at him. In her other hand, she held his brandy.

"Sorry, I couldn't find the crackers." She set the beverage on the dresser near the doorway. "Meanwhile, you're messing up the plan. You were supposed to drink this and go back to sleep. On the couch." Reflections of firelight danced in the amber liquid laced with God knows what. "You were going to think you'd passed out again due to the head wound, and I was going to take you to the hospital where I could play nurse. We'd spend some quality time together, and you'd see I'm perfect for you."

Shock, and the gun, had him frozen in his tracks. Marilyn was his boss's daughter. She'd been the little girl in pigtails who'd trailed after him and his brothers in the park, or played dolls with Becca. In the years since, she'd grown into a confident woman—or so he'd thought. He couldn't believe she would be obsessed with him, let alone stalk him. Looking back, though, he could see things differently, could recall signs of her interest in him. She'd managed to show up at the law offices more and more often this past year, supposedly to see her father but often inviting Matt to lunch. As an interior decorator, she'd even offered to decorate his new house for free, not that he'd taken her up on it.

"How were you going to explain away Gwen?" He didn't dare look down at the woman he loved. He didn't want to draw Marilyn's attention to her. He already suspected what Marilyn must have planned. The picture of the tombstone she'd sent was indication enough. He just wanted to see how far the woman's madness went.

"The man I paid should be here soon. While we're at the hospital getting you checked out he'll deal with her. He'll even take the body away and dispose of it." She waved her free hand as if swatting away a fly, but her other hand still held the gun. "Once you're free of her, I'll help you build the life you always wanted."

But he'd already been building the life he always wanted—with Gwen.

GWEN LOVED EVERYTHING ABOUT MATT'S HOME, ESPECIALLY HOW IT had come to feel like home to her too. Tonight, she loved that it was such a short drive from his parents' place. As they'd pulled up to the curb in front, she'd still been riding high on her realization that she loved Matt and she wanted to fight for a place beside him —a place filled with laughter, light, passion, and beneath it all, a strong bond that held it all together.

She'd dropped her purse near the front door and raced up the stairs, peeling off her coat and scarf along the way, unable to keep the smile from her lips. He'd told her he wanted her. Forever. Well that's what she wanted too. No more punishing herself for not being there for Jenny. She'd be there for the people who remained in her life. For Matt. She'd find a way to balance career and family. Heck, he did it, so she could too. And facing her fears was worth it.

He was worth it.

And apparently their stalker thought so, too, because she'd made her move while Gwen had been turning on the fireplace in the darkened bedroom. The moments before she'd been knocked unconscious came back in a sudden rush. She'd taken off her coat and scarf, then bent to turn the key that turned on the fireplace and heard a noise. She'd turned to investigate and a blonde woman had come at her with a fireplace poker. There'd been searing pain and then blackness.

Now, she thought she heard voices. She blinked her eyes open. Matt was on his knees beside her, his hands at chest level, palms out. His attention was on something or someone on the other side of the room. Gwen turned her head slowly, wincing at the pain in her temple, but couldn't see beyond the bed. But she heard the woman from across the room.

"I know a man who'll do just about anything for less than the price of a cheap car. Gwen will simply disappear. If anybody digs deep enough, all signs will lead to Louise Pritchett. That ex-client of yours was already suspected of one murder, so it won't be a leap to connect her to Gwen's, especially when the police find evidence that she's obsessed with you. You and I will be free to live our lives together."

"That's cold, Marilyn," Matt said, rising to a standing position without moving his hands.

*Marilyn.* Gwen's suspicions had been correct. The woman must be holding a gun on Matt since his hands were up like that.

"It's fitting." The calm casualness in Marilyn's tone was chilling. "She's worth less than a hunk of junk. She's pathetic, actually. No personality, no warmth. Hell, when I broke into her house during the Pritchett trial, thinking I could use something against her to help your side, the only personal item I found was a measly little shoebox shoved into a corner of her closet. Good thing you're smart and didn't need my help, though I would have liked to have been useful." She paused, and when she spoke again, her tone was harder. "But there was that one picture of you and her in Jamaica in there. Had a date on the back. I asked the receptionist at Daddy's firm about that trip, and she told me all about how happy you were the next week when you returned. That's when I knew I had to be even more proactive, that I needed to push her away. After all, I'm the one you're supposed to be with. I've known it since elementary school. I know what it takes to be a successful lawyer's wife—just look at my parents."

Matt's jaw clenched. "And how will Rich and Deena take it

when you're arrested for breaking and entering, double assault, and attempted murder?"

Gwen had to fight to keep still as a surge of fury ran through her. The woman was actually contemplating murdering her and disposing of her as if she were trash. She'd never even met the woman. Her brain rebelled at the thought of losing her future, her life, as Jenny had. And the thought of losing Matt? Her heart thumped harder. He understood her in a way she'd never experienced before, and somehow, despite her emotional walls, they'd forged a bond. He'd become important to her, and she couldn't face losing him, just when she'd found him.

*Then fight for him.*

The urge to move was strong, but she forced herself to remain still as her mind ran through the possibilities. Her best defense was the fact that Marilyn couldn't see her from her vantage point and didn't know she was conscious. At this angle, the bed protected her. First, she needed to free her hands. Cataloguing her resources, she realized she had precious little to work with. She'd dropped her purse by the front door and her scarf and coat in the bedroom in her eagerness to get ready for Matt. But in the pocket of her jeans—

"Stop right there." Marilyn's command was firm. Gwen had been inching her bound hands toward her side pocket and froze before realizing the words had been directed at Matt, who'd been gradually inching away from Gwen and around the end of the bed, closer to Marilyn.

His voice was calm and steady as he issued his own command. "Put the gun down. Nobody has to get hurt. You and I can simply leave. Together."

*No!* Everything inside of Gwen wanted to scream the word. She guessed he probably wanted to protect her by getting Marilyn out of here, but what would the obsessed woman do when she realized he wasn't going to be hers for long? Gwen couldn't let him sacrifice himself to keep her safe.

Her fingertips resumed their quest toward her pocket and she felt the small lump of the gift she'd received earlier. The keychain with the right tools for any occasion.

Marilyn's voice was triumphant as she responded to Matt's plea. "I knew you'd come around. We were always meant to be together. A couple of times back in high school, I saw you in the park with some girl or another and knew one day it'd be me you were kissing. Hell, even our initials are the same. It was meant to be."

"You obviously saw things more clearly than I did." Matt took a step forward, his hands outstretched toward Marilyn. Was she giving up the gun?

Gwen fumbled with the tool until she found something sharp, then started sawing at whatever had bound her wrists, ignoring how it sliced her fingers as she got it into a position where she could apply pressure against the bonds. Her wrists ached at the awkward angle, but she ignored the pain and kept cutting.

"I was a couple years younger." There was a dreamy note in Marilyn's voice. "You never looked my way, but I knew I would get your attention, just like I had during the Christmas play. I just had to be patient. Now, we can fill those other frames with pictures of us, and they'll cover our big, beautiful tree each year. Our wedding, our kids, our pets…"

"It sounds beautiful." Matt took another step away from Gwen, toward Marilyn, and Gwen yearned to rise up and stop him. She kept sawing, even as warm liquid coated her fingers. She'd nicked something as she worked.

"It will be beautiful, except I had to use some of the frames on *her*." Marilyn's tone turned hard again.

"You don't have to think about her anymore." Matt attempted to keep Marilyn's focus on him. "You have my complete attention now."

"Good. Because it's time for you to settle down. Even Daddy said so. He's going to make you partner soon, but he wanted to make sure you were going to set stakes here permanently. I knew it was time for us to get closer. That's when I started attending your trial in November. But I saw how you looked at *her*. And then I found out about Jamaica. I knew then that she wasn't going away that easily. The day you won in court, she was the loser, and yet you looked at her like you wanted her."

Gwen's heart caught in her throat. Had Matt's feelings for her really been that transparent? He'd professed his desire to date her, to get to know her, but she hadn't taken him seriously then. They'd lost so much time because of her stubbornness and blind focus on her career. She'd make it up to him if they both got out of this alive.

"But that's over now," Marilyn said. "You have me. And I promise I'll be all you ever need."

"I'm sure you will." Matt took another step toward Marilyn. Gwen bit her tongue to keep from shouting at him to stop. He was only a few feet away from a crazy woman and her gun. The bullet wouldn't miss if she fired.

Gwen sawed faster and felt some give in the rope.

"But we don't need to kill her to make her go away." Matt took yet another step. "You already tormented her with the picture of her sister. Surely that's enough."

Marilyn laughed humorlessly. "You'd think so. But you only spent more time together. You and your White Knight complex. No, it'll be better for us if she's no longer around to distract you. But don't worry. I hired someone else to do the dirty work. Killing her is beneath us, and if anyone gets caught, it'll be the guy I hired."

"And Louise Pritchett? How did she become involved in this?"

"I needed a scapegoat. And since she was a client at Walters and Hammond, I was able to access her bank data. There's a paper trail that shows the man I hired was paid from her account. Daddy said one day that she had been interested in you while she was your client. It was easy to encourage the woman to pursue you, and I gave her Gwen's address, told her that's where you lived. All of this was done anonymously, of course. She was pretty angry that you would pay attention to the woman who prosecuted her. Unfortunately, she went a little overboard, drew too much attention to herself."

"And the woman at the soup kitchen?"

"I paid the dirty homeless woman to give you the boxes."

"But how did you know we were there?"

"Followed you from your house. I was hoping to bump into you at brunch, but when you called Daddy to say you couldn't make it, I figured I'd better see why." She scowled. "I've been patient long enough, but this is our time together. You belong with me."

Gwen felt the cord give way and her fingers tingled as the blood rushed into them and the device she'd been using dropped to the floor with a soft thud that resounded in the quiet that had followed Marilyn's pronouncement.

"What's going on?" Marilyn's question was followed by the grunts and cries of a struggle.

Gwen pushed to her knees, willing her numb limbs to work properly. She was finally able to look over the bed and spied Matt struggling to get control of Marilyn's flailing arms.

"You bastard! You liar!" Marilyn spewed at him as she fought. Gwen's first impression of the pretty blonde was that she was beautiful except for the expression on her face and the darkness in her heart.

She spied the gun on the rug near the fireplace and crawled toward it. Her bloody fingers were slippery, and she couldn't grip it correctly at first try. She wiped her palms on her pants and tried again, this time making sure she had a good grip as she aimed it toward Marilyn.

Gwen ignored the various pains and throbbing in her head and hands and rose to her feet. "Stop!" she called out. Marilyn stopped struggling and sent a fierce snarl Gwen's direction.

Matt let go of Marilyn and shifted toward Gwen. His gaze

raked over her, pausing on her wrists and the gun. "You're bleeding."

"I'll be fine. Cut myself getting loose. I owe your family another thank-you for the handy gadget."

Matt's laugh was rough with emotion, but it was the sweetest sound in the world, considering Gwen thought she might not ever hear it again.

Downstairs, the front door opened and Becca's voice rang out. "Matt? Gwen?"

"Up here," Matt called back. "And we caught our stalker."

The sound of two sets of footfalls preceded Becca and Diego appearing in the bedroom. Becca's eyes shot from Matt to Marilyn to Gwen. "You guys left so quickly, I didn't get a chance to secure your house first. Looks like you should have waited for us."

"Looks like they handled it," Diego said, his gaze taking in the scene. He withdrew something from his back pocket. Handcuffs.

"Mostly," Matt said. "Marilyn hired someone to dispose of Gwen more permanently. If we wait around a little while, I suppose we'll catch him too."

As Diego restrained Marilyn and pulled out his cell phone to call the police, Gwen lowered the gun and handed it to Becca. Matt immediately pulled Gwen into his arms.

"I'll get blood on you." Gwen tried to pull away.

He only held her tighter. "I don't care. I need to hold you, probably for a very long time."

She slid her fingers up his back and held him close, inhaling his familiar, reassuring scent. "I'd like that."

He dipped his head until his lips were at her neck and let out a shuddering breath. "I don't know what I would have done if anything had happened to you."

"Ditto," she said.

He laughed and squeezed her tighter. "Counselor, you're going to have to do a lot better than that."

She pulled back within the circle of his arms to look him in the eyes. "How about I love you? And I need you. And I don't want to let you go. Ever."

He grinned. "Ditto."

She'd received the best Christmas present she could wish for—peace, love, and the hope of many more days and nights with Matt Haney.

# UNTIL DEATH

A MINDHUNTERS HOLIDAY NOVELLA

*For Tim.*

*Every day I'm with you is a celebration of love.*

# CHAPTER 1

SHE HADN'T NOTICED HIM. THAT SHOULDN'T PRICK JAKE ROSALES'S pride but it did, especially since his entire body came alive at the sight of Dr. Rachel Montgomery. Though they'd only met once, recognition punched him in the sternum the moment she pushed through the front doors of the Hotel del Corazon.

His gaze drank her in as she crossed the lobby. Silky blonde hair hung to her shoulder blades and a red coat did little to hide her trim waist and gently swaying hips. Long, jean-clad legs ended in cowboy boots. She looked fresh and vibrant, despite the fact it was ten o'clock on a chilly February night.

The Hotel del Corazon—hotel of the heart—was a colorful old-world style jewel on San Antonio's popular River Walk. Its terra-cotta floor tiles and wrought-iron accents reflected the signature Spanish-colonial decor of South Central Texas. It occupied a prime location overlooking the river with its barges full of tourists, dinner parties, and mariachi bands complete with horns, strings, and dancers in full skirts or charro suits.

Rachel seemed oblivious to it all. She progressed to the reception desk without glancing left or right. She walked under the exquisite ironwork chandelier without glancing up. She didn't turn her head to take in the plush brown leather chairs arranged artfully in the cozy area where Jake was seated near a massive river-stone fireplace with a blazing fire. She walked as if she were a woman on a mission, spine straight and lips set in grim determination. The small black duffel bag hanging from her shoulder bobbed against her side with every long, purposeful stride. She was braced for impact—but from what or from whom?

Jake had one guess: Dr. Bryce Schafer, Chief Technical Officer of S&R Biotech, Jake's brother's business partner, and the subject of Jake's informal investigation. From his surveillance, Jake knew Bryce had contacted and seen Rachel multiple times since early January. The pair had dated briefly in undergraduate school a decade ago before breaking up. It seemed they'd reunited in recent weeks.

*Damn.* From what Jake had learned of Rachel, she was an excellent doctor and all-around good person. He hated to see her involved with a potential criminal. Jake's brother Jeremy believed Bryce was stealing from the company, and Jeremy's wedding, including all the events leading up to the big day, was an opportunity to get a closer look at Bryce. Jake's gut churned at the thought that Rachel might be here to meet the man in his hotel room—and then she confirmed it.

"I believe Dr. Schafer left something for me," she told the receptionist. The woman behind the counter smiled and handed her an envelope. Rachel opened it, slid out a keycard, and stared down at it for a long moment, turning it over in her hand. She murmured her thanks, pivoted, and headed for the bank of elevators to her left. She pressed the UP button, closed her eyes, and took a deep breath. Her lips began to move silently. He could have sworn she was counting slowly to ten. A moment later, she stepped into the elevator and the doors closed.

When Jake first met Rachel at his brother's engagement party two months ago, he'd been struck by her poise and charm. At the time, he'd been dealing with too much of his own shit to want to drag anyone down into the abyss with him, but she'd somehow become a blip on his radar that night. The memory of her laugh and bright smile had occasionally broken through the black clouds that had lingered since witnessing the shooting death of his partner last fall. San Antonio Police Officer Floyd Lancaster was dead because Jake had failed him. Jake had been careful to keep people at a distance while he came to terms with one of the most horrific incidents in his life. He shouldn't be thinking about a woman with golden hair and a beautiful smile. He should be focusing on the task at hand, and how he was about to meet with Jeremy and his fiancée, Adriana, for drinks and an update on Jake's surveillance of Bryce.

Instead, he found himself watching the elevator doors, willing them to slide open and Rachel to step out. He shook his head at himself. Rachel was none of his business. But Bryce had recently become his business, and Jake hated to see her hurt by whatever Bryce was mixed up in.

He glanced at his phone and saw a text from Jeremy saying they were running late returning from their parents' house. So when the empty elevator car returned to the lobby, Jake stood and crossed to it. With a muttered curse, he punched the button for the tenth floor, where he knew Bryce was staying, along with most of the wedding party. Jeremy and Adriana had invited their families and closest friends to join them on the River Walk for several days of activities leading up to the wedding, and so several had arrived today in anticipation of the fun that would start tomorrow.

At the end of the hall, he stopped at Bryce's door, deciding on an excuse for knocking. He could say he was hoping Bryce would join him for a drink, a best-man-meets-fellow-groomsman bonding ritual? He leaned forward to listen, but no sounds came from within. Suddenly, he heard the sound of quick footsteps against the tile on the other side of the door. Rachel's sexy boots came to mind and he backed away from the door just as it swung inward.

Rachel Montgomery, in the flesh. Once again, she seemed entirely unaware of his presence and irritation pinched at him. One of her hands gripped the duffel bag at her shoulder, and the other held a cell phone. Her head down, Rachel's attention was on her phone as her thumb scrolled across the screen.

"Rachel?"

Her head popped up. The flash of fear that crossed her features slammed into him, and irritation was replaced with alarm. Had something bad happened? Had Bryce hurt her? Jake's entire body tensed at the thought, ready to leap into action. He glanced over her shoulder but only caught a peek of red rose petals strewn across marble tiles before the door closed behind her.

She blinked, and then her blue-green eyes widened with recognition. "Jake, right? Jeremy's brother?" It disappointed him that she knew him only as the groom's brother and best man, but that would change soon.

Jake nodded. "We met at the engagement party a couple months ago. And you're one of Adriana's bridesmaids?"

Her smile, which had been blooming, faded when a deep voice emanated from the phone in her hand. *"You've reached Dr. Bryce Schafer, Chief Technology Officer of S&R Biotech. Leave me a message and I'll get back to you as soon as I can."*

Rachel's attention snapped back to the phone. She put it to her ear, suddenly all business. "Bryce, I don't know what's going on, but I'm here at your hotel room, as summoned. And you're...not. Call me when you get this."

The tightness inside Jake relaxed. If she'd been planning to meet Bryce here for sexy times, it hadn't gone according to plan. In fact, her entire demeanor was dialed to supremely annoyed. She tossed the phone into the large black bag at her shoulder and yanked the zipper shut.

"Everything okay?" he asked.

"Adrenaline." She gave a throaty, self-deprecating laugh that had his abdomen tightening. "And frustration."

"Is this about Bryce?" His gaze went to the closed door.

"Do you know him?"

"Only through Jeremy."

"Right. They're business partners."

"But I don't know the guy well," Jake said.

Though Bryce was one of the groomsmen, he hadn't attended the engagement party just before the holidays. He'd been out of town on personal business. One of the reasons Jeremy had agreed to Adriana's idea to host several pre-wedding events this week was so they could find out what Bryce was up to. According to Jeremy, Bryce had been acting strangely, disappearing more and more in recent weeks. Once, he'd blown up at Jeremy when confronted about some chemicals that had gone missing from S&R Biotech's lab. Those chemicals were expensive and important to their research.

After quietly interviewing Bryce's coworkers, employees, and previous girlfriends, Jake couldn't say he was impressed with the guy. The man was good at researching new drugs, but he apparently had an ego the size of Texas and the greed to match. According to his business acquaintances and exes, he thought he was above reproach. One had even thrown around the word *narcissist*.

Something about Bryce had always set off Jake's alarm bells, including the fact that he could get physical when things didn't go his way. Though they'd been friends since college and co-owned S&R Biotech, when Jeremy had confronted Bryce, it had nearly come to blows.

Jake searched Rachel's face. "Did he do something to you?"

Her blonde hair slid across her shoulders as she shook her head. "No, nothing like that. The frustration is self-directed. I should have expected this kind of behavior." She frowned. "I thought he'd be different this time, and that's my fault."

"Maybe you're being too hard on yourself." Even the smartest of people, like his brother, was susceptible to Bryce's charm. "The guy's clearly an idiot."

A smile curved her lips. "Thanks. Are you here to meet with him too?"

"No. I was about to grab drinks with Jeremy and Adriana and thought I'd see if anyone else from the wedding party wanted to join us."

"Well, you can count Bryce out. He's not here. It was his idea to meet and then he didn't bother to show up. Told me he'd leave me a key so I could let myself in, but why wouldn't he be here?"

"Maybe he was detained. Work, or a business meeting?" Unlikely at ten o'clock at night. Besides, Bryce was in business with Jeremy. His brother had shut down their labs for the week of the wedding and most of the wedding party had checked into the hotel that afternoon. It was Jake's understanding that Rachel had to work a couple more mornings at her clinic across town, and had opted to sleep at home those nights.

Rachel looked behind her at the room's closed door as if contemplating the possibilities. "Something, or *someone*, detained him, but it wasn't business. It's a scene set for romance in there. Except for the broken champagne glass."


RACHEL SHOULD HAVE IGNORED BRYCE'S DEMANDS. AFTER ALL, they'd broken up. Again. Two days ago, she'd discovered he'd been texting another woman pictures of himself, along with suggestive messages. Rachel had ended things immediately.

She'd put in several hours at the Pecan Grove Community Health Clinic that day and wanted nothing more than a glass of wine and a warm bed. But Bryce had insisted she stop by, whatever the hour. With the wedding activities gearing up tomorrow, she'd decided to appease him, if only to clear the air between them before they bumped into each other in front of their friends. She didn't want to be responsible for ruining Adriana's wedding experience.

But Bryce had obviously enjoyed champagne—and likely other things—with another woman while waiting for Rachel's arrival. What the actual fuck? Was he trying to shove his sexual prowess in her face?

"A broken glass?" Jake asked, pulling her attention back to the attractive man in front of her. His dark hair had a wave to it that was slightly mussed and totally sexy. Brown eyes held flecks of gold that seemed to warm to liquid as he studied her. "Maybe someone needs assistance? Did you check every part of the suite?"

"The bathroom door was closed. And I suppose there's the closet too. I didn't even think someone could be hurt. I just wanted to get out of there." She fumbled in her bag for the keycard, her fingertips nudging aside her stethoscope and wallet before she found what she wanted. She quickly opened the door.

Laying a hand on her shoulder, Jake stopped her just inside the entryway. "Hang tight here and let me check things out. I'll let you know if someone needs medical attention."

He picked his way across the blood-red rose petals strewn across the entryway, his gaze surveying the living room. A bottle of champagne was open and chilling in an ice bucket. A tray of bite-sized, decadent desserts, including large, sumptuous strawberries and chocolate truffles, sat on the coffee table. The window beyond overlooked the glittering lights of downtown, reflected in the dark waters of the San Antonio River.

He disappeared into the bedroom and Rachel imagined what he was seeing. The sheets were tangled as if the bed had been used in a rather vigorous manner. A half-filled champagne glass sat on the side table. An empty, cracked one lay on the rug by the bed. Had he found anyone in the bathroom?

Unable to stay still any longer, she crossed the living room and stood in the bedroom doorway. "Is everything okay?"

Jake emerged from the bathroom. "Nobody here or in the

closet. No clothes or personal items, either. It looks like whoever was here left." He crouched on the rug beside the broken champagne glass and pulled out his phone to take a picture. He zoomed in on the image of the red lipstick print on the rim.

"I wondered about that too," Rachel said. He glanced over his shoulder at her, and his gaze dropped to her lips. "It's not my color."

He rose and crossed to her. As he leaned closer, she sucked in a breath and inhaled his masculine scent. A jolt of awareness hit her in the abdomen and sizzled a path to her more sensitive parts—parts of her that hadn't throbbed with an ache like this in a long, long time. For a moment, she thought he might kiss her, and she suddenly wanted to immerse all of her senses in him with an intensity that shocked her.

The scientific portion of her brain marveled at her body's reaction. She barely knew Jake. Months ago, they'd enjoyed a conversation, shared a few laughs, and toasted the bride and groom. And yeah, she'd had some butterflies flutter in her stomach during that conversation and he may have played a starring role in her dreams that night, but she hadn't seen him since. So why did he seem so familiar? Why was her body reacting so strongly to him? He had to be emitting some pretty intense pheromones.

Jake stood so close she could see a small scar on his chin, hiding beneath the five o'clock shadow that darkened his jaw. His easy smile gave him a boy-next-door look, but it was his eyes that kept her from looking away. Caramel-brown and fearless, they watched her with a combination of curiosity and concern—and no doubt caught every nuance, every nonverbal communication, every wince or blush.

And then he sniffed her.

The fantasy bubble burst and she jerked back. "What are you doing?"

"I don't smell champagne. It wasn't you drinking from this glass."

"No kidding." Her cheeks were on fire as she spun away to move back to the living room.

Jake followed on her heels. "I'm sorry. I shouldn't have done that."

"Sniffed me? Why? It was a good guess that it was my lipstick on that glass, seeing as I bumped into you while coming out of his room. It's also fairly obvious that unless Bryce took up wearing red lipstick, a woman was in this room with him. But you could have just asked. It wasn't me. It's equally obvious that Bryce and his mystery woman are long gone, despite his demand that I meet him here tonight."

And that was the root of her anger. She'd allowed Bryce's lack of regard for her feelings and his habitual deception back into her life. She didn't know why his behavior surprised her. The man had always put his own needs first.

She stopped by the coffee table and eyed the ice in the champagne bucket. It was still more ice than liquid, so it hadn't been sitting there that long. A glint of metal caught her eye and she moved closer and picked up a silver chain. A heart-shaped locket dangled from it, icy water dripping from its tip.

"Is that yours?" Jake asked.

"Never seen it before." The freezing metal bit at her fingers as she opened the heart. "There's nothing inside."

An empty heart. How appropriate, considering that's how she'd been feeling lately. In fact, if she hadn't been feeling so lonely, she never would have let Bryce back into her life a month ago. She'd only wanted some companionship, especially since one of their mutual friends was getting married and Rachel hadn't had anyone else she could ask to be her plus-one. The invitation to be a bridesmaid at Jeremy and Adriana's Valentine's Day wedding had spurred Rachel to try to reconnect with a man who didn't know how to love anyone but himself.

Completing her residency in the trenches in Chicago's Cook County and then returning to her hometown of San Antonio to join the Pecan Grove Community Health Clinic had consumed all of her mental and physical resources, all of her waking hours and some of the hours she should have been sleeping. She'd tried dating, but none of the men had seemed as driven and serious as her. Or they hadn't understood why she had little time for them. Or they'd only been interested in her looks. When Bryce began to pursue her, she'd been willing to risk her heart, to see if she could find a connection, and had been disappointed yet again.

So why wasn't she crushed? She was a tiny bit hurt, sure, but it was nearly a relief to have discovered those texts. Bryce wasn't worth her time. Maybe she wasn't shocked because she had expected him to disappoint her, as before. Better sooner rather than later.

She turned the empty locket over in her hand. At least it was only an empty heart and not a broken one. She examined the outside. No initials or identifying marks. Had it been a gift from Bryce to a woman? If so, why had it been left here?

"Are you okay?" Jake stood so close to her shoulder that she nearly jumped. She'd gotten lost in her thoughts.

"Yeah." She let the locket slide to the table. "Kind of relieved, actually. Deep down, I didn't really expect this thing with Bryce to work out."

"So why are you here?"

She huffed out a laugh. "That's a good question." She turned to face him and examined his features. He was easy to talk to and easy to like. "I'm clearly wasting my time." She'd only come at Bryce's request, to leave him a few things he'd left at her place, but if he wasn't here, she wasn't going to bother. He could seek her out for a change.

Jake glanced at his watch and she admired his long fingers and the dusting of dark hair on his forearm. "Adriana and Jeremy are supposed to meet me in the bar for a drink. Why don't you join us?"

Rachel had intended to meet with Bryce as quickly as possible and head home to the tiny one-bedroom guesthouse cottage she rented about fifteen minutes from downtown. A bottle of wine awaited her there. A hot guy with powerful pheromones awaited her here.

She smiled. "A drink would be nice."

He unleashed his smile this time, and its power hit her full force. Her skin tingled as if his mouth sent whispers across it.

*Nice* was too mild a word to describe Jake Rosales. Interesting, yes. Sexy, for sure. Reckless, quite possibly. Jake placed a hand at her lower back to guide her from the room, and she was suddenly feeling a little breathless and a whole lot reckless.

# CHAPTER 2

THEY TOOK THE ELEVATOR IN SILENCE, BUT EVERY CELL IN JAKE'S body was aware of the woman at his side. Rachel's light scent filled his head. He couldn't help the smile that curved his mouth at the thought that she'd come tonight to talk to Bryce, but was heading to the bar with *him* instead. He vowed to help her put the unpleasantness with her ex out of her mind.

His smile faded at the thought of the empty hotel room on the tenth floor. Where had Bryce gone?

Looking for any excuse to touch her, Jake briefly put his hand at the small of Rachel's back again to guide her off the elevator at the lobby level. His hand heated at the light touch, and he wanted to leave it there, especially when she sent a soft smile his way. He forced himself to let go as they entered the bar. They took a booth along the windows that looked out over the twinkling lights of the River Walk. The dark wood and romantic lighting lent an intimacy to the setting that only heightened Jake's awareness of the beautiful woman sitting across from him. Her light eyes and honeyed strands of hair reflected the flicker of the flame from the table's single candle.

"Should we wait for Jeremy and Adriana?" Rachel asked.

He shook his head. "His last text said they were still at my parents' house. Probably got cornered by one of my relatives. My aunts are particularly interested in how long it's going to take for them to start having babies."

Rachel laughed. "I imagine you have a lot of family in town for the wedding."

"We have a lot of family in town, period." The Rosales clan had spread across South Central Texas over several generations. One had even fought at the Battle of the Alamo.

A waitress appeared to take their orders and then disappeared. The lightness of a moment ago had dissipated.

He ducked to look into Rachel's downcast eyes. "What's on your mind?" Was she thinking about how she'd been stood up?

Rachel rolled her eyes. "I'm sorry. I'm so rusty at this." She gestured to the space between them as if that would explain what the hell she was talking about.

He blinked. "Rusty? At drinking?"

Amusement twinkled in her eyes. "Yes, drinking—with a hot guy in a bar on a weekday night. This isn't my normal."

"Hot guy?" He couldn't stop the grin that split his face.

"Yeah, well, don't let it go to your head." She looked down at her fingers, which toyed with a cocktail napkin. "If it weren't for Adriana, I'd probably never go out. As it is, we only get together every few months."

"But you two are close?"

"Close enough that she asked me to be a bridesmaid, sure, but I think that's because I was part of her circle in college. She and I had a lot in common. We were both limited on funds and had to find some creative ways to entertain ourselves while everyone else was going out and partying."

Jeremy and Adriana's group of friends had gone to Texas A&M together years ago, most of them Pre-Med at the time. Adriana had only recently moved to San Antonio, and she and

Jeremy had connected right away. Things had moved quickly since then.

Rachel shrugged. "We all got busy, I guess, but kept in touch from time to time. Adriana, Lauren, Cecilia, Emma, and I were all study buddies."

"A bond forged in blood, sweat, and tears, I'm sure."

She grinned. "Something like that. But I definitely focused on studying, which is why I'm not used to having drinks with a hot guy in a bar. Give me a workshop to present to colleagues, or a visiting doctor to impress, or a patient to talk to and I'm in my element. But a casual drink?" She shook her head and met his gaze. "Like I said, I'm rusty. And a bit lazy."

"I think you're doing just fine. And lazy? Really?"

"I was seeing Bryce, wasn't I? I'd conveniently forgotten why I'd ended it years ago." She snorted. "I guess I should be grateful that he reminded me."

His eyes narrowed in thought. If he'd had to choose a word to describe Rachel—heck, if he'd had to choose ten words to describe her—he wouldn't have picked lonely. And yet, that's what he was sensing from her now. Her sad smile tugged at his heart.

"What?" She tucked her hair behind her ears in a nervous gesture that set off another tug in his chest. She looked up gratefully when the waitress arrived and set their drinks in front of them. Jake took a sip of the high-quality anejo tequila he'd ordered.

Rachel drank from her margarita and licked a fleck of salt from her lip. "Your turn. Tell me something deeply personal so I'm no longer embarrassed."

"No need to be embarrassed. I like hearing about you." But Jake took mercy on her and changed the subject, carefully avoiding anything deep or personal. No way was he going to scare her off right when he had her where he wanted her. "I hate weddings."

Her eyes widened. "What?"

"Don't tell my family, okay? All this craziness has made our lives nuts for weeks. I'm glad there's only a couple more days and then it will settle down."

"It doesn't have to be crazy."

"That hasn't been my experience."

"It depends what the bride wants, I suppose. Adriana always wanted the craziness, as you put it. Most brides want to feel special and cherished."

"You wouldn't make your groom crazy?" He was surprised that he truly wanted to know. What kind of woman was Rachel Montgomery? Had she dreamed of her own wedding? He'd glimpsed optimism, determination, and strength, but what made her truly happy?

She seemed to give her answer some thought before speaking again. "I think it depends on what the two people want, together. It's the connection between them that's key, the mutual appreciation and understanding of each other. Celebrating that is important, sure, but I don't think it's as important as the life they're building."

Hearing her take on it brought to mind Jake's parents. Vida and Ernesto Rosales had been married for forty years, and easily had another forty in them. They'd always kept it simple, focused on love, family, and enjoying the little things.

Jake turned his glass on the table, watching the glint of gold in the liquid. "Well, there's one good thing about this wedding."

"What's that?"

"It's what brought us together tonight." He lifted his glass in a toast. "To the unexpected."

Rachel touched the lip of her margarita glass to that of his tumbler. "To the unexpected." She took a sip, set her drink aside, and leaned forward on her elbows. "You want to know what else is unexpected?"

He leaned forward to shorten the distance even more and smelled the lime on her breath. It made him want to pull her close and taste her. "Yes."

"I'm enjoying myself. I certainly didn't expect that when I drove here tonight." Her gaze dropped to his mouth, and when their eyes met again, a shot of desire hit him at his core.

He sat back to give himself room to breathe, and took a swallow of his drink to cool the flames she'd fanned. "Tell me something else unexpected, something few people know."

"I grew up dirt poor on the wrong side of the trailer park."

"Here, in San Antonio?"

She nodded. "It wasn't all bad. But things took a definite turn for the worse when I was thirteen. That's when my mom died." She hurried on, focusing on the brighter side of what must have been a tough time in a young girl's life. "Even then, I had my older sister Catherine and my dad. Unfortunately, Dad went to jail when I was sixteen."

"That must have been rough." An understatement, but he got the sense she wasn't looking for pity.

"Alcohol fueled some horrible choices." She shook her head as if erasing whatever images were playing out in her memories.

"Were you put in foster care?"

"Briefly. As soon as she could, my sister took me in."

"That's pretty amazing."

"Yeah." Her soft smile spoke of her love for her sibling. "Catherine lives in Chicago now. She followed me when I was accepted to medical school there and stayed because she has a great job with SSAM. They're a private agency that hunts down violent criminals who've disappeared or fallen through the cracks in our justice system. Important work, for sure."

Jake had heard of SSAM, also known as the Society for the Study of the Aberrant Mind. Many law enforcement officials were aware of the expertise SSAM agents could offer in cold cases. Until three months ago, Jake had planned to become a detective and had filed their information away as a potential future resource. All of that was up in the air now. Still, Rachel looked so proud of her sister that he nearly told her about his job with the SAPD. Instead, he stopped himself. Such a confession would only lead to questions he didn't want to answer, and a look of disappointment in her eyes when she realized what he'd done—or failed to do—had cost a man his life. So he kept the conversation focused on her.

"So you have no family close by?" He couldn't imagine such a thing. His parents were an active part of his life. Beyond that, he had dozens of aunts, uncles, and cousins within shouting distance.

"Dad was released from jail recently. I see him about once a month but it's probably different than what you have with your parents. He doesn't really know me after missing so much of my life." Again, loneliness echoed in her wistful words and his heart squeezed.

*Don't get too close.*

The warning came from a deep-seated sense of self-preservation that had served him well in the past. When it came to the investigation he was supposed to be focused on, Rachel was still a resource to be mined. After all, she'd been close to Bryce in recent weeks.

But the warning came too late. Every moment he spent with Rachel pulled him in closer.

JAKE WAS AN AMAZING LISTENER, AND THAT WAS WHY RACHEL TOOK a long drink from her margarita rather than continuing to blather on about her past. It wasn't that he didn't seem interested, but she was doing all of the talking. Before she could attempt to refocus the conversation on him, however, she heard a familiar voice.

"Well, this is a surprise." Jeremy clapped Jake on the shoulder.

Rachel stood to embrace Adriana.

"I see you've already got drinks," Adriana said. "I could use one after the day we've had." She signaled to the waitress and slid onto the bench Rachel had vacated.

Jeremy slid in next to his fiancée and rolled his eyes. "We had a snafu with the flower people."

The only vacant seat was next to Jake, and a tremor of anticipation rippled through Rachel, awakening her senses. She sat. Her thigh brushed against his and she sent him a quick sideways look, but he didn't seem to notice. Neither did the others, as they were ordering a pitcher of margaritas from the waitress. Jake didn't shift away, either, so neither did she, though the contact had her body aching for more.

"The flower people," Jake said with a grunt after the waitress left. "Sounds like a horror flick. Attack of the flower people."

"Don't go into the fields alone," Rachel said in a theatrical voice. Jake laughed.

Jeremy's eyes widened at the sound. His gaze moved between the two of them, his curiosity evident. "How'd you two end up here together?"

"I thought you were with Bryce," Adriana said.

Rachel opened her mouth, not sure what she was going to say, and nearly jumped as she felt a large, warm hand on her thigh. Jake squeezed her leg lightly in support.

"Bryce is an idiot," he said. He left his hand where it was and a rush of moist heat to her feminine parts had her cheeks burning. Thankfully, the others seemed to think her reaction was in response to Bryce's idiocy, and not the touch of the man beside her.

The ends of Adriana's long, dark hair brushed the tabletop as she sat forward. "What happened?"

Rachel hoped her shrug was nonchalant. "I made a mistake letting him back into my life. End of story."

"When, exactly, did that story end?"

"A couple days ago. He'd been texting another woman, and they weren't innocent texts." After another supportive squeeze on her leg, Jake withdrew his hand. Rachel nearly whimpered at the loss.

Adriana's jaw dropped. "That bastard. Who's the woman?"

"No clue. And honestly, I don't care. I dodged a bullet by discovering it early on."

"So what brought you here tonight?" Jeremy asked. "Did you decide to check in to the hotel with the rest of us instead of waiting a couple days?"

Rachel shook her head. "I still have to work tomorrow morning, so I'm headed home after this. Bryce insisted on meeting tonight and I thought it might be good to clear the air so we could both move on. When I told him I had to work until late, he said he'd leave a key. But he wasn't in the room when I went up. I bumped into Jake and he invited me for a drink."

Jeremy scowled. "I wonder where Bryce went."

"Well, I'm glad you ditched him." Adriana cast Jeremy a look under her thick, dark lashes. "No offense, baby. I know he's your friend."

Jeremy grunted. "And business partner." A look that Rachel couldn't decipher passed between the brothers.

The waitress dropped off the pitcher of margaritas and empty glasses, but Rachel waved off a refill when Jeremy lifted it in question. She needed to drive home soon. She had hoped the waitress's interruption would derail their talk of Rachel's ex-boyfriend, but it wasn't to be.

"Bryce can certainly be charming when he wants to be," Adriana said, looking thoughtful. "He had a different woman every month back in college. Except for you, of course. I believe that lasted a few months, right?"

Rachel nodded. Bryce had been attentive and wonderful until he'd grown bored of her.

"I was surprised when I heard you were seeing him again," Adriana said. "I didn't know you'd kept in touch."

"We hadn't, until the wedding."

Adriana winced. "Sorry."

Rachel waved a hand. "Don't apologize. I thought maybe he'd be different. After all, we'd all gone our separate ways for years. Most of us have grown and changed."

Jeremy and Bryce had focused on careers in pharmaceutical

research. Adriana had gone into hospital administration rather than attend medical school.

Rachel shook her head. "Who knows what he was thinking? He certainly wasn't thinking with his brain."

Jake snorted. "Like I said, he's an idiot."

Rachel sent him a grateful smile. "I should head home." She slid out of the booth, trying not to notice how cold her thigh was without Jake's pressed up against it.

"We'll talk more at the dress fitting tomorrow," Adriana promised. "And then I have a fun surprise in store for lunch."

"The groomsmen are meeting up too," Jeremy said. "I wonder if Bryce will be there."

The brothers shared another look at the mention of Bryce's name, communicating in a silent language that Rachel didn't understand.

Jake got to his feet and helped her into her coat. Her skin tingled where his fingertips brushed her neck and pulses of pleasure coursed up and across her scalp. He handed her bag to her. "Can I walk you to your car?"

"I'd appreciate that." She said goodbye to Jeremy and Adriana and walked with Jake to the street exit of the hotel to wait for the valet to bring her car around. "Thank you for the drink, and for being such a good listener. In fact, I think I did all of the talking." A sedan pulled alongside the curb where they waited. "That's me. Thanks again."

On impulse, she leaned in to kiss his cheek. The friction of his five o'clock shadow against her lips made her shiver.

Before she could turn away, he reached out to cup her cheek. The pads of his fingers were rough against her skin and sent another shiver through her. "There's no need to thank me. It was my pleasure."

His gaze dipped to her mouth as if he were going to kiss her. Her breath caught in anticipation and the butterflies in her stomach beat their wings wildly.

Instead, he took a step back. "Good night, Rachel. I look forward to seeing you tomorrow."

As she tipped the valet and slid behind the wheel, the butter-flies were still swirling in a vortex. This was the anticipation, the excitement she'd been searching for. She'd initially dreaded what tonight would bring, but that had changed when she'd bumped into Jake Rosales. He'd brought the unexpected into her life and she wanted more.

# CHAPTER 3

THE NEXT MORNING, RACHEL WORKED A COUPLE HOURS AT THE clinic, which was experiencing its normal winter weekday rush. Pecan Grove's receptionist, Teresa, stopped Rachel after she'd seen several patients.

"Don't you have somewhere to be? Some kind of bridesmaid duty to perform?"

Rachel finished making a note on a file and closed the folder. "I can see a couple more of the drop-ins before I leave."

Teresa made a shooing motion. "Go. Get out while you can. It's busy, but a little slower than expected for flu season. Dr. Rain can handle it." Melissa Rain was covering extra hours while Rachel was wrapped up in wedding festivities. Adriana had planned three days of fittings, luncheons, bachelor and bachelorette parties, and, of course, the rehearsal dinner, all leading up to the big event on Valentine's Day. Rachel couldn't fault her friend's excitement.

"Call me if you need anything."

Teresa smirked. "You know I have it covered. Just remember to have fun. You don't take enough time off for yourself."

"Yes, Mom." Rachel smiled. The part that would be fun was

seeing Jake again. There was something equally comfortable and mysterious about that man.

Several minutes later, Rachel parked in a downtown garage where the daily rate was less expensive than the hotel's accommodations. Besides, the short walk along the river would be pleasant.

She headed to the river level, one story below the city's street level. Though it was February, Texas had relatively mild winters, and San Antonio was expected to reach sixty degrees by lunchtime. Rachel had opted for jeans, a cotton shirt and a light sweater for a bit of warmth. There was no railing or wall along much of the walkway, so one had an unimpeded view of the water, which shimmered in the sunlight.

She gazed up at the hotel and briefly considered knocking on Bryce's door and confronting him about how he'd lured her there and then ditched her, but she found she didn't really care. Last night had actually turned into a great evening. Besides, she'd left the duffel bag that had the belongings Bryce had asked for in her car. She was a little surprised Bryce hadn't texted or called her by now. At the very least, he'd wanted his remaining belongings yesterday.

She pushed thoughts of Bryce from her mind. Today, she was looking forward to time catching up with Adriana and her fellow bridesmaids. And, later, Jake.

She walked through the River Walk entrance into Hotel del Corazon and found Adriana and their group clustered in the lobby. The bride-to-be rose and greeted Rachel with a kiss on the cheek. "I wasn't sure you'd make it after that pitcher of margaritas."

"I only had a sip. Besides, I wouldn't miss getting a sneak peek at your dress."

Adriana beamed. "I can't believe there are only two more days before I become Mrs. Jeremy Rosales." Her friend was glowing. Adriana's long dark hair was loose around her shoulders and her dark eyes were alight with excitement.

A twinge of envy pinched at Rachel's gut and she ignored it. "How's everything going? No glitches today, I hope."

Adriana pulled a face. "Jeremy's mother seems stressed. Maybe you can sit beside her at the fitting? You're so good at talking to people. My mom is looking forward to seeing you again, too." Rachel had met Adriana's mother a few times, but hadn't seen Joanna Whitley since the A&M graduation a decade ago.

Rachel spent a few minutes catching up with Emma and Cecilia, both of whom now lived in Austin and had gone into a family practice together following medical school.

"Oh! Our ride's here." Adriana clapped her hands to get the group's attention. "Mimosas and fresh fruit await in the limo."

Soon, Adriana, her sister and maid of honor Francesca, and their mother Joanna piled into the back of the limousine. Jeremy's mother Vida, Rachel, Emma, and Cecilia followed. Adriana was the center of attention, smiling, bubbly and the picture of a blissful bride.

Once the car was moving toward the dress shop and each of them had a mimosa in hand, Adriana tapped a long, manicured nail against her glass to signal a toast. "I'm so happy to have my sisters back together again—my sister by blood and my Aggie sisters. It's been way too long since we've all been together." She raised her glass. "To good friends and family." Everyone cheered and sipped their mimosas.

Rachel silently counted the members of their group. "Aren't we missing one?"

"Lauren couldn't make it today." Lauren Foley had been another member of their pre-med circle of friends. She worked at S&R Biotech as their sales rep, a position that had better suited her talents. Her knowledge of the medical industry was helpful, but she'd always preferred personal interaction to research.

"Sales emergency?" Emma said. Beside her, Cecilia snickered.

"Yesterday afternoon, she called to say she was starting to come down with something," Adriana said, ignoring their remarks.

"Anything I can do to help?" Rachel asked.

"Just a stomach bug or something. She said she needed a day or two to rest. She'll probably be at the bachelorette party tomorrow night. If not, I'm sure she'll be fine by rehearsal the next night. But I already gave her the bridesmaid gift I got her, just in case. Which brings me to these." Adriana opened the canvas bag at her side and withdrew several small boxes wrapped in silver paper. She handed one to each of her bridesmaids. "These are my way of thanking you for being here to stand up for me and support me in this journey." Her eyes turned teary and she sniffed. "I know we don't see each other as often as we used to, but you are all amazing women, and I'm honored to have you at my back."

Simultaneously, the women unwrapped and opened their boxes and, with a chorus of oohs and ahhs, held up the contents. They'd received identical gifts. When she saw hers, Rachel froze. Her fingers gripped the box so tight they turned white. Around her, the other women were exclaiming over the beautiful silver necklaces, opening the heart-shaped lockets, lifting their hair and turning to help each other put them on.

Rachel pulled her locket from its box and held it up so that it dangled in front of her face. She examined it until she confirmed what she suspected. It was identical to the one she'd seen in Bryce's room. Her stomach turned over. "You said you already gave Lauren hers?"

"Yes, last night. We met for dinner, but she left early when she wasn't feeling well. I decided I'd better take the opportunity to give Lauren her gift early."

The pieces started clicking into place. Rachel's thoughts went to the lipstick on the champagne glass. Lauren's? Was she the one whom Bryce had been texting in recent weeks, too? While he'd been trying to rekindle things with Rachel, had he also been working on Lauren? Anger rose up inside until she reminded herself that she owed the woman a debt for saving her from making a huge mistake.

"With the wedding on Valentine's Day, I thought these would be appropriate," Adriana was saying. "Some day, when you find your happy ending, your heart will be as full as mine." She lifted her locket from where it lay, tucked beneath the collar of her shirt, and opened it to show a picture of her and Jeremy. Rachel smiled along with the others, but inside, her thoughts were whirling.

Thankfully, it wasn't long before the limousine pulled up to a dress shop with several bridal gowns of varying shapes and sizes in the window. The women had sent in their measurements weeks ago so their gowns could be prepped, but this would be an opportunity to make the final nips and tucks. Adriana had thought it would be more fun with all of them here together—minus Lauren, of course. Confronted with the new information about the necklace, Rachel had to wonder if Lauren had truly been ill, or if her sudden illness had been an excuse to meet Bryce in his room.

Refusing to dwell on her ex or his trysts, Rachel let herself be swept away by the excitement and motion around her. The dressmaker and two assistants took the bride, mothers of the bride and groom, and bridesmaids to the back in small groups for their fittings. For those waiting their turn, there was tea and more champagne waiting on a table beside a pair of plush velvet couches. Emma and Cecilia were in the front of the store, admiring dresses. Joanna and Francesca were whisked away with Adriana into the changing rooms. Vida Rosales sat alone with a delicate teacup steaming with chamomile tea, watching the action with an air of concern, a furrow deepening on her forehead.

Rachel took a seat next to Adriana's future mother-in-law. "It's good to see you again, Mrs. Rosales."

"Rachel, wasn't it? Please, call me Vida." Mrs. Rosales turned inquisitive brown eyes on her. Jake had worn a similar expression when he'd focused on her last night. "I remember you from the engagement party."

"It was fun celebrating with you all."

"Yes, well, it's a time for celebrations, I suppose. A whole week of them." She pursed her lips and watched a harried assistant emerge from the back rooms, grab a measuring tape, and disappear again. "So much celebration. Everything's moving so fast."

"You think Jeremy and Adriana are going too quickly."

"They just started dating four months ago."

"At least they knew each other in college, even if Jeremy was a couple years ahead of us." Rachel smiled. "Adriana always had a talent for making things happen when she put her mind to it. She's very focused. She was usually the organizer of our study group, making sure we had a schedule and stayed on task."

The line in Vida's forehead smoothed as she smiled thoughtfully. "She's been quite the whirlwind in Jeremy's life. The word you used...focused." She nodded. "Adriana's definitely focused. She pulled this all together. Not that Jeremy wasn't just as involved, of course. My sons are motivated, too."

Rachel thought of what Vida's other son had said about hating weddings. "Even Jake?"

Vida's smile dimmed. "Jake's been a little lost lately. He doesn't like to talk about it."

"I'm sorry to hear that." Her conversation with Jake had been focused on her last night, and now she wondered if that had been on purpose.

"He's had a struggle, but he'll find his way. He always does." Vida punctuated her affirmation with a sharp nod.

Before Rachel could question her more, Adriana emerged from the changing area looking regal in a white dress fit for a princess. Crystals covered the bodice and shimmered as she moved. The skirt was full and trailed behind her for at least six feet as she took a turn around the room.

Watching from behind Adriana, Joanna exclaimed her delight and Francesca's eyes watered. Emma and Cecilia moved from the front of the shop to admire the dress, adding their praise.

Rachel grinned. "You look beautiful."

A moment later, Rachel and the remaining women were called

back to try on their dresses. The raspberry-colored silk slid across her skin, making her feel sexy and elegant. Studying herself in the mirror, she imagined Jake standing at her side in his tux, or leading her to the dance floor at the reception with his hand at her back. He'd pull her into his arms and hold her close, maybe even lean down to kiss her. A light flush turned her cheeks pink and her eyes darkened as her pupils widened with arousal.

The dressmaker's assistant appeared and the fantasy dissipated as the woman circled Rachel. She worked efficiently, pinning the fabric in a couple places. Within a few minutes, she'd excused Rachel to change.

"Now that the details are finalized, it's time to relax and have fun," Adriana announced once they were all dressed in their street clothes again.

"And eat." Emma rubbed her hands together in anticipation.

"And drink." Cecilia lifted a glass of champagne.

"Just wait until you see what I have planned for us next." Adriana grinned and clapped her hands like a little kid on Christmas morning.

The limousine was waiting when they emerged from the dress shop. The mimosas they'd had earlier had been replaced with pure champagne for the ride back to the hotel. The conversation was animated and everyone was feeling relaxed.

"Too bad Lauren's missing all the fun," Adriana said.

"Oh, I doubt she's missing all of it." Emma nudged Cecilia. The two dissolved into giggles.

"What do you mean?" Adriana said. "She's sick."

Cecilia snorted. "Surely, it's not a coincidence that Lauren and Bryce are both MIA today. They do work together, after all."

"Maybe they ran off to Vegas," Emma added. "Love is in the air, right?"

Adriana scoffed. "They wouldn't dare. The wedding is only a couple days away."

"Still enough time for a quick trip to Vegas."

The joking stopped as they pulled up in front of the hotel. Adriana led the group through the lobby, straight back through the bar, and through the rear exit to the River Walk. Rachel guessed they were headed toward one of the many wonderful restaurants that lined the waterway. But then she caught sight of the flat boat decked out in a long, rectangular, white-linen-covered table set for a party of at least a dozen.

Adriana smiled. "Welcome to our private lunch cruise. Right this way, ladies. The guys will be along soon, but there's no reason we can't get this party started."

They boarded the barge and a server immediately appeared with two pitchers of margaritas, traditional lime and frozen strawberry. At this rate, and without any food in their stomachs, they would all be drunk before the boat pushed away from the dock.

Rachel's gaze skimmed the sidewalk that ran along the river until she caught sight of Jeremy and his five groomsmen, his dad, and Adriana's father, headed their way. Jake wore jeans and an untucked, button-down shirt, a pair of sunglasses dangling from the V at his neck that drew attention to the tanned column of his throat. She imagined pressing her lips there. The butterflies awakened in her stomach as his gaze found hers and he smiled. He looked every inch the dangerously hot guy she'd had drinks with last night.

"Still no sign of Bryce," Emma said from beside her.

Rachel hadn't even thought to look for Bryce. She only had eyes for Jake.

JAKE SPOTTED RACHEL RIGHT AWAY. THE SUN'S RAYS CAUGHT HER hair and turned it to liquid sunshine. As he met her gaze, she smiled, and it took his breath away.

Beside him, Jeremy followed Jake's gaze. "You sure you can trust her? She was seeing Bryce, after all. She might have been consorting with the enemy."

Inside, Jake was itching to leap to Rachel's defense, and that told him everything he needed to know. He'd always trusted his gut when it came to people, and he'd rarely been wrong. By all accounts, Rachel appeared to be one of the good people in the world, caring and nurturing, rarely taking time for herself, to the point it nearly hurt her.

"You don't trust her?" he asked Jeremy. "You knew her in college. As I recall, when I first told you Bryce was dating her again, you expressed true shock."

His brother shrugged. "She's smart. But it seemed like bad judgment for her to go back to a guy who hurt her."

This time, Jake got defensive on her behalf. "You mean like the bad judgment you showed when you went into business with him?"

Jeremy sighed. "He's got a way of worming his way into people's lives. He doesn't seem to have any qualms about using people to get what he wants."

Jake hated that his brother's wedding week was tainted by lies and deceit. "Still no word from the golden boy?"

"No." Jeremy's jaw clenched. "He's not answering or returning my calls. No explanation for his absence. Nothing about S&R's missing chemicals and drug samples, or the files that disappeared from our computers last week." His scowl deepened.

"Maybe Bryce knows I've been digging up information on him at your request, or that you suspect he's up to something. Maybe he grabbed what he could and went into hiding." Had Rachel heard anything from Bryce today? Jake was eager to talk to her, and not just to pick her brain about Bryce's whereabouts and activities over recent weeks. He found himself wanting to get to know her.

Jeremy shook his head. "I've been careful not to treat him differently while we sort out the truth. But standing Rachel up like that made me wonder if he was feeling the heat. You didn't tell her why you went to Bryce's room last night, did you?"

"No."

"Good. Keep it that way and maybe she'll let you in. Bryce had a reason for getting close to her in recent weeks. I want to be sure we can trust her, that she isn't part of his plan, before we share anything else with her."

Jake nodded, but it didn't sit right, keeping things from Rachel. While he didn't want to share the reasons he was on leave from the SAPD, he didn't think it was necessary to lie about his investigation into Bryce's activities. But he'd defer to his brother for now. "Let's focus on getting you married."

Jake greeted his mom and dad, who were settled in their seats at one end of the table. The bride and groom were holding court in the middle seats, where they could visit with everyone. Jake headed for his chair, demarcated by a name card at the far end of the table. Jeremy had ensured that he would be seated beside Rachel. Across from her, an empty chair waited for Bryce. Despite the reminder of the man's disappearance, there was good humor in her eyes and a healthy blush to her cheeks.

"You look good," he said.

"Got a good night's sleep, thanks to someone who helped me put things in perspective before I went home." She gestured to his place next to her and he pulled out his chair. "Looks like I get to talk to that someone again. Did you set this up?"

"Maybe." He winked, and then sobered, tipping his head toward the empty chair. "Did you ever hear from Bryce?" Her smile dimmed and he instantly regretted the question.

"No. And that's probably a good thing." She leaned in to whisper, "The current rumor is that Bryce and Lauren might have run off to Vegas together."

He caught a whiff of her scent and a hint of champagne on her breath that made him want to kiss her. As her words sank in, he jerked his gaze to the other end of the table where, sure enough, there was another empty seat and no sign of Lauren Foley. "She's missing too?"

"Well, I don't know if the Vegas part is true, but apparently, she's the one he met with in his suite last night."

"How do you know?"

She tugged the collar of her shirt aside and revealed a silver locket identical to the one from Bryce's room. "Adriana gave these to each of her bridesmaids this morning—except for the one she gave Lauren last night when it appeared she wouldn't be well enough to attend today's events."

"Interesting." Aware others were watching them, he didn't reach out to touch the necklace, or to run his fingers along her neck, though he was aching to touch her.

She pulled her collar back into place. "That's what I thought."

Their conversation broke off as Jeremy made a short speech to the group, thanking them for sharing in their happiness. A pair of waiters began laying out the fixings of a family-style Texas barbecue, complete with bowls of coleslaw and ranch beans and platters of cornbread and every manner of barbecued meat, from beef ribs to chicken to pulled pork. Delicious aromas filled the air and his stomach growled.

"Your mother is lovely, by the way," Rachel said after they'd filled their plates. The breeze blew a strand of hair across her face, where it stuck to her lips and caressed her jawline. Jake experienced a moment of ridiculous jealousy over a strand of hair. She efficiently tugged it back into place.

He cleared his throat and tried to focus on their conversation. "Mom's great. She and Dad have run a successful restaurant for twenty-five years, so she's used to people taking her orders. It's been hard for her being relegated to the sidelines." From the other end of the table, his mother met his gaze and arched a brow at him. Jake gave a short shake of his head when he caught the twinkle in her eye, silently conveying his message not to meddle in his budding relationship with Rachel, if that was what this was. Part of him really hoped that was what this was. His mother only smiled wider and saluted him with her margarita glass.

Rachel's laugh turned his attention back to her. "She's probably used to wrangling two rambunctious boys, too, from what she's said. She's very proud of you both, though she expressed some concern about you."

"Me?"

"Something about losing your way recently?"

"Oh." His good mood slipped away.

"I spilled my guts to you last night. If you want to talk about it, I'm a good listener." Concern took over her expression.

"I don't."

"Okay." Hurt rang loud and clear in the single-word response.

Silently, he cursed. But he couldn't let her in, couldn't let her see that side of him. His failures were his own, and he wouldn't put that burden on anyone else.

"The offer stands if you…." Her words trailed off and she went still, her head back and her wide eyes locked on the bridge they were passing beneath. A shadow moved over her features and she shivered as the stone bridge blocked out the sunlight.

He reached for her fingers and found them chilled. "What is it? Rachel?"

She blinked and looked at him, shock in her eyes—shock and fear. "I thought I saw him."

"Who?"

"Bryce. On the bridge." As they emerged from the other side of the wide, stone arch, they looked back, but nobody was there. "He seemed like he was glaring at me, like he was angry."

"You're sure?"

"He was wearing a hooded sweatshirt and dark sunglasses, but yeah, something about the way he was looking at me gave me a chill." He rubbed a hand in a circle on her upper back, hoping to soothe her. "But I have to be wrong, right? Why would he be there instead of here?" She glanced at the empty chair across the table from her.

They weren't that far from the hotel, so he supposed it could have been Bryce. He glanced back at the bridge again. A family of five was crossing, and stopped to look out over the water. There was no man in a hooded sweatshirt and dark glasses. Had she really seen Bryce in disguise or had he simply been in her thoughts and some corner of her mind had conjured him? Either way, he was going to keep his eyes on her. As Jeremy had stated, Rachel might be the key to figuring out where Bryce was and what he was up to.

"Join me for dinner tonight," Jake said.

Her surprised gaze focused on him. "What?"

"After this, there aren't any scheduled events until the bachelor and bachelorette parties tomorrow." And he didn't think she should be alone, but he didn't want to add to the fear that was still etched on her face.

"I was going to go home after this. I'm on the schedule to work the morning shift again tomorrow."

"There's a great Tex-Mex place across the river from the hotel. We could walk around and play tourist until dinner and then give it a try."

"Maybe."

To distract her, Jake kept up the conversation as the lunch wrapped up. After a few minutes, the barge pulled up to the dock near the hotel. Rachel and some of the women were assisted off first. Jeremy and Adriana had opted to stay a moment longer and finish their margaritas. Jake was about to step off behind Rachel when he was stopped by his mother.

"Give me a hand up?" his mother asked from beside him.

He reached out and helped to steady her until she was on the sidewalk, though she had great balance and his dad was right behind her if she'd needed help. As he joined his mom on the side-walk, his eyes narrowed on her. "What's with the delicate flower act?"

Though they were on solid ground, she leaned into him as if

she were still off balance. "You going to tell me what's up between you and the doctor? I like her, by the way."

His gaze found Rachel farther along the pathway that bordered the river, walking with Emma and Cecilia toward the hotel. "I like her, too, Mom, but it's complicated."

"Relationships usually are, *mijo*. Until you fall in love, and then things are pretty simple."

Fall in love? Was that what he was doing? He enjoyed Rachel, wanted to be around her as much as possible, but love? He'd just met her.

His mother apparently read his mind. "Your father and I knew each other only a few days before we knew we were meant to be together."

"Mom—"

A woman's scream pierced the air and the smile fell from his lips. His head jerked up, and his gaze searched for Rachel while his heart lodged in his throat. A flash of dark clothing caught Jake's peripheral vision as a man in jeans and a navy blue hooded sweat-shirt ran away from the group, ducking into the cover of the hotel's landscaped foliage as he took a shortcut to the stairs that led to the street level. He was carrying a purse—Rachel's purse, he realized.

"Stop him!" Emma pointed toward the stairway that led to the street level above the river. The guy was nearly out of sight. Two of Jeremy's groomsmen took off toward the stairs and the third pulled out his phone, probably to call the police.

Jake's gaze again searched the sidewalk where Rachel had been walking. When he couldn't immediately locate her, adrenaline hit his system like a drug. He took off at a run, covering the distance in a matter of seconds. A light-haired figure in the water swam for shore, her movements heavy and awkward from the water-drenched clothing she wore. *Rachel.*

"He pushed her!" Cecilia was trying to kneel in heels and a tight skirt, reaching for Rachel.

Jake's only focus was on getting to Rachel and pulling her from the water. As he got close, her fingertips clutched the edge of the sidewalk that lined the waterway. His knees hit concrete and he nudged Cecilia out of the way so he could grab Rachel's hand. Jeremy appeared at his side to take Rachel's other hand. Together, they pulled her from the murky water. As she knelt on the sidewalk, river water poured off her and soaked his shoes. It was frigid. Jake pulled her to her feet. Her cotton shirt was plastered to her body and her sweater hung, heavy with liquid, from her slender frame. She was soon standing in a puddle, violently shivering.

He cursed and pulled her into his arms and murmured shaky words into her wet hair. "You're going to be okay. I'll keep you safe." It would be his new mission in life.

# CHAPTER 4

THE ANGER BURNED. RACHEL WELCOMED THE FLAMES BECAUSE THEY heated her from within when her exterior felt like she'd just taken the polar plunge. While the February day's air temperature had been pleasant during lunch, the freezing river water bit at her muscles with sharp teeth. If Rachel got her hands on the asshole who'd nearly yanked her shoulder from its socket as he'd snatched her purse, she would tear him apart. And then shove him into the river.

She could have sworn the asshole had been Bryce, but hadn't managed more than a quick glimpse of dark clothes and even darker glasses before she'd gone into the river. Whether Bryce or some stranger, it had been the same man she'd seen on the bridge. But why the hell would Bryce snatch her purse and push her into the river?

Jake pulled her into the hotel and across the lobby. Soaked as she was, every step was work and her jeans chafed at her skin. If she hadn't worn her boots again today, her shoes probably would have been lost in the river. Instead, they were heavy with river water. Adriana, Emma, and Cecilia fluttered around her, asking if there was anything they could do. Of course, it was too late to change what had happened. Someone had thought to snag a towel from the hotel's pool area and wrapped it around her shoulders.

"I got this," Jake told the bridal party firmly, ending their chatter. He leaned over to say something to Adriana and the women fell back as he led Rachel to the elevator.

When he pushed the button, Rachel snapped out of her haze. "Where are we going? My car's not here. I didn't park in the hotel's garage." She wanted to go home and change. On the other hand, Jake's arm around her felt pretty damn good.

"We're going to my room. Unless your car key was in your pocket or you have a spare hidden away on you." His doubtful gaze traveled over her.

Her purse—oh God, her keys, her licenses and credit cards, her cash. The mugger got them all. She muttered a string of curses.

Jake tugged her closer against his side. "As long as you're safe, that's all that matters. You can shower and get warm and dry in my room. Adriana's going to bring a change of clothes for you. You're about the same size, right?" He pulled her into the elevator with him and the doors slid shut, blocking out the world. He looked down at her wet boots. "I'll have her bring shoes, too."

His thoughtfulness brought tears to her eyes.

"Come here." He wrapped his other arm around her as she stepped closer, folding into the warm, comforting heat of his chest.

In that moment, she knew she was falling for this man. They'd forged an immediate, easy bond. But the doctor in her knew the intensity of emotions that often accompanied the aftermath of an adrenaline rush could make one prone to bad decisions. Experiencing the phenomenon full force, in Jake Rosales's arms, was heady stuff.

He didn't seem to care that she was soaking his shirt with dirty water. He didn't ask about the mugger. He wasn't worried about the wedding guests left behind in the lobby. He only cared about her, about making sure she was safe and warm. Except for her sister's love, Rachel had never been the subject of someone's focus and care, and it touched her to her core. She ignored the aches that were surely going to be bruises within a matter of hours and pressed closer to him, turning her head to inhale him and press a kiss to his collarbone.

He inhaled sharply before he stopped breathing altogether. His hands moved into her hair and he cupped her face, his gaze scanning hers.

The elevator dinged and the doors slid open. He released her enough to guide her off the elevator, but kept hold of her hand, as if sensing she needed to hold on to him. He stopped at his room, but his gaze moved down the hall, toward Bryce's door. "Hang on a minute."

She stayed by his door, watching as he went to knock on Bryce's. No answer.

With a grim set to his jaw, he returned to her side. "It was worth a try."

"If I still had my purse, I could have given you the keycard," she said. But she didn't have her purse.

"It's okay. If he doesn't turn up soon, we'll have the manager check the room." He pulled out his key and unlocked his room. She realized with surprise that his fingers were trembling.

She walked past him as he held the door open for her. The room had a slight woodsy, spicy scent to it. Jake's scent, she recognized. She found it immediately soothing. "It's looking more and more like Bryce did this, isn't it? I can't believe he would steal my purse."

"And push you in the water," he bit out. "Let's not forget that part." Despite the anger in his voice, he reached up and pushed her damp hair out of her face with a gentle hand. "I only caught a glimpse of the guy from behind. Did you get a good look at him?"

"It all happened so fast. But yeah, I think it was Bryce." She remembered the surprise of someone grabbing her arm and yanking it backwards, separating her from Emma and Cecilia.

She'd caught a glimpse of her stunned reflection in his glasses before his lips had pressed into a firm line and he'd shoved her shoulder, sending her backward toward the river. His other hand had been on her purse strap. "Why would Bryce want my purse? I was perfectly willing to bring him his things. Okay, maybe not *perfectly willing*, but I would have done it. I obviously tried."

"Maybe he needed money."

"And he wouldn't just ask one of us? None of this makes any sense."

Jake disappeared into the bathroom and she followed, watching as he retrieved a stack of fresh towels from beneath the sink. He set them on the counter and turned on the water in the shower, making sure it started to heat. Again, she was struck by his thoughtfulness in taking care of her.

When he turned to her, there was compassion and concern in his expression. "Warm up. Take your time. I'll be right outside if you need anything." He left, closing the door behind him to give her privacy.

*I'll be right outside if you need anything.*

She needed him. Needed his arms around her again, holding her together like he had in the elevator. Because now that she was standing here alone, she felt a little shaky, like she might fall apart at any moment. Adrenaline letdown was the likely culprit. She forced herself to stand a little straighter. Jake had been gentle and understanding but she had to be strong on her own. She'd learned long ago to stand on her own two feet and hold her head high. Some days, forcing steel into her spine had been the only way she'd made it through.

*One. I am okay.*

*Two. Inhale deeply.*

*Three. I will relax.*

She peeled off her clothing as she counted through her anxiety and fears. The soaked jeans clung to her like a second skin.

*Four. Exhale slowly.*

She swiped the side of her hand in a swath across the steamed-up mirror and examined herself. Her eyes were wide, skin pale, breath too fast.

*Five. Inhale deeply.*

*Six. Exhale slowly, releasing the stress and negativity.*

A glint of silver drew her attention to her neck, where the heart-shaped locket hung to the tops of her breasts. Just like that, any calm she'd been on her way to achieving dissipated. She touched the heart. A second later, she yanked the chain over her head, and set the necklace on the counter. She didn't want any more reminders of Bryce, or Lauren, or what they might or might not have done with each other, or to her. Whatever was going on, she didn't want to be involved.

She stepped under the hot spray and took her time showering, needing several minutes just to warm up and feel human again. She shampooed her hair and rinsed, letting the heat seep into her scalp and bones.

As she thawed, the ramifications of recent events began to hit her. Someone had taken her money, her ID badges, her credit cards, and even her feeling of safety.

With an angry flick of her wrist, she shut off the water and stepped out of the shower. Through the door, she heard voices in the outer room and recognized Jake's low drawl and then Jeremy's reply, though she couldn't make out the words. The hotel room door closed. A second later, there was a knock on the bathroom door.

"Rachel?" Jake called through the barrier. "Jeremy brought a change of clothes for you."

She wrapped herself in one of the towels Jake had set aside for her and opened the door. He seemed to search her eyes for evidence that she was herself again.

"I'm okay." Her words were as much for her benefit as his. "I'm the doctor, remember?"

"Adriana wanted to check on you herself, but she's dealing

with some overwrought bridesmaids. I guess her mother is having a bit of a freak-out, too. Something about bad luck ruining the wedding." He held out the plastic bag containing dry clothes.

As she reached for the bag, his gaze narrowed on her forearm. He took her hand gently, turned her arm over, and exposed a red mark that was the beginning of a bruise.

"I'm okay," she repeated. "I think the purse strap caused it."

"Bullshit. The mugger caused it when he tried to take your purse." A muscle in his jaw clenched. The fierce look in his eyes promised retribution if he ever caught the perpetrator. With the lightest of caresses, he ran a fingertip over the red mark. "Does it hurt?"

"Not at the moment." She steeled herself against a shudder of desire as he traced it again. She was tempted to tell him about the opposite shoulder, where Bryce had shoved her, just to see if he'd press his lips there to soothe the ache.

"Probably because you're still in shock."

"More likely because I can't think of anything else when you touch me like that."

His nostrils flared slightly and his eyes darkened with a heat that echoed what she'd been feeling. In the next instant, he'd put his hands on either side of her neck and tugged her gently toward him. That was where the gentleness ended. The moment their lips touched, her body went up in flames. She'd thought they'd had heat before? That had been nothing compared to what happened when he kissed her.

She sucked in a necessary breath through her nose and inhaled Jake. Her sweet addiction.

*Jake. This.* This was what she'd been searching for.

His tongue slid intimately against hers. He cupped her head to tilt it at the angle that would take the kiss yet deeper. A wildness filled her belly and spread like fire through her. She pressed closer. Bands of steel held her along his length, but she couldn't get close enough. Only her towel separated the rest of her skin from his touch, and she was tempted to let it drop to the floor.

Reckless. Dangerous. Possessed. He made her want to feel all the things she'd never experienced before.

A groan filled the air between them. She couldn't have said if it was hers or his, but she was starting to feel shaky for an entirely different reason. He pulled away just far enough to look into her eyes. The fingers of one hand had sunk into her hair, making her scalp tingle at the contact. The others were splayed across her back.

"Damn." His quiet exclamation was part wonder—and all frustration. She knew then that he wasn't going to take this any further, and braced herself against a wave of disappointment. He slowly released her.

"I should get dressed." She took a step backward toward the bathroom. The bag slipped and she grabbed for it. Jake's sharp intake of breath alerted her to the way the edge of her towel had come open, exposing her thigh. But he didn't invite her back into his embrace, so she retreated. "I'll be right back."

She closed the door behind her and leaned back against it, tempted to thunk her head against the wood. Instead, she did what usually helped when she was confronted with new situations. She made a plan of action. She'd dress, call her credit card companies, contact her landlord to get a new key, a locksmith to get her into her car….

Her gaze landed on the silver locket where it lay on the counter. Yes, it was a reminder of Bryce and Lauren, but it was also a gift from Adriana, a symbol of love and hope. She put it on, refusing to let Bryce's actions control hers. After dressing in the clothes Adriana had sent for her—soft, faded jeans and a T-shirt with a band from Austin splashed across it—she rejoined Jake. Her lips tingled as she remembered their kiss, but he seemed to have become all business.

He gestured to her to sit on the bed and handed her a cup of coffee he'd made with the hotel room coffee maker. "In case you're still cold or shaky." He ran a hand over his head, looking a little shaky himself. "I can't believe I let this happen. I should have been by your side."

She released a harsh laugh. "You can't have known I was going to be mugged and pushed into the river, especially in broad daylight with other people around. How the hell could you have known Bryce was capable of that?"

JAKE COULDN'T LET IT GO. RACHEL WAS WRONG. HE SHOULD HAVE known she could be in danger. Shitty things happened to good people all the time. As a cop, he knew that. As former military, he knew that. He'd obviously learned nothing when he'd lost his partner.

A light touch at his shoulder brought him back to the present. "Jake? I'm going to be fine. Please don't beat yourself up about it anymore." Her hand moved down his arm and she interlaced her fingers with his.

She was trying to soothe him. She'd gone through hell today, and yet she was trying to take care of *him*.

He let go of his anger and forced a smile. "Okay, but I'm not letting you do anything alone until we catch Bryce." He squeezed her fingers. "Think we can go over what happened? Or do you want to go straight down to the lobby? There's someone from the police department waiting to take your report." He scanned her face for signs of shock. "If you need more time, I can stall them." But, every minute that passed, her assailant got farther away. Bryce got farther away. Still, he wouldn't pressure her.

"No, I can go. I know time is of the essence."

"You're allowed a minute or two. You were the victim of a crime. It was enough to rattle anyone."

"You'd think I could have taken this in stride," she muttered.

His body tensed. There was a story, a dark one, behind her statement. "Why?"

She shrugged. "I've been through worse. A guy once held me at knifepoint and forced me to stitch him up. You'd think this was a walk in the park—or a swim in the river—compared to that."

He ducked down to look into her eyes. "You were held at knifepoint? What the hell?"

She pulled away and fished in the bag for the shoes Adriana had sent for her. "I don't want to talk about it. Like I said, it was worse."

He turned her so she'd meet his gaze. "Violence imprints on your brain the way nothing else can." He had a flash of his partner hitting the ground, already struck by several rounds while Jake was still getting out of the car and drawing his weapon. It had happened so fast, and yet it replayed in slow motion in his head all the time. "You're not wrong to react, Rachel. You're allowed to be shaky once in a while. Hell, I'm shaking on the inside, too."

"I kept a cool head the first time. Now, I'm not feeling cool at all. I think I'm getting worse at this rather than better."

His finger brushed over her cheekbone. "You did fine. You survived, which is the most important thing."

She turned away with a sigh. "As much as I'd like to hide here all afternoon, I should call my credit card companies and all that fun stuff." She looked around and cursed.

"What's wrong?"

"I was looking for my purse, which is, of course, long gone."

"We can handle the phone calls later. Let's go down and talk to Detective Osborn first. Maybe Oz will help me track down Bryce too. This investigation has taken a violent turn, so I'd appreciate the help."

"Oz? Investigation?" She studied him.

Fuck. He'd let the truth slip. He saw the moment understanding dawned. Something shuttered in her eyes and her expression hardened.

"You're investigating Bryce?" she asked, her voice hard.

He couldn't meet her gaze. He felt the newfound bond between them crumbling to dust. The lips he'd nibbled just minutes ago were now pressed in a firm line.

She shoved to her feet. "Oh, my God. *That's* why you were outside Bryce's door last night. And that's why you were so willing to have a drink with me." She shook her head. "I thought we'd formed a connection, that you were just interested in me and would eventually tell me about yourself. I'm such an idiot."

"Let me explain." He stepped toward her.

She shoved her hands through her damp hair and spun away. "No. I have to go."

"I'm with the SAPD," he tried, hoping she was listening. "But I'm currently on leave."

"How nice for you."

"Not really. It's a pretty shitty time in my life, actually." As the weeks had passed, he'd gotten better at coping with the pain and guilt, but it hadn't gone away. It probably never would. He should have been ready for anything, should have stopped Floyd from getting out of the car and drawing his weapon on the man before Jake could back him up. But Jake had taken a moment to radio their position and report they'd located the odd character who'd been lurking in a quiet neighborhood. Neither of them had expected immediate gunfire.

"So that gives you license to take advantage of me?" Rachel asked, oblivious to the direction of his thoughts. "You could have just come out and asked me about Bryce. You could have asked me anything. Instead, you led me to believe we were getting close." She headed for the door, but he was right on her heels. "Don't follow me," she said over her shoulder.

Hell, no. He was sticking to her like glue. "At least let me walk you to the lobby." Later, he'd figure out how to convince her to keep him around longer than that.

She jabbed her finger at the DOWN button and whirled to face him. "I'll be fine on my own."

"*No* isn't an acceptable answer when a violent criminal is targeting you. Nor is it okay to say you'll be fine on your own. You don't know what Bryce is capable of. Today should be example enough of that." Again, Floyd's shooter came to mind. No way would he make the mistake of underestimating a potential criminal again.

With an exasperated huff, she turned when the elevator arrived and got on. She didn't argue or block his way, which he supposed was progress. They rode to the lobby in silence. Jake couldn't help remembering how she'd willingly walked into his arms the last time they'd been in this elevator, or how she'd kissed his neck. Which brought to mind the kiss in his room. His body tightened with the memory of holding her. What a difference an hour made. Now, she'd iced him out. In her eyes, he'd likely been just as bad as Bryce, building up her trust before blowing it to bits with secrets.

*No.* He refused to believe he was anything like Bryce Schafer. Given the chance, Jake would keep Rachel in his life, and in his bed, on a more permanent basis. And he'd take care of her heart, too, because it was a big, generous heart that deserved protecting. Unfortunately, she thought he'd stomped all over it.

"I'm sorry, Rachel."

She cast him a sideways glance but didn't reply. Her shoulders were hunched, her body tight with tension. She was closing herself off from him and he felt a moment of panic.

"I shouldn't have withheld part of my identity from you, but it's a long, complicated story. And I wasn't sure I could trust you."

This time, she turned a glare on him. Shit.

"Not you, per se," he quickly added. "I couldn't trust what kind of relationship you'd developed with Bryce. You were clearly here last night to meet him, and Jeremy believes Bryce is stealing from the company, robbing his best friend. Everything I've learned about the man indicates he doesn't care about anybody but himself."

Her glare dissolved into a contemplative frown. "Stealing from S&R would mean he's stealing from himself, too. Why would he do that?"

"Greed."

She released a puff of breath. "You have evidence of this?"

"Not yet. That's why I've been watching him. He's been acting strangely, but Jeremy and I have nothing concrete yet. Just some missing chemicals and files, a few instances where he's dropped a lot of money on something extravagant."

"But no solid evidence?" The door slid open on the lobby level and when he didn't answer her, she stepped off the elevator. "Good luck with your investigation, but please leave me out of it."

Jake watched her walk away. The moment she passed the registration desk, Adriana and several other members of the wedding party, including the groomsmen who'd tried to chase down the mugger but had returned empty-handed, descended on her. They pulled her to a chair by the fireplace and plied her with questions and exclamations of concern. Jake hung back, knowing he wasn't welcome at her side. Besides, Rachel had told him he was basically unwanted here. But he couldn't leave her. Not only had he promised he wouldn't leave her while Bryce was possibly wreaking havoc in her life, but he didn't want to leave her side.

"Is that your woman?" a familiar gravelly voice said.

*His woman.* Jake's gut clenched, knowing she'd been so close to being his woman and now he'd blown it. Jake turned and shook hands with the man who'd supported him when Jake had questioned everything about himself. "Good to see you, Oz. Small world."

Detective Robert "Oz" Osborn grunted in his typical gruff manner. "Don't act like this was a coincidence. Apparently, you summoned me."

"Summoned? You're not exactly Batman."

"Close enough. And he and I have never been in the same room together. Just sayin'." His eyes narrowed. "You want to tell me why I'm here?"

"I wanted the best." While Rachel had been in the shower, Jake had called the police department to report her encounter and make sure someone he trusted to do a thorough job was appointed to the task. While a mugging didn't exactly warrant the attention of a homicide detective, aggravated assault did fall within Oz's purview.

Oz tipped his head toward the sitting area in the lobby. "I assume the lovely blonde with damp hair is Dr. Rachel Montgomery, victim of the assault and mugging?"

"That's her." Not that he'd describe her as a victim. She was one of the strongest women he knew. Currently, she was sitting tall, her chin up, doing a damn fine job of holding up under pressure. In fact, from where he stood it looked like she was the one reassuring her friends, rubbing Adriana's shoulder and forcing a smile. Still, Jake's desire to protect her was strong.

"Did you request the surveillance footage like I suggested?" Jake asked. He'd shared with Oz that the hotel's security cameras might have caught the mugging if they were functional and pointed in the right direction. He'd also hinted that he wouldn't mind seeing footage from last night, especially from the parking garage, in case it caught Bryce driving off somewhere with someone.

Oz held up a flash drive.

Jake grinned. "You *are* Batman."

"I helped the hotel discreetly handle a theft problem with one of their employees last year, so they owed me a favor."

"And now I owe you."

"Nope." He shook his graying head. "The department wants you healthy, wants you back. That's how you repay me."

Not wanting to go down that road, especially not here, with so many people possibly watching, he jerked out a nod. "Doing my best."

"What happened to Floyd wasn't your fault. It could have happened to any of us."

Jake gestured to the business center around the corner, off to the side of the lobby. "How about we see what's on that drive?"

The *center* was a counter with two stools, a phone, a couple desktop computers, and a printer. Jake stood where he could keep Rachel in his sightline while Oz opened the drive on one of the computers, clicked on a folder marked with today's date, and found a file labeled River Walk View.

Oz watched the footage for a few moments, and then sent Jake a disappointed look. "Looks like the attack happened just a few yards out of range."

Jake leaned over his shoulder. "Try the one with yesterday's date, the file labeled Parking Garage Exit. Some time in the evening hours before ten o'clock."

Oz clicked and the screen displayed the exit gate in the hotel's parking garage. Several cars came and went as Jake watched. The image was a little grainy, and amber-colored due to the dim lighting in the garage.

"What are we looking for?" Oz asked.

"A black Lexus." After weeks of tailing the guy, he easily spouted off Bryce's plate number. The camera angle allowed at least a partial view of the rear of the cars, including the license plates, as they exited.

With one eye on the video footage and the other on Rachel and her friends, Jake filled Oz in on his suspicions about Bryce, the man's mysterious disappearance yesterday, and his equally puzzling, violent reappearance today. When the time stamp in the corner showed nine-twenty at night—about a half hour before Rachel had arrived at Hotel del Corazon, a Lexus that looked a lot like Bryce's car pulled up to the gate and a man who could have been Bryce leaned out his window, looked right and left, and slid a card into the slot. The gate opened and the man drove through. The whole thing was about twenty seconds long. They couldn't tell if anyone was in the passenger seat or the back of the car. Bryce Schafer had been alive and well at nine-twenty last night. He'd left the hotel. So where was he now? And where was the woman he'd met with?

"Can I watch that again?" Jake asked.

"That's the guy?"

"I think so."

Oz replayed the portion with the Lexus. Jake's eyes were drawn to a dark stain on the forearm of the man's light-colored sleeve as he reached out to slide his card into the slot that would open the gate.

Oz froze the image on a frame that best showed the sleeve. "You thinking what I'm thinking?"

"I'm thinking that looks like blood."

# CHAPTER 5

THE GROUP GATHERED AROUND HER SUDDENLY WENT QUIET. RACHEL looked up as the sea of concerned faces parted and Jake and another man came into view.

"Rachel, this is Detective Robert Osborn." Jake introduced his companion. "He's a colleague and friend of mine. We call him Oz."

She stiffened at the reminder that Jake hadn't trusted her enough to share this part of his life. He'd been SAPD, a cop. And he'd been using her to investigate Bryce. It still stung that she'd thought they'd formed an instant connection, but it had all been in her head. Instead, she realized now that he'd never trusted her. There could be no connection without trust.

Osborn took the seat across from her and leaned forward, his kind gaze meeting hers. "I understand you've had a difficult day."

She looked at Jake, remembering how he'd been a bright spot in her day—until he'd betrayed her. "You could say that."

"Jake tells me you might know your attacker, that it could be a Dr. Bryce Schafer?"

Osborn proceeded to ask for a description of the assailant and an accounting of the events of the day. She did her best to provide all of the details, shuddering as she got to the part where she'd gone underwater. The memory of sinking into the cold river, the water closing over her head, had her swallowing hard. She felt a hand at her shoulder, and knew that it had been the hand that had pulled her from the water. Jake. He'd moved to her side. Despite her declaration that she could do this by herself and her anger at him for misleading her, she felt better having him here.

"You and Bryce recently broke up?" Osborn asked.

"You could say that, though I'm not sure we were ever really together. We were only dating for a few weeks before I broke it off a couple days ago. I guess I'd describe it as a trial run."

"Which he failed," Emma muttered from somewhere behind her.

"Miserably," Cecilia added. "Of course, it doesn't take much to turn his head."

Osborn's gaze remained on Rachel. "He was involved with another woman?"

She shrugged. "Probably. When I went to his room to talk to him last night—his idea, not mine—it looked like he'd already met with another woman." She glanced at Jake, remembering how he'd been there with her. It had felt like he'd been there *for* her, too. But that could have been wishful thinking. "I found a silver locket there." She lifted the necklace that hung at her neck. "It was identical to this one."

"Lauren," Emma said with a nod. "It had to be her he was meeting with."

"Lauren?" the detective asked.

"Lauren Foley," Cecilia put in helpfully. "F-O-L-E-Y."

"We don't know that for sure," Adriana said. "She said she was sick."

"She always was an opportunist," Emma added. "Remember when she stole my boyfriend senior year?"

Cecilia nodded. "She's always been competitive."

"Has anyone heard from Lauren today?" Osborn asked.

Adriana shook her head. "I texted her a get-well message this morning, but she didn't respond. I assume she's resting."

Emma snorted. "Or in Vegas."

"With Bryce," Cecilia added.

Detective Osborn stood. "I'd like to ask her a few questions."

"I'll try calling her now," Adriana offered. Cell phone in hand, she stepped aside to place the call.

From beside her, Jake leaned in to speak so that only Rachel could hear. "By the way, Oz and I watched security footage from the hotel's cameras. It shows Bryce driving out of the parking garage at about nine-twenty last night."

She glanced at him and saw the regret in his eyes. He was extending her an olive branch by sharing information with her. She nodded in acknowledgement of the offering.

"Still no answer," Adriana said.

"I'll speak to the hotel manager and have someone let us into her room," Osborn said. "In the meantime, perhaps you all can wait nearby. I may need to talk to you again." He shared a look with Jake and then headed for the reception desk.

Was Bryce with Lauren now? Part of Rachel wanted to confront the pair.

"I want to go with him," Jake said, "but I don't want to leave you alone here."

She shook her head. "I'm not alone. I'm surrounded by hotel staff, friends, and your family. And there's a wall between me and the river."

He didn't laugh. "I'd feel better if I had you at my side."

She would too, but she wasn't ready to admit her weakness for him. "I can go with you."

It was his turn to shake his head. "I don't want you anywhere near where Bryce might be, especially after what he did to you."

"Fine. I'll stay here. I need to talk to Adriana, anyway." Rachel spotted the bride-to-be heading into the hotel bar with Jeremy, the rest of her bridal party, her parents, and Vida and Ernesto Rosales.

"Don't leave the hotel. And don't go anywhere alone. Promise me." His expression showed his concern, and she hardened her heart against the softening she felt.

"I promise. I certainly don't want to end up in the river again." She hid a shudder.

"Thank you." His gratitude surprised her into meeting his gaze. That was when he surprised her again by leaning down to capture her lips in a kiss that was hot and urgent—and over much too quickly. When he pulled back, there was a lingering heat in his eyes. "I know you're angry with me, but I'll make it up to you. That's *my* promise."

He was striding toward the elevator before she could even think how to respond.

"THANKS FOR LETTING ME TAG ALONG." JAKE RODE WITH OZ AND the hotel manager to the tenth floor.

"Come back to work and this could be your glamorous life every day," Oz said.

Jake snorted and then shook his head. "I think I'm nearly there. I miss the part where I help people." He'd felt ineffective since leaving. Investigating Bryce had given him some sense of purpose, but what would happen when all of this was settled?

Osborn eyed him. "You were close to making detective, weren't you?"

"I was on that track." He only had another six months of service as a patrol officer before he could apply for detective.

"Seems to me that's the best way you could help people. I meant what I said before. What happened with Officer Lancaster could have happened to any of us."

Jake wasn't so sure, but he bit his tongue. Besides, they'd arrived at the tenth floor. They headed toward Lauren's room, which was at the opposite end of the long hall from his and from Bryce's. At room 1028, the manager knocked. There was no answer, and a do not disturb sign hung on the door. They tried again.

Jake spoke up this time. "Lauren, are you in there? It's Jeremy's brother, Jake. Everyone's worried about you. Please open up or we're going to force the door open. We just want to make sure you're okay."

When there was still no answer, Oz nodded at the manager, who slid his master key into the slot, and then stood aside. Oz and Jake had taken a few steps into the room when they saw her, a blonde laying across the bed in sexy red lingerie, the comforter beneath her soaked in a congealing puddle of blood. It appeared she'd been shot in the chest.

"That's Lauren Foley," Jake confirmed when Oz sent him a questioning look.

There was no doubt she was dead. Her eyes were open and she was pale and unmoving. The smell of blood and death was the next thing to hit them. That was quickly followed by the sound of a gasp echoing in the silent room. Jake whirled and his gaze locked onto Rachel's pale face.

Her hand dropped from where it covered her mouth. "Somebody shot Lauren?"

Jake quickly shifted to block her view and backed her into the hallway where the manager was standing. The man was looking pretty pale, too.

"We'll be calling for a forensic team," Jake told the manager. "You might want to make arrangements to keep people away from this floor, or at least this room." The manager nodded and hustled away.

He turned to Rachel and forced himself to unclench his jaw. He wasn't angry with her so much as he hated that she'd seen the body. "You promised you'd stay downstairs with the others."

"I figured I'd be safer sticking close to you. Besides, I thought if Lauren was sick, I might be able to help." She swallowed hard.

"And yeah, maybe part of me wanted to confront Bryce if he was here. But I never expected *this*."

In his time with the SAPD, he'd seen a few scenes like the one inside that hotel room. Hell, he'd seen worse while serving in the military. But for Rachel, this expression of raw violence was new. He thought of Bryce's sleeve and the dark, wet stain on it. Now he wondered if it had been Lauren's blood, and if the man was capable of murder.

Oz emerged from Lauren's room and slid his cell phone into his pocket. "Detective Brock, the crime scene techs, and the coroner are on their way." Jake knew the other homicide detective as well. In fact, Oz and Brock had been mentors as Jake had explored the possibility of making detective.

"I'd like to stay." Jake examined Rachel's face. She was still in shock. "I'll have Jeremy take you back downstairs, okay?"

"I can stay, too." But her words were shaky.

"I don't want you near this. Besides, you'd be the best one to break the news to the others."

Her eyes widened, and she nodded. "Okay."

He made a quick call to Jeremy, telling him nothing about what they'd found in Lauren's room. He asked that he come to the tenth floor, alone, as soon as possible. He hung up and saw Rachel, arms wrapped around herself, gazing absently toward the door to Lauren's room.

She caught him looking at her and shook her head. "I know I was mad at you before, but at the moment, I'm kind of glad you have SAPD connections. Poor Lauren."

"Oz will help her find justice."

Her gaze turned thoughtful. "Are you a detective for the SAPD, too?"

"No, but I wanted to be." He braced himself for the usual follow-up questions about why he was no longer on that track, but she didn't probe. Instead, she surprised him by understanding his need for space, and maybe offering forgiveness.

"I'd like to hear more about it sometime, when you're ready." Her expression was still guarded, but no longer completely shut off. It encouraged him, and he offered yet another olive branch.

"Maybe tonight, if you let me drive you home."

She gave him a soft smile. "I'd like that. But it looks like you'll be here a while."

"Not too long. I don't have the authority to process the scene, after all." But he did want another peek at what had happened inside, and Oz's thoughts as to whether Bryce could have been involved. "When I'm done, I'll take you home to get some things."

A wrinkle of confusion creased her forehead. "What do you mean?"

"You're not staying by yourself while a killer is out there."

Down the hall, Jeremy rushed off the elevator and, spying them standing there, hurried toward them. "What's going on?"

"Lauren's been murdered," Jake said.

"What?"

"I'll explain more later. Can you take Rachel downstairs to the others?"

"Of course."

Jake sent his brother a look of gratitude. "Don't let her out of your sight." He gave Rachel a quick kiss on the forehead and breathed in her scent. "It's going to be okay. Go with Jeremy now."

She nodded mutely and let him hand her off to his brother. Jake watched until they got on the elevator.

He moved to the doorway of Lauren's room, careful not to touch anything. He wished he could work the case. He missed feeling useful. "I'm at your disposal, Oz."

Oz grunted. "If only you were officially working for the SAPD again."

"I'll be working on that soon."

"Glad to hear it. You still can't work the case."

"I'm here if you need me, even if it's to fetch you a coffee." When he was back on the job, it would be a different story.

. . .

"Are you okay?" Jeremy gazed at her with concern.

"I will be," Rachel said.

But Lauren would never be okay again. While Rachel had never been close to the woman, and Lauren had likely been involved with Bryce behind Rachel's back, Lauren didn't deserve what had happened to her. Nobody did.

"By the way," she continued, "I know Jake was investigating Bryce for you. He didn't want to tell me. I just wish he hadn't hidden his true motives."

Jeremy grimaced. "Don't blame him for that. I asked him not to tell you. I wasn't sure we could fully trust you. But Jake says you're good, and that makes you good in my book." Hearing that Jake had defended her, and that he hadn't wanted to lie to her, melted the rest of the ice she'd built up around her heart. "Plus, you ended up in the river. I doubt Bryce would have done that if you were working with him."

She lightly punched Jeremy's arm. "You know me better than that."

"Yeah, I do. I shouldn't have doubted you. Accept my apology?"

"Don't let it happen again."

"Wouldn't even think of it." Jeremy draped an arm over her shoulder as they entered the hotel bar and crossed to the large table where Adriana was surrounded by her parents, future in-laws, bridesmaids, and groomsmen—everyone except Jack, Bryce, and Lauren.

Adriana looked up as they approached. "Is Lauren still sick?"

Rachel's lip quivered and she bit down hard, but she didn't have to respond because Jeremy did it for her.

"I'm sorry," he said. "She's dead. I wish I didn't have to break the news this way."

Adriana froze. As Jeremy's blunt statement sank in, the rest of the group around her erupted with questions and exclamations.

"I don't understand," Adriana said. "I thought it was just a virus." Jeremy moved to hug her.

Rachel shook her head. "She wasn't sick. She was murdered." More questions filled the room and she raised her hand to signal for silence. "Jake's up there right now, trying to get more information. I don't know anything else."

"This is horrible," Emma said, swiping at her tears. "I feel bad for joking she'd gone to Vegas."

Cecilia nodded and blew her nose into a napkin. "Me too." Her jaw dropped. "Was it Bryce?"

"It is odd that he disappeared at the same time," Rachel said. "The two of them worked together at S&R, so it makes sense they knew each other. But why would he kill her?"

"We should postpone the wedding until we figure this out," Vida Rosales declared. "We all understand."

Adriana sobbed into Jeremy's shirt.

"We can decide that later," Jeremy said.

Adriana lifted her head with a hiccup and pressed her lips together. "No. I'm not going to let anyone steal our dreams. It's our special day and nobody, including Bryce, is going to ruin it. Lauren would forgive us, I'm sure. She was a good friend. And we'll honor her, of course. We can have a special ceremony for her."

Rachel sighed and sank into a seat, murmuring her thanks when Emma pushed a glass of water toward her. "I just don't understand how this escalated."

Adriana shook her head. "They both had tempers. Maybe things got heated. Hell, she was probably jealous and angry, since Bryce wanted to meet with you. Like Cecilia said, Lauren was a competitive woman."

Rachel's head whipped toward her. "We'd broken up. She had no reason to be jealous. He just wanted to talk and get some of his things back."

"I'm glad it isn't you they found dead upstairs. What if he didn't really want to talk when he asked you to come to the hotel? What if you had showed up when he was enraged?" Adriana glanced around the group. "We all have to take extra care of each other."

Emma snorted. "I think you two have safety covered. You each have your own personal bodyguards. So lucky."

Cecilia nodded. "The Rosales brothers are legit white knights." She smiled at Jeremy, and then turned to Mrs. Rosales. "You did good. They're nothing like Bryce."

"Nothing," Emma agreed, and started crying again. "Poor Lauren." There was a long moment of silence as they grieved for their friend.

Adriana stood suddenly and straightened her spine as if going into battle. "If anything, what happened to Lauren proves that we never know how much time we have left, so we should grab at happiness wherever and whenever we can."

Jeremy stroked a hand over his fiancée's back. "So true." He smiled wearily. "Life is short. Whatever you want to do, we'll do it."

"The wedding is on," Adriana announced, and swiped at a tear before looking up at Jeremy. "I want to make you my husband as soon as possible." She glanced around the group. "The bachelorette party is still on for tomorrow. We'll find a way to honor Lauren there."

Jake entered the bar and approached the table as Adriana made her announcement. He looked concerned, but sent a small smile of reassurance Rachel's way. "Can we make that party a group event instead of splitting up into guys and girls? I think it would be safer."

"Sticking together is probably wise," Jeremy agreed. "We should have a group event instead of separate parties tomorrow."

Adriana looked as if she might object, but, seeing the brothers' expressions, relented. "The more the merrier. I'll figure out some-thing and send the details out to everyone." She looked at Rachel. "I guess you don't have your phone. Or maybe you'll get it back soon."

At the reminder of all that she'd lost today, her stomach

clenched again. But at least she hadn't lost her life. She glanced at Jake, sending him a silent plea.

He read her thoughts. "I can take you home now."

As Rachel said her goodbyes, Emma caught her eye and mouthed the words, *white knight*.

# CHAPTER 6

RACHEL'S HEAD WAS STILL SPINNING. JUDGING BY JAKE'S SILENCE AS he walked her to the hotel garage and unlocked his silver pickup truck, he was still processing what had happened too. Other than saying he'd take her home long enough to grab a few things, he hadn't spoken.

"I wish we could get into my car," she said as they drove past the parking garage she'd chosen that morning. "I have my duffel bag there and it has a change of clothing. You wouldn't have to take me home." It also contained her stethoscope and a few first aid supplies for emergencies.

He glanced her way. "In the military, we called that a go bag or a bug-out bag. We had to be ready to go in an instant."

"You were in the military?"

"Before joining the SAPD, I was Army. I didn't get a college scholarship fresh out of high school like Jeremy did and my parents didn't have a lot of extra money left over after running a restaurant, no matter how successful it was." It seemed both she and Jake had faced challenges growing up and overcome them.

She appreciated that he was sharing a piece of himself and wanted to keep him talking. "Your mom must have been relieved when you left the military. Of course, when you came back you joined the police force."

"She was still worried about my safety, but at least I was back home. Plus, I came out of it all with a handy skillset. If you really need your bag, I can break into your car." He shot her a mischievous grin.

She laughed, happy to feel this easy with him again. "That's okay. I can get a few things from home."

"Will we need to break in?" His wink said he was still teasing.

"Thankfully, the landlord has a spare key hidden in the yard." They fell into a comfortable silence. Unfortunately, her brain wouldn't settle. She bit her lip, not wanting to revisit the scene of Lauren's murder in her mind, but full of too many questions to avoid it. "Did you find out anything else after Jeremy and I left you on the tenth floor?"

He looked out the driver's side for a moment, avoiding her probing gaze. "We probably shouldn't talk about it."

She tried to bury her disappointment but failed. "You still don't want to share things with me, don't trust me with details? I played your game the other night. The least you can do is return the favor."

This time, he looked at her. "Game?"

"At the bar. You asked me to share something unexpected, something nobody else knew. It's your turn."

A muscle jumped in his jaw. "It's not that I don't trust you. It's that I want to protect you. And me, too, I guess."

She softened. "You can tell me anything, Jake. About you, about work, about whatever."

"Some of it's pretty ugly. You might run the other way."

"Give me some credit. My medical career started in downtown Chicago. I work in a community clinic in a poverty-stricken area of town where people don't always have the means or the will to care for themselves. I've seen and heard some pretty ugly things."

He was quiet for a long time before he spoke again. "My partner died. It was my fault."

She bit back a gasp. Inside, her heart squeezed for him. "I'm sure that's not true."

He sent her a sad smile. "I appreciate you saying that, but you don't know the story."

"No, but I know you. Or, at least, I feel like I do. And Detective Osborn—Oz—seems to know you, too. I don't get the sense he blames you for whatever happened either."

He shook his head. "I should have been there. That's all there is to it."

She was certain there was so much more, but he wasn't ready to share. "Thank you for sharing at least that much with me. And I hope, over time, you realize that what you could contribute to our community by being in law enforcement far outweighs anything that happened. The world needs more men like you."

He shook his head but didn't argue. She'd consider that a win.

"What about the rest?" she asked a moment later. "What else did you find out about Lauren's death?"

He was quiet a long moment, but when he sighed, she knew he'd decided to share his findings. More progress.

"Lauren was shot once in the chest at close range, probably within the past twelve to twenty-four hours," he said. Well within the timeframe Bryce had been missing. "There was blood in the bathroom, too, which indicated the killer hung around afterward and cleaned up before leaving."

"That seems so...cold. But that means there could be DNA evidence, right?"

"Probably. But it'll take weeks, if not months, to get the results. In the meantime, we still don't know where Bryce is. Finding him is the key right now—both to this mystery and to making sure he's not a threat to you. That's why you're coming home with me tonight." He pulled up to the curb and parked where she indicated but didn't get out of the car. Instead, he turned to look at her. "I'm going to keep you safe. I'm not going to leave you to face this alone."

She shivered, but not from fear. Anticipation thrummed beneath the surface of her skin.

"You might not trust me yet, but you can trust that," he added. On some level, she was aware that his need to protect her stemmed from what had happened to his partner, and his perceived failure.

"I know I'm safe with you." She held his gaze, wanting him to understand that she trusted him with her life.

He gave a sharp nod. "Let's get your stuff and go to my place." Her body tightened at the thought of staying overnight with him. She wanted him with an ache so fierce it scared her.

Her tiny guest cottage was tucked behind the larger house owned by two married doctors she knew from the hospital. She and Jake walked along the driveway to the cobblestone walkway that led to her door. Twilight colored the sky a deep purple that was nearly black. Shadows played tricks with her eyes and she was glad Jake was at her side as she retrieved her spare key from under the flowerpot beside her door.

Jake slid her a glance. "That wouldn't fool most criminals."

"Not much crime in this neighborhood."

She opened the door, flipped on the lights, and came to a sudden stop. The living room had been tossed. She rushed to her bedroom. Drawers hung open and linens had been stripped from the bed and left in heaps, a far cry from how she'd left her house this morning.

"Rachel? Damn it, stop! Let me check things out first." Jake growled out his command and pushed past her. His eyes were everywhere as he checked the bedroom, bathroom, and closet. "All clear. But if it hadn't been...."

If it hadn't been, she might have been attacked. She hadn't even considered that the intruder might still be here. She wrapped her arms around herself. The one place she'd truly felt safe had been violated.

"One," she whispered. *Be aware of who you are.* "Two." *Inhale deeply.*

"What are you doing?" Jake had his phone out and was dialing.

"Breathing exercises. After my mom died, a school counselor taught me how to use them to relax." Despite her efforts, her breathing was becoming rapid and shallow.

Phone at his ear, Jake ducked down to look into her downcast eyes. "What's three? Tell me, Rachel."

Some part of her realized he was trying to pull her back from the edge of panic. Fear clawed at her lungs with long, sharp nails. "Three is try to relax."

He ran a hand down her arm. "Hey, you're going to be okay. Keep counting." He broke away as he spoke to someone on the other end of the line.

*Four. Exhale slowly.*

*Five. Inhale deeply.*

*Six. Exhale slowly, releasing the stress and negativity.*

When Jake hung up, he glanced at her again. Apparently, she looked calm enough, because he gave her a tight smile instead of trying to talk her down.

"There are bloody bandages in the bathroom and a first aid kit on the counter. I'm guessing they're not yours?"

"No. You think he's hurt?" A chirping sound drew her attention to her bedside table and, recognizing the sound, she rushed toward it. "It's my phone."

"I thought you said it was stolen along with your purse."

"It was." She picked it up and searched the area for her purse and its other contents. She found it on the kitchen counter and immediately checked for her other belongings. "My wallet's here, but my keys are still missing." She looked at Jake in disbelief. "Bryce did this?"

Her phone chirped again and she scrolled through the recent activity on the screen. "A text from Adriana just came through with the new, combined bachelor-bachelorette party info and something about a tribute to Lauren. There's another text from Bryce."

He looked over her shoulder. "From about an hour ago."

"*I'm being framed,*" she read aloud. "*I didn't shoot Lauren.* I suppose standing me up and stealing my purse doesn't necessarily mean he killed Lauren. What if he *was* framed?"

"You're so willing to believe the best in other people. It's a gift. But my gut's telling me this is another of Bryce's lies. Besides, how did he know she was shot unless he was in her room?"

She blew out a breath. "That's what my gut says, too."

His phone rang and he pulled it from his pocket to look at the screen.

"Who is it?" she asked.

"It's Oz." He answered with a quick greeting. His lips pulled downward as he listened. "Where?" His gaze shifted to her. "Pecan Grove Community Health Clinic?"

The hairs at her nape rose.

"We'll be right there," Jake said. "And Oz, someone broke into Rachel's house too."

After he hung up, Rachel pounced on him. "Something's wrong at the clinic?"

"The cops found Bryce's car in the parking lot."


Pecan Grove Community Health Clinic was on a smaller street, just off the main road and away from the evening traffic. Ten minutes after Rachel had hastily packed an overnight bag, Jake pulled his truck into the clinic's parking lot. The night was dark, the area lit only by a couple streetlights. It was also cold now that the sun had set.

"We've got to stop meeting like this," Oz said as they joined him beside Bryce's shiny Lexus. His tone was dialed to sarcasm, but his attentive gaze surveyed Rachel. Jake saw the consideration and doubt in the man's eyes. She was still a person of interest in whatever was going on with Bryce, and now there was Lauren's murder to consider. Hell, if Jake had been investigating the case, he'd have been suspicious, too. She seemed to be at the center of everything. But deep down, he knew she couldn't have done anything illegal, and that Bryce had dragged her into his mess. She certainly didn't need to break into her own clinic. Besides, Jake had been with her all afternoon.

"What have you got?" Jake asked.

"First, there are these." Oz held up a set of keys.

"You found them!" Rachel exclaimed.

"Don't get too excited. They were used to get into the clinic, which was picked over. Looks like he disabled the alarm, made a mess inside, then left out the back on foot. Could be our officer showed up while he was inside and he couldn't make it back to his car."

"What time did the clinic close today?" Jake asked Rachel.

"Five," she said.

"We can't be more than two hours behind him. He's certainly not acting like an innocent man."

"Not at all," Rachel agreed.

"Bryce sent her a text to say he's being framed for shooting Lauren," he explained to Oz.

Oz's brows went up. "Well, since her murder hasn't gone public, I'd say he has to know something about it."

"Unless someone from the wedding party or hotel notified him," Jake said. "But I checked and everyone swears they haven't been in contact with him."

"Wait. You said Rachel got a text?"

"We found her cell phone, purse, and wallet in her house," Jake said. "Along with signs Bryce had cleaned and bandaged himself in her bathroom. He must not have had the supplies he needed to deal with his wound."

"That's odd, since the mess inside the clinic indicates something similar."

"Maybe the wound was too serious for him to bandage effectively at my house," Rachel suggested. "A lot of my first aid supplies, including a suture kit, were in my medical bag, which wasn't at home. He would have known he could find better equipment here. And since he had the keys, it would have been easy to get in."

"Or maybe he took your purse because he needed to get into your house and the clinic," Jake said thoughtfully. "Maybe this is about more than bandaging a wound."

Rachel frowned. "It must not have been a life-threatening wound, anyway. Otherwise, he wouldn't be moving around so much, wouldn't have mugged me, and probably would have gone to the hospital, even if he was a murder suspect."

"I'd like you to look around inside," Oz told her. "We need you to tell us if anything is missing. But don't touch anything. There's one room in particular that seemed to be his focal point. I have a patrol car on the way to Bryce's house, in case he fled to somewhere familiar. Another is headed to the S&R offices."

"Tell them to approach with caution," Jake warned. He didn't want what had happened to his partner to happen to anyone else.

Jake was first inside the clinic. While the officer on the scene had cleared it, he wanted to double-check it himself to make sure it was safe for Rachel. And yeah, part of him wanted to make sure the asshole hadn't left her any more messages. If the guy had been framed, why not come forward and let the police sort things out? Jake found the room that seemed to be of key interest to Bryce. A syringe lay on the counter with a bottle of a clear liquid nearby. Bloody gauze pads were scattered near the sink. A white men's dress shirt with blood on it lay on the floor. An instrument table was left cluttered with the items one might need for...hell, he wasn't sure. But Rachel would know.

He returned to Rachel's side. "It's okay to go in." He let her walk ahead of him this time, wanting her to form her own impressions of the scene. At the doorway to the room where Bryce seemed to have spent the most time, she stopped. "Theories on what happened here?"

Her narrowed gaze continued to sweep the room, pausing on various items. "I'd say he sterilized and stitched a wound." She pointed to the small bottle next to the used syringe. "That's an antibiotic."

"Based on the blood on the shirt he left behind, the wound was his left forearm. Would he would be able to stitch that?"

She thought a moment. "He's right-handed, so yes. It would be difficult, but not impossible if he was determined."

"Let's hope the patrol officer finds him at his place." He'd sleep better if he knew where Bryce was, and that the guy was behind bars, unable to get to Rachel.

While Jake called Jeremy to fill him in on Bryce's latest adventures, Rachel called her coworkers to inform them about the break-in and police investigation. As he hung up, he overheard her assuring them she'd be there in the morning to clean up the mess. Bryce's mess. Jake could strangle the guy.

Back in the parking lot, they were about to climb into Jake's truck to head to his place when the radio from Oz's car announced a code. Jake paused, recognizing the alert and the address. He'd been at that house often enough in recent weeks.

Shots fired on an officer. Bryce Schafer's home address.

Heart in his throat, all too aware of what an officer-involved shooting could mean, his eyes met Oz's. The detective picked up his radio to confirm the details with dispatch. He turned to Jake, his gaze understanding. "Nobody was hurt. A man fired as the officer approached the door, but the officer took cover. Suspect fled from the rear of the house on foot and got away. He matches Bryce's description."

Jake put an arm around Rachel's shoulder, wishing he could always keep her this close, this protected. One thing was sure, he wasn't leaving her alone tonight.

# CHAPTER 7

THEY WALKED INTO THE RESTAURANT TUCKED INTO THE CORNER OF A strip mall and Rachel immediately perked up. Her stomach growled, reminding her that, despite everything, she was human and still alive. Then again, the enticing scents of roasted meat, onions, and fresh tortillas would have been enough to pull her back from the brink of death. The ambience, a kaleidoscope of color and lively music, delighted her other senses.

"I hope this place is okay." Jake looked unsure.

"It's fantastic. It's got an old-world charm and smells wonderful."

He grinned. "Great. Vida Loca is my parents' restaurant. The name means—"

"Crazy life." Rachel returned his smile. "I grew up in San Antonio too, remember? Plus, fluency in Spanish comes in handy in my line of work."

"Yet another unexpected surprise." As he held the door for her, Jake informed her that Vida and Lou Rosales had run the restaurant for decades and it was still going strong. His pride in his family's success was obvious. That he wanted to share this part of himself with her made Rachel feel even closer to him.

They were greeted warmly by the hostess, who was apparently one of Jake's younger cousins. "It's good to see you," Lisa said as she led them to a table. "Your parents will be pleased to hear you stopped in. It's been quiet around here."

"Probably because they've been staying at the hotel." Jake winked.

"Nearly had to kick them out and force them to take a few days off. Must run in the family."

So, Jake was a workhorse. Rachel would have guessed that about him, given the way he'd agreed to investigate Bryce for his brother, even during his personal leave from the force. Rachel's smile slipped as she remembered that he hadn't been at work in months because he blamed himself for a horrible incident. Would he ever be able to move past it? She studied him as he ordered a "sampling" of menu items that was enough to feed an entire mariachi band.

His gaze narrowed on her. "What? I can see the wheels turning."

"I'm thinking about why you left a job you clearly loved."

He turned his water glass on the table, watching the ice shift. "I figured we'd eventually get back to that."

"We don't have to talk about it if you're not ready."

He studied her and sighed. "I don't want to hide anything from you. Not anymore." That touched her more than he could know.

"I saw the way you reacted when we heard about the shooting at Bryce's house." Thankfully, the officer had been okay. But Jake's situation had obviously ended differently. "Were you hurt?"

"No." He leaned back and tapped a finger on the table in an uncharacteristic sign of nerves. "My partner was. Floyd Lancaster. He was shot and died at the scene." He went quiet for a moment, lost in some memory of that traumatic day. "Some said I didn't do enough to protect him. There was an investigation and I was cleared but it was…rough. Floyd was a friend. I was supposed to be backup when he confronted a suspect. Floyd jumped out of the car and the guy had a gun in his hands before I could get in position. I should have been there."

"Or he could have waited."

His gaze pinned her. "He's the one who lost his life. He lost everything."

"Because he decided not to wait. And because some guy you didn't expect to be violent came out shooting. Floyd's death is a tragic loss, but it wasn't your fault. In fact, you might have been killed, too." She reached out to wrap her fingers around his tapping one and hold his hand. "I can see that you cared. I can also see you miss being a cop. Don't let Floyd's choices change yours."

His brown eyes shuttered. "I can go back any time."

"Then why haven't you? Or maybe it's difficult to constantly deal with people who could be thieves, psychopaths, or killers. That must be tough."

"You learn not to trust lightly. And to appreciate the people you can count on, like family." He looked around the restaurant. "It's a gift to have strong family roots."

She thought about Vida's pride in her sons, and her concern that Jake find his way through a tough time. "But you *are* going back?"

He shrugged. "I kind of like having the time off to relax."

She snorted. "Liar." He was obviously meant to protect and serve.

"Hey, if I hadn't been on leave, I couldn't have looked into the stolen files for Jeremy, and then I wouldn't have had the opportunity to get closer to you. And that's something I don't regret at all." His fingers entwined with hers and he leaned closer, tugging her forward until their lips could meet. His kiss was short and sweet, a promise of more to come.

They enjoyed a delicious meal of the best authentic Mexican food Rachel had ever eaten, during which several of the cooks and waiters came over to say hello. After they were finished, Jake hugged his cousin goodbye and walked Rachel to his truck.

"Where to now?" she asked as he slid into the driver's seat beside her.

"Home? My home, that is."

"Yes, please." She leaned over and kissed him and the heat that had simmered between them all evening flared. When she pulled away, sparks of desire danced in his eyes. Without another word, he started driving.

Five minutes later, they pulled up to an apartment building and he shut off the engine. The two-story brick building stretched across several acres. It was a bit weathered with time, but otherwise a nice location.

"Told you it was nothing special." He sounded almost defensive.

"The setting doesn't define the person," she said. "Remember that I grew up in a run-down trailer."

The defensiveness faded and he smiled. "Want to see the luxury that awaits?"

Inside, he set her bag on a chair and locked the door. His apartment was neat and clean, the furniture comfortable, if sparse. He seemed to have a bare-bones approach to life. The personal touches, such as framed pictures of family on a shelf and a guitar on its stand in the corner, indicated he only kept close what he needed, what he enjoyed or valued. It made her feel all the more privileged that he'd kept her close these past couple days.

"Thank you for being with me tonight, through it all," Rachel said, unsure how to express exactly how much it meant to her. Despite finding out he'd kept some things from her, she was feeling a connection with him she'd never felt so deeply, or so quickly, with any other man. She chose to show him with her actions. She stepped close, waiting for a cue as to how she should proceed, or if her advances would be welcome. "And thank you for giving me a place to sleep tonight."

"My pleasure." He scanned her face, and a breathless moment

passed until he reached for her. She walked into his arms, her mouth meeting his as if it belonged there. The kiss was gentle, a reassuring warmth that had her relaxing into his embrace. Soon, though, her body demanded more. Her fingers traced his shoulders and wound their way into his short hair. She tipped her head to slant her mouth in a more satisfying angle. She flicked her tongue across his. He groaned and his arms tightened around her. One hand came up to cup the back of her head, as if reluctant to be parted even a few inches from her. He backed her against the wall and devoured her until they were both panting.

He drew away to study her eyes. "Do you want to see the rest of the place?"

Rachel knew what he was really asking. He wanted to be sure she knew what she was getting into if she said yes. "Yes."

"Thank God." He took her hand and led her to the bedroom. She caught a quick glimpse of his kitchen and a small dining area on her way to the master bedroom. Again, neat and tidy ruled here, but it was also warm and inviting—like Jake's arms when they were around her.

They stood by his bed, stripping each other until they were skin-to-skin. Her eyes widened when he removed a revolver and ankle holster from around his leg and placed it on the dresser.

"It's just a precaution," he said. He pulled her into his arms and all thought of guns and safety fled as his heat enveloped her.

Her breasts pressed against his chest, her nipples hardening at the contact. She fell sideways with him to the soft mattress. His hand drifted down her side and his fingers gripped her bare hip before sweeping over her bottom and trailing down her thigh. When he reached her knee, his hand pulled it up so that her thigh lay on top of his, leaving her sex exposed to his questing fingers. He stroked her with a sense of purpose that made her cry out his name.

. . .

HIS NAME ON HER LIPS MADE JAKE'S ERECTION THROB WITH A NEED that bordered on pain. Her ragged breathing matched his, as if they'd both just run for their lives, but he couldn't stop kissing her. He needed her more than air. She didn't just kiss him back. She challenged him, and he loved it. She bit his bottom lip gently, and then licked it. Another hungry growl rumbled in his throat. Her expression as he found her sensitive core mirrored his own—desire, frustration, and promise. He turned the tables on her, kissing her with all the pent-up passion he'd been restraining. She planted a hand at his shoulder, rolled him to his back, and straddled him. Her wet heat pressed against his length and had him gasping for breath.

"Hang on a second," he managed, and reached for his bedside drawer to retrieve a condom. He hurried to put it on. He throbbed, impatient to sink into her.

She gave a sound of encouragement and continued to devour his mouth. One of his hands moved downward to grip her butt cheek as he aligned her with him. He entered her slick, tight heat and his entire body rejoiced at the contact. She cried out against his lips and quickened the pace, riding him as he arched into her.

He watched her, enthralled by her abandon, trying to stall his own release until she found hers. She was strawberries and cream, her nipples pink and pebbled, her smooth skin flushed with pleasure. Next time, he'd explore every inch with his mouth.

*Please, God, let there be a next time.*

She quickened the pace and he stroked the nub at the center of her desire in the way he was learning she liked. A moment later, she tensed and cried out her release.

"Jake!" she shouted as she tightened around him.

He grinned against her skin, liking the way his name sounded when she lost control. His grin turned into a groan when she quickly regained the upper hand. She smiled wickedly and pressed her mouth against his, shifting her hips until his body demanded its own release. He threw his head back into the pillow, his entire body exploding with a rush as he came into her.

She slumped against him, and he turned his head to kiss her, his lips not wanting to be separated from her for more than a moment. He felt her lips curve beneath his.

Her eyelids were heavy as she looked at him from beneath long lashes. "God, I needed that." Her cheeks turned pink and her eyes widened. "Did I just say that out loud?"

He grinned. "I heard it."

She dropped her forehead to his chest. "What you must think of me. I don't usually move this fast."

"Look at me, baby."

She lifted her head to meet his gaze.

He never wanted her to feel regret with him. It was too wonderful between them to take for granted. "That was perfect. Take in the good moments whenever you can."

She smiled. "Sounds like an excellent life motto."

"It is." It had certainly gotten him through some difficult times. He pulled her head down to his and kissed her slowly, gently. He breathed in the scent of her, of him, of them together. She didn't seem in a hurry to leave his bed, which was perfect because he intended to keep her there as long as possible.

She rolled to her side and he tucked her up against him, his long legs entangled with hers as their breathing, and their bodies, relaxed. She was quiet for so long he thought she might have fallen asleep.

"What do you think he was looking for?" she asked.

His eyes shot open. He hated that he hadn't been able to distract her for long before they'd returned to the topic of Bryce, but it was inevitable. "You think he's looking for something?"

She turned to face him. "The way he trashed my house? And while nothing was missing from Pecan Grove, I could tell he'd rummaged around in the clinic too. So yeah, I think he's looking for something, and not just suture materials."

"The same thought crossed my mind." He'd intended to go back over both scenes tomorrow, when he took her to work at the clinic, but it appeared she wanted to have this conversation tonight. "Could it be something he gave you?"

She'd mentioned Bryce had sent her a lot of little gifts over the past few weeks, while trying to insert himself back into her life. Jake smothered the jealousy that threatened to rise to the surface. Rachel was his now. She was in his arms, in his bed. *His.*

Her fingers traced a heart-shaped pattern on his chest. It was soothing, but he doubted she was even aware of what she was doing. Her forehead scrunched as she thought. "There were flowers. And chocolates."

"Not very creative. What else?"

"A couple of little things here and there. A lollipop bouquet."

"A what?"

"You know, one of those bouquets made out of cookies or fruit? This was made out of lollipops of different flavors and colors, each wrapped in cellophane. It was pretty. I left it on the front counter at work, where the staff and patients could enjoy it."

"Was there anything else with it? Maybe a note?"

Her cheeks turned bright red. "Something about how he looked forward to licking me like a lollipop, long and slow."

He swallowed hard. "Sounds like he wanted you bad. He's not going to have you." His hand moved over her hip.

She wriggled against him. "No, he's not. But his actions make it even stranger that he had an affair with Lauren at the same time he was pursuing me."

Or the guy could simply be a narcissistic asshole. Jake was betting on the latter. "Anything else?"

"He took me to lunch a few times. Had me come to the S&R research lab once for a tour. Bragged about some drug he was developing that was going to make him a lot of money." She shook her head. "Maybe he's not looking for something. Maybe he was just looking for me."

They were interrupted when his cell phone rang with the chime he'd reserved for his brother's number. It was the middle of the night, which never bode well.

"I have to take this." Jake leaned across her to reach his phone on the bedside table. He took advantage of the position to press a kiss to her bare shoulder and she shifted beneath him, making him hard all over again. She gave him a wicked grin as the evidence of his desire pressed into her belly. He'd hoped to have another chance to make love to the beautiful woman in his bed before morning. But those hopes were dashed as he answered and sensed panic in his brother's opening statement.

"I'm at the hospital," Jeremy said without preamble.

"What's wrong?" Jake pushed to a sitting position against the headboard. Beside him, Rachel sat up too, examining his face as if she could read his thoughts there.

"Adriana was acting weird, almost like she was drugged."

"Did she take anything out of the ordinary?" Rachel asked, apparently overhearing Jeremy's statement.

"Not that I know of."

Jake put Jeremy on speakerphone to save him from having to translate. He'd let the two doctors talk to each other directly.

"She'd been drinking alcohol off and on all day," Rachel said.

"She'd slowed down in the past couple hours, though." Hope and doubt fought each other in Jeremy's words. "We had a round of drinks in the bar after you guys left, to toast Lauren's memory. I insisted she eat something, but she didn't feel like going out. We ordered room service. A short while later, she wasn't feeling well. She went into the bathroom and vomited. She came back to the bed and passed out."

"She lost consciousness?" Rachel's worried gaze met Jake's.

"For a few seconds. I was able to rouse her, but she was mumbling gibberish."

"What's going on now?"

"We're still at the hospital. They're running tests and have her on an IV. She seems much better at the moment."

"I think you were right to take her to the hospital."

Jeremy exhaled. "Thanks. I think so too. I guess I just needed to hear it, since she's asking to go back to the hotel."

"We'll be right there," Jake said. After hanging up, he began gathering items of his and Rachel's clothing, discarded in their determination to get each other naked.

Rachel's forehead crinkled. "Do you think this could be another attack by Bryce, that he somehow tried to drug her?"

He handed her clothes over and began pulling on his own. "The guy's been doing some pretty reckless things. But it would mean he'd have to be at the hotel, which is risky when he's wanted for questioning. But if he's capable of murder, shooting at a police officer, and stealing from his own company, I doubt drugging Adriana was a big leap for him at this point."

Which led him to his next question—what would Bryce do next?

# CHAPTER 8

Rachel blinked as she and Jake walked through the sliding doors and into the bright lights of the ER. They spoke with a nurse and followed her directions to a room in the back made up of three walls and a curtain. As they approached, they heard the sounds of a gentle argument through the closed curtain.

"But I'm fine now," Adriana said.

"A half hour ago, it was a different story." Jeremy's fear and frustration were evident in his hard tone. "We're not walking out of this hospital until you're completely in the clear."

"But we have things to do. The bachelor-bachelorette party, for one. Since we merged them, we need to make sure the new plans are in order. You're sure Rachel and Jake are on their way? Maybe they can help."

Rachel took that as her cue and pulled the curtain aside. Adriana was seated on an exam table, looking tired but otherwise healthy. Feisty, even. Rachel felt a wave of relief. Thank God Bryce's craziness or greed or whatever hadn't claimed another person.

Jake strode straight to his brother to hug him tight. After, he took Adriana's hand and squeezed it. "Everything okay here?"

"Getting there," Jeremy said at the same time Adriana said, "Yes."

Rachel took her friend's free wrist so she could assess her pulse. It seemed strong and steady. Definitely a good sign. "I'm glad you're feeling better."

Adriana turned pleading eyes to Rachel. "You're a medical doctor. Explain to my husband-to-be that my vitals are fine and I'm taking up a bed that someone probably needs more than I do."

"He's concerned because he loves you. You might as well humor him. Enjoy the attention. Besides, losing consciousness is a big deal. It can be a sign of something serious."

"I just needed to purge whatever was making me feel that way. The effects are already wearing off, and I haven't lost consciousness again. Please don't let this ruin my big day."

Rachel would have pointed out that Bryce's odd behavior and Lauren's death had already cast a huge shadow on the festivities, but she didn't want to upset her further. "How did this happen?"

"I don't know. We were just chilling in our room, having a lovely dinner. I started feeling weird. I lay down for a bit, but didn't feel better. I suddenly felt like I was going to throw up."

"She was getting worse," Jeremy said, and stroked a hand across Adriana's brow. "I started thinking about how Lauren had been feeling sick the night she died. Maybe that had been a way of getting her to go to her room, where the killer could get to her."

"You mean Bryce could get to her," Adriana muttered fiercely. She looked up at Jake. "Have the police found him yet?"

"No." Jake's tone was frustrated. "They attempted to reach him at his house, but he got away." And he'd shot at the officer on the scene. Jake was probably giving Adriana and Jeremy the sanitized version to prevent further worry. Still, she saw the concern that knit his brow.

"Maybe a night in the hospital wouldn't be such a bad idea,"

Rachel told Adriana. "There'd be people to watch over you. I doubt Bryce would make a move here."

"I can stand guard outside the door," Jake offered.

Adriana shook her head. "Like I said before, I'm not letting him ruin my wedding plans. Besides, Jake's going to catch him before he can do anything else. Please tell me you've made progress." Adriana looked at Jake.

"Working on it." Jake sent his brother a glance.

"Maybe we should let him get back to it," Jeremy said.

Adriana turned to Rachel. "I heard he broke into your house and clinic. How bad was it?"

"It's a mess," Rachel admitted. "But it's fixable."

"Why do you think he'd do that? It just doesn't make sense."

"Jake and I think he was looking for something. Oddly enough, he left my phone on my nightstand. Even texted me."

Adriana sat up straighter, her interest piqued. "What did he say? Did he explain what's going on?"

"He said he'd been framed."

Jeremy stiffened. "Framed? By who?"

Rachel shrugged. "Didn't say. I assumed it was bait so that I'd agree to meet with him." And then he could hurt her like he'd hurt Lauren and Adriana.

Adriana shook her head. "There's got to be a reason he's targeting you, or seeking you out. What could he want?"

"I wish I knew."

"Please don't agree to see him if he calls. Don't even talk to him. He's dangerous. I don't want to lose another friend."

"Of course not." Rachel squeezed Adriana's hand. She'd learned her lesson and wanted to stay as far away from Bryce as possible.

"Until we figure out what Bryce is after or find him and put him behind bars, we're all in danger," Jake said.

"I think that's enough talk about him for tonight," Jeremy said. He leaned down to kiss Adriana's forehead. "I want you to relax so I can get you healthy and get the heck out of here."

Jake slid a hand around Rachel's waist. "How about we get a cup of coffee and give these two some privacy?"

Rachel followed Jake through the curtain and out into the ER. She said hello to a nurse she recognized and took Jake to the cafeteria, interlacing her fingers with his.

"Adriana looks okay, right?" he asked. "I don't like seeing Jeremy so stressed."

She saw the lines of worry for his brother and wished she could ease his burden. "She looks great. It seems she's on the mend, but the tests will show more." Such as whether she'd been drugged or poisoned.

Though it was after midnight, neither of them would likely be sleeping tonight, so they purchased a couple cups of coffee and a piece of coffee cake to share. The dining room was empty at this late hour except for a couple helicopter pilots from the emergency airlift crew and a few nurses on break. Rachel and Jake took a table near the back.

As they ate, her phone vibrated against the table where she'd laid it. She looked at the screen to see who would be texting so late and froze.

She looked up sharply. "I just got another text from Bryce."

"What does it say?"

*"I'm sorry. Let's meet. I'm hurt. Need a doctor."*

*Go to the hospital,* she texted back.

Jake smirked. "Maybe he'll actually show up while we're here and we can take him into custody."

"If only we were that lucky." She read his reply text aloud. *"Too dangerous. Need to see you. Only you. Bring your medical bag."* She looked up. "Sounds like maybe he is wounded."

"We figured as much by the blood and bandages at your house and the clinic. But that doesn't mean you have to be the one to treat him. He's probably a cold-blooded killer. Wait." He set his coffee down and reached for her phone. "Can I see that?"

She handed him her phone.

Jake read the message again. "He asks specifically for your medical bag."

"Oh my God," she murmured as she remembered. "One of the things he left at my house is in that bag. I forgot all about it. But it was so insignificant. It couldn't be what he's after."

"It may be insignificant to you but seems pretty damn important to him. What was it?"

"A keychain flashlight. How could that be anything of interest? Certainly not worth killing anyone over, or mugging them and shoving them in a frigid river."

"Where is it now?"

"I attached it to the zipper of my go bag, as you called it. I figured a flashlight might come in handy in an emergency."

"He asked you to bring some of his things to his hotel that first night, right?"

"Yeah."

"Could be he'd hoped to get it back from you then." Jake rubbed the dark stubble on his chin. "When that didn't work out, maybe he figured you'd put it in your purse. Could be why the purse was snatched."

"And when he didn't find it in my purse, he searched my house and clinic."

"And didn't find it either of those places."

"When he couldn't find it, he must have figured the only place left was with me or in my car, which he couldn't find because it's still parked downtown, in a public garage." She pushed her coffee aside. She didn't need any more caffeine. Her nerves were already buzzing at the thought they might have finally discovered what Bryce was after.

Jake looked equally excited. "Maybe that's why he left your keys in your clinic. He probably hoped you would take the bait about him being framed, and agree to meet him. When you showed up, he likely planned to corner you or follow you from the clinic. When the police showed up instead, he chose to run."

"I wonder what's so important about a flashlight."

Jake stood and grabbed their coffees. "Let's go find out."

As they were already near downtown, it took less than ten minutes to get to the garage and pull alongside her car. Jake made her wait in the passenger seat while he scoped out the area and made sure Bryce wasn't lying in wait and that they hadn't been followed. Jake circled her car and then lay flat on his stomach on the cold concrete to look beneath the vehicle. She turned to glance around the garage. She didn't see anyone, but that didn't mean Bryce wasn't there, watching.

Jake returned to his truck and opened her door for her. "I don't see anything suspicious."

As she got out, a shudder ran through her. Had Bryce planned to kill her that night she went to his room? Somehow, he'd ended up with Lauren instead.

"Hey, wait." Jake pulled her around to face him and ducked to look into her eyes. "You're okay and you're going to stay that way. I'll make sure you're safe."

"I know. I trust you." She stepped forward and pressed a kiss to his lips. "And I greatly appreciate you being here." She wanted to get this over with and get out of here as quickly as possible. The dark corners and dirty smells of the parking garage turned her stomach.

Rachel unlocked her car and searched through it. Nothing seemed to be missing or disturbed. It was just how she'd left it. She found her duffel bag in the trunk.

She pointed out the five-inch-long flashlight keychain dangling from the bag's zipper. "This is it."

Jake studied it, unscrewed the end, and turned it over. A thumb drive fell into his open palm.

Her jaw dropped. This had to be what Bryce had been after.

"Let's go." Jake started back to his truck.

"What about my car?"

"We'll leave it here for now. You're not leaving my side until this is settled." He held the passenger door open for her.

"Where are we going?"

"The hotel. It's the closest place I can think of with a computer where we can look at this thing."

A couple minutes later, they again pulled into a parking garage, this time at the Hotel del Corazon. He led her through an empty lobby. It was now almost two in the morning, and there wasn't even a hotel employee manning the reception desk. Jake gestured to a stool and she took a seat while he loaded the drive. She dismissed the spike of adrenaline that hit her system at the thought of unraveling this mystery, but it wasn't so easy to ignore the man leaning over her shoulder. Jake's solid warmth made her want to lean into him.

Rachel stared at the computer screen with shock as words and numbers popped up. "It's not even password protected?"

"What am I looking at?" Jake's eyes narrowed as he read the screen.

She took over the mouse so she could scroll through pages and pages of data and notes. Vaguely, she was aware of Jake observing their surroundings, leaving the document interpretation to her while he kept watch.

After several long moments, she leaned back. "Wow. Jeremy and Bryce were researching a drug for treatment of mood disorders."

Jake nodded. "Jeremy mentioned something about that months ago. But it didn't go anywhere. He said the data didn't show it as viable."

Rachel shook her head. "That's not what this shows. Bryce must have altered the data he gave your brother. These reports show a very healthy outcome. And the drug had some alternative uses that would be lucrative, too."

"Lucrative enough to lie to my brother and sell out his own company?"

"If money is the motive, I can see far-reaching applications for this drug in pharmaceutical markets. And if he was looking to sell to people who might not have such altruistic motives, it rivals opioids in the potential for prescription drug abuse." She glanced at Jake. "Bryce would know how to maximize various revenue streams."

Jake called Jeremy and left a message when he didn't answer, briefly filling him in on where they were and what they'd discovered. After, he called Oz, gave the detective a quick update, and asked him to meet them at the police station immediately.

"Let's go." Jake put the drive in his pocket and took Rachel's hand, pulling her with him toward the door that led to the parking garage. She had to jog to keep up with him, but she was just as eager to get the evidence to the police.

"I can't believe Bryce would kill for this." She thought of the man she'd once known, the man she'd hoped had changed. Obviously, he hadn't changed—not for the better, anyway.

"Plenty of people have killed for money or drugs." Jake clicked his key fob to unlock the doors of his truck from several yards away. "Or to cover a crime."

A deep voice spoke from behind them. "Or to keep a bitch of a bride from getting her grubby hands on it."

Jake froze and Rachel jerked to a stop at his side. From between Jake's truck and the car parked next to it, a dark figure emerged. It was Rachel's worst nightmare—Bryce with a gun.

"Put the gun down," Jake said. At the same time, he slowly stepped to the side until he was standing in front of Rachel.

Bryce sneered. "Aw, that's sweet." His gun was now pointed at Jake, which suited Jake just fine. He didn't want Rachel in the line of fire. Still, she was close enough to get hit by a stray bullet if Bryce started firing. Or, if he hit Jake and then kept going, Rachel would be next. Jake either needed to get to the gun strapped to his ankle or defuse this situation before it escalated.

"You can't win in this scenario," Jake said.

"Really? I have the gun. That makes me the winner."

"Is that the same gun you used to kill Lauren?" He noted the silencer on the end. That must have been how Lauren was shot without anybody hearing it.

"It's the same gun, but I didn't kill her. I found it in her room, when I found her."

Jake nodded. "Oh, that's right. You said you were framed. If you turn yourself in, you'll be able to argue your case. But if you kill me or Rachel, you'll definitely go to jail for murder."

Bryce laughed harshly. "Looks like I'm already headed that way. Everyone thinks I killed Lauren. What's another couple killings added to the list? And with what Rachel has—something that's *mine*, by the way—I can disappear and no one will ever find me."

"Don't do this, Bryce." Rachel moved closer to Jake, and he shifted to keep her behind him.

"I won't, sweetheart. As long as you hand me that thumb drive. I saw you park and rush inside. Caught the light of the computer through the lobby windows. I know you know what's on that drive. I can't let you turn it over to Jeremy or the police."

"And after we give you the flash drive, then what?" Jake demanded, already knowing the answer but stalling. "You're just going to let us go?"

Bryce shrugged. "With those files, I'll have enough money to charter a private jet out of the country. I can start a new life. I've always landed on my feet."

"Why did you kill Lauren?" Rachel asked. Jake could feel her anger vibrating through her chest, against his back.

"I told you, I was framed. I'm guessing the real shooter had a silencer on this gun, or someone in the hotel would have heard the shot. Find the silencer and you'll find the shooter."

A shot rang out, piercingly loud as it reverberated throughout the garage. Bryce's gun clattered to the concrete and he crumpled to the ground, his knees hitting before he slumped over. Blood began to pool beneath him.

All of this happened in a matter of seconds, and Jake's instincts took over. He shoved Rachel between him and his truck, pressing her head down.

"Stay low," he ordered.

He heard someone running toward them and spotted Adriana hurrying toward the truck, her cheeks pink and her eyes wide. She had a gun in her hand, aimed toward Bryce as she called out to them. "Are you guys okay? I thought he was going to kill you."

Rachel straightened. "Is he dead?" She started to move toward Bryce and Adriana. Jake grabbed her wrist and pulled her back behind him. "I have to check if he's alive," she protested.

"Stay here," he said. "I'll check." Jake shot her a look that told her to stay near the truck, and moved to check Bryce's pulse. He picked up the man's limp wrist. There was no sign of a heartbeat. He shook his head and Rachel put a hand to her mouth. They both looked toward Adriana.

Adriana stepped closer. "He's dead?"

"He's dead," Jake confirmed.

"Did he explain why he stole the company files?" Adriana asked.

"He didn't have the chance." Jake eyed the gun in Adriana's hand. Her fingers were white as she gripped it tightly. He didn't feel he could safely reach for the gun strapped to his ankle while she still held hers. He reached out for her hand. "How about I take that?"

She backed away. "I think I'll keep it. It makes me feel safe." There was a wild look in her eyes that he didn't think was entirely due to the shooting.

"What are you doing here at three in the morning?" he asked. "I didn't know you were released from the hospital."

"I left. Jeremy brought me home a little while ago, but I couldn't sleep."

"So you thought you'd take a stroll through the parking garage with a gun?"

"Of course not. The gun was just a precaution. I knew Bryce was still out there somewhere. I heard your phone message to Jeremy, and that you were headed to the police station with some kind of evidence. I figured I'd try to catch you down here and maybe go with you. This affects me just as much as it does you."

"And it was too much trouble to wake me?" Jeremy called out. He strode toward them from the direction of the hotel.

Adriana looked at him with surprise. "I thought you were sleeping. I'd already put you through so much tonight with the trip to the hospital. I figured I'd let you rest. I knew Jake would catch you up in the morning."

"I heard you leave. What's going on? And where did you get a gun?"

She shrugged. "My suitcase. I take it everywhere. Daddy taught me how to shoot when I was a girl. Having it makes me feel safer."

"Why don't I know about this?" Jeremy's expression hardened to stone. "Just one more thing I feel like I didn't know about you. There's been a lot of that lately." He took a step closer and Adriana raised her gun to aim it at Jake.

"Stop right there," she said.

Jeremy stopped. "I should have seen the signs. I was trying to figure out why Bryce used my login to steal the files, and now it's clear. You stole them."

Adriana turned to aim the gun at Jeremy. Jake's heart caught in his throat. Behind him, Rachel gasped. Jake could imagine what must be going through her head. Adriana was one of her best friends, after all.

Bryce's gun had fallen too far out of Jake's reach. Still on his knees beside Bryce's body, he bent slightly to his side, inching his hands closer to his ankle where his gun was in its holster.

But Adriana saw the movement and swung her gun to aim at him. "Get up," she ordered. "Hands up, where I can see them."

Jake pushed slowly to his feet, his hands out in front of him. "So Bryce wasn't lying. He was being framed—by you."

"Why?" Jeremy asked, looking stunned and angry. "I gave you everything you could want."

"Not everything. I wanted my own sense of security and financial freedom. And don't act like Bryce was some innocent. He learned what I'd done weeks ago, but did he report it to you?" She laughed. "Nope. Instead, he and Lauren worked together to blackmail me. But even that wasn't enough. He decided to steal a copy of the data for himself."

"But he wouldn't kill Lauren," Rachel said. Jake mentally cursed, hating that she'd drawn attention to herself. "Not if he was working with her. He said he was framed."

Adriana grinned. "That was the one truth he told. Lauren was a backstabber. I killed her. She deserved what she got."

"But Bryce running away messed up your plan," Jake said, willing Adriana to focus on him again.

"He was supposed to be found with Lauren's dead body. I tried to knock him out when he discovered her, but he got away." She snorted. "Cut him pretty bad, though, when the lamp broke. Since he ran, I set up his hotel room to make it look like he'd met with Lauren there and that they'd fought."

"The locket," Rachel said. "And the lipstick in Lauren's shade." The ruse had worked, as all signs had eventually led them to discovering Bryce and Lauren's connection. "Why not just kill him?"

"Because Bryce still had his copy of the files somewhere," Jake guessed. "You couldn't have any evidence that might point to you floating around."

Adriana grinned. "And now I know where it is. Hand over the drive." She held out her free hand, her gun now aimed at Jake.

"Adriana," Jeremy pleaded, "you don't have to do this. We can figure this out." The barrel of the gun swung back to Jeremy and Jake's blood ran cold.

"It's gone too far," Adriana said. "I can't go to prison. I'm sorry I lied to you."

"Lied?" A strangled sound came from Jeremy's throat. "You're threatening to kill my brother. And then what? Kill the rest of us, too? I thought we were in love. We had our whole future in front of us."

"I can't go to prison," Adriana said again. "I care about you, but I learned a long time ago that survival is the first priority. I promise I'll make your funeral beautiful, honey. I'll make it look like Bryce shot all three of you and I came onto the scene just in time to take him down. Sadly, I didn't arrive in time to save any of you."

Jake knew Adriana's end game would be deadly for all of them. With the gun pointed at him and his loved ones, however, there wasn't much he could do without someone getting hurt. Still, he had to try.

Jake reached for his gun. Unfortunately, his brother lunged toward Adriana at the same time. Another shot went off, the loud noise resounding throughout the garage. Time slowed. The memory of his partner being hit as Jake scrambled to get out of the car and get his weapon, of Floyd's body falling and Jake unable to move any faster or delay the inevitable, made his heart pound harder. He leapt for Adriana. He ploughed into her, grabbing her wrist and knocking her to the ground. They fell together and he landed on top. He used his weight to knock the wind from her as he wrestled the gun from her grip.

Where had the bullet she'd fired gone?

As he gained control of her weapon, Adriana stopped fighting him. Using his body as an anchor to pin her, he glanced over his shoulder. Jeremy was on the ground. Rachel knelt beside him. His brother's pants were soaked with blood.

"No!" Jake shouted.

Jeremy reached for his wounded leg. Seeing the movement, Jake felt a rush of relief. Jeremy wasn't dead, but there was still so much blood. He wasn't out of the woods yet. His wave of relief quickly transformed to adrenaline when Adriana resumed her struggle beneath him. He shifted his weight to rise, but kept the gun trained on her.

"Don't move." He ordered her to stay on the ground as he pulled out his phone and dialed 9-1-1 to request an ambulance and police at his location.

"Hold this tightly to your leg," Rachel was saying to Jeremy as Jake hung up. While Jeremy did as she asked, she hastily unzipped her go bag and pulled out a strip of black material with a short rod attached. Jake realized it was a CAT—a combat application tourniquet. Rachel looked up to see him standing over her. "This is just temporary until the EMTs get here. He's losing too much blood."

Jeremy was losing more than that. He was starting to lose consciousness. Rachel quickly tied off the tourniquet, working efficiently and calmly to save his brother, all while speaking words of encouragement and praise. When she was done, she wiped her brow with steady hands, heedless of the blood she smeared on her forehead. Her smile, however, was shaky, an indication of the adrenaline and fear coursing through her body. The sound of an ambulance approaching on the street level outside the garage was a welcome one, but it didn't compare to the loud beating of his heart. Jake knew in that moment that it beat for Rachel. He was falling hard for this incredible woman.

# CHAPTER 9

JAKE DIDN'T WANT TO DISTURB THE WOMAN IN HIS ARMS, AS THERE
had been precious little sleep during the twenty-seven hours since
his brother was shot, but the surgeon was approaching. He needed
to speak to Dr. Mendoza about Jeremy's condition. He shifted
slightly, trying to extract himself without waking Rachel. Of
course, her head came up immediately.

"What's wrong?" she mumbled. She looked tired and slightly
grumpy to have been woken—until she got her bearings. The look
of concern she'd worn since they'd followed the ambulance to the
hospital, the one that sleep had temporarily erased, quickly
morphed her features again. To Jake, she was still the most beautiful woman in the world.

"The doctor's here." Jake tipped his head toward the surgeon
and Rachel stood with him to face the news. She'd been by his side
for the entire time they'd been at the hospital, except for a few
hours they'd gone to his house to catch a few hours of sleep and a
change of clothes, and he was grateful she was still here with him.

Dr. Mendoza gave them a tired, yet satisfied, smile. "Jeremy
came through surgery with flying colors. He's in recovery." Relief

nearly knocked Jake's legs out from under him. He wasn't sure he could handle losing Jeremy, or delivering any more bad news to his parents, who had left a short while ago to seek out breakfast in the hospital cafeteria.

If only Jake had been quicker, faster, somehow superhuman, and could have stopped Jeremy from charging Adriana, maybe Jeremy wouldn't have been shot. Maybe he could have saved his parents the stress and grief yesterday had brought as they waited for Jeremy to stabilize and go into surgery.

Of course, it could have been much worse. If he and Jeremy hadn't acted, they would have been dead alongside Bryce, who'd apparently messed with the wrong woman.

Adriana, of all people. Jeremy's bride-to-be.

Hell, today would have been Jeremy and Adriana's wedding day, Jake realized. Instead, the groom had gone through emergency surgery to remove the bullet and save his leg and the bride was in jail. Not even close to the happily-ever-after Jake had wished for his brother.

"Prognosis?" Rachel asked.

"It's good that you were there and acted so quickly," Dr. Mendoza told her. "He might have lost the leg. Or, worse, his life."

Jake's arm tightened around Rachel's shoulders and he kissed her on the top of her head.

She wrapped her arms around Jake's waist as she spoke to the surgeon. "So you were able to save his leg?"

Mendoza nodded. "It seems so. The next day or so will be critical, of course. We'll know more about how well he's healing. But at the moment, he's stable."

"Is he awake?" Jake asked.

Mendoza grinned. "A little groggy, but awake and asking for you. They're moving him from post-op now. One of the nurses should be by shortly to take you to his room. I'll check on him regularly and keep you updated. In the meantime, keep the stress to a minimum."

Jake sent a quick text to his parents to let them know Jeremy would be receiving visitors soon. "I don't know how we're supposed to keep his stress low when today would have been his wedding day," he muttered.

Rachel nodded. "Not going to be easy. I'm so sorry for you all."

He folded her into his arms and took comfort in breathing in her scent. It was so familiar to him now. "You have nothing to be sorry about. You saved the day. Hell, you saved my brother. The bad stuff was all Adriana." He reluctantly let her go as Oz walked into the waiting room.

"How's your brother?" the detective asked.

"Pretty good, considering," Jake said. "He just got out of surgery and they're about to take us back to see him."

"If you have a second, I'll catch you up."

"Definitely." He'd love to hear what Oz had learned so he could explain to Jeremy what the hell Adriana had been thinking.

"We spent most of yesterday interviewing Adriana and putting the pieces together. Apparently, she had stolen company data and had made arrangements to sell it to a rival pharmaceutical company in China. Lauren Foley, as a sales rep for S&R Biotech, intercepted a call one day and learned of Adriana's plans. Lauren was in a casual sexual relationship with Bryce, and shared with him what she'd learned. It appears the two decided to turn the tables on Adriana and profit from the situation, rather than seek the help of law enforcement."

"The two were colluding *and* sleeping together?" Rachel asked, incredulous. "They both meant to backstab Adriana and Jeremy."

"And Adriana didn't appreciate being bossed around," Jake muttered. "They were moving in on her territory."

Oz nodded. "She'd already paid Bryce a ton of money to keep quiet, and now he was threatening to sell the plans out from under her."

"And with her planning to marry Jeremy, Bryce had even more

leverage," Rachel said. "But if Bryce and Lauren were dead, all of her problems would go away."

Jake's hand tightened at her waist. If he hadn't followed Rachel to Bryce's room that night, would she have tracked the clues to Lauren's room and found her murdered? Would Adriana still have been there, and would she have shot Rachel?

"Adriana couldn't track Bryce down after he fled Lauren's room," Oz continued. "When Bryce kept showing up at Rachel's home and clinic, she figured Rachel must have the copy of the files he'd stolen, so she waited and watched. The flash drive had a copy of the formula and data from a drug they'd recently been developing at S&R."

"Her trip to the ER was to lure us back, to see what we had found," Jake realized. "Because I'd kept Jeremy updated, she knew we'd nearly bumped into Bryce at Rachel's house and the clinic, and she wanted to make sure we didn't find him or the files first. She faked that she'd been drugged."

"That fits with what we've learned," Oz agreed. "I'll need to talk to your brother, of course, to get the remaining pieces of the puzzle, but it can wait until he's a little stronger and clearheaded. We've got enough to file charges against Ms. Whitley."

*Ms. Whitley.* Adriana would never be Mrs. Rosales, and Jake felt some relief that at least they'd stopped her before the plan had gone further. If Jeremy had discovered her duplicity later, after the wedding, she might have found more creative, less detectable ways to deal with him.

After Oz had left with a promise to swing by later in the day, when Jeremy could receive more visitors, Jake turned to the woman who'd been by his side for several days straight. It was incredible how Rachel had become a part of him. He couldn't imagine going through this without her. Spending so many hours together, many of them filled with danger or emotionally-charged situations, had a tendency to strip down everything else and show a person what was important.

"I had the files all these weeks," Rachel said. "If only I'd realized sooner, or seen through his plans, I could have handed everything over to the police. We could have avoided all of this."

Jake pulled her against him. "Bryce knew you wouldn't suspect him of anything because you think the best of people."

She scoffed, her breath a puff of hot air against his neck. "Obviously, to a fault."

He pulled back to look into her eyes, wanting her to see how serious he was when he told her how much he believed in her. "Not at all. It's a gift. You're a healer. In fact, you healed a part of me I didn't want to recognize was broken." His hands came up to cup her face and he kissed her tenderly, trying to convey all of the feelings in his heart to her.

A throat cleared nearby, and he reluctantly pulled away. "I can take you to see Mr. Rosales now," a nurse said. She sent them a soft smile and then led them down several corridors to a private room.

Jeremy's face was pale, even a little green, but he was propped up in bed and his eyes were open. He smiled weakly.

Jake bumped knuckles with his brother. "Good to see you, man." His throat was thick with emotion.

"Good to be seen," Jeremy said. "I don't remember everything, but I think Adriana shot me?"

Jake nodded solemnly. His brother's bride had shot him, had planned to kill them all. What could he say in response that wouldn't sound ridiculous?

Rachel reached out to squeeze Jeremy's fingers. "She won't be hurting you anymore. They've got her locked up, and she's admitted enough that I doubt she'll be released any time soon."

"I guess I was unconscious and lost a day. That would make today Valentine's Day." He grimaced. "It would have been my wedding day."

"At least it wasn't your funeral," Jake said.

.   .   .

RACHEL OBSERVED JEREMY WITH A DOCTOR'S TRAINED EYE, AND THEN as a friend. He seemed stable and on his way toward healing. She couldn't help wondering how his heart would fare, though. Still, she was amazed when, within minutes of their arrival, Jake had his brother laughing—quickly followed by groaning—at some silly joke.

"*Mijo!*" Vida Rosales rushed into the room and stopped on the other side of Jeremy's bed, where she fell across Jeremy's chest and embraced him. "We've been praying for you."

Jeremy grinned. "It obviously worked, Mama."

She cupped his face, searched his eyes, and then straightened and slapped him lightly on the shoulder. "Of course, it did. An amazing doctor had something to do with it, too." She looked at Rachel and swiped at a tear. "Thank you, again."

"I could never thank you enough," Jeremy told Rachel, reaching over to hold her fingers.

Rachel smiled. There was a time she might have accepted the gratitude, and then backed out of the room to leave the family to themselves, but Jake's arm was around her waist, holding her in place at his side, as if she belonged there. She was surprised to realize that it felt right. She'd found the connection she'd been looking for all along.

"I'm sorry, everyone," Jeremy said. "I brought that woman into our lives."

"And you're the one paying for it," Jake said. "No need to apologize to us. I just wish I'd seen Adriana's link to Bryce and the stolen files sooner."

"We were so wrong about her," Ernesto said from the end of the bed. Their father shook his head. "I refuse to say the woman's name any more. She fooled us all, son."

"But looking back, there were signs," Jeremy protested, determined to beat himself up. "She'd been acting strangely for weeks. I thought she was just stressed about the wedding plans, and she always had an excuse for her odd behavior. She'd also been acting needier than usual, always wanting to be by my side and demanding I take more time off from work."

"She was trying to keep you away from work and Bryce so you didn't learn what she was doing," Rachel guessed.

"I just can't believe all of this was going on under my nose," Jeremy said with a shake of his head.

Jake squeezed his brother's shoulder. "You'll need time to heal. Time and family."

Rachel realized Jake was speaking from his own recent experience with pain and disappointment. He was coming out the other side of his own personal tragedy due to the loss of his partner. She had no doubt that with such a strong, supportive family, he and his brother would heal together. And, if he'd let her, she hoped to remain by his side to help.

As if reading her thoughts, Jake added, "I'm learning that we can grieve and learn from our experiences, but eventually we have to move on. There's too much left to do in the world, and so many ways we can help people." He grinned at her. "Someone wise and beautiful taught me that."

After a few more minutes of visiting, a nurse came in to ask that they give the patient time to rest.

"You guys go home and rest, too," Jeremy told them. "I'm not going anywhere, and I'm in good hands." He asked his father and Jake if they'd stay behind a moment.

Vida and Rachel left them to talk.

"Thank you again for everything," Vida said. "And for staying with us. I rested easier knowing Jake had you by his side. Those two boys are as close as brothers can be without being twins."

"I'm glad I could help," Rachel said.

"Do me one more favor?"

"Sure. What do you need?"

"Get Jake out of here. Feed him. He needs some time away from this place."

Rachel shook her head. "I doubt he feels like going anywhere."

He'd likely want to hang out in the waiting room for a couple hours until his brother felt like having visitors again.

"He doesn't always know what's best for him. It's Valentine's Day. Go celebrate each other. Celebrate life. Besides, he needs you now, needs you in his life."

"Jeremy's hurt, this ordeal with Bryce was exhausting…. It's not a good time to celebrate anything."

"On the contrary, it's always time to celebrate, especially if we're celebrating love. Love always wins."

*Love always wins.* Rachel had gone into this week hoping to make a connection with someone. Had she been lucky enough to find more, to find love?

Jake and his father caught up to them.

"Dad says you guys are heading home for a break," Jake said to his mom. "I don't think he's going to let you change his mind on that one."

Vida nodded. "I recommend you find some way to relax too." She sent a significant look Rachel's way.

Ernesto and Vida said their goodbyes as the four of them passed through the hospital doors and into the bright, cool February day. Rachel and Jake watched as the older pair headed toward their car.

"I can take you home if you want," Jake said.

"No." Rachel turned her face up to the sunshine.

"You don't want me to take you home?" He sounded disappointed.

She breathed in deeply and exhaled through her mouth. She was ready to walk confidently into her future.

"You're doing your counting, aren't you?" he asked, looking puzzled as he turned her toward him.

"No." She smiled. "I was enjoying a moment of clarity. I don't need to count this time. I just need you."

She reached up and unlatched the locket Adriana had given her. She walked a few steps to the nearby trashcan and laid it on the lid.

Maybe someone else would find solace in the necklace. Rachel planned to fill her empty heart in other ways.

Feeling lighter, she turned back to Jake. "I want to pick up some takeout and go to your place. I want you to hold me in your arms for hours. That's all I want for Valentine's Day."

He grinned. "I'm about to make your dreams come true." He took her face in his hands and kissed her.

She breathed him in, inhaling her future. She exhaled slowly and her lips curved beneath his. "Happy Valentine's Day."

THANK YOU FOR READING UNTIL DEATH. I HOPE YOU ENJOYED IT! If you'd care to leave a review, they are always appreciated.

FOR MORE MINDHUNTERS HOLIDAY NOVELLAS, BE SURE TO CHECK out CHRISTMAS STALKING (available now) and WICKED NIGHT (available April 2019), or the entire collection of three novellas in DEADLY HOLIDAYS (Available in digital and print April 2019).

AND IF YOU MISSED RACHEL'S SISTER'S STORY, CATHERINE AND MAX found their happily-ever-after in ACCEPTABLE RISK.

ACCEPTABLE RISK (MINDHUNTERS, BOOK 5)

TO REPAY A DEBT, RESOURCEFUL RECEPTIONIST CATHERINE Montague has been living a lie. Her secret betrayal eats at her conscience. She knows what she has to do to reclaim her life, but revealing the truth could mean losing everything, including the agent she's fallen in love with.

For sexy ex-SEAL Max Sawyer, hunting killers gives him a sense of fulfillment he never would have found if he'd followed the path that was his birthright. However, when his latest mission goes horribly wrong, releasing a hardened criminal in Max's hometown of San Antonio, Texas, it'll take all of his charm to convince the beautiful and resilient Catherine to serve as a buffer between him and the painful ties from his past.

Amid a manhunt, the re-emergence of a serial killer, and the activity of an organized crime ring known as the Circle, Max and Catherine may be the only ones who can set things right again. That is, if Max can forgive Catherine for her deception before a killer claims her. But is mercy a risk he's willing to take?

# WICKED NIGHT

## A MINDHUNTERS HOLIDAY NOVELLA

*For my readers,*
*who enjoy seeing good triumph over evil*
*as much as I do.*

# CHAPTER 1

"I GOT THIS." FIONA ELLIOT STEELED HERSELF AGAINST THE elements as she walked the downtown streets. The crisp October wind was only a breeze by Chicago's standards, but it was strong enough to bend her like a willow. "You just enjoy the end of your solitude."

Through the phone, her best friend and boss, Vanessa Knight-Crandall, laughed. "I'm just ready for the critter to pop out. This bed rest stuff sucks."

"At least it's not the strap-you-to-the-bed kind." It was the take-it-easy, restricted activity kind, but Vanessa wasn't one to be tied down.

After the health scare Vanessa suffered a few months ago, Fiona had taken on most of the workload at the gallery—happily. Currently, things weren't going as smoothly as she might have liked, but there was no way in hell she'd let her friend worry about anything other than having a healthy delivery.

"And you have me to handle stuff at the gallery," she reminded Vanessa for the umpteenth time.

"And to make sure I get all the latest celebrity gossip magazines."

"You know it. So, relax and enjoy your quiet time. You just focus on bringing that amazing baby girl into the world."

"Nice try, but I'm not telling you the gender."

"Fine. Keep your secrets."

Vanessa's laughter ended on a wistful sigh. "Only a few weeks to go."

As Fiona crossed with the light at State Street, a gust blew her auburn hair into her face. Hooking a finger through the stray strands, she swiped them from her field of vision, securing them behind her ear. She cursed as the motion dribbled coffee—from the cup held in that same hand—down her suede jacket. She never should have left on the morning quest for caffeine from her favorite coffee shop, or let down her messy ponytail—both efforts to relieve the headache that was pushing at her skull.

"What was that?" Vanessa asked through the cell phone Fiona clutched to her other ear. Her question was followed by an amused snort. "Sounded like you cursed Mother Nature. I thought you loved autumn."

"We've apparently skipped straight to winter." She picked up the pace as the soaring downtown skyscrapers that surrounded the Chicago Loop district channeled the chill through the streets until it was a steady hum in her ears. At least the gallery was only a couple blocks away. There, she could regroup. She lived upstairs and could change her jacket before getting back to work.

And, after work, play, which would require another change of clothing. A thrum of excitement made her skin tingle and lightened her mood. Her latest piece was calling to her, and long-sleeved shirt, thick overalls, fire-resistant apron, and welding gloves and helmet were her standard uniform when she was creating in the back room. She could lose herself in the piece of metal she was shaping into some semblance of the sculpture that lived in her head. To date, she'd made enough money from her art to invest in the higher-priced equipment, such as the TIG welder that gave her more control and let her work with a variety of metals. Until her art generated more income, her bread-and-butter job was in the adjacent gallery Vanessa owned, selling other artists' work.

Fiona had met Vanessa when they'd worked together at a New York City gallery. They had bonded over a common love of all things art, and then had moved to Chicago together to follow Vanessa's dream of opening her own gallery. After three years here, Fiona thought she had adjusted very well despite the occasional bouts of homesickness—for New York, not for her native Iowan roots. Those roots might as well have been anchored in dust. She'd long ago fallen under the spell of big-city life.

But she was beginning to think her recent restlessness was deeper than simply missing New York. The Windy City had many of the same perks as the Big Apple. More importantly, it offered her an opportunity to follow her passion at the Ortega-Knight Gallery. Vanessa had opened the gallery in honor of a mutual friend who'd died way too early in life. It was a privilege to work there in a capacity Fiona loved. So why was she feeling unfulfilled and lonely?

She shook her head at herself and returned her attention to Vanessa. "The sudden change from summer temps to arctic chill is wreaking havoc with my body." Her headache throbbed in testament.

"That's because you're built like a dancer, all graceful limbs and no fat. I, on the other hand, could heat the whole city right now." Vanessa was eight months pregnant and complained regularly that it felt like an alien had invaded and taken up residence in her body. Still, she glowed with happiness. And heat.

A handful of crisp, golden leaves chased each other along the sidewalk, riding a swirl of wind. With the rainstorm they were expecting by the end of the week, those leaves would be decaying in the gutter soon, and fall would be over before it had even begun.

"With Halloween tomorrow night, Mother Nature gave us a reprieve as long as she could," Vanessa said.

"At least the weather will be perfect for showcasing our latest exhibition. The rain and wind fit the *Wicked Night* theme." The products of up-and-coming artist Orlando Reyes's eerie-but-creative genius had been on display for two weeks, and Fiona was intimately acquainted with them, as it had been her job to prepare them for display and then sell the public on the macabre offerings.

"True."

"Sold a couple of his big-ticket items in the past couple days," Fiona said. "It was good that we booked him before he became famous." Orlando's name was becoming a big draw in the art world. She mentally patted herself on the back for having discovered him before his work had been featured in a prominent art magazine and lauded by a well-known director of horror flicks. Orlando's use of recycled trash to create his three-dimensional art was an added appeal to collectors who wanted to make a statement about environmental awareness and recycling.

"He'll love hearing that." Vanessa's tone held respect, but also a touch of sarcasm. She was well aware that Orlando's ego was part of the package they'd signed on for during this month-long exhibit.

"He definitely will," Fiona agreed.

Orlando was temperamental and demanding, and these sales would only feed his ego. She much preferred working with his low-key and efficient assistant, Charlotte, whenever possible. However, she hadn't been able to get in touch with either to confirm Orlando had arrived in Chicago as planned yesterday, and that was stressing her out.

"There are plenty of new pieces I've been holding back," Fiona said. "I've been saving them for the Halloween bash." The party would be the unveiling of Orlando's most unique pieces. The storage area just behind the art gallery was crammed with art, and it had started to overflow into her work area in the next room.

The shrinking space had been a source of mild irritation for weeks, but it would be worth it to make a splash.

"So everything's going okay?"

"Absolutely." And if it weren't, there was no way she'd worry Vanessa. She just needed to confirm with Orlando or Charlotte that he made it to Chicago yesterday, and that he'd actually be at the party tomorrow night, as well as the interview she had scheduled that afternoon. A vibration trembled through her palm. "Hang on a sec. I'm getting a text."

Fiona pulled the phone away and, still clutching her coffee, swiped with her pinky finger to retrieve the incoming text. The sender's number was unknown. A picture was attached.

Upon viewing the attachment, she stumbled toward the closest building and leaned against the cold concrete. Her legs started shaking, and she sank to the sidewalk, leaned back against the building, and set her coffee beside her. She couldn't stifle a low moan. Around her, people continued to walk the sidewalk, talk on their phones, and otherwise ignore her.

"Fi?" Vanessa's voice broke through the image that had burned into her brain. "Is something wrong?"

Fiona put her on speakerphone so she could communicate as she flipped to the picture again, her mind not wanting to acknowledge what her eyes were seeing. "I...I don't know. Someone sent me a picture."

"What kind of picture?"

"A woman. A redhead." *Like me.* "She looks glassy-eyed. Dead, maybe. At the very least...broken." Her voice cracked on the last word. There was no sign of life, no spirit left in the woman's vacant stare. And from beneath the red silk scarf tied around her neck emerged ragged, bloody gashes. Three of them marked her neck and chest, as if she'd been mauled by some beast. Congealed blood ran in rivulets from the marks, down the sides of her chest and soaked into her shirt. "It's horrible."

"Forward it to me."

Fiona cleared her throat and reminded herself she wasn't going to worry Vanessa about anything. "No."

"Fi, I can help."

"I don't want this stuck in your head, too." She wouldn't be forgetting the image any time soon. "I won't do that to anyone, let alone my best friend, and especially not while she's eight months pregnant."

"I'm on restricted *activity* not restricted interaction."

"No."

"Then send it to Noah." Vanessa was married to Chicago Police Detective Noah Crandall. Conveniently—or inconveniently—he was a homicide detective. He would know what to do.

"Yeah." She blew out a breath. "Yeah, okay. I'll send it to him."

"Promise me."

"I promise." A moment later, she hung up, intending to forward the text to Noah. But involving him wouldn't stop the shivers, or the horrors that haunted her after seeing that image. What did she have to do with a broken and battered woman? Dear God, was the woman dead? If she wasn't, she had to be in a lot of pain.

Unless the whole thing was a hoax. Movie makeup could be amazingly lifelike. And it was almost Halloween, the season for tricks and treats. And some people sent things to the wrong numbers. This might not even be meant for her.

She clung to these facts, pushing up from the ground and taking a moment to lean against the building before picking up her purse and her coffee, and resuming her walk. Anxious to reach the shelter of the gallery, she quickened her pace.

Another vibration shook the palm that still gripped her phone.

As she read the screen, her brief moment of hope shattered. The text hadn't been sent to the wrong person. It had been intended for her.

*Fiona, you inspire me.*

.  .  .

THERE WASN'T ENOUGH COFFEE IN THE WORLD TO GET DETECTIVE Greg Marsh through this morning. Still, it was worth a try. He glared at the empty pot in the break room and willed the machine to drip ebony manna into his mug. The machine lacked the motivation to comply.

"Long day?" Detective Noah Crandall asked as he walked in and eyed the standoff.

Greg grunted. "And it's only ten o'clock." He leaned back against the counter. Perhaps if he ignored the coffeepot, it would give in for wont of attention. Reverse Psychology 101.

"Are you coming or going?"

"Going. As soon as I can, anyway. Worked a scene around midnight. Just got done interviewing people."

"Let me guess." Noah pushed a couple of buttons and something lit up on the machine. "Mountains of paperwork and no happy ending."

"You can tell that from my expression?" He must be slipping. He was usually good at hiding his thoughts and feelings, a skill developed at a young age, when revealing his true thoughts or feelings hadn't ended well.

"More so from the desperation with which you were eyeing that empty coffee mug. And the murderous glare you sent the machine."

"Unfortunately, you're right."

Noah winced. "Then I hate to ask you for a favor, but you do owe me."

"Do I?" Greg raised a brow. It was the other way around and the amused spark in Noah's eyes said he was well aware. Greg had covered several shifts for him when Vanessa had a health scare a couple months back. They'd thought she would miscarry, but she'd rallied, and the doctor had ordered her to take it easy. Greg's smirk fell away and he straightened from the counter. "Oh shit, is it Vanessa? The baby?"

"No, no. They're fine. She's getting tired of being home, though."

"I can imagine. What do you need?"

"I really do hate to ask, but we could use a favor." Noah snatched a mug from the drying rack by the sink as the hiss and bubble of the coffee trickling forth gave Greg renewed hope for mankind—or at least his own survival.

"What kind of favor?"

"Do you remember Vanessa's friend from a couple months back?"

"Fiona?"

"That's the one." Noah filled Greg's mug before seeing to his own.

Hell yes, Greg remembered Fiona. She wasn't the kind of woman a man could forget. Her spirit was as beautiful and vibrant as her smile. He could still feel the small of her back beneath his fingertips as he'd escorted her to her apartment door, above the gallery where she worked. He could see her soft, fiery red hair swinging against her shoulders as she'd turned into his arms, the flash of green eyes as she'd laughed with him. The softness of her incredible mouth when he'd kissed her.

Greg frowned. "Yeah, I remember her. Why?"

"I know that blind date didn't work out so well. Stupid idea, I guess, but Vanessa and I thought you'd be good for each other." Noah's gaze turned speculative. "You never did say what went wrong, and Fi's been unusually closemouthed about it."

What went wrong was that everything had felt too right. Greg had cut the strings before either of them regretted it later. He'd thought of her many times during the past several weeks, but he'd carefully squashed any impulse to contact her again. While he enjoyed the occasional date, a relationship didn't fit in with his line of work. His heart had been halfway hers before the night was over, triggering all kinds of alarm bells, so he'd ended things.

But in the quiet hours of the night, he wondered about Fiona and the spark of passion they'd shared.

He tried to casually sip his coffee while mentally urging Noah to get on with whatever favor he intended to request. The silence drew on until Noah realized he wouldn't get any answers about the blind date.

"Anyway, Fi needs some help," Noah finally said. "Possibly of the law enforcement variety."

He froze. "Is she okay?"

"Sort of." Noah took his sweet time adding three sugar packets to his mug.

*For God's sake....* "Sort of?" He gestured to Noah to elaborate.

"She's physically okay, but shaken up. I received this from her about an hour ago." Noah fished his phone from his pocket and handed it over.

Greg examined the image she'd forwarded. It showed a woman with red hair—not as dark or silky as Fiona's—her neck bound in red silk, her upper chest etched deeply with several marks, as if claws had scraped away her flesh, trying to get to her heart. The woman stared, glassy-eyed, into the camera.

"Some kind of sick prank?" Greg hoped against hope. Or maybe it was one of those living art things.

Noah shook his head. "It was followed by a text that said, '*Fiona, you inspire me.*' Sounds more like a stalker than a prankster to me. Besides, I can't think who would want to prank her this way."

"Tomorrow's Halloween. Maybe someone just wants to scare her." A single, beautiful woman living alone in a drafty studio apartment above an art studio that was empty except for business hours.... Yeah, Fiona Elliot was a prime target.

Noah shrugged. "Maybe. But I'd prefer to err on the side of caution. Vanessa's asking me to help, but I'm swamped trying to wrap up some cases before the baby arrives. And with the pregnancy in its final weeks, I'm trying to be there for her as much as possible, you know?"

"Sure." Actually, Greg didn't have a clue what it was like to be there for a pregnant wife, having never had a wife or children. He didn't know how Noah managed it. The last thing Greg needed was another person to need him. But this was Fiona, one of the most independent women he knew, and she was asking for help.

"You want me to look into this?" Greg asked.

Noah exhaled a relieved breath. "I would appreciate it."

He handed the phone back and pushed away from the counter, turning to top off his mug. It was going to be a long day after a long night. "Forward the messages to me and I'll see what I can do. I'd been thinking about calling her again, anyway." *Shit.* Why had he admitted that?

Noah grinned. "Yeah?"

He sighed. "Yeah."

He hadn't decided what to do about his unrelenting thoughts about Fiona, but once the words were out of his mouth, it felt right. The sudden spark of anticipation was the same feeling he got when he was pursuing a hot lead that could change everything.

# CHAPTER 2

During her lunch break, Fiona's phone vibrated against the battered wood counter that lined her workshop's wall in a large back room of the Ortega-Knight Gallery, rattling enough to win her attention away from the sketch she'd been working on. The screen lit up with the incoming message. A shudder of distrust and anxiety slithered through her as the photo of the woman in the red scarf came to mind. Would every text now elicit an unwanted Pavlovian response?

She forced herself to pick up the phone. A whoosh of relief moved through her, chasing away most of the fear. The text wasn't from some stranger, but from Vanessa.

*Someone from CPD is heading your way about your mystery texts. Told Alyssa to let him in.*

Alyssa was their part-time help, and was manning the store while Fiona took her break. Before she could wonder if the *someone* Vanessa referred to would be Noah, she heard the light clip of a man's dress shoes against the concrete floor behind her. She turned, her heart catching at the sight of the man who'd starred in many of her thoughts and dreams over the past several weeks.

"Is this your work?" Detective Greg Marsh's rich voice resounded off the tall, bare walls and vibrated through her limbs. His gaze swung from a metal sculpture in the corner to her, and then took a leisurely cruise down her body, surveying her long-sleeved T-shirt, overalls and work boots. Her abdomen tightened with awareness.

He was one of those quiet, watchful men who knew how to wield his intensity to his advantage. He waited patiently for her answer, seemingly oblivious to the chemistry that threatened to combust whenever they were near each other. Or maybe he wasn't so oblivious, given the slight flare of his nostrils and the bobbing of his Adam's apple.

She squared her shoulders and attempted to gather her suddenly scattered thoughts. "Detective Marsh. To what do I owe the pleasure?"

He muttered something under his breath.

She narrowed her eyes on him. "Excuse me?"

"I said, 'stubborn woman.' You can't call me Greg? After our kiss, and how close we came to—"

"I thought you wanted to go back to being near-strangers." She had interrupted to halt his words, but couldn't stop the flush that crept up her cheeks at the sudden memory of a searing kiss that might have led to so much more. Let him talk about anything but the humiliation of him walking out on her after she'd invited him into her bed. She supposed she should be grateful he'd stopped instead of taking all that she'd offered and then walking away, but she couldn't seem to summon an attitude of gratitude.

With another bit of muttering, accompanied by a shake of his head, he stepped farther into the room. His gaze moved back to the sculpture she'd been fashioning into a man and woman locked in a passionate embrace. She'd been pleased with the amount of motion and expression she'd captured in the bits of bronze and steel she'd entwined as if the couple was dancing. His diverted attention gave her the opportunity to study him. His dark brown hair invited her fingers to travel through it and his wide shoulders would be more than enough to lean on.

She bit the inside of her cheek to force herself to focus. "I was expecting Noah."

"I know." A muscle jumped in his jaw. He clearly didn't appreciate that he'd been second best. Interesting—and confusing, given he'd been the one to call things off after their blind date. "He's wrapped up in a case."

"And in their baby," she guessed.

"Neither of them warned you I was coming?"

"No." Vanessa's text had been suspiciously vague and last minute. She would likely blame the lapse on preggo-brain, while in actuality, the happy couple was probably attempting round two of matchmaking among their friends. They were all bound for disappointment.

"I saw the texts you received," he prompted when she simply stood there. "You could have called me for help. After all, I've tasted your strawberry lip gloss." His gaze dropped to her mouth. Again, she had to force herself to ignore the electricity that arced between them.

"And decided you didn't like it."

He stilled. "I decided nothing of the sort. I said we shouldn't move forward, but I didn't want to move backward."

Stunned, she could only gape. Had she misread things? No. He'd been very clear in his text the next morning that he'd had a good time on their date but wasn't interested in anything else. *I enjoyed our date, but I don't think we should let this go further.*

She'd figured she'd been too forward for the stoic detective who never seemed to act without taking the full measure of such action. She, on the other hand, had always been a *carpe diem* kind of gal. They weren't the good match Vanessa and Noah had sold her on.

"Calling you about something like this seemed like a burden you wouldn't want to bear," she said. "You made it pretty clear you didn't want more contact with me." She'd been disappointed, and frankly, a little hurt that he hadn't wanted to give it another shot. At least a second date. She'd thought they'd clicked, especially when he'd had his mouth on hers, kissing her with a sense of urgency and desperation that had resonated all the way to her soul.

Something like regret flickered in his eyes. "My life is complicated." And, damn, that sounded like pity in his tone.

She tried for a nonchalant shrug. "I suppose it's better to know up front that it won't work. Why waste our time, right? Truthfully, I was relieved." At least in part. She'd felt an immediate connection with Greg. He was handsome, intelligent, sexy and intriguing—a potent combination. An artist had to risk opening his or her heart to the world in order to experience things more fully and stimulate creativity, and Fiona had long ago adopted a motto of *frivolous fun*. The serious-but-sexy detective standing in front of her didn't have a frivolous bone in his body. He would have seriously cramped her style—or so she told herself.

"Fiona—" His hand came up as if reaching for her.

Though he hadn't taken a step to close the distance, she took a quick step back and shoved her hand through her hair, tugging loose the ponytail as she put some distance between them. Two pills had knocked her headache on its ass for a couple hours, but now it was returning with a vengeance. "Forget about it."

He dropped his hand. "It just wouldn't work."

"I get it." She was a complication. That stung, but she managed an indifferent shrug. "It's not worth your time."

"On the contrary." His eyes held her captive and it wasn't pity she found there but heat and regret.

She held her breath, waiting for him to complete his thought, to say that maybe he would give them a shot. Instead, he turned to survey another of her recent works, an eight-foot-tall silvery tree, created out of aluminum, that dwarfed her, though she was nearly six feet tall. Greg was several inches taller than her, all lean muscle, and the sculpture didn't look so intimidating next to him.

His gaze moved back to the life-sized dancing couple, and he studied her work in silence. She'd taken a blowtorch to it to bring out the blue-green tones in the bits of copper. Then, she'd polished it until it glimmered as if the couple danced in the moonlight. She tried not to look at his short, dark hair, or his muscles that flexed as he maneuvered around the piece. No way would she admit she'd pictured him when she'd sought inspiration.

He ran a hand down the arm of the sculpted woman, the earth-human blend of iron and copper, twisted together to mimic muscles and sinew. Fiona shivered as if he'd touched her skin.

A small smile tipped his lips. "Huh."

Defensiveness prodded her chin into the air. "What?"

"I expected it to be warm, but it's not." His gaze lifted to meet hers. "You give the illusion the metal is alive."

Some strange emotion flooded her at his look, which was part awe and part understanding. Fiona's family had been shocked and disappointed to learn she'd wanted to be an artist. No, those words were too mild. They'd laughed her out of Iowa, especially when they'd learned the medium she'd chosen was metals, a material she'd fallen in love with during shop class in high school. Which was just as well, since she'd needed to leave the small town she'd grown up in to find herself. She loved everything about the big-city life she'd found in New York, the freedom and openness of it, the way she could lose herself in the crowd.

Her metallic sculptures reflected the anger, frustration, and beauty of the world—anything that touched her senses or stirred her emotions. To her, the metals were alive and strong, nearly breathing. Her sculptures were also both rigid and pliable, a dichotomy she found fascinating. A healthy balance of strength and flexibility was how she'd adapted and survived. Her art was both an outlet for her rebellious energy and her life's work.

That Greg understood her message, that he saw beneath the surface level to the artist she was, was a surprise—and she wasn't sure she liked it. She'd had him pegged, fitted his square self into a square hole. But now, well, she'd have to reevaluate. Except that he'd told her she didn't have a place in his life, so why bother?

"Beautiful," he murmured. When she turned to see which sculpture had captured his fascination this time, his gaze was on her. His eyes were filled with wonder and admiration. Her pulse quickened. She hadn't realized how close they now stood to each other. Had she moved? Had he?

He reached out and flicked a finger beneath a strap of her work overalls, then tugged lightly. His knuckle brushed at the shirt she wore beneath, and she swore she could feel his touch as if she were wearing nothing at all. She held her ground, but her breath caught at the surprising, casual flirtatiousness of the move.

He grinned. "Nice outfit."

She cleared her throat. "I was working a little during lunch. It has a lot of pockets for storing odds and ends while I'm working. It's also for protection, for when the sparks fly." She was babbling, and forced herself to stop. Sparks were definitely flying between them. The overalls hugged some of her curves—all of the important ones. She'd never been more aware of that, or felt more vulnerable, than now. Too bad she'd taken off the fire-resistant apron that added another layer of protection, because she definitely needed insulation from this man and the desires he stirred up.

She forced herself to take a step back, and his finger plucked free of the strap. His grin faded and she almost regretted putting distance between them. Almost. He'd made it clear he didn't intend to pursue a relationship. He was here for something else entirely. She had to remember that, no matter how he made her feel when he was around.

She quickly changed the subject. "So, Noah and Vanessa sent you here to do what, exactly?"

"To help." He scowled, the heat in his eyes evaporating. Was he reluctant to be ordered to assist her, or still ticked that she hadn't called him first? She couldn't get a read on him.

"Okay, so help. Do you think the woman in the photo is dead? She certainly looked dead."

"If she was a local murder victim, I'd have heard about it. It's not your usual crime scene. Too staged."

"So, she's not local, or she's not a murder victim?" Hope fluttered in her chest, jarring loose some of the tightness that had taken up residence since she'd received the texts.

"Could be either." He shrugged. "Or it could be that she's just not the usual victim."

"Like, the victim of a cult or a serial killer or something?"

"Let's hope that it's nothing that serious." But he obviously wasn't ruling out the possibility. "I'll ask around and check with other precincts. I'm also working on tracing the number from which the texts were sent. And Noah's contacting SSAM to see if they know of anyone investigating similar murders."

"SSAM? Manchester's organization?" The Society for the Study of the Aberrant Mind had helped Vanessa when she'd been in need, targeted by a killer. Started by Chicago businessman Damian Manchester to find his daughter's murderer, the private organization was well versed in unusual crimes committed by unusual criminals, particularly serial killers.

Greg nodded. "In the meantime, have you received other strange messages of any kind lately? Pissed anyone off, or maybe attracted an admirer? Anything out of the ordinary at all?"

She thought for a moment. "No, nothing." In fact, her life had been too status quo for her liking, contributing to her restlessness.

"Any idea what the messenger meant by that second text, about you inspiring him?"

"Not a clue. As an artist, I hope my work makes people think and feel more deeply, of course. But I would never want anything like this to happen." She shuddered at the thought that something she'd created might have inspired a murder—or, at the very least, a staged photo meant to frighten her.

"You're good at making people feel."

She ignored the pleasure his comment gave her. "You'll keep me posted if you find out anything?"

"And you'll tell me—*me*, not Noah—the moment you receive the next communication." He hadn't said *if* she received anything else. He was expecting further contact.

"Of course."

"You still have my number?"

"Yes." Though she hated to admit it.

"Use it."

AN HOUR LATER, GREG HAD SETTLED BEHIND HIS DESK AT THE precinct. He was off the clock and should have been home resting, but he was spending his own time investigating Fiona's strange texts. A few yards away, Noah's desk was empty, but that wasn't unusual. Detectives worked unpredictable shifts and were often out, processing crime scenes, interviewing suspects for their cases, or beating the bushes for leads. Or maybe Noah had gone home to take care of his very pregnant wife.

Fiona hadn't been far from Greg's thoughts, and while he'd never pictured having a wife and kids, the image of her slender body rounded with his child suddenly took hold. His usual defenses were down, which was to be expected. Whenever he saw Fiona, her beauty sucked his breath and his good sense away. And her sense of humor, her sarcasm, her art work...well, he found everything about her sexy as hell.

He hated that he'd hurt her. He'd caught the quick little flashes of pain and distrust in her eyes before she could hide them. By breaking things off before they'd begun, he'd only been trying to shield her from hurt down the road, when he wouldn't be able to commit to both her and his job, but he'd failed. Today,

Fiona had worn her sarcasm like she wore her overalls—as another layer of defense—but he'd seen the awareness in her eyes. It only made him want to peel away those defenses, even when his job should be his priority. The only thing he wanted out of life was to make a difference where he could, and he had no room for distractions like Fiona. Unfortunately, his body didn't agree.

He sipped at another cup of coffee and tried to focus on the texts. Earlier that morning, before going to see Fiona, he'd put out feelers based on what he already knew. The silk scarf around the victim's neck had to be something that would stand out for any homicide detective. He checked his emails and his voicemails, hoping his attempt at tracking down the mystery woman had led somewhere. One of his messages was a reply to his request to trace the phone number from which the texts had been sent. Unfortunately, the technician had little to report.

"The phone was a burner," the man said when Greg called him back, hoping to get more details. "Sorry, but it looks like a dead end." Unfortunately, it wasn't just a dead end for Greg. It was a red flag. Nobody would go to the trouble of obtaining a burner phone for a Halloween prank. He'd no sooner hung up with the tech lab when he looked up to find a fellow CPD detective stopping at his cubicle.

Detective Luke Safford's expression was grim. "Just got a call about a body. Heard you were looking for something in particular and I thought this one might interest you."

"You think it might be the woman in red?" But in his gut, Greg knew. Somehow, the mystery woman had been located.

"Might be. Person who called it in mentioned it looked like she'd been sliced or something."

"Sliced, not stabbed?"

"Yeah, the wording caught my attention, too. Also mentioned a red scarf."

*Shit.* Fiona would no longer be able to pretend this was a prank.

He hated to be the one to burst her bubble of hope. "Want company on this one?"

One side of Luke's mouth tipped upward. "I'll drive."

Fifteen minutes later, they pulled up to a warehouse not far from the area of downtown Chicago known as the Loop. Greg glanced at the address on the slip of paper, then back up at the large, vacant building. It had once been a candy factory, but had shut down a decade ago. The shore of Lake Michigan was within a few miles. Other than the calls of seabirds, the traffic from a street farther away, and the hum of machinery from a nearby warehouse, the place was practically deserted, though it was late afternoon on a typical workday.

"Perfect place to dump a body," Luke murmured. Greg had been thinking the same thing.

Outside the main entrance, a man in an oversized coat, ball cap, and work boots waited with the first officer on the scene. Greg and Luke acknowledged the officer, who introduced them to the other man, a Mr. Louis Nelson, the property's caretaker.

"You discovered the body?" Greg asked Mr. Nelson.

"Yeah," Nelson responded. "Owner installed a motion-sensor video camera here at the front and one on the loading dock around the side. Usually a cat or something sets it off, so I didn't pay any attention to the initial alert last night. Had some free time today, so I scrolled through the alert and saw a strange car pull up to the loading dock's door. A woman got out and looked around a bit, then went inside the building. Didn't see her come out again."

Luke looked up from the pad where he'd been jotting notes. "Can we get a look at that footage?"

Nelson nodded. "Got it on an app on my phone." God bless modern technology.

Greg and Luke shared a look as the man loaded the footage from the previous night and showed them his phone screen. Luckily, there was a floodlight that lit up the area at night, so even though the recording was made during the dark of night, they caught a glimpse of the woman's features as she looked around. She could be the woman from Fiona's text. She paced the parking lot for a minute before glancing at her phone. Then, she went to the side door next to the loading dock and let herself in. They watched for several minutes, but she never reappeared.

"There were no other alerts?" Greg asked.

"Nope," Nelson said. "Never came out." And apparently, neither did the killer. Not through either of the main doors, anyway.

"Is there another entrance?"

"No, but I found a broken window on the other side of the building. Low enough that someone could have crawled through. Wasn't broken when I was here last week."

"The woman's car?"

"Parked around back." Nelson led them around the building to the blue compact car parked by the loading dock.

Careful not to touch the vehicle, Greg peeked in the windows. On the floor of the front passenger seat was a rectangular container that looked like a tackle box. He doubted this woman had come here to fish.

Greg glanced up at the darkening clouds. They were expecting rain for the next few days, and the wind was blowing it in fast. "Crime scene techs better get here soon before the weather worsens."

Luke glanced at his watch. "Last I heard, ETA is fifteen minutes."

"You notice what the woman wasn't wearing in the video?"

"A red scarf."

"The killer must have added that little touch. I want a look at what other touches he added." Greg retrieved protective booties and gloves from Luke's trunk. The loading dock's door creaked on its hinges as he pushed it open. The faint smell of sugar mixed with dust and rusting machinery filled the air.

Luke gestured toward a back corner. "Nelson said he found her over there." They clicked on the flashlights they'd brought from his car. There was no electricity inside the building, and any daylight that made it into the room was filtered through windows that had been covered with butcher paper. Except for the one, broken window near the body. A beam of light poured in like a spotlight. They headed in that direction.

"What would bring someone here, especially in the middle of the night?" Luke's question echoed Greg's thoughts.

Greg grunted. "She was either meeting someone she trusted or up to no good."

They found her body lying on the hard, cold concrete in the corner. Here, the sunlight through the broken window provided some relief in the dimness of the factory. She was exactly like the image Fiona had received. A red silk scarf was knotted around her neck. Three nearly parallel gouges marked her chest. Her eyes were open, her stare vacant and unseeing.

Careful about where he stepped, Greg crouched near her body and aimed his flashlight at her head. "You see this?"

Luke shifted to glance at where Greg had aimed the beam. "Is that a bump?"

The side of the woman's head, behind her ear, had a large bump and a line of dried blood. "Looks like she may have been knocked out before she died."

The creak of the door from the other side of the factory announced the arrival of the crime scene team. Greg and Luke went outside while the team set up lights and cameras as if the woman were a model in a fashion shoot. Greg waved one of them over and led them to the victim's car. The tech reached into the glove box and removed a registration slip, and then handed it to Greg.

"Amber Lockett," Greg read aloud. "Address is in Springfield."

"She's a long way from Springfield," Luke said.

"But why?"

The tech examined the tackle box and drew it out to pop it open. Inside, a variety of tubes of oil paints and several paintbrushes of different sizes and widths, as well as cleaning rags filled the trays and compartments. The smell of turpentine wafted into the air.

"She was an artist," Greg said. Amber looked like Fiona, was an artist like Fiona, and had apparently come into contact with the same killer as Fiona. Greg vowed that's where the similarities would end.

Fiona wouldn't end up dead.

# CHAPTER 3

AFTER HER LUNCH BREAK, FIONA WORKED THE FLOOR OF THE gallery, grateful for the steady stream of customers. Keeping busy helped her avoid thoughts of the texts and the man who'd returned to her life as a result of them. During a break, she made a quick call to Charlotte about the interview she'd set up for Orlando.

"You'll make sure he gets here within the hour?" Fiona crossed her fingers.

Charlotte sighed. "I can't promise, but I'll try. He disappeared to visit some friends and take in the local scene as soon as we got here. You know how he is." Translation: Orlando had been out late partying. The man was frustratingly flighty.

"This interview's really important." Fiona reiterated the pertinent information, as well as the time for tomorrow evening's event, before hanging up. It was the best she could do, other than declaring him a missing person and having the police look for him. Thoughts of police had her thinking about Greg again, and, with a groan of frustration, she threw her energy into selling a piece to the next person who walked through the door.

An hour later, the soft sound of a door chime told her she had a new arrival. Neil Ramsey, a reporter who wrote an arts and events column for a local newspaper and its accompanying blog, had agreed to do a piece on Orlando for tomorrow's party. He turned in a slow circle, taking in the overall impression of the gallery, and then grinned.

"I love what you've done with the place." He winked at her.

His easy manner made him instantly likeable. As he extended his hand, his appreciative male gaze slid over the deep purple dress she'd changed into after her working lunch break, before darting back to her face. He had the sleek look of a runner, his shoulders not as wide as Greg's. His scent was different, too. Nice, but not nearly as yummy.

She returned his smile and shook his hand. "Fiona Elliot."

*Arts Daily* was a wide-read blog and Ramsey's story would ensure a healthy attendance for tomorrow night's event, as well as in the weeks to come, when *Wicked Night* would still be on display even after the haunting season ended.

"I'm so glad you could fit us into your schedule," she said.

Neil pulled a notebook and pen from the side of the camera bag slung over his shoulder. "It'll be tight to get something written up tonight, but I already posted a brief teaser on the blog based on what you told me, and I've been researching your artist." He glanced around. "Will he be here soon? An interview with the artist, especially someone as ostentatious yet mysterious as Orlando Reyes, is vital to the story."

"He should be here any moment." She hoped. Neil frowned and Fiona mentally cursed Orlando's inability to keep a schedule. She scrambled to fill the gap until Orlando arrived. "I'm sure he's just running a few minutes late. He won't want to miss this. We're thrilled you're offering to feature his show on your blog. In the meantime, let me show you some of his work." She gestured to the twelve-foot wall behind them, where an image of a snarling were-wolf seemed to leap from a frame and claw at the viewer. "Orlando knows how to add the fright factor. He uses mostly recycled scraps of plastic, paper products, and other materials to make his work three-dimensional."

Neil pulled his camera from his bag and snapped a few pictures. "He has a way of making the stuff of nightmares come alive."

Fiona led him around the wall to another area, where she'd set up a life-size vampire with blood dripping from its fangs as he bent over a woman in his arms. The tip of his fang just barely brushed the woman's exposed neck. "As you can see, he likes to use popular images from films and recreate them, put his own twist on them."

"Must be why his work is so trendy in Hollywood."

Fiona nodded. "One famous horror director has several of Orlando's pieces in his personal collection. This one was done primarily with various types of plastics. The cape even flows if it catches a breeze."

"There's almost a sexual energy to this one."

"Many of the pieces in *Wicked Night* are macabre, but also sensual. Orlando believes sexual tension can be mysterious, and sometimes painful." And the artist should really be conveying that message himself. Fiona tamped down a flash of impatience. She'd have to put in another call to Charlotte if Orlando didn't show up soon.

Neil finished taking a picture and leaned in for a closer look at the vampire's cape. "Is that a garbage bag?"

"It is." Fiona led him through the rest of the gallery, commenting on various pieces and checking her watch when Neil wasn't looking. "We've been rolling out a couple new pieces each week, to keep the momentum rolling."

"He's got a real skill for transforming refuse into something interesting," Neil complimented. "But I'm looking for something unique, something different. Something to inspire me, Fiona."

She froze. She scanned his expression but could see nothing but interest—in both her and the art. There was no malice behind his word choice. Still, the reminder of that text left her chilled. *Fiona, you inspire me.*

She forced words past her too-tight vocal cords. "Inspire you?"

"Something especially creepy and provocative for the Halloween season. Maybe I can get a sneak peek at one of the pieces you'll unveil at the party tomorrow night?"

"We saved some of the best for those who are planning to attend. Those looking for a truly wicked night won't be disappointed." She removed her phone from her pocket as she felt the vibration of a text.

*Be there soon. Both of us.* Charlotte had succeeded in rounding up Orlando. Fiona exhaled in relief.

Meanwhile, Neil seemed intent on getting an exclusive. "I can hint at that with a sneak peek. I won't post pictures of whatever you show me until tomorrow morning. I can lead in with another teaser tonight. It'll create interest and serve both the blog and your gallery. If the pieces you've held back are as dark and brooding as the others, this will be the creepiest place in Chicago to spend Halloween night."

"That's what we're hoping for." With Orlando on his way and Neil on board, Fiona finally started to relax. It was all coming together.

Deciding to trust Neil, she led him through a door that went to the back rooms. Her work area was through a door to the left, and the storage area that held the rest of Orlando's pieces was to the right. Straight ahead was the rear exit to the alley.

She stopped at the door on the right. "As you'll see, Orlando likes to toy with all of the observer's senses."

"Even taste?"

"Absolutely. Poison apples."

"That, I have to see."

"And taste, if you dare." She grinned and pushed open the door to the storage room. She flicked on the light. Neil followed her inside, eagerly raising his camera lens to capture the pieces that crowded the room. "The candied apples are actually apples coated in melted cinnamon candies and displayed on a rotted-looking tree." The shiny apples had been delivered by a local vendor that morning, and Fiona had hung them herself to the specifications Charlotte had provided. Now, they were ripe for the picking. Beneath the tree, a figure of a pretty woman with a mischievous look in her eyes held an apple out to them.

"She's made mostly of paper-mache and scraps of fabric," Fiona said as Neil leaned in for a closer look. The woman was clothed in torn white cloth, as if she wore a toga that had been nearly ripped from her body.

"Her eyes are so lifelike. And I'd swear she's inviting me to do more than take a bite of her apple." Neil leaned toward Fiona conspiratorially. "Is Orlando really as debauched as the rumors say?"

Fiona hid her surprise that he would ask such a question. Then again, he was a reporter. "I suppose you'll have to judge that for yourself when you talk to him. But I find him reasonable enough." That wasn't exactly true, as she'd had to walk a fine line of shutting down his advances while also doing some long-distance ego-stroking when he'd wanted to back out of the exhibition a month ago, citing the venue wasn't big enough. She'd talked him down and sent him the data on the customer traffic she anticipated, as well as detailed plans for advertisements and their Halloween event highlights. He'd sent her black roses the next day. And the man *had* shipped all his pieces according to her instructions and timeline. Of course, the timely and organized parts were likely due to his assistant's efforts. Perhaps Fiona should send Charlotte roses.

"I heard he hosts sexual fantasy parties," Neil pressed.

Fiona had heard similar rumors but had shrugged them off. "Many of the world's best artists have been eccentric in some way."

"Eccentric doesn't always translate to good art. I have to warn you that my readers expect me to be brutally honest in my opinions. If I don't believe *Wicked Night* is wicked enough to satisfy the creep factor on Halloween night, I'll have to say so in my blog post."

"Of course. We chose you for this interview because of your reputation for providing the public with honest opinions—with panache, of course."

He grinned. "Of course. May I look around?"

"Be my guest, but I can only permit a couple pictures for the blog. The rest are going to be surprises for those who attend *Wicked Night*. Please forgive the tight fit and the poor lighting. These weren't meant to be seen until I move them onto the main floor tomorrow. You're truly getting the first look."

Fiona held back to text Charlotte as Neil moved forward to explore.

*Where are you? The reporter's almost done.*

She bit her lip and waited, but there was no reply text. Damn. She'd have to continue to stall or reschedule.

"I've found the one I want to feature," Neil called out. He'd rounded a corner and only the top half of his head was visible over a shelving unit.

She moved around to view what he was looking at. He'd gone into his photographer's stance, shifting as he took pictures from various angles. A bare-branched silver tree stood taller than them both. A mix of fabric and plastic sheets were draped and flowed from its branches, as if it were a ship preparing to take sail. For this one, Orlando had directed her to place a fan somewhere out of sight so that the piece would seem to move in the wind. The plastic was full of holes and tears, and thin enough that light could be seen through it. It looked like something made from skin. This was her favorite of Orlando's pieces. It was unique, not some interpretation of a pre-existing character from a film or book.

Neil paused to lower his camera as he rounded the tree. "I wonder what this is supposed to mean."

Fiona followed him to the back of the tree. Something between a moan and a gasp squeaked out of her throat as she spied what had caught his attention. A red silk scarf, identical to the one the woman in the text had been wearing, was caught in one of the branches. From a nearby branch dangled a Polaroid picture on a red string—a picture that was both similar to and different from the picture Fiona had received. Another woman who appeared to be dead, with parallel marks ripping open the flesh of her bare chest, but definitely a different woman. Written at the bottom of the Polaroid in red Sharpie: *Still inspired by your fierceness.*

Neil caught the strange noise she'd made and looked at her sharply. "This isn't supposed to be part of the piece?"

"No. Definitely not." It hadn't been there when she'd unpacked it and set it up according to Orlando's directions.

She backed away on wobbly legs. "Don't touch anything. I need to make a call." She was already fumbling to find Greg's phone number, praying he would know what to make of this.

Neil was taking more photographs, but she didn't care. She only knew she needed Greg. Now.


GREG WAS STILL WORKING THE SCENE WHERE AMBER'S BODY HAD been found. After Fiona's call, however, he hauled ass to get to her. Ten minutes later, he was standing in the gallery warehouse, in the room across the hall from where he'd seen Fiona earlier that day.

The storage room was one of the strangest, most surreal scenes he'd ever seen. What he supposed qualified as art filled the room. A half-dressed vixen, tortured faces, a devil frolicking with maidens. Stark, dark, and hinting of violence and sex, the overall effect was chilling. These had to be Orlando Reyes's *Wicked Night* pieces.

"If I could fire you, I would," a man's voice reverberated off the walls, pulling Greg farther into the room until he rounded a corner. The guy standing before him wore a top hat, dark velvet suit with a bright orange silk shirt, and several rings that flashed in the low light as he gesticulated wildly, his hands nearly bumping

Fiona's face as he yelled at her. "You're obviously not very good at your job. I thought I could trust you."

*Oh, hell no.* Greg's primal protective instincts had his fists tightening at his sides. He stepped forward.

Without taking her eyes off the wild man, Fiona shifted closer to Greg. Energy—a maelstrom of anger, impatience, and fear—seemed to vibrate through her. The man berating her was in full-on tantrum mode, not paying any attention to Greg or the other people in the room. A thirty-something woman in dark clothing hovered in the corner, her hands gripped together in front of her. A well-groomed man with a high-quality camera stood to the other side, taking in the scene with great interest and occasionally snapping pictures of Orlando. At least, Greg assumed the gesticulating man was Orlando Reyes, from what he'd found online during his web search at the station earlier.

"You assure us you have everything under control and then I arrive to find everything is totally fucked up!" Orlando flung the statement at Fiona. "This whole thing is off. We're leaving. Charlotte." He snapped his fingers in the air, presumably to summon the woman in the corner. She jumped to comply.

Greg leaned down to speak in Fiona's ear. "Want to make some introductions before I deck him? It'd be the polite thing to do."

His pounding heart calmed somewhat at the quirk of a smile she shot him. Then, she put a placating hand on his chest that sent his pulse into a gallop again. He was hit with two thoughts at the same time. He'd do anything to have this woman touch him, and he'd do anything to keep her safe. The surge of protectiveness, quickly followed by an irrational rush of possessiveness shocked him, but as it settled in his chest, as he saw her gratitude for his support loosen the tightness in her features, it felt right.

She frowned at whatever expressions she'd seen cross his features and pulled her hand back. "I was just explaining to Mr. Reyes that this might be a crime scene, so I shouldn't immediately remove the objects that were added to his pieces." Her statement both filled in the gaps for Greg and added a calm reminder to the upset artist that he needed to take a chill pill and let the police do their job. "Greg, this is Orlando Reyes and his assistant, Charlotte." She tipped her head toward the other man in the room. "Neil Ramsey is a reporter here to do an interview. Everyone, this is Detective Greg Marsh. He's here to help."

Orlando's eyes narrowed. "You're too late to help. Someone ruined my work."

Fiona nodded. "I'm sure Detective Marsh will clear this up as quickly as possible and you'll have your art back under your control. In the meantime, perhaps you'd like to join Neil in our conference room for the interview? He's hoping to have content go live tonight so that all your admirers will be chomping at the bit to get to tomorrow night's event. I'll have Alyssa bring coffee."

Orlando rolled his shoulders, closed his eyes, and sucked in a breath through his nose. His nostrils flared. When he opened his eyes again a second later, his lips curved, though his expression was still dark with ill temper. His outward demeanor changed so quickly that Greg nearly applauded. "That would be lovely, Fi. Let's make that happen, shall we?"

"Absolutely," Fiona said with a patient smile.

Orlando turned to Neil. "Let's find this conference room." Charlotte leapt from the corner and followed Orlando, who was now completely jovial as he clasped Neil on the shoulder and spoke of his excitement for Halloween event. But over the other man's head, Orlando shot Fiona a warning look that spoke volumes. *Clear up this mess quickly or else.*

The *or else* had Greg bristling, eager for a fight. He'd spent years learning how to control his own feelings and channel them into investigations, but the threats to Fiona seemed to test his limits, showing just how far she'd gotten past his defenses. Increasingly, he got the feeling he was fighting a losing battle when it came to ignoring their connection.

He relaxed as the trio exited and he was left alone with Fiona and some rather disturbing art. "That guy's a piece of work."

Her heavy sigh morphed into a giggle. The crease between her brows returned as she looked toward the door where Orlando, Neil, and Charlotte had disappeared.

Greg reached out and touched her jaw, waiting until she raised her troubled gaze to his. "I didn't like how he was talking to you." He couldn't seem to keep the growl from his voice.

Her expression softened. "I've dealt with difficult people before. I'm in sales, remember? Making people happy is what I do."

"I don't care about those people. Are you okay?"

Her green eyes sparked with determination. "I will be."

No, she wouldn't be. The news he had yet to share with her wasn't good.

He took her hand and squeezed it. "We'll make sure of that." He let go of her rather than pull her closer, as he wanted to. "Now show me what you found."

She led him around a large metal tree with its branches draped in what looked like—*Jesus*—human skin.

"It's only treated fabric and plastic," she said, following his gaze. "Orlando likes to titillate the senses."

On the rear branches, he saw what had worried her—as if the other items in this room weren't reason enough for concern. Whoever had sent her the text had obviously been here, on the gallery's private property, and left their mark in the form of a disturbing photo and a red silk scarf. Greg used his phone to take pictures, and then called the crime lab to have someone come over to process the items. Perhaps they could find prints.

"When would this have happened? When's the last time you saw this piece in its"—he swallowed a cough—"normal state?"

"Yesterday, about midday, I guess. I was in here, unpacking, dusting, and getting things ready, and then took a late lunch break. After that, I had work to do in the gallery. Today, I worked in the gallery and on my own stuff in the other room instead of coming in here. I needed some time to process those texts, and I find that working with my hands helps." Her chin went up as if bracing herself for criticism that she'd take some of her workday to create her own art. Maybe Orlando would give her hell for taking a day off from the event prep, but Greg wouldn't judge her.

He smiled. "I get it. I have a cabin on Lake Michigan that I go to when I need to process something. It's quiet. Chopping wood out back is therapeutic. As is taking my boat out on the lake."

"That sounds lovely." She smiled back and they shared a moment of peace before she looked back at the tree. Her brow creased again. "I haven't been in the storage room today until Neil —he's the reporter who was here—came by to gather information and pictures."

"So this happened between yesterday around lunchtime and about an hour ago. Any reason to suspect Neil?"

She shot a startled look at him. "I don't think so, but I barely know him. He's a well-respected reporter for *Arts Daily*. I contacted him for this interview. Nearly had to beg because of the timeline, so I don't think this would be his doing." She gestured toward the tree with its scarf and dangling photograph.

Greg stepped closer to the photo. "Different woman." Which meant there was likely another victim out there, somewhere, undiscovered.

"Apparently, he's still inspired by me," she muttered, referring to the writing on the bottom of the Polaroid.

"I'm inclined to believe it's the sick voices in this guy's head that truly inspire him to kill."

"If killing is what he's doing. This could still be some kind of prank, right?"

He hated to snuff out the last bit of hope in her eyes, but she had to know the extent of this. "We found the victim from the picture that was texted to you."

She raised her hand to her mouth, but couldn't stifle her gasp. "What?"

"I just came from a crime scene. She was murdered in an abandoned factory within the past twenty-four hours."

"Did you identify her?"

"Amber Lockett from Springfield, Illinois. Sound familiar?"

"No." She released a slow breath. "What's this about, Greg?"

"Hell, if I know." Unfortunately, all he did know was that a
killer was involving Fiona in his grisly plans. After the discovery of
Amber Lockett's body, Greg had already been formulating plans in
his mind. This latest picture settled it. He was taking a couple days
off from work to devote to keeping Fiona safe. "We might have a
serial killer on our hands, and you're the only one he's reaching
out to. Until we find this guy, you and I are going to stick together
as close as that dancing couple you're sculpting. "

# CHAPTER 4

FIONA'S EYES NARROWED. "WHAT DO YOU MEAN, STICK TOGETHER?"

His declaration clearly wasn't well received, but Greg planned to take the choice out of her hands. Her safety came first. A killer's fascination with her could quickly change from inspiration to desperation. Something had triggered this killer to go after at least one beautiful woman linked to the art world, possibly a second woman, and he wasn't about to let Fiona be the next victim.

"You've got a couch upstairs, right?" His own body reacted at the thought of spending his nights beside Fiona in the tiny apartment where he'd dropped her off after their date.

"You can't stay there." Wariness flashed across her features.

An unpleasant thought hit him. "Do you already have someone living with you?"

"No, but—"

The tightness in his chest loosened and he bit back a triumphant grin. "Great. All I need's a pillow."

She held up a hand. "Oh, no. That's not happening. You are not staying the night at my place."

Yes, he was. And maybe the next night, too. But he didn't need to belabor the point now. He had hours left in the day to convince her to let him move into her life. He marveled at how welcome the idea was after all he'd done for weeks to shove thoughts of her from his mind. "Fi, I'm exhausted. I'm hardly going to seduce you. I'll be another barrier between the killer and you." Her face paled but he had her attention and she wasn't arguing. "Now, I'm going to talk to Orlando and the others while they're still here, and then you and I can talk more. Will you be okay?"

She gazed at Orlando's tree. "I suppose I could be worse." She could be dead. Yeah, it could be much worse.

Greg wasn't comfortable with her being hurt by this at all, and he was going to catch the person who had involved her in this. In the meantime, he didn't want her in the storage room, obsessing over the woman in the photo. "Can you help me out?"

She looked back at him. "Anything."

"I need the names of anyone who would have had access to this area in recent days. Employees, cleaning people, vendors, or anybody else you can think of who might have a key or other means to enter without being seen."

"Of course."

"Are there any security cameras?" His gaze searched the corners of the room but didn't spot any.

She bit her lip. "No. I mean, there is one at the back entrance, but it hasn't worked in months. It was one of the things on my to-do list." Her expression was troubled.

"Show me all the entrances and exits."

She led him to the rear exit, pointing out the defunct camera when she opened the door. He stepped out into the alley and checked the lock. It had been damaged to the point anyone could have gotten inside.

Fiona cursed beneath her breath. "We could have been robbed." He didn't point out that she could have been murdered.

"When's the last time someone entered through here, that you know of?" he asked.

"Except for deliveries, I'm the only one who comes in from the alley. Well, Vanessa does when she drives herself because there's a little room to park back here, but she hasn't been in this week and lately, Noah's been dropping her off. Alyssa, our part-time sales and reception person, usually comes in through the front entrance, on the street side. A delivery truck brought the last of Orlando's pieces a couple days ago. That might have been the last time we used this door. I remember making sure the door was locked after they left."

He looked up and down the alley. There was a dumpster and bits of papers and trash, but no signs of life. He nudged Fiona back inside. "So as far as you know, nobody's checked this lock in two days and you hadn't been in the storeroom since yesterday, around lunch?" She nodded and he mentally cursed.

She wrapped her arms around her waist. Her voice was soft when she spoke again. "I live right upstairs. Someone dangerous came inside the building and I never knew it."

He itched to pull her into his arms but restrained himself. "The important thing is that you're okay. And I'm going to be sleeping on your couch, so you'll be safe tonight." She didn't argue, and he took that as a good sign.

"Anything else I can do—besides call a locksmith?"

"Would you wait out front for the crime lab person to arrive while I interview the others, and then maybe show him what we're working with?" Having a task would give her something to occupy her mind.

"Yeah, sure."

He followed her through the back hallway to the door that led into the gallery.

She nodded toward a wall of windows on the other side of the spacious main room, where they could see Neil, Orlando, and Charlotte. "That's the conference room. It's more of a classroom most days, where we offer art classes."

"Call that locksmith immediately. I want that fixed by

sundown. And line up someone to fix that camera." He waited until she nodded and then turned toward the conference room, watching through the windows as Orlando paced, Neil helped himself to coffee, and Charlotte sat in a chair at the table, writing on a notepad.

Behind him, Fiona spoke to the young woman who'd been manning the storefront. "Alyssa, can you find me a number for an emergency locksmith, please." Her voice faded as Greg reached the open door to the conference room and other voices dominated.

"Not bad for trailer park trash, eh?" Orlando's demeanor was completely different now that he had an eager audience. Across the room from him, Neil finished doctoring his coffee and then moved back to the table, where a mini-recorder sat, capturing every word. Charlotte sat nearby, doodling on her pad of paper.

Neil shook his head and smiled. "My readers are going to love your underdog story. Thank you for opening up."

Greg stepped into the room and closed the door. "I hope you'll open up to me, too."

Orlando's smile faded and his black eyes turned steely. "All I know is someone defiled my work. I'm the victim here."

Out of Orlando's line of sight, Charlotte rolled her eyes, but looked away when she saw that she'd drawn Greg's attention. She was probably in her early thirties, dark hair pulled back into a twist, pretty in an understated way. The dried paint beneath her short nails indicated she was also an artist. How long had she been working for Orlando, and how well did she know him?

Greg focused on Orlando first. "Defiled is quite a powerful word, Mr. Reyes. So is victim."

"I sent my work here. Fiona was supposed to be caring for it, setting it up to my specifications. Some stranger altered my work and messed with my creative vision. What would you call it?"

Greg took out a flip-notebook from his shirt pocket, a gesture meant to both intimidate and remind Orlando who was in charge. "And where were you for the past two days?"

"None of your business."

Charlotte cleared her throat to draw his attention. "We were in Savannah at an artist retreat until yesterday morning, when we took a flight here. We were able to check in early at the hotel. After that, he rested."

Greg arched a brow toward Orlando. "You were tired enough to need a mid-morning rest?"

Orlando's scowl deepened. "She mentioned the retreat. I'd just finished a piece that had wrung me out emotionally—not that you'd understand anything about that." His gaze flicked dismissively over Greg. "Do you have any idea what it takes to be an artist?"

Greg held his anger in check and gave the man a smooth smile. "Why don't you enlighten me?"

Orlando snorted. "Not worth my time. But I was at the hotel, catching up on the sleep I'd missed. Ask Charlotte."

At Greg's glance, Charlotte nodded, but she didn't make eye contact. She'd gone back to doodling.

Orlando smirked. "See?"

"You didn't recognize any of the items that had been added to your piece, or the woman from the photo?"

"No."

Greg turned to Neil. "And you? Where were you between yesterday morning and this afternoon?"

Neil shrugged. "I was out of town until last night, finishing up the post that's on the blog today. You can check my rental car reservations or ask my contact at the art museum in Minneapolis. I got back late, posted my piece, and met a friend for breakfast. I slept a little and worked at home until I came here. Until I saw Fiona's reaction, I didn't know there were things added to Mr. Reyes' piece. I thought it was part of his design."

Orlando grunted.

Neil's eyes narrowed. "Is there something more serious going on?" It seemed his reporter's instincts were kicking in.

Instead of answering, Greg turned to Charlotte. "Anything to add?"

Her glance flitted from Greg to Orlando, and then back again. "No, nothing." Greg didn't believe her, but it would take digging and trust-building to decipher which part of Orlando's story had been a lie.

"Do any of you know a woman named Amber Lockett?" Greg asked.

"I do," Neil said. "What's this got to do with her?"

"How do you know her?"

"She has an independent arts blog. I've seen her a couple times at local events, though I don't really know her, other than we share a love of the arts. She often branches out into other media like films and food." He frowned.

"What is it, Mr. Ramsey?"

"You'll see if you check out her blog that she's rather, uh, critical. She likes to stir the pot, and her audience likes it too."

Orlando leaned back in his chair and cackled.

Greg shot him a look. "Something's funny?"

"I just realized who you're talking about. Artsy Amber, right?" Orlando's question was directed at Neil.

Neil nodded. "That's the name of her blog."

Orlando snorted. "She spews shit whenever she can."

"And she spewed about you?" Greg asked Orlando.

The man nodded. "All over me and my art."

"How do you feel about that?"

Orlando's eyes twinkled with a mixture of malice and mischief. "Free speech is a right in this country. As an artist, it would be pretty hypocritical of me if I didn't respect everyone's right to communicate their opinions and feelings."

"Was that Amber in that picture?" Neil asked. "I didn't get a close look."

"No," Greg said. "But I'm sorry to inform you that we did find Amber earlier today. She'd been murdered." He carefully studied the occupants of the room as he dropped that bomb. Their expressions displayed varying degrees of surprise, but none of them were particularly saddened. He handed each of them a business card. "Thank you for your help. I'll be getting your contact information from Fiona in case I have any other questions, but please call me if you think of something."

"What about the claw marks on the woman's chest?" Orlando asked. Dark humor danced in his eyes. The man was baiting him— and enjoying it.

"What makes you so sure they're claw marks?"

"The note written at the bottom points in a certain direction. *Still inspired by your fierceness.* I would have thought it was pretty clear."

Greg narrowed his gaze, tired of Orlando's games. "And I would have thought you would volunteer information that might help catch a killer."

"Yes, well, I had assumed, as an officer of the law, you would be thorough in your questioning. Guess I was wrong."

Greg forced his clenched jaw to relax. "I could take you to the station and question you. Would that be thorough enough for you?"

"Maybe you should ask your girlfriend." The sneer marring the man's handsome face indicated he'd seen the spark of attraction Greg struggled to hide whenever he was around Fiona. Orlando's gaze moved to the door. "Speak of the devil."


Fiona stood in the doorway with a plate of cookies. Her gaze moved from Orlando, whose expression spelled trouble, to Greg, whose face was, as usual, unreadable. However, artists knew to look at a person's eyes for the truth, and Greg's conveyed a mixture of concern, distrust, and frustration. Directed at her? No, he had to be reacting to Orlando, who was skilled at bringing about those emotions in other people.

She set the plate on the conference room table. "Did I miss something?"

"How about you and I talk in private?" Greg turned to the rest of the group, who had fallen silent. "The rest of you can go on with your day, as long as Fiona knows how to get in touch with you."

Neil slung his camera bag over his shoulder and came forward. "I can't say it's all been a pleasure, but it sure has been interesting." He gave her a soft smile. "My piece will be posted within a couple hours. I'll keep any talk of murder out of it, though I may mention something about surprises."

"Thank you." A weight lifted off her chest as she watched Neil leave. The last thing she needed was for this incident to cast a negative light on tomorrow's event.

"Oh, I don't know," Orlando said, looking thoughtful. "A little scandal never hurt anyone."

She bit back her annoyance. "I don't think that's entirely true. Amber was certainly hurt."

Orlando surprised her by nodding. "Keep us posted on how things are going."

"I will. And the event starts at eight o'clock tomorrow night. I trust you'll be here, since you're the guest of honor."

"Wouldn't miss it." He snagged a cookie, and then leaned in and placed a quick kiss on her lips. It was over before it even registered or she could think to react. With a snap of his fingers toward Charlotte, Orlando walked out with his assistant close on his heels.

Once Fiona was alone with Greg, she crossed her arms over her chest. "Want to tell me what that dark cloud over your head is about?"

Greg shook his head. "I'm wondering just how deep into this mess you are."

"Well, since the killer of not one, but possibly at least two women, has been contacting me, and I apparently inspired the killings, I'd say I'm in pretty deep."

His eyes studied her. "Orlando seems to think you have another reason to know what that message on the Polaroid means."

*Still inspired by your fierceness.* She started to shake her head, but stopped. She couldn't deny the cold brick of ice that had formed in her stomach since she'd read the words. Out of self-preservation, she'd convinced herself that her initial reaction had been wrong, because the alternative meant her work had been used to harm someone, and that was unacceptable.

He kicked out a chair. "You're shaking. Sit down."

She sat.

He took a chair and turned it to face her. Sitting forward, his elbows braced on his knees, he looked into her downturned eyes. "Tell me what's going through your head."

She blew out a shaky breath. "I think, maybe, the killer was referring to a piece I worked on years ago."

"Why?"

"It was named *Fierce.*" She pulled her phone from her pocket and loaded a photo of the piece, taken when she'd premiered it two years ago. She held it out to show him. The steel creature had snapping jaws and a mouth full of sharp teeth, as well as two paws, raised in the air as he reared on two legs as if about to strike. At the ends of the paws were sharp, three-inch claws. She'd purposely rusted the steel to add to the grimy, chilling effect. "If you scroll forward, there are a couple more photos."

He studied them in silence, ending on the picture of her solemnly laying a hand on its back, as if trying to soothe six feet of metal beast. He handed the phone back to her. "Powerful image. Like I said before, you're amazing at putting emotion into your work. I'm guessing something inspired you?"

"He was a monster from my nightmares." As with all her pieces, she'd drawn on her current emotions when designing. In a fit of anger at the world, just after her beloved aunt, the woman who'd basically raised her, had succumbed to the cancer that had ravaged her body, she'd designed this thing—a rusted cancer monster she could tame.

"Whatever prompted this design must really have done a number on you." He spoke so softly she thought she might have heard the compassion in her head. But it was enough to keep her talking.

"*Fierce* represented my inner fears and insecurities after cancer took my Aunt Dee. She was the person I felt closest to in this world. This sculpture represented both the thing that took her from me and the rage inside of me, eating me from the inside."

"That must have been a horrible time for you."

She swallowed, remembering the nights she'd cried herself to sleep, knowing she'd lost the only family that had ever mattered to her. "I wanted to unleash on the world, but I couldn't."

"So you unleashed in your workroom."

"It was the darkest piece I ever worked on." And it had wrung her insides out. She'd often ended the workday in tears, emotionally gutted. But it had been worth it. The process of creating *Fierce* had been purifying, cleansing.

"Where is *Fierce* now?"

"Vanessa convinced me to put it in a special charity auction. It sold."

"That must have felt amazing."

"It did." She smiled as the dark memories were replaced with a much lighter one. Vanessa and Noah had taken her out to dinner and they'd toasted with champagne. "Raised some money for cancer research. Best thing I've ever done." Creating that piece had been therapeutic in so many ways. Her happiness faded. "And now women are dead because of it."

He reached for her hand. "Hey, listen to me." He squeezed her fingers until she met his gaze. "If the killer hadn't used your sculpture as inspiration, he would have found another weapon. He's only using you to justify his bloodlust."

His words broke through, and she nodded. Evil existed in the world, and that wasn't her fault. A killer's obsession could be used to attempt to justify all kinds of horrific behavior.

Greg squeezed her hand again. "Neil said that the first victim, Amber Lockett, was a blogger in the art world who'd been critical of many artists. How well do you know your art friends? When I asked you before, you couldn't think of anyone who might feel scorned or jealous. How about now? Any enemies? Or anyone who might use you as a scapegoat to go after Amber?"

"None I can think of. Besides, this person seems to be more of an admirer than an enemy, right?"

"It can be a fine line between obsession and violence. Which is why I intend to stay close until we figure out who's behind this."

*Close*, meaning in her tiny studio appointment, on the couch only a few feet away from her bed. Every movement as he shifted during the night, every soft snore or puff of breath, would echo in the small space between them. But she didn't argue. She wanted him there. She wanted him close.

# CHAPTER 5

GREG MEANT WHAT HE SAID. HE INTENDED TO STICK LIKE GLUE TO Fiona. Not that it was a hardship. The view from where he'd been sitting for the past hour was perfection. Through the wall of windows that separated the conference room from the gallery, Greg watched as Fiona explained the nuances of one of Orlando's 3-D works to a young couple.

Judging by their mode of dress, the number of glittery rocks on the woman's neck and fingers, and the Rolex on the man's wrist, they could afford to purchase whatever piece they wanted. The art in Greg's apartment was more of the whatever-had-been-on-sale at the department store variety, purchased hastily when his parents had announced an impending visit and he'd needed to decorate to convince them he was fine on his own. The last thing he needed was his overanxious mother worrying about him. It was one of the reasons he'd learned to disguise his emotions at an early age. But that didn't mean he couldn't appreciate why other people might drop a lot of money on a piece of art that spoke to them— like Fiona's art. He could see spending a few paychecks on some- thing she'd poured her emotion into, something she'd shaped with

her own hands. He loved that she lost herself in designing something new, that she left a piece of herself in each work of art. Her
creative spirit called to his no-nonsense one like yin went with
yang. And he was growing tired of fighting the pull toward her.

While he'd watched Fiona work her magic with customers,
Greg had remained in the conference room, touching base with his
contacts via his cell phone and working on a laptop he'd borrowed
from Fiona. Online, he'd researched the sale of *Fierce* and made a
call to the organization who'd sponsored the charity auction. He'd
found another picture of her beside her sculpture. Her red hair
had been scooped into a messy bun that was chic and unassuming.
The look, as well as the artfully applied makeup and flowing white
dress, made her look like Hollywood royalty. Or a goddess of fire.

*Fierce* had sold for tens of thousands of dollars to a retired businessman and it had been shipped to the man's house along the
shore of Lake Michigan, an hour north of Chicago. Fiona had
downplayed her contribution to the charity, and he felt a surge of
pride in her accomplishment. She was an interesting blend of
contradictions—fire and determination when confronted, but
gracious and understated when it came to her own achievements.
He enjoyed all of her many facets.

His cell phone rang. His eyes still on his enigmatic redhead, he
answered the call.

"Noah told us you have a hot case right here in Chicago," Holt
Patterson said after greeting Greg. Holt worked for SSAM as a
mindhunter, spending his days creating psychological and physical
profiles of killers based on crime scenes.

"I'd hoped I was wrong about this." Greg ran a hand over the
back of his neck and leaned back in his chair. "But it's looking
more and more like we have a serial killer on our hands."

"Haven't been able to think of much else after that description
you left on my voicemail." Holt was referring to Greg's description
of the picture of Amber Lockett that had been sent to Fiona.

"So, it rang a bell?" Greg leaned forward in his chair, feeling the usual stirrings a lead generated. His pulse thumped louder in his ears, his blood ran hotter, and his focus sharpened.

"More like a gong. It was unique enough that I called a contact at the FBI's Behavioral Analysis Unit. The red scarf tied around the neck? The parallel gouges in a woman's chest? My contact says it sounds like a handful of murders the FBI worked across the southern states, from Mississippi to Georgia."

Greg stilled. "Handful?"

"Five, at the last count, scattered across several states. Local law enforcement was struggling to put the pieces together until they saw a pattern and asked the BAU for a profile of the scenes."

He released a slow breath. He'd suspected they were dealing with a serial killer, but not one so prolific. His gaze tracked Fiona through the window, reassuring himself she was okay. She'd finished selling one of Orlando's 3-D paintings to the young couple, and now she stood in front of a sculpture of dancing skeletons, chatting with an older woman. Fiona was animated as she told some story, her hand gestures and dancing eyes bringing it to life.

*She's safe.*

The locksmith she'd called had arrived several minutes ago and was replacing the broken lock at the rear of the building. And Greg had called someone to repair the security camera, which should be addressed in the morning.

Still, there was no way he was leaving her alone until the killer was caught. She was a precious, bright light, and there were too few of those in the world—in his world—these days.

"Please tell me the FBI figured out who's doing this," he said.

Holt sighed. "Unfortunately, no. No identification or significant leads. The killer's still at large. But if these murders were in the south, what would bring him here?"

*Fiona.* "I'd love to compare notes, especially as we likely have another victim." Greg filled Holt in on the latest development, including the Polaroid hanging from the tree in the storage room.

He'd enlisted a crime scene tech to check things out in the gallery's storage room. As there wasn't much to process, they'd already come and gone. "What can you tell me for now?"

"The murders in the south span the past eighteen months. There's a definite progression as the killer perfects his technique. I'm waiting on the rest from my contact but should have it soon. Can you stop by tomorrow morning to discuss it? I should have a profile sketched out by then. It'll be rudimentary, though."

"I'll take what I can get." As they spoke, Greg put him on speaker so he could forward the texts Fiona had received, as well as the photos taken that afternoon in the storage room. "This latest one is probably an undiscovered victim. The initial text depicts a woman named Amber Lockett. CPD identified her body earlier this afternoon."

"Sure looks like the crime scenes from the south. The victims were posed similarly." Holt confirmed Greg's worst fears. A serial killer was interested in Fiona.

"Amber was identified as a blogger from Springfield. We're still getting information on her." Luke was out pounding the pavement, freeing Greg to work near Fiona in case something new—or the killer—popped up. "And then the most recent picture was hanging in the storage room this afternoon. Anything you can share could help me protect Fiona. Time is of the essence."

"Absolutely." Holt paused. "The other five murders were committed over an eighteen-month period, about one every four months, but this would make two within the past few days? That's a heck of an accelerating timeline. And now someone's involving your friend. Why her? Why now?"

"We're wondering the same thing. It may be related to a sculpture she produced two years ago." He told Holt about *Fierce*. "I'm working on reaching its owner and tracking the piece down."

"The sale coincides with the timeline of when the first victim disappeared in Georgia."

"Fiona thinks the markings on the women's chests match the claws she constructed, though she can't be sure."

"The victims I know about were sliced up with some kind of metal claws. But the fatal wounds were blows to the head."

"Knocking them unconscious would make it easier to pose them and create the image the killer wanted." An artist who used dead bodies as his medium. *Christ.* "I think this person is fascinated with the art world."

"Like Fiona. Bring her by SSAM tomorrow morning. In the meantime, make sure she's taking appropriate safety measures."

"Oh, I will." Greg planned to be Fiona's most dependable safety measure.

"SEVEN?" FIONA'S LEGS TURNED TO RUBBER. SHE SANK INTO A CHAIR in the conference room. She'd spent the late afternoon and early evening trying to pretend she wasn't watching Greg through the windows as he worked. But she had no idea this was what he'd been discovering while she'd been trying to focus on selling Orlando's pieces.

Greg leaned against the table in front of her and waited until she met his gaze. His look was hard as steel. "This isn't about you."

"Except that it is. Somehow. Somehow seven women are dead, nearly identical parallel claw-like marks across their chests that seem to have been produced by my creation." With a trembling hand, she pushed her hair from her forehead.

"There's no proof *Fierce's* claws made those marks. I haven't heard back from the man who purchased the piece. It could still be intact, for all we know."

"Doesn't matter. Either way, the killer's not done, and I'm still *inspiring* him." Her stomach churned and threatened to expel its contents. A chilled bottle of water was placed at her elbow and she looked up at Greg. "Thanks."

He crouched in front of her, his hands on her knees as he studied her features. "Drink."

She unscrewed the top and took a small sip, then a larger one. Her stomach settled a bit, but her hand was still shaky.

His sharp gaze swung to the windows. "It's nearly seven o'clock. Closing time, right?"

"Yeah."

"Lock up and go lie down. You've had a rough day."

She snorted. "Not as rough as some have had it." Those poor women. Why would they be a target? Who was interpreting her artwork as a license to kill?

"I'll carry you upstairs if I have to."

The thought of being held in his arms, against his broad chest, sent a ripple of awareness shimmying across her skin. She sent him a small smile. "Is that a threat?"

He didn't reply, but his eyes darkened with heat and desire. Her smile faded and her breath caught. He'd really carry her to her apartment. And then what? Her abdomen fluttered at the possibilities. But she had more pride than to give in to her hormones. He'd rejected her once. Though he was sending mixed signals now, it was safer to assume she'd be rejected again and operate as if they had no future. The next day or two was going to be tough if he truly insisted on staying by her side. She didn't think she had the strength to resist him if he made the slightest effort to pull her into his arms—not that he'd make any advances on her.

Then again, the way he was looking at her now was a touch possessive, a touch concerned. All of it thrilled her.

"I'll go lock up," she said.

He rose. "Good. Just let me pack up here. Don't enter your apartment without me." The reminder that a killer could be in her apartment—had, in fact, been in the storage room without anyone knowing—had her stomach clenching again.

As he shut down the laptop and pulled together his paper

notes, Fiona sent Alyssa home, turned out the main lights, and locked up.

The stairs to Fiona's studio apartment were tucked behind a wall of art, hidden from view unless one knew where to look. She waited at the base, looking up the darkened staircase. She flicked on the light, half-expecting to see a man at the top, waiting for her, *Fierce*'s sharp metal claws in his hands, ready to slice open her chest.

"Ready?" Greg stood behind her, studying her. Steadying her.

She shook off the horrifying image and nodded. With Greg at her back, she could face whatever was ahead. "Ready."

She used her key to let them in, immediately feeling better as the familiar sights and smells of her cozy studio apartment surrounded her. At first glance, the place might seem cluttered, but every item there had purpose and meaning to her. And with only five hundred square feet to play with, she thought she'd done quite well restricting her passion for art.

She watched as Greg's gaze drifted across the colorful throw pillows lining her Goodwill couch, then to the small, galley-style kitchen with quirky 50s décor, and finally landed on the queen Murphy bed that was currently down, but could fold up into the wall when she did her yoga. She hadn't had time to make it up this morning and the sheets were in disarray. As if the sight of the bed singed his eyeballs, his head jerked back to the living area and its small, scarred coffee table, the surface of which was a mosaic made of broken ceramic tiles. She'd designed it herself, making the base out of scrap metals. She and Vanessa had smashed plates from the thrift store and used the bits to make the tabletop.

"Cozy," he said.

She'd accept that as a compliment. "Thank you. You probably didn't notice much last time you were here, with our lips locked together and all." She couldn't resist provoking him with the reminder that he'd been here before, when he'd walked her to her door, kissed her as if he desperately needed all the oxygen from her lungs, and then walked away from her.

"Yeah. I didn't notice much other than you that night." His gaze drifted to her mouth.

Her lips tingled and her skin warmed. She supposed she should be flattered that he'd lost himself in her to the point he hadn't observed his surroundings. Greg didn't seem the type to lose himself in anything.

He seemed to come to his senses with a shake of his head. Or maybe he was reminding himself that he didn't want to kiss her anymore.

She turned in a circle. "Well, welcome to my humble abode. I suppose *mi casa es su casa*—for tonight, at least. It's not much, but it's home."

"And it's close to work." Humor tugged at his mouth. "Guess it won't take long to check for intruders, either." He could see every part of her studio apartment from the front door. There wasn't even a closet. No walls. Just a bathroom and a tall wardrobe cabinet next to her bed. He opened each and perused them briefly. No boogeymen hiding there. He moved to the refrigerator and she watched with amusement as he checked that, too.

"No popsicles staging a coup?" she asked. "I'm pretty sure Ben and Jerry are slowly trying to kill me."

He slid her a that's-not-funny look, but it quickly softened as he studied her. "You look dead on your feet. I was looking for food. You know, nourishment? You need to eat something."

His need to feed her was just plain sweet, but she could see the lines of fatigue pulling at his own features. Had he worked a full shift and then dealt with her stuff the rest of the day? She'd been so focused on how he was disrupting her life that she hadn't considered until now what he was setting aside to be here for her.

She shrugged. "I despise grocery shopping."

"I can see that." Back at the couch, he scooped aside her filmy curtains to eye the fire escape. No boogeymen there, either, apparently. He tested the locks on the windows and apparently found them up to his satisfaction. "I have a friend from the force who's set up watch across the street. You need anything while I'm gone, call me immediately and wave out the window. He's parked right across the street."

"Gone?" A tremor of alarm wove through Fiona, tightening around her breastbone and squeezing. "You're leaving?" She'd just accepted he was going to stay on her couch and now he was going to desert her. Again. Her heart plummeted to her toes.

"I'm going to run home and pick up a few things. I'll grab dinner for us both on my way back." He came forward to run his hands down her arms, and then squeezed her hands. The personal contact was comforting. "Hey, you'll be safe. I'll be back within the hour. The broken lock at the rear exit is fixed and there's a new deadbolt." He tossed her a shiny new key. "I'll make sure Noah gets a copy to Vanessa. Keep this window and your door locked." He jabbed his finger toward each, respectively.

As if she'd want to open either to the elements. That morning's breeze had tried to bend her in half, and throughout the day, the wind had built into something that howled like a wild animal as it whipped around the edges of the downtown buildings.

He nudged her toward her bed and she gratefully sank onto it. "Rest. I'll be back soon with sustenance."

*And then what?* She wanted to ask the question but was suddenly so tired she couldn't think. Fatigue overwhelmed her and she curled up on her side. Greg grabbed the afghan from the end of the bed and tucked it around her. Aunt Dee had knitted it for her, and it always felt like a hug. She took comfort in its bright fall colors and soft yarn.

"Apartment key?" he asked.

"Purse." Before her eyes drifted closed, she saw Greg reach for her purse on the kitchen counter.

"I'll lock the door behind me."

It seemed he'd just left when suddenly he was by her side again, a paper bag in each hand. Wonderful smells came from within. Raindrops glistened in his hair and on his coat and she glanced at the window, where rivulets of water were illuminated by a flash of lightning. Thunder boomed.

She pushed herself into a sitting position and stretched. "That was fast."

"An hour. I would have let you sleep, but you need to eat." He hefted one bag.

"Are you feeding an army?"

"Didn't know if you wanted Chinese"—he lifted the other bag —"or preferred burgers and fries, so I brought both."

"Either one is great." She studied the bags and recognized the logos of nearby restaurants. Two of her favorites. On their blind date, they'd talked about food and somehow, he'd remembered the smallest of details. Acknowledging his thoughtfulness would be a little too intimate, would make her too vulnerable, yet her heart became a puddle in her stomach. She could no longer pretend she wasn't interested in Detective Greg Marsh. But that didn't mean she was going to crumble at his feet, either.

He nudged aside the art catalogues on the coffee table, the only table in her tiny apartment. "I forgot to ask your preference before I left. I texted you because I didn't want to wake you if you'd crashed. Since you didn't answer, I just brought both."

She retrieved her phone from the kitchen counter, near her purse. "I guess I never took it off vibrate. After those awful texts, every time my phone made a sound, I jumped."

"Understandable. There's nothing else from your admirer on there?" His face was tight with concern.

Reluctantly, she scanned her messages. "No." She set her phone aside, face down. She would have changed her number, but she figured the killer would only find another way to contact her. Obviously, if he'd killed seven women, he was determined. "What can I get you to drink?"

"I'll take one of those sodas I saw in there." He removed the food options from the bags and laid out a feast that made her mouth water and her stomach rumble. He picked up a burger and unwrapped it while she grabbed a couple of cold sodas and joined him on the couch.

She hadn't had much of an appetite all day but suddenly, she was starving. "I may be hungry enough to eat both meals." They dug in for a couple minutes before she came up for air. "Thank you for taking care of me."

"Any time."

She snorted and soda nearly came out her nose.

His eyes narrowed. "What?"

"*Any time?* Weeks ago, you literally told me you never wanted to see me again."

He grunted. "I'm pretty sure I didn't say that."

"Okay, maybe not literally. Close enough, though. So now that I'm in danger, you changed your mind? I think you've got a white knight complex."

He brushed the burger grease from his fingers onto a napkin. "Maybe."

She tipped her head, interested that he'd accept her diagnosis so readily. "It would explain why you became a detective." Despite what had happened on their date, he'd be there for her if she needed him. The sense of security flooded her with warmth.

"A long time ago, I made a commitment to helping others."

At the expense of forming relationships, apparently. "Something happened to someone you cared about," she guessed.

He met her gaze. Wariness tightened his features and, underneath, weariness, as if she'd stirred up an old pain. Sensing he wasn't ready to let down his defenses, she squashed the urge to run her fingers over the lines and soothe him.

"You don't have to tell me about it," she said when he didn't elaborate. To prove she didn't need his response, she resumed eating.

After a long silence, he spoke again. "I shouldn't have pushed you away."

She stopped mid-chew, sure she'd heard him wrong. She forced herself to swallow while she chose her words carefully, because forgiving him meant they had something to build on. She wasn't sure she wanted to build something just to watch it crumble.

"Well, I can't disagree with you there." She poked at the chow mien in her container as she fought to keep things light. "So, what are you missing by being here with me? What's a night in the life of Detective Marsh like?" Curiosity was the artist's curse. She wanted to know what made him tick, what episodes had colored his life, provided shading and marbling and rough spots, and all the features that made him interesting.

And why she hadn't been good enough to warrant a second date when their chemistry had been off the charts.

"Pretty boring," he said. "Case files and the occasional ballgame on TV before restless sleep."

She pictured him rolling around in his bed. Did he sleep in boxers? In the buff? Beside another woman? She stabbed her food a little harder than required. "Nobody's missing you at home?"

"I'm not missing anything or anyone," he said. He waited until she met his gaze. "That evening with you was an anomaly. When I told you I couldn't date you, it was because you'd be a distraction from my job. I don't do relationships beyond a few dates."

"Have you tried?"

He frowned. "No."

"No serious relationships at all?" Fascinated, she set her food aside and turned to face him on the couch, pulling her feet up underneath her. "Why not?"

"Most people don't understand the long hours and how this job grinds down emotions until they're dull, until there's nothing left. I saw what it did to my mother when my father dedicated his life to a career on the force. It nearly broke her."

"First of all, I object to you lumping all women into one basket. I'm not your mother."

His lips twitched. "Definitely not."

"Second of all, I've seen plenty of non-dull emotions from you." Her skin flushed at the memory of his touch on her skin, on her lips. "You seem convinced that you can't find room in your life for more than your job."

He nodded. "I always thought so, yes." Because of what he'd observed with his parents? Apparently, she'd have to show him there was a different way to be.

"Then I apologize."

Startled, he stilled. "For?"

"Sounds like you like quiet evenings with no upheaval. Sorry I'm stirring the pot."

"I don't mind." He seemed surprised by the admission and she nearly grinned.

"Truly? You seem uncomfortable around me sometimes. Like I might make you share secrets against your will."

He pondered that for a moment. "I see how open you are in everything you do. Your expression of feelings, both in words and through your art, is genuine and honest and I can't help but think my feelings are...."

"Constipated?" she tried when he seemed at a loss.

He laughed, a rich baritone that slid across her skin like Aunt Dee's handmade blanket, warm and familiar. "I prefer the term *private*. I don't like to talk about myself."

"How about our kiss? Want to talk about that?"

His gaze dropped to her mouth and then he looked away as if he couldn't let himself go there. "I suppose we should."

"Well, I'm not twisting your arm. It's not like I want to talk about something that was so distasteful to you. It's just that I want to know how I misread the cues, and maybe make sure it doesn't happen next time." She really wanted to kiss him again, but not if he was going to run away.

"Distasteful?" He made a sound that was part strangled groan, part laugh. "Not at all. At the time, I was afraid of getting involved with anyone."

"*At the time.*" She tipped her head to the side and studied him, trying to ignore the wild fluttering in her chest. "And now?"

"Let's just say I've recently had someone open my eyes to more of what the world has to offer." He winked before peeling the paper away from a set of chopsticks and poking them into a carton of Kung Pao shrimp.

She had to blink several times to realize she'd really seen what she thought she'd seen. The stoic, intense Detective Marsh had actually winked. His statement was one of the best compliments she'd ever received, and, in a way, he'd admitted he had feelings for her.

Holy hell.

For a while, they ate in companionable silence, but inside, her mind was a tempest. There was suddenly a crack in the door he'd slammed shut after their date. Getting to know him a little bit more gave her a tingle of hope—and made her want to throw that door wide open and really shake up his world.

# CHAPTER 6

EARLY THE NEXT MORNING, FIONA PACED HER LIVING ROOM, WHICH required exactly four steps in each direction. Movement seemed to help settle her nerves. The nervous energy felt an awful lot like fear, and she hated that. Then again, it was Halloween, a day designed for fear. She couldn't help wondering what the killer would have in mind for her today. Had he already claimed another victim?

Greg had been a perfect gentleman, sleeping on the couch, though it didn't exactly fit his tall frame. He'd been so exhausted that he'd crashed shortly after dinner. It made her feel safe to have him there, looking out for her. And after he'd opened up to her a little, she'd felt closer to him.

Still, she hated needing anyone, even the sexy detective. Most of all, she hated that she wanted him. She wasn't about to invite him into her bed when she wasn't sure what kind of response she'd get. Open herself up to rejection again? No, thank you. He'd have to make the next move. Unfortunately, she wasn't the patient type and a methodical man like Greg moved slowly, cautiously. Then again, he'd stroked her cheek to wake her this morning. She'd been ordered not to leave her apartment until he returned from his errand, even to go downstairs to her workroom or the gallery. And so, she paced. Did the man not understand how much work she had to do for tonight's event?

Glancing out the window, she spied the car of the off-duty friend Greg had mentioned. The officer was standing guard while Greg was gone.

A knock on her door made her jump. Greg had her key, so who was knocking? Tentatively, she moved to the door and looked through the peephole. The face of her handsome, sexy detective was outlined there. She hurried to open the door and had to restrain herself from jumping on him like an eager puppy.

"Did you forget your key?" she asked.

"*Your* key, and I didn't want to assume I should use it again. Besides, I figured you'd be awake by the time I got back and might be dressing or something." A slight flush reddened his cheeks. "Any contact from the killer?"

Instinctively, her hand went to her pocket, where her phone was silent. "No. If he had, I would have contacted you right away, as per your instructions."

"I appreciate you following the safety protocol, both on that and on staying here while I was gone."

"Better safe than sorry, but now that you're back, I have a show to put on." She was about to push past him and head down the stairs to the gallery when he took her hand.

"Relax. Alyssa just arrived and I've got reinforcements coming."

"Reinforcements?"

"Vanessa—"

She planted her hands on her hips. "Tell me you did *not* bother a woman who's expected to give birth at any moment and is supposed to be taking it easy." The thought of her partner toddling down here to set up dozens of pieces of art—many of them heavy or awkward to lift—horrified her. "Vanessa needs to rest."

"She has her doctor's permission to be here as long as she sits on a stool and doesn't move."

Fiona rolled her eyes. "Like that's going to happen."

"Noah will be here to keep her in her seat. He's expecting to do the grunt work while she puts her feet up and tosses out orders. If she fails to comply, she's not allowed to attend tonight's event."

"That might work. But I'm right here. I can do the work."

"Not this morning. They'll get things started while we're gone. I'll explain on the way. Grab your jacket."

Fiona was torn between getting out of Dodge and staying to help Vanessa. She dug in her heels. "I'm not sure I should go anywhere."

"We have a meeting at SSAM."

"Why didn't you say so?" Some of the heaviness that weighed on her lifted. Maybe with SSAM's help, they'd lock away this killer before tonight's event and she could relax and enjoy herself. And nobody else would be murdered.

Fiona had been to SSAM's offices once or twice before in her two years in Chicago, accompanying Vanessa to see some of her friends there who had helped in the investigation in New York City that had helped take down a serial killer. That case had resolved the murder of Natalie Ortega. The ache of grief for the friend they'd lost was always part of Fiona's heart, as it was part of Vanessa's.

As the building was only a few blocks away, they opted to walk. Autumn's bite was even deeper than the day before, especially after last night's storm, but she'd worn her longer coat. Besides, the shock of cold was welcome. Within twenty-four hours, Fiona's perspective had changed entirely. Today, it was simply good to be alive to tip her face to the sunshine that pushed through gaps between the buildings.

Beside her, Greg's long strides ate up the sidewalk. He'd so readily become her shadow and shield, and she'd let him. Somehow, she'd let him in when she hadn't needed anyone since she was six years old and got lost in the mall in Iowa City. Her mother had nearly left without her, berating her for wandering off when she'd simply lost sight of her mother, who'd *wandered off* into a restaurant to have a drink.

To this day, Fiona couldn't touch the hard stuff because the smell of alcohol reminded her of her parents. She could still feel the mall security guy's hand gripping her shoulder as her mother spat the accusation at her, telling her that leaving her at the mall alone for a few hours might teach her a lesson. When her mother had turned to leave without her, Fiona had howled with fear. That's when the mall security guard had pulled her gently to the side and asked if she'd wanted to go with her mother because there were other options if she was being neglected or abused. And hadn't *that* made her mother snarl. She'd lit into the man. In the end, the police had called Fiona's extended family to intervene. It had been Aunt Dee who'd taken her under her wing, given her a haven a few streets away to run to when things got bad.

Fiona shot Greg a sideways glance, but his gaze was on the strangers they passed on the sidewalk. He was as quiet as ever. How had he spent his hours away from her this morning? Last night, they'd studiously avoided discussing the murders further, and Fiona had appreciated the reprieve. She wasn't sure she'd have been able to sleep otherwise. But now, in the light of day, on the way to SSAM to profile a serial killer, she was ready to talk.

"Any news from your sources this morning?" she asked.

"Yes, but it can wait until we're in the meeting." He reached out and squeezed her hand, then surprised her by continuing to hold it.

Since they were close to their destination, she didn't pursue the topic, but she was worried he'd confirm her worst fears, that she'd been linked to the end of seven beautiful women's lives. Their lights had been extinguished, and some asshole wanted her to share in the credit. Two minutes later, the building was within sight. Instead of going in, however, Greg took her hand and led her across the street to a coffee shop nestled against the yoga studio where Fiona occasionally took classes with Vanessa and some of the SSAM crew.

Greg held the door open for her. "Thought I'd treat you to breakfast, since I crashed on your couch."

"I think that's my line." She stepped up to the counter and they placed their orders, but she insisted on paying. "Your White Knight fee." When he grimaced, she cocked her head at him. "You don't like that?"

"You're perfectly capable of saving yourself. I just want to help."

His faith in her abilities released a little burst of happiness in her chest. She resisted the urge to run a fingertip along the groove that had formed in his brow. He was only thirty-five, a few years older than her, and yet the knowledge shining in his eyes reflected lifetimes of hard-won experience.

When their coffees and breakfast selections were ready, they settled at a table in the corner with Greg's back against the wall so he could see everyone coming and going. The shop was bustling with its usual weekday morning crowd, and some patrons were even in Halloween costumes. Greg watched an older gentleman dress up his coffee with creamer and sweetener at the condiments counter, and then two young mothers settle near the window with their toddlers in tow, handing them juice boxes before clasping their own mugs like lifelines.

Apparently satisfied their fellow patrons weren't threats, he turned back and caught her studying him. "What?"

"Just wondering what thoughts are going through your head." She shrugged. "I people-watch, too, but I consider it part of my job as an artist. I study life so I can capture it in my work."

"You watch for emotions, or to study personal details or flow of motion. I watch for the out-of-place." His grin was humorless.

"You expect danger everywhere you look."

It was his turn to shrug. "Too many times, my expectations are met. Besides, it's my job. I like to know what's going on around me so I can be prepared."

She picked at the muffin in front of her. "What made you that way, do you think?" She held her breath, willing him to answer and let her in.

He paused for a moment before looking again at the mothers with their toddlers. "The way I was raised. My dad was a cop, and he raised me to be vigilant." He paused, but looked like he would say more. Fiona could see the moment he decided to share whatever was haunting his expression. His eyes cleared and he met her gaze directly. "My mother was in and out of institutions. Depression and anxiety could cripple her, which crippled the whole family. My dad and I never knew what might set off an episode, what might make her feel unstable enough to want to leave for long periods of time."

"I'm so sorry. That must have been difficult on all three of you."

He nodded. "It was. We managed. She eventually found a medication that helped—when she takes it. But yeah, there was a lot of upheaval when I was younger. And I love her, so...." He shrugged.

"So, you gravitated toward a career in a field that literally thrives on order. You needed predictability." An idea struck her with the force of an electrical jolt. "That's why you don't want to date me, isn't it?"

His eyes narrowed. "What do you mean?"

"I can come across as a little scattered at times." She grinned. "Come on, you can admit it."

His mouth curved. "Maybe, but I kind of like it. And I thought I could handle it, handle dating you and keeping my life compartmentalized. But then there was the kiss." His gaze lifted to meet hers and her breath caught.

*The kiss.* Her body tingled at the memory. "I was taken aback, too. Again, it was unpredictable. I take risks, whereas you have enough danger in your life. I make you shudder."

He sipped his plain black coffee. "I'm not sure *shudder* is the word I would use."

"But it's probably difficult, for someone like you who tries to keep things orderly, to be with someone like me, who occasionally craves a bit of chaos. What if I told you I find your quiet confidence, and your desire for order, incredibly sexy?"

"Funny." But it was heat, not humor, that leapt to his eyes.

"I mean it. You have a way of making me feel calm and steady. Every force in the universe needs balance, and maybe you're mine. And maybe I'm yours."

He held her gaze for a long moment. "I'd say we have a dilemma."

"Right. Because you'd be the one taking the greater risk, getting involved with me. My motto is frivolous fun and yours is…not." She leaned forward and tried on her sexiest smile. "But you can't resist me."

A grin tugged at his lips. "True."

"Ah-ha! A confession!" She leaned back and gave him some space, but she wouldn't let him totally off the hook now that she had him here. There was something in him that called to her, something that made her want to help him see the world differently, to enjoy the world he worked so hard to protect.

And him protecting her? She'd be stupid not to make the most of that opportunity.

He was a man who needed a mission, someone to save. Unfortunately, she wasn't the type of woman who wanted a protector. But she was becoming more and more interested in bridging the gap between their philosophies. He was a man who needed some fun, especially after what he'd shared about his upbringing. And, if she had to admit a flaw, she could use a little more structure in her life.

They could learn a lot from each other, if he'd open himself to the possibilities.

.  .  .

GREG LOOKED AT HIS PHONE ON THE TABLE AS HE HEARD THE CHIME of an incoming text. He scanned the information and his stomach twisted.

"What is it?" Fiona asked. The teasing from a moment before was gone as fear flashed across her face.

"Luke, the detective investigating Amber Lockett's murder, identified the other victim this morning, and he just sent information about her."

"The victim in the picture that was hanging from Orlando's tree?"

"Yes."

"Is that why you had to leave the apartment for a couple hours? Do you have to be at work, investigating or something? If so, I can take care of myself."

"No doubt, you can. But I'm here, and I've made arrangements, so we're good." He'd taken personal time off to help her. And if he was being honest, he liked being with her.

"Arrangements?"

Reluctantly, he told her the truth. "I took a few days off from work." She gaped.

He stood and gathered his half-full coffee cup, intending to toss it in the trash. While he needed the caffeine after a restless night on Fiona's couch, the bitter taste had turned to ash on his tongue after the information he'd just received.

She came up behind him to throw her trash away. "I'm not comfortable with you taking personal time off for me."

He turned to her suddenly and cupped her face. "Nobody makes me do anything I don't want to do. Besides, Chief's been after me to use some of the personal time I've got saved up, so you're helping me, actually. Let me do this, please. I need to."

Her hands came up to grip his wrists. "Okay, okay. I'll help you by letting you help me." Her lips curved in the soft smile he loved. He nearly kissed her then. Everything in him wanted to taste her lips again. Instead, he drew on his inner strength to let her go, sifting his fingers through her hair before totally releasing her. Touching her settled the angsty need that normally resided within him. Perhaps she was right. Perhaps they made a good team, two opposing forces complementing each other.

"I'll tell you more at SSAM," he said. "Holt promised he'd have a preliminary profile drawn up."

Outside, they crossed the street, entered the lobby of the SSAM building, and caught an elevator ride to the fifth floor. Greg leaned against the wall next to her as they ascended. Damn, she smelled good, like sunshine, the autumn wind, and coffee. Thankfully, she was too preoccupied to notice how he studied her.

He didn't regret sharing what he had with her. In fact, it had felt like a burden had been lifted. His mother's depressive episodes had shaped much of the first half of his life, but they'd also made him who he was today. He was stronger for what he'd gone through, as were his parents, once his mother had found a good therapist. He suspected Fiona's own struggles had made her stronger, too.

The elevator doors opened and they faced glass doors that led to the SSAM waiting area and a counter, behind which a beautiful blonde smiled in greeting.

"Hi, Catherine," Fiona said to the receptionist.

"Good to see you." Catherine's smile faded and concern knit her brow. "Although, I guess it would be better if you didn't have a formal reason to come here. How are you holding up?"

"As well as can be expected. As you can see, I have my own personal bodyguard, so nothing to worry about." Fiona patted Greg's biceps and his muscles twitched in response.

Catherine grinned and offered them coffee, which they declined, and then walked to a door where she pressed her palm to a security pad. It unlocked with a click and they followed her into a hallway that branched off into several offices. She stopped at the third one on the right and waved them ahead of her.

Dr. Holt Patterson rose from behind his desk and extended his hand in greeting. Fiona and Greg took turns shaking it. His office was full of books, his laptop was open on his desk, and a photo was perched on top of a haphazard pile of folders. Within the frame was the portrait of a happy family. Holt's arm was around a pretty blonde who held a newborn baby boy. In front of the couple, a boy who had the gangly limbs of a pre-teen mugged for the camera.

"Thank you for making this a priority," Greg said. "I know you're busy."

"Please, take a seat," Holt told them, and they sat in the two chairs facing his desk. Greg wondered how many grieving or worried families Holt or Damian or any of the others had offered advice, hope, and solace to over the years. As a detective, Greg had been in a similar position many times. But the kind of monsters SSAM dealt with made the experience ten times worse.

"Anytime we can stop a killer," Holt continued, "especially one who's taken so many innocent victims, I want to make it a priority. And since it's a friend of a friend who's at risk, it moves right to the top of the caseload." He smiled softly at Fiona. "I know we haven't formally met, but Sara says she hopes to see you at yoga again soon."

"I look forward to it," Fiona said. "And congratulations on the new baby."

Holt's gaze moved to the family picture and he smiled. "Thank you. They remind me regularly that, while there's evil in the world, there's plenty of good. So let's get your situation sorted out and put a killer behind bars so you can get on with your lives too. Anything new to report?"

"CPD identified the second victim this morning," Greg said. Beside him, Fiona leaned forward, listening intently. "The woman's boyfriend came by when she hadn't responded to his texts. He found her in her bed. Similar scenario with the red scarf and claw marks across the chest. Signs of blunt force trauma to the back of her head."

"Who was she?" Fiona asked. Worry clouded her expression.

"Marlene Marlowe."

Her jaw dropped.

Greg stiffened. "You know her?"

"I know *of* her. She's an up-and-coming artist in the area. I didn't recognize her from the picture, but I would have known her work anywhere. She works in metals, like me. I was going to offer to feature her at the gallery in the coming year."

"I'm sorry." His words were useless, but there was nothing else to say to soothe the ache in her eyes.

Her expression hardened. "I want to nail this bastard to the wall."

Holt smiled grimly. "That's what we all want. I developed a partial profile based on what you'd already sent me, and I received the files on the five other murders, the ones that occurred over the past two years across the southeast, this morning. I'd like more time to look over each of those files more carefully before making an official report."

"But unofficially?" Greg pushed. Time was of the essence. That was one of the reasons he'd left Fiona alone that morning, to make sure Holt had all the information he needed.

"Unofficially, I'd say we're dealing with an organized killer who knows ahead of time how the act is going to go down, who the target is, what the escape route will be, and how to dispose of evidence. He also knows how to lure victims where he wants them."

"And we still don't know how," Greg said. "Somehow, the killer lured Amber to a deserted factory in the middle of the night. He also knew not to go near the security cameras."

"Exactly. He's smart and careful. Our subject likely has a career in, or at least a strong interest in, the arts. From what I've read of the cases in the south, most of the women were linked to the art community in some way. One was attending classes at a local university, one worked at an art store, one was an art teacher at a school in a large city."

"So, we need to find what the five women had in common and we'll find the killer," Greg said.

But Holt's head shake squashed his hope. "The FBI tried. But that doesn't mean we can't take a fresh look at it. In the meantime, I'll add that we're looking for a tightly-controlled type of person who has stuffed feelings down deep for a long time. Most likely, the killer is from Georgia, where the killings seem to have begun. There would be few outlets for his aggression, and something triggered the murders, maybe failure in his artistic endeavors."

"Or in his sexual conquests?" Fiona asked.

Holt shook his head. "I don't believe so. The scenes don't indicate this is sexual in nature. The women weren't abused or used sexually. I'd say, in this case, murder is a release valve, an expression of power." Holt's gaze went to Fiona. "You've apparently given this person the self-worth to turn the valve. The slashing would indicate a need to mark his prey and dominate. He's probably proud he's releasing the beast inside of him, especially since he seems to need your approval. The text and note about you inspiring him are indications of that as well."

"I most definitely do not approve," Fiona muttered.

Holt nodded. "Of course not. But based on the fact this person is sending you pictures of his conquests, much like a cat would dump a dead bird at your doorstep, he's trying to please you. And that may be how we can catch him."

Fiona leaned forward. "How?"

"By showing you don't approve, we may draw him out."

Greg's insides went cold. "Or piss him off enough that he'll go after Fiona. Rejection by his idol? He won't take that well."

"There is that risk, but if you control the location and the narrative, you should have the upper hand."

Greg had worked hundreds of cases in his years as a detective. At age thirty-five, he had more than a few years of experience behind his badge. He liked to think he could remain professional, no matter what—or who—crossed his path. But this killer was after Fiona, and that made him want to set aside his badge and go after him with everything he had.

"You're talking about tonight's event, aren't you?" she asked.

Holt nodded. "I'm guessing the killer will be there, or at the very least, will be watching from somewhere nearby."

They looked up as Catherine knocked on the open door. "I've got someone here to see you. He said you were expecting him?" A dark-haired man in a hooded sweatshirt and jeans stood behind her, his hands in his front pockets and his expression carefully shadowed, as if he was used to hiding his innermost thoughts. But beneath the brim of his ball cap, his dark eyes caught everything.

Holt stood. "Come in, Nico. This is Fiona Elliot and Detective Greg Marsh."

Greg shook Nico's hand, but noticed Holt had left off the other man's last name in his introductions. On purpose? Everything about Nico indicated he didn't want to be known.

As if sensing Greg's questions, Holt explained. "When you said you had trouble tracking down the owner of Fiona's sculpture, I called for reinforcements. Nico knows how to find anyone or anything without drawing attention to himself."

Greg would guess Nico's pedigree included special forces or government experience—maybe both. "Did you find the man who bought *Fierce*?"

Nico frowned. "The guy migrates to Florida during the fall and winter. I checked, and he's been there for the past month." Greg's mounting disappointment was wiped away by Nico's next statement. "But I found the piece itself." He pulled a phone from his pocket and handed it to Fiona. "Is that your work?"

Her eyes widened and she nodded. "That's *Fierce*. Is that someone's living room?"

"A den, actually."

"How did you get this?" Greg asked, his impression of the man improving by the second.

There was a bit of humor in the twist of Nico's lips. "Since you're a member of our esteemed law enforcement, I don't think either of us wants me to answer that. Let's just say the owner's summer lake house is about an hour north of here. That's where he keeps this piece. Interesting work, by the way," he said to Fiona. "Appropriate name. There are more pictures there. Holt said you wanted to see the claws and teeth, in particular."

She examined several more photos before looking up, happiness sparkling in her eyes. "Nothing's missing. It wasn't my work that harmed those women." Her brief moment of hope dissipated, and she sagged. "That doesn't make them any more alive, though."

"While I'm glad you're feeling less guilty about something you shouldn't feel guilty about," Holt said, "*Fierce* obviously spoke to the killer. We have to figure out why. Where else was this piece featured?"

Fiona thought a moment. "Only at the event and in an article about the auction. And some online promotion and blogs, I guess. There was a picture of *Fierce*, along with the other pieces."

Holt jotted down a note as she rattled off the name of the magazine. "Anything else?"

"They included brief interviews with each of the artists about their pieces. I shared a little bit about my journey as an artist, and the struggles I've overcome, with family, loss, and self-doubt, and how my sculpture reflected those battles. God, is that what inspired this person? Is that why they're obsessed with *Fierce*? So, I *am* responsible."

Greg shook his head. "Not in the least." She avoided his gaze and he waited until she looked at him. "A gunsmith or knife-sharpener doesn't deal a final blow, and creating that work of art doesn't mean you took those lives. He would have gone on quietly repressing his anger until he burst at some point, in some way—likely, the end result would still have been homicide. You have no reason to feel guilty. In fact, at the moment, you might be the only hope we have of catching him before he kills again."

Holt nodded. "Your piece might have given him a motivation,

but without it, the killer would have found something else to inspire or mutilate. The goal was release of inner emotions, and that led to murder."

Nico added his agreement. "Murder, dominance…they become compulsions for some people, evil people, and those desires find a way to express themselves." There was a wealth of experience in his eyes, before his expression became shuttered again.

A few minutes later, after thanking Holt and Nico for their help, Fiona and Greg started back to the gallery. The walk was quiet as they each digested information discussed at the meeting. While part of Greg's brain reviewed the psychology of the murders, the rest of him was braced for danger. He scanned the face and body language of every person they passed on the street, searching for any threats.

Fiona broke the silence. "From what Holt said, the killer's going to make contact with me at some point, possibly tonight."

"I won't let him hurt you." Greg vowed it with a ferocity he felt all the way to his soul.

She huffed and shot him a sideways glance. "I'm not sure you could stop him. He seems pretty determined, not to mention successful."

"We'll make a plan."

"Does it involve you, me, and a killer?" She was trying for humor, but he didn't smile. "I mean, this guy already feels he has a special bond with me. Why not make it a ménage a trois?"

He jerked to a stop. "Stop that."

She stopped and turned back to him. "What?"

"Making jokes. Your safety isn't a joke to me." Just the thought that someone had forced such a bond on Fiona had him thinking murderous thoughts of his own. She was a bright light in this dark world. Too many lights were being snuffed out by evil every day, too much darkness swallowing up people like his mom. It was up to people like him to keep the lights burning bright. "And I don't think that we should use you to catch a killer. We'll find some other way."

"The killer's already using *me*. It's not as if he's simply going to back away."

He resisted the urge to fold her into his arms and keep her safe there forever. "You're actually considering getting involved in this?"

"I already am involved."

"I don't like the thought of you antagonizing this person and putting yourself in more danger."

"Aw, you care." Her eyes softened.

"I do." Goddamn it, he shouldn't be admitting this. He looked away, suddenly feeling uncomfortable. "You would really risk your life?"

"To save another woman, or two, or five, or a dozen from a fate like those others? Hell, yes." No hesitation. This was the reckless-ness he'd sensed within her on their date, the sense that he could easily lose himself in her vitality, in her utter strength and confi-dence that she knew her purpose. He'd never known another woman like her.

"If he does feel some kind of bond, he'll see your cooperation as a betrayal."

"That's the whole idea, right? That'll draw him out."

Greg couldn't stop the growl that rose up in his throat. "Because you'll become the target."

"Not sure sitting back and letting him do what he wants—in my name—is any safer." This was personal for her whichever way he sliced it. All he could do was protect her.

He sighed. "So, we set a trap."

"Tonight. I'll post something on social media. Something provocative." She nodded, decision made, and turned to resume walking.

"And I'll make sure to have backup in place."

She looked over at him as they crossed at the next light. The art gallery was finally in view. "You do know this guy's not actually an animal, right?"

He shook his head. "He *is* an animal. He's worse, because he has free will and yet he's *choosing* to kill. He knows the difference between right and wrong, but chooses wrong anyway. And it's my job to stop him."

Instead of entering through the front of the gallery, they headed for the back alley and the rear entrance that led to the warehouse portion. He took her elbow to slow her so he could examine the alley before they entered. All was clear. Using the new key, she let them through the back door. Greg turned back to lock it, and then engaged the brand-new deadbolt he'd had the lock-smith install. Unfortunately, the camera repairman hadn't had time to fix their other security problem yet, but that gave Greg a reason to continue to stick close to Fiona. When he turned, she had stopped in the hallway and was watching him.

"So, I post a message and then what?" The uncertainty in her eyes was so unlike her that it tore at him.

"We get ready for the *Wicked Night* party." Where he would keep a close watch. At least this way, she'd be in one place, with fewer unknowns. "And I become your shadow."

"He might not even show his hand tonight."

"Then we'll wait him out. Eventually, his compulsion will push him to act. And I'll be there when he does." As she opened her mouth to object, he hurried on. "Let me be there for you. I wasn't before, and that was a mistake. I want to be with you now."

She cocked her head at him. "What kind of time commitment are we talking here, Detective? Endless nights on my couch?" Or in her bed.

"Whatever it takes."

# CHAPTER 7

*WHATEVER IT TAKES.*

Greg meant what he said, and apparently Fiona realized it. Her gaze turned molten and her lips parted as if she were going to respond. Instead, a split-second later, they'd each taken a step forward and she was suddenly in his arms.

His hands fisted in her luxurious red hair as her scent surrounded him. Her taste tickled his tongue like the most tempting of sweets. Awareness of the soft woman in his arms, pressing close to his body as if she wanted him to absorb her—and he would have if it was in any way possible—shot through him like a double espresso. His nerve endings sizzled as the heat between them soared.

She moaned and his arms squeezed her tighter to him. She came up on her tiptoes, her breasts sliding across his chest. Even through their clothes and jackets, he felt the friction and groaned deep in his throat.

He waited for the usual internal objections to rise up. The connection between them, deeper than anything he'd ever felt, had stopped him from pursuing her weeks ago. How could he know after one date that he wanted this woman in his life forever? Somehow, he had, and it had scared the bejesus out of him. Now, desire had flooded out the fear. All that was left was a deep need for the woman in his arms. Unfortunately, there was still a tingle of apprehension in the far corners of his mind. How could he make sure he didn't lose her when he had to focus on his career? And how did an introvert like him live up to Fiona's standards of living life to the fullest when he craved control and order?

Fiona pulled away just enough to search his face. "Hey, where'd you go? I felt you mentally pull away just now."

"Habit." She'd read him so easily, demolishing his defenses. "I'm no match for you, Fiona Elliot."

The corners of her mouth kicked upwards. "Stick with me. I'll teach you how to let go, relax, and have fun." She slid her fingers into his hair and pulled his mouth down to hers again.

The passion between them threatened to combust. He tipped his head to better capture her mouth. His hands slid down to grip her hips, skimming her long, lean frame along the way. His fingers itched to touch bare skin.

Perhaps being defenseless wasn't so bad. Something about the spark of life in her spoke to the calm within him. She was feisty strength, a backbone of steel much like the metals she worked with.

"Fiona?"

At the sound of the door between the hall and the gallery opening and a woman's voice calling Fiona's name, Greg released the woman in his arms and stepped back, gasping for breath. Damn. He'd let himself get caught up in the passion again, forgetting to be cautious. His hand slid beneath his open jacket to touch the gun strapped to his shoulder.

Fiona stopped him with a hand on his chest. "It's Alyssa."

Greg dropped his hand back to his side. "She must have gotten an alert when the back door opened." At Fiona's questioning gaze, he explained, "The security guy couldn't fix the camera yet, but I talked to Noah and he was going to install a low-tech alarm this morning. It'll alert whoever's in the front area with a soft chime when someone opens this door. He or Vanessa must have told Alyssa about it."

As the assistant saleswoman approached, Greg put more distance between him and Fiona. "I know you have work to do. I'm going to do a security sweep of the building, but I'll be nearby. And Noah and Vanessa, too, of course."

"Actually, you just missed them," Alyssa said. "Vanessa said she was starving so they left through the front. Early lunch break. They said there was a cop sitting in a car out front, for security."

"So, there's nobody else here?" Greg asked.

"Well, that's why I came looking for—" Alyssa was interrupted when Orlando burst in, coming from the direction of the gallery.

"There you are." Orlando's tone was accusing as his gaze landed on Fiona. Had he thought she'd been hiding from him?

Greg started to step between them, but Orlando was too quick. He gripped Fiona's shoulders, his eyes wide as he took in her appearance. His medium build was accented by another black suit. This time, the shirt beneath was blood red—about the same color as the silk scarves the killer's victims had been wearing.

"You didn't have to come this early," Fiona said.

"I was worried." Orlando's mood flipped on a dime.

"I'm fine, Orlando. What's wrong?"

"I slept in so that I'd be refreshed for tonight." Based on the reports he'd read of the man, it was more likely he'd been out all night partying and had overslept, but Greg bit his tongue and kept his thoughts to himself. "When I woke, I found a note from Charlotte. She said she had to help at the gallery, that there was a problem and you needed her."

"I haven't spoken to Charlotte, and I don't think she showed up here." Fiona and Greg both looked to Alyssa.

Alyssa shook her head. "I haven't seen her. We locked the doors to the usual customer traffic so we could set up for tonight, but I'm sure she would have knocked, or called."

"And there's no problem?" Fiona asked.

"No."

"Did you try calling her, ask for an explanation or location?" Greg asked Orlando. Maybe the poor, overworked assistant simply needed an excuse for a break.

"Of course. She isn't answering." Orlando's gaze swept over Fiona. "Are you sure you're okay, sweetie? You seem a little flushed. You must be going as crazy as I am with the police not finding anything helpful in this investigation."

Greg gritted his teeth at the not-so-veiled insult and fought the urge to remove the man's hands from Fiona's shoulders. Orlando was way too close to her. And he'd definitely be sending someone to look for the missing Charlotte. She was involved in the art world, and fit many of the characteristics of the killer's other victims.

"Everything's under control," Fiona assured Orlando. "You can go do whatever you need to do, but make sure you're back here by eight tonight. As for Charlotte, I'm sure it was a miscommunication. She's probably running some last-minute errands and will show up eventually. Really, you don't have to worry. We've got this."

She reached for Greg's hand and brushed her thumb over his wrist. It was meant to be soothing. Instead, her touch set his pulse racing as he thought about her lips there—and then touching other parts of his body.

Orlando dropped his grip on Fiona's shoulders and glared at her hand on Greg's. "Okay, then. If you're okay, where do we stand on *Wicked Night?*"

"I was about to check on everything," Fiona said. "Vanessa's been here, overseeing things." She looked to Alyssa for confirmation.

The young woman took the hint and nodded enthusiastically. "Everything's almost ready."

Orlando kept his gaze on Fiona. "I thought you were handling everything."

"I am." Fiona dropped Greg's hand, defensiveness straightening her spine as she pasted on a gracious smile. "Guests will start arriving at eight tonight. The catering company has confirmed, as well as the valet service we hired for the evening. As you intended, Vanessa and I want this to be more than a viewing. We want it to be an *experience*. Something everyone in Chicago—hell, in the entire art world—will be talking about."

"Yes, I saw Vanessa in the gallery before they left. She had some man hanging my paintings, but he seems inexperienced."

*Poor Noah.* Greg nearly grinned. Orlando's appearance on the scene must have been what prompted Noah and Vanessa to escape for a lunch break.

"He was just helping out until I could take over," Fiona said.

"Well, you're here now." Orlando looped an arm over her shoulder and pulled her away from Greg, toward the gallery. "Shall we get to it, then? I have specific ways the audience is to experience my collection."

"Through all five senses. I have your notes."

"Exactly. But I have a few changes."


A MAN'S PRESENCE SHOULDN'T BOTH CALM AND EXCITE HER, BUT Fiona found that Greg held that amazing power. Though he stuck mostly to the sidelines throughout the day, she felt his eyes on her while she worked to rearrange things according to Orlando's directions and set up the gallery. It was comforting. And intoxicating. She'd spent a lot of her mental energy wondering if he'd kiss her again—or if he'd do more than that next time.

In the early afternoon, after Orlando had given his directions and left, Fiona took a deep breath to steady her nerves. There would be no undoing what she was about to do. She had a fifteen-minute break and Greg was on the phone. It was the perfect time to sit down at the computer. There, she crafted a message to the killer. If it took announcing her displeasure with the killer's actions to lure him out into the open, then she'd do it.

She selected a photo of a red silk scarf that looked as if it were dancing in the wind. She shared it on all of her social media platforms with a single message that she thought might provoke a reaction from her so-called admirer.

*Looking for inspiration in a world that wants to use my fierceness for its own evil purposes. I will never let evil win.*

She messaged Neil to ask that he boost her efforts by sharing her message on his social media accounts. Hopefully, her words would have a butterfly effect and they could lure the killer and stop him before he killed again. She went back to preparing the gallery, using the activity to avoid thinking about whether a killer was reading her message.

By five that afternoon, Fiona sent Alyssa home for a break and then sat down next to Vanessa on a stool at the customer service counter. She sighed with relief. Vanessa passed her the plate of cheese and crackers she'd been nibbling on. Noah and Greg had adjourned to the conference room to discuss something, but they still watched through the windows. All day, whenever Vanessa so much as shifted on her stool, Noah's eyes would narrow on her as a reminder not to move.

"Thank God we're on schedule," Vanessa said, stroking a hand over her burgeoning belly.

"Considering how the past couple days have gone, it's a damn miracle," Fiona said.

Vanessa sent a wave toward the conference room window. "He watches you like a hawk."

She followed her friend's gaze and smiled, seeing how even as Noah and Greg bent their heads together in discussion, their eyes were on Fiona and Vanessa. "I could say the same about your husband."

Vanessa chuckled. "He thinks I'm going to pop at any moment."

"You are." She wrapped her arm around her friend's shoulders and squeezed. "Thanks for being here today. I know it's exhausting."

"Don't think you'll talk me out of being here tonight. I'm not about to miss the fun stuff after working all day."

"You mean ordering people around."

"I'm so good at it." Vanessa laughed and plucked another cracker off the plate Fiona held. "You're saving my sanity by letting me be bossy. You didn't need me here today. You've done such a fabulous job all on your own."

Around them, the gallery had been transformed into Orlando's vision of a wicked night. Life-sized sculptures made from recycled plastics, fabrics, and other materials practically begged a person to touch them. Wall art that was a mixture of oil paint and recycled bits seemed to reach out to grab the viewer. No matter how creepy Orlando could be, he was an excellent artist.

Fiona observed her friend. "Go take a nap, though, okay? Rest for a while." They had locked up the gallery for the day in preparation for tonight's event. Now, they had a couple hours before the door opened to those art lovers who had bought tickets, looking forward to the devious delights that the *Wicked Night* exhibition would bring. Soon enough, there would be a couple hundred people walking through those doors.

And the killer could quite possibly be among them.

She felt Greg's eyes on her and looked his way. He was frowning. Crap. He'd seen her smile slip. In answer to his questioning gaze, she forced another smile to indicate she was fine. Unfortunately, he didn't take the hint and stood.

Vanessa pushed to her feet, too. "Looks like they're wrapping things up. I'll rest if you rest, okay?"

"Deal." Fiona planned to lock herself in her apartment, put up her throbbing feet for a while, and then shower and dress for the event. At the thought of two whole hours of relaxation, she nearly moaned with ecstasy.

"See you tonight," Vanessa said as Noah appeared at her side with her coat. "I know you're in good hands."

The pair exited through the front door of the gallery and Greg immediately locked it behind them. Fiona felt a ripple of awareness move through her belly. She and Greg would be alone until Alyssa showed up to let the caterers in at six-thirty. Fiona was dusty and achy from a full day of moving art around and angling the lights until everything was perfect, but at the thought of Greg in close quarters with her, alone, she suddenly felt a flood of warmth throughout her body that loosened her muscles and made her ache for an entirely different reason.

She gestured toward the stairs. "I have to get ready for tonight. I assume you're coming?"

Was it her imagination or had his eyes turned a darker shade of blue? Her body heated at the memory of their kiss. Screw trying to hide how she felt about this man. If he was going to be in her orbit indefinitely, he was going to damn well acknowledge these feelings they had for each other. Besides, the kisses they'd shared—both weeks ago and earlier that day—indicated he cared a whole hell of a lot. Maybe he'd finally admit it. Maybe he needed a little push.

She let her hips sashay as she climbed the stairs in front of him. And when he nudged her aside at the door to her apartment, she refused to move far. Her breasts just might have brushed his arm.

He cleared his throat. "Wait here a minute while I make sure it's safe." Yep, he was definitely as affected by her as she was by him. He returned within a few seconds. "It's safe."

*That's what you think.*

He watched as she locked the door and then he settled on her couch.

"Can I get you anything?" she asked. *Me?*

"No, thanks."

She went to the refrigerator and grabbed a couple of bottled waters, tossing one to him before downing her own. "Sweaty work, moving all those creations around. I feel dirty all over."

His gaze had locked on her throat when she drank, but it shot to her eyes and narrowed when she spoke. "What are you doing?" His deep voice sent shivers of anticipation straight to her core.

She shrugged innocently. "Just commenting on my day." She started stalking toward him, slow and predatory. Inside, she was twisting with need for this man, worried he might reject her yet again. But she'd come to believe that what they shared was worth the risk. "Since you're sharing my space, I thought it was only polite to make conversation."

His attention traveled over her, taking her in from head to toe.

"Unless you'd prefer something other than talking to occupy our time," she said.

When he didn't reply, didn't do anything but continue to devour her with his gaze, she continued forward, not stopping until she was standing in front of where he sat on the couch. She dropped to her knees and slid her palms up his thighs. He stiffened. The rapid thumping of his pulse in his neck gave her courage to continue.

"When you kissed me, you left me imagining all kinds of scenarios," she said. "In fact, the kiss from our blind date left me with *weeks* to imagine what I'd do if you were mine."

Her hands moved to his waistline, where the pouch that held his handcuffs was strapped to his belt. She removed his handcuffs. Her gaze shifted to his, but he didn't stop her. In fact, he seemed intrigued, and aroused. Definitely aroused, judging by the hard ridge in his pants.

Fiona weighed the handcuffs in her palms. Now this was some metal she hadn't experimented with before. Her body pulsed with excitement.

"You want me to stop?" she asked when he continued to study her silently.

"God, no." He choked out the words.

She grinned. "As I was saying, I have some ideas. I think you'll like them." Or maybe he was a vanilla guy. But he didn't strike her as such. Not that she was flavorful in a crazy way, but she could be butter pecan or mint chocolate chip on occasion. A little variety was good for the artist's soul.

Something in his expression changed and the heat in his eyes flared to a flame. "I do enjoy creativity on occasion."

She delighted in the sudden light feeling that pervaded her, like bubbles effervescing beneath her skin and lifting her up. God, she needed this, needed to feel free of the weight of recent events. She was in the mood to test someone else's limits for once, to be in control. Or to surrender and let him take complete control, if she could convince him to give in to the passion she sensed broiling beneath the surface.

"But not those," he said, indicating the handcuffs. "Not this time, anyway. I want to touch you, and I want you to touch me."

A shiver of anticipation moved through her, followed by a thrill of triumph as she realized what he'd said. She set the handcuffs on the table behind her and pressed her palm over his heart, feeling the cotton of his shirt, the light imprint of his buttons, and more. A pounding pulse. Heat. The guy was like a radiator, and she was a cat who wanted to curl up on him.

She slid her fingers up over his pecs and to the side of his neck, her body extending along his. With a light pressure, she drew him closer, his head bending down until his mouth met hers. During it all, his eyes never left hers. Only when she licked his lips did he let his eyelids slide closed.

He groaned his surrender and his body came alive. His hands went to her hips and he tugged her closer until she was in his lap, straddling him. Unfortunately, she'd worn jeans today, knowing she was going to get dirty. It was too thick a barrier, and she wanted all of their clothing gone, now. Still, she pressed against his pelvis and could feel the full, hard length of his arousal beneath her. This was what she'd wanted from him since the day he'd walked into her life. This man who was quiet and strong on the outside, but thoughtful and protective on the inside. He was everything she wanted, everything she needed.

She held him to her like a lifeline, encircling his shoulders with her arms and then sifting her fingers through his hair. He groaned as her nails gently scraped his scalp. He rocked against her and she needed him inside of her, wanted him to soothe the relentless throbbing there. His hands gripped her waist but she wanted them on her ass, on her breasts. Hell, she wanted them everywhere. Now.

As if reading her thoughts, his palms moved and she nearly whimpered, but they didn't travel where she wanted them. Instead, they slid up her back and into her hair and fisted gently. With a groan, he pulled his lips from hers to look into her eyes. He held her by his grip in her hair, firm, but not painful. Another thrill ran through her.

"Tell me what you want," he demanded. His words tickled her moist, sensitive lips. "I'm not the type of man for one-night stands with someone I'm supposed to be protecting. So, you make the choice now. What do you want?" Guilt and honor danced in his eyes.

She wanted this man to lose control with her. "I want you. I want more than one night. And I definitely want more from you than protection. I've wanted you since the night you laughed and drank and shared with me. But only if you want that, too."

"I want that. I want you. Always you." With a growl, he pulled her mouth back to his and, not breaking their frenzied kiss, twisted sideways to lay her back on the couch.

He began peeling away her clothing, kissing his way along her skin as he bared it. She gasped and arched into him when his mouth found one aching nipple and suckled. His hand found the other and together, they brought her to the edge of paradise. She was nearly panting as she pulled his head away from her aching breasts so that she could help him remove his clothing. As he shed his pants, he produced a condom from one of the pockets and she nearly shouted with relief. He was always protecting her.

He sheathed himself and knelt between her parted legs. He cupped her cheek before bending to kiss her gently. But she didn't want gentle. She wanted his full weight on her, him inside of her with an urgency she'd never felt before.

"Don't you dare stop," she said.

He exhaled a rough laugh and bent his forehead to touch hers. "I don't want to stop."

"Good. Don't."

He leaned up to smile down at her. "You're bossy."

She reared up to nip at his lips. "Just wait until we try the handcuffs."

He arched a brow. "I don't think we need them. I've got you right where I want you." And then he entered her with deliberate slowness.

She moaned. "Who said I'd be the one wearing them?" The wicked man. He thought he had all the control. Well, two could play at that game.

She gripped his hips and arched into him, taking him into her until he stretched her and filled her completely. He hissed out a breath. One hand came up to tease her rigid nipple. A moment later, he replaced his hand with his mouth. Her breath caught as his fingers found the bundle of nerves between her legs. With him filling her and his fingers working their magic, he had her shouting his name within seconds. The shockwaves reverberated through her as he started pumping into her. She clenched around him and sent him over the edge. He shouted her name and her lips curved as he collapsed against her.

# CHAPTER 8

A<small>N HOUR LATER,</small> F<small>IONA AWOKE SUDDENLY.</small> H<small>ER EYES SHOT OPEN AND</small> she lay still as she tried to sort out where she was and why she seemed to be pinned down. Her smile bloomed as awareness returned.

Her couch.

Greg.

And the hottest sex of her life.

*It wasn't just sex.* The whisper moved through her brain and she froze. How had she let him back in so easily? When he resolved this case and locked away the killer, would he come back for her or walk away like he'd done before? Old self-doubts, the ones that had been instilled long ago, when she hadn't even been good enough for her parents to love, reared their ugly head.

His head lay at her heart, his soft puffs of air teasing her bare nipple. She lifted her head and spied their clothing strewn about the floor. The clock on the wall said she only had a half hour before she was supposed to be downstairs to make sure everything was going smoothly with the caterers. Not long after that, guests would start arriving.

"Please tell me the event is cancelled." Greg's voice was relaxed and raspy with sleep, but there was an underlying tension that she was coming to know well. They were both aware of what dangers the night might bring. He pushed himself up to his elbows to look down into her face.

Her gaze drifted over his strong jaw, his wide, sculpted shoulders. An artist's dream. Her dream. Every instinct within her urged her to hole up in the apartment and spend the night enjoying his hard body.

She sighed. "Not cancelled."

"Pretty please?" He leaned down and kissed her neck.

She swallowed a moan. "Maybe after? I'd be up for more fun, if you are." She wanted to keep the tone of their conversation light, nonthreatening. She didn't want him to run again. Instead, he was frowning as he rolled to a sitting position.

"Yeah, fun." He shook his head as if he couldn't believe her words. Or maybe he couldn't believe he'd allowed himself to have fun.

She rose and started gathering clothing. "I thought you didn't want anything more."

He ran a hand over his head. "I didn't. Or I didn't think I could."

"But now?"

He scraped a hand across his jaw. "I think I might be willing to try."

She froze. "What about why you backed away from me in the first place? Those problems don't suddenly go away."

"No, they don't. I didn't see how I could balance my job with a relationship, especially not after seeing how my dad tried to juggle caring for my mom, a son, and his career."

"I'm plenty busy with my own career. I don't need a man beside me twenty-four hours a day." Not after the killer was caught, anyway.

He gave a soft smile. "I'm realizing that. And I think if anyone can ride out the ups and downs of being involved with a cop, you can. You're fearless. But you're the one with the *frivolous fun* attitude. Are *you* ready for a relationship?"

She glanced at the microwave clock and grimaced. "Not at this very moment. I have to move my ass if I'm going to make it to my own event on time."

She grabbed the last of her clothing, tossed it into her dirty clothes hamper and grabbed her dress from the wardrobe cabinet before disappearing into her bathroom to take the quickest shower ever.

Greg's words followed her. Had she closed herself off to the possibility of a real relationship, hiding behind an attitude of frivolous fun? Damn her parents for making her feel less than worthy of a happily-ever-after. She conjured Aunt Dee and focused on those memories instead. Aunt Dee had lost her husband before Fiona had even been born. Still, she'd had pictures of the man and their happy times together. Her aunt wouldn't have wanted her to shut herself off from any part of life. In fact, she'd been the one to tell Fiona to embrace every moment, every experience, as valuable. That was the artist's creed.

So why did opening herself fully to Greg feel like a risk?

Because losing him, losing their connection after it had filled up all of her hollow parts, would leave her wrung out and empty.

When she emerged from the bathroom fifteen minutes later, after showering, applying makeup, and slipping into her little black cocktail dress, she couldn't look at Greg. But she felt his eyes on her as she scurried about the room, donning black sapphire earrings and a matching necklace. While guests had been encouraged to come in costume if they so desired, she'd chosen to keep it simple. She wore a witch's hat and a wrist cuff created by a local artist friend. The cuff was made in the image of a spider's web that crawled halfway up her forearm. A black sapphire spider sparkled in the center.

"Are you going to talk to me?" Greg asked.

She looked his way and was momentarily stunned speechless

by the sight of him in a suit and tie. He must have had Noah bring him a bag earlier. "Probably."

He stepped closer and examined her face. "You wanted me to open up to you, but I guess I went too far."

And that wasn't fair of her. He had done what she'd asked of him. "I'm just processing a lot. You touched on a hot button I didn't know I had."

He gave her a half smile. "Ditto. But that's what makes us a great pairing. We balance each other. You're the one who told me that."

"We do." She gave him a quick kiss, hoping it would speak for her when she couldn't find the words to express the confusing emotions he'd unexpectedly stirred up. "I have to get downstairs, but we'll talk later. I promise."

Within an hour, the gallery was alive with conversation, music, food, and alcohol. Fiona felt Greg's eyes on her as she moved about the crowd that had gathered to celebrate and admire Orlando Reyes's *Wicked Night*. A DJ played dark, throbbing music that matched the art—all part of Orlando's five-senses artistic vision. The gallery was an adult-oriented haunted house of sorts, but with a splash of sex and sin thrown in. Tonight, sight, sound, touch, smell, and even taste permeated the human psyche.

Fiona maneuvered through the crowd, soaking it all in. Near the bar, she heard exclamations of pleasure from several people who'd just been served the signature blood-orange-inspired cocktail she'd had a mixologist develop for the event. Screams of delight echoed as one of the live actors she'd hired to wear some of Orlando's art startled the guests by moving. The cinnamon-candied apples hanging from the twisted metal tree tantalized the taste buds and had people picking their own—part of the touch and taste portions of the senses. Fog from the back room filtered through the door near a marble headstone, along with an earthy, musky scent Orlando had chosen to diffuse throughout the gallery and tickle the noses of the patrons.

As the mist grew higher, Greg stepped up behind her and spoke in her ear. "I don't like this. It's hard to keep a visual on you." His deep, rich timbre and warm breath tickled her neck. If she could escape, she'd pull him up to her apartment and bury herself in him again. Or vice versa.

"I'm afraid it's necessary," she said over her shoulder. "Besides, Noah's here, too."

"Noah's distracted keeping an eye on his wife."

"I saw Holt and that Nico guy by the door earlier."

"I asked them to be here as backup." Greg growled. "I had no idea the lights would be so dim. And what's with the strobe light?" In one corner of the gallery, flashing lights added to the eerie effect. One of the live actors, an acrobat contortionist dressed as a skeleton, was using the lighting to full effect, and judging by the crowd's reaction, he was a big hit.

She sighed. "I can't do anything about it now without ruining the whole party."

Before Greg could grumble any more, Orlando, wearing a black three-piece suit, neon green shirt open at the collar, approached. Greg faded into the background again, retreating to a position not far away, but far enough to give her room to mingle and work.

Orlando had added a handlebar mustache to his ensemble and resembled an old-time villain. Was he a villain who'd killed seven women in cold blood? He gripped her arms and leaned in to kiss her on each cheek. "We did it. Of course, my work is what drew them."

"Of course," Fiona readily agreed. His work, combined with her efforts, had made the night a big success. A tingle of awareness had her looking over his shoulder. She caught Greg's gaze, his head tipped in question. She gave a short jerk of her head to indicate she was fine.

"So, you're happy?" she asked Orlando.

"Almost." He ran a fingertip over his mustache.

*Almost?* What more could she do to please him?

His smile hardened. "If only my family back in Georgia could see me now. I'd love to rub their noses in this."

She froze for a second, and then forced herself to speak. "You're from Georgia? How did I not know this about you?"

"Dropped my accent years ago. I don't like to talk about it, though I did do a tour of cemeteries throughout the south a couple years back. Nothing like the above-ground cemeteries in New Orleans for inspiration."

*Inspiration.* There was that word again. Panic crept in and she looked around for Greg. Across the room, Neil was chatting with Vanessa, who was planted on a barstool alongside Alyssa. Greg and Noah were mingling with the crowd, but their gazes roved about the room. There was one person missing who should be enjoying the party.

"Where's Charlotte?" Fiona asked, pleased the music disguised the tremor in her voice. "I haven't seen her this evening."

Orlando scowled. "She's an ungrateful bitch. I got rid of her."

Greg had never felt so useless. He could only watch from a distance as Fiona worked the room, charmed potential patrons, and probably angered a killer. He wanted to give her space to work her magic. So when Orlando had approached her, Greg had gritted his teeth and backed away—and fought the urge to punch a wall when the asshole leaned down to kiss Fiona's cheeks.

As if she felt Greg's frustrated gaze, she looked up. He tipped his head in question, begging her to signal that she needed his rescue. Instead, she gave a subtle shake of her head. She had this. Orlando's come-ons were expected and she could deal.

Greg bit back disappointment.

"Someone kick your puppy?" Noah stopped at Greg's side with a knowing smirk on his face.

"No, but somebody kissed my woman."

Noah's brows shot up. "Your woman. That was fast."

Greg's gaze surveyed the room as he stood with Noah, both of them watching for threats. "Not so fast when you think about how our first date was months ago. I was just too stupid to act on it at the time."

"And now?" Noah asked.

"Now, I'm going to going to be smart." He'd always been the type to follow through once he'd made a decision. And he'd decided Fiona was good for him, and he would be good for her. He was no longer going to let his parents' relationship influence decisions about his own future.

"Looks like we both got lucky when it comes to women. Smart, strong, creative. In fact, I'm going to go kiss my wife now, and show her how appreciative I am." Noah slapped him on the shoulder and crossed the room to Vanessa.

Greg was well aware of how strong Fiona was, and that she didn't need his help. He was falling for a feisty redhead. He never had a chance.

A smile curving his lips, he looked back at her. The smile fell away as he noted her demeanor had changed. Her body was rigid, and concern knit her brow. In a flash, he was moving toward her.

"Everything okay here?" He inserted himself beside her, angling so that Orlando couldn't get his paws on her again so easily.

Orlando turned a grin on him that barely disguised his disdain. "We're simply celebrating my success."

"Maybe your assistant would like to celebrate with you," Fiona said. "Charlotte got all of the pieces here on time. Where *is* Charlotte?"

Greg understood her meaning immediately. "She's still MIA?" He'd had a uniform go by the hotel earlier looking for Charlotte, but she hadn't answered, and nobody there had seen her since that morning. With nothing to go on, he'd asked patrol units to keep their eyes open for someone matching her description and prayed the killer hadn't claimed another victim.

Orlando shrugged. "Doesn't matter anymore. She's gone."

Fiona sent Greg a worried look, but before they could question Orlando further, a trio of female fans dressed as French maids approached, surrounding him and gushing about the sensuality of his work. Orlando said something in French and signaled to a waiter to bring a tray of champagne flutes over. He proceeded to hand them out as if they were candy and the women were trick-or-treaters.

Greg bent to speak in Fiona's ear. "You think he killed Charlotte?"

She shook her head. "It's hard to believe, but...maybe? He said he's from Georgia, and toured the south a couple years ago. It was part of the inspiration for *Wicked Night*. He also said something about getting rid of the *ungrateful bitch*. He meant Charlotte."

Alyssa approached, wringing her hands and looking anxious. "Fi, can I speak to you a minute?"

Fiona frowned. "What is it?"

"There's a problem with the caterer."

While Fiona was engrossed in a party-related problem, Greg went to join Noah, Holt, and Nico, who were now congregating near the door. "I may need backup," Greg told Noah and Nico. He looked at Holt. "And I need your read on this guy."

Holt scanned the crowd. "Which guy?"

"Orlando Reyes. He's been saying some suspicious things to Fiona."

Noah's expression darkened. "What kind of things?"

"Apparently, he grew up in Georgia."

"Something he omitted from his online bio," Noah muttered.

Greg nodded. "And he said something about getting rid of his assistant. Nobody's seen Charlotte since this morning, when she left the hotel on foot."

"I'll head to the hotel," Nico said. "If there's any trace of her, I'll find it." He was gone in an instant, moving through the crowd like smoke.

"How can we help?" Noah asked.

Greg's gaze found Orlando. "We're going to have a chat with the guest of honor."

Fiona had just resolved the issue with the caterers when her phone buzzed. Dreading another issue, she reluctantly checked the screen and saw a text from Vanessa.

*It's time. I need your help.*

The stool where Vanessa had been sitting was empty. Fiona's gut clenched as her fingers flew across the screen in a hasty reply. *Time? The baby's coming?* In the time it took to receive a reply, she'd nibbled off her lipstick.

*Yes! Don't tell Noah. He'll only panic. I need you.*

*Where are you?* Again, an interminable wait.

*I snuck away to the restroom in the back. My water broke. I don't know what to do.*

They had a private, employees-only restroom in the warehouse portion of the building, at the back of the storage room. Fiona looked around for Noah and thought about grabbing him first. But Vanessa had worried about his panic, and had expressly ordered her not to tell him.

Still, she hesitated. She doubted the capable detective would panic. It was more likely he'd be overprotective, which was also probably not what Vanessa needed either.

Noah was also deep in conversation with Greg, Holt, and, apparently, Orlando, whom they'd pulled into the conference room. What was going on? Either way, it looked like the guys had Orlando well in hand. He wouldn't be able to follow her if he was tied up with them. She would be safe.

And Vanessa needed her. She could assess the situation and text Noah after she reached her friend.

During her internal debate, another text came through. *Hurry!*

Fiona's feet were moving before she could reconsider. She

dodged guests as she made her way to the back, her thoughts only on her best friend, the baby that was about to enter the world, and the risks they had already faced. Vanessa was like a sister, and she'd do anything for her.

She shoved open the door to the storage room and maneuvered around the remaining sculptures and paintings that would be rolled out in the coming weeks, as *Wicked Night* would still be on display. She made her way toward the bathroom at the rear of the room. Light came from beneath the closed door.

"Vanessa? Honey, are you okay?" She knocked lightly, and then tried the doorknob, but it was locked.

She heard a noise behind her. Before she could turn, something hit her head. Excruciating pain spiked into the side of her skull and radiated outward. Her legs gave out as if her brain no longer communicated with her muscles, and the floor rushed toward her face. More pain shot through her cheek as it connected with cold concrete.

And then everything went black.

# CHAPTER 9

"Wake up, beautiful Fiona," a soft voice called, followed by a throaty, feminine laugh.

"Charlotte?" Fiona stirred as something cold and scratchy slid across her neck and down her chest. Her eyes blinked open.

She struggled to focus on the face that hovered above her. There were two faces. No, three. And they were swimming. Her head throbbed like a son of a bitch. She reached for the spot that ached, but realized both hands moved in unison in front of her.

Her wrists were bound.

Her eyes opened fully as she remembered the pain, and then falling to the storage room floor. But she didn't remember being handcuffed.

And then her fingertips brushed against silk fabric at her neck. She looked down and saw the scarlet scarf. Fear turned her muscles to gelatin.

"Good, you're awake." Charlotte's three images finally coalesced into one solid being.

Fiona pulled herself into a sitting position, her gaze darting around. She winced when the movement made the throbbing intensify. "Where is he?"

"Who?"

"Orlando."

Another laugh, and suddenly Fiona's blood ran as cold as the cement floor she was planted on.

"He's not here," Charlotte said. "It's just you and me."

No Vanessa either, Fiona surmised as the truth hit her. "You stole Vanessa's phone to text me?"

Charlotte shrugged, and her dark eyes glittered. "I had to get you alone somehow. That detective was sticking to you like paint on a canvas."

Her stomach twisted as she remembered the empty stool where she'd last seen her friend. "How did you get Vanessa's phone? Did you hurt her?"

Charlotte's mouth tightened. "I wouldn't do that. She's pregnant." As if that logic made any sense when she'd killed seven women for no other reason than they were artists. Of course, there had to be some reason that made sense in Charlotte's warped mind.

"She's not having her baby?"

Charlotte shrugged and the dark *Scream*-style cloak she wore shifted like a specter. A mask was pushed up over her head. Such an outfit would have allowed her to move about the party without anyone knowing. "No idea. But she was fine last time I saw her. She was tired. I helped her upstairs to lie down in your apartment. And then I helped myself to her phone."

Fiona sagged with relief. At least her friend was okay. "My apartment. That's where you got the cuffs." She studied them and recognized them as Greg's. *Greg.* Where was he? He'd be so angry she'd left the main gallery. But he couldn't be angrier with her than she was with herself.

"That's what you get for playing sex games with the detective."

Charlotte's eyes darkened. "You shouldn't trust him. You can't trust any man. Or woman, for that matter. I thought I could trust you. And then you showed your true colors. You're just like all the rest."

Charlotte raised the short rod in her hands. Fiona had thought it was a hammer, but now she realized it was so much more. It was hammer-like in the handle, but it was what was at the end that had a scream crawling its way up her throat. The end had been fashioned into a metal paw with sharp claws, nearly identical to the ones Fiona had made for *Fierce*. Charlotte had modified the concept into a razor-sharp weapon. This was what Fiona had felt against her neck and chest when she'd awoken.

"You like it?" Charlotte held the club up so the metal caught the light as she turned it in her hand. "I made it myself. I modeled it after your sculpture."

A shudder ran through her. Shit, shit, shit. She was in trouble. She swallowed and tried to speak calmly. "I recognize it."

"I saw it in the magazine. *Fierce*. What you said about that piece, in that article, inspired me. That's why what you did is such a disappointment." Charlotte touched the claw to Fiona's cheek, light enough that it didn't draw blood—yet.

Greg wouldn't get here in time. He was focused on Orlando as the potential killer. Survival would be up to her. At one point, Charlotte had admired her, had been inspired by her. Fiona would use that.

Fiona turned her head, as if studying the claw. "It might have been modeled after my piece, but it's unique. And the welding work is excellent. You have the makings of a great artist."

"You think so?" Charlotte's anger morphed into surprise. Just as quickly, her delighted smile twisted into something ugly. "My mom said I'd never amount to anything. So did Orlando. But half the pieces out there are mine." She jerked her head toward the gallery.

"Orlando was stealing your work and taking credit?" No

wonder Charlotte was angry. "I can understand why you'd be upset with him, but why take it out on those women you killed?"

Her face contorted with rage. "They deserved it. Bunch of fakers and thieves. I couldn't kill Orlando without anyone suspecting me, but I could take care of the others."

"They did what Orlando did?"

She shrugged. "Sometimes worse."

Enough to justify their deaths? Fiona wanted to demand an explanation for Charlotte's heinous behavior but worried about pressing her too far. Fiona just needed to build trust, or maybe stall the young woman long enough for Greg to come after her.

"They made me so mad," Charlotte continued. "Made my inner fierce come out, you know? Like yours did. When I saw your sculpture, I knew you'd understand. Sometimes you can't keep the hurt in any longer."

"Those women hurt you?"

"Guys, I expect it from. Girls don't have an excuse for treating each other like they did. We're supposed to support each other. They mocked me. Or stole the show away from you or someone else I cared about." She was lost in memories for a moment before she suddenly locked eyes with Fiona. "The anger, the frustration... The only thing that made it better was this." She raised her weapon and Fiona stiffened her muscles against an instinctive flinch. "But I was wrong about you, too. You didn't understand. You let Orlando boss you around. Then I saw your post online today." Her face twisted again, this time in disgust and disappointment. "You're as horrible as the others."

"I only did that so I could meet the person I was inspiring."

"That's a lie."

"No. Really. It's *you* who inspire *me*. To follow through with your goals, no matter what the cost? That's true passion. And you did it all with an artistic flare."

"I thought the scarves were a nice touch." Charlotte touched the scarf around Fiona's neck, then ran the fabric through her finger-tips. "And they're a symbol that nobody will bind me anymore."

"DID YOU KILL CHARLOTTE?" GREG STALKED TOWARD ORLANDO.

He'd managed to pull the guest of honor into the conference room, away from the noise and crowd. He was ready to beat the truth out of the man, but that wasn't his style. Besides, there were witnesses. Noah and Holt had followed them.

But Orlando must have seen Greg's desperation and rage, because instead of using sarcasm and ego—his usual weapons—he flipped from arrogant bastard to amiable confidant. Unfortunately, it wasn't the confession Greg, Noah, and Holt had been expecting.

Orlando snorted. "Kill her? God, no. I fired her."

"Before or after she disappeared this morning?"

"Just about two hours ago. She came back to the hotel and went on some crazy rant about how she was done with people disre-specting her. Something about how anybody can say anything on social media, but that it wouldn't protect them. I told her to get my suit from the hotel's cleaners, and she laughed. *Laughed.* It was her fucking job, and she wasn't willing to do it, so I fired her."

Something hard and cold settled in Greg's gut, as if he'd swal-lowed a rock. "How long has Charlotte been your assistant?"

Orlando thought a moment. "Three years, maybe. I don't know. She was an art student who showed up at my door wanting a job. Looked up to me like she was some kind of mutt needing rescu-ing." He shrugged. "She did a good job for cheap, so I kept her."

He paced to the side table that held the coffee pot. "Did she go on the tour of the south with you, the one you told Fiona about?"

"Yeah. Why?"

He stopped as his eyes landed on a piece of paper, the one Charlotte had been doodling on, in the trash can. He picked it up and straightened it out. Among the various squiggles and faces she'd sketched were three jagged lines, like claw marks.

Greg whirled to Holt. "Keep him here. I have to find Fiona."

Noah was right on his heels and they spread out to search the sea of faces in the gallery. The flickering strobe lights, grim artwork, and thick crowding of costumed bodies assaulted his senses and slowed him down, but the urgency roiled up inside him. He needed to find Fiona *now*.

Where would a killer take her? Where could Charlotte get her alone? At some point, the killer had accessed the storage room to manipulate Orlando's artwork, using the tree to display the latest victim. Charlotte had been standing there that day. Would she have gone there again?

As Noah headed in the direction of Fiona's apartment, Greg took the opposite route. He pushed through the crowd and made it to the door that led out of the main gallery and to the back rooms.

After the noise of the party, the relative quiet and stillness of the hallway was a shock to his system. It was dark, too. He raced to the storage room door and listened, but couldn't hear anything beyond the muted throb of bass from the party. He drew his gun, turned the knob, and pushed open the door as quietly as possible. He quickly ducked inside and pressed himself against the wall. It was just as dark in the storage room as in the hallway. From somewhere in the back of the room, he heard a voice, but couldn't make out who was speaking or what was said. He crept around the pieces of artwork, praying he wouldn't knock anything over and draw attention to himself.

There! He could make out a figure in black. Charlotte? Her back was to him. There was some kind of club in her hands. As she raised it, the dim light reflected off the end, and he could make out razor-sharp claws.

"Stop!" he shouted, his gun aimed at the figure. She spun to face him, club raised. Charlotte's face was that of a crazed attacker. "Drop it," he ordered.

"Greg, don't," Fiona's soft voice came from behind Charlotte, on the ground.

*Fiona.* His heart flip-flopped in his chest. The rush of relief weakened his limbs, but he held his aim on his target. He took a quick look, needing to see Fiona. She struggled to her knees behind Charlotte, swaying a bit. From the light of a bathroom behind her, he could see blood dripped down her neck, near her ear. She was hurt and her hands were bound in front of her. *Goddamn it.*

"She's a killer," he bit out.

"I know, and she deserves to pay, but not this way. Charlotte, stop this," Fiona pleaded with the young woman. "Don't let what Orlando or anybody else did ruin you entirely. Don't let it hurt anyone else."

"They deserved it," Charlotte screamed. "They deserved to die, and you do, too. You're taking their side, *his* side." She glared at Greg. Suddenly, she spun and raised her weapon.

"Get down, Fi!" Greg shouted as he raised his own.

He saw Fiona dive to the side and land hard as he fired at Charlotte, aiming for the center of mass. His bullet struck her in the back. The club fell to the floor with a clatter and she crumpled. Fiona was crawling away, her movements awkward with her hands tied, but putting distance between her and Charlotte.

"Greg?" Noah called out from the storage room door. He came to stand beside Greg, his own gun drawn. He blinked as his eyes adjusted and landed on the black heap on the floor. "Is that Charlotte?"

"I shot her," Greg said. "She was about to kill Fiona."

Noah nodded and started moving toward Charlotte's body. "You take care of Fiona."

Greg holstered his weapon and kicked the club away from Charlotte before rushing to Fiona's side. He dropped to his knees beside her and took her hands.

"Jesus. Are those my cuffs?" He scrambled to get the key from the holder at his belt.

"She got them from my apartment." Fiona sent a frightened

glance toward Noah. "Please check on Vanessa. Charlotte said she walked her upstairs to lie down, but she also took Vanessa's phone to text me. I want to make sure she's okay."

"I'm right here," Vanessa said from the doorway. "Noah told me to stay out there."

"I'm not sure why I bothered," Noah said, a smile in his voice.

She stepped farther into the room. "Me either." Her eyes widened as her gaze landed on Fiona's bloodied face and neck. "What's going on?"

"Charlotte was the killer," Fiona said, gesturing to Charlotte's body.

"Oh, my God. Is she dead?"

Noah rose from where he was crouching over her. "There's a pulse. Go call for an ambulance."

Greg finally managed to unlock the cuffs and Fiona wrapped her arms around his neck, pressing her forehead into his neck. She was shaking within his embrace and he held her tight. Then again, it may have been him shaking.

After a long moment, she pulled back. "I just needed you for a minute. Now we can do your job."

"We?"

"I'll shut down the party and you'll take statements or arrest Charlotte, or whatever the hell needs to be done. I want to help those women find justice. I'm ready to give my statement." Her hair had come down and was wild around her face, except where blood from her head wound had matted it to the side of her neck.

Greg cursed. "I'm taking you to the hospital."

"I'm okay." She managed a tremulous smile. "I am. A little shaky, but that's why you're here. You're rock steady. My rock."

"You may have to convince me of that last part. I'm not feeling so rock steady at the moment." He was starting to shake now that the rush of adrenaline was over.

"I'll hold you until you are," she promised, wrapping him up in her arms again. "Until we both are," she said into his neck. "We make a good team."

"You're damn right." He took a deep breath filled with her scent to steady himself. "I'm still taking you to the hospital."

"Or we could just go back to bed. We should have stayed there, like you said earlier." Sirens were already sounding from the direction of the back alley. "Of course, that was the couch. This time, we'll try the bed."

He huffed out a laugh and then gave her a quick, hard kiss on the mouth. "No place I'd rather be. But first, the hospital. And then, when this is all over, I'm taking you on a date."

She laughed, and it was the most beautiful sound. "A date? Our last date didn't end so well."

"I was an idiot."

"But you've changed?" She gave him a teasing smile.

"Absolutely. You changed me."

"It had better not be a date at the hospital."

"A real date with food and wine and anything you want," he promised.

"Even some frivolous fun?"

"As long as it ends with you in my bed."

Her lips curved into the smile he'd come to love, the one he wanted to see first thing in the morning and last thing at night. "No place I'd rather be."

# EPILOGUE

*THREE MONTHS LATER*

CHICAGO WAS HELD FIRMLY IN JANUARY'S ICY GRIP WHEN VANESSA and Noah brought their daughter, Breanna Natalee Crandall, into Fiona's workshop for a rite of passage.

"This might get messy," Fiona warned.

"From what I've seen, she likes messy," Greg said.

"It's her first work of art and she's only nine weeks old," Vanessa said with a laugh. "I'd expect a bit of mess."

"There's nothing clean about having a baby," Noah said, but the sparkle in his eyes spoke of his pride and happiness.

They'd had an intense few months, but things were evening out. Charlotte had healed from her gunshot wound and was immediately carted off to prison, where she'd confessed to seven counts of murder as well as various other charges she'd incurred along the way, including the attempted murder of Fiona. In the meantime, Orlando had used his association with a serial killer to his benefit, and the fame had only added to his standing in the world of horror.

Fiona took the baby's bare feet, one at a time, and pressed them gently into the shallow pan of swirled colors of nontoxic paint before putting them against the canvas they were going to frame. Breanna chortled in her typical easygoing manner.

"She's already an art lover," Fiona said.

"I'm going to hang that over the crib," Vanessa said. She held Breanna while Fiona washed the baby's feet over the sink.

Fiona kissed the baby's clean toes and inhaled her soft scent. Some day, she'd have this, she vowed. She'd have love, and family, and everything she'd ever dreamed of. All signs indicated she would have it with Greg.

Vanessa turned the baby in her arms. "It'll look great near the mobile you made her. The metallic symbols make soft tinkling sounds when I spin it. She loves that. You're going to spoil her with all these unique works of art."

"And I'll keep spoiling her." Fiona had poured a lot of love into the mobile, and she had a lot more to give. "There's a lot of beauty in this world, and I want to make sure she knows it."

"And a lot of fun too," Greg said, coming up behind her and sliding his arms around her waist.

While the new parents bundled Breanna in a coat and blanket to prepare for their drive home, Greg turned Fiona in his arms and nuzzled her neck.

"I meant what I said last night," he said for her ears only. "I love you." The proof gleamed in his eyes as he met her gaze.

"And I meant it right back. I love you, too." She knew it was love. Just as she knew it was the lasting kind of love. The wicked night that had finally brought them together had been followed by months of beautiful nights in each other's arms. And there were many, many more wonderful, loving nights to come.

## ALSO BY ANNE MARIE BECKER

The Mindhunters Series
Only Fear
Avenging Angel
Deadly Bonds
Dark Deeds
Acceptable Risk
End Game

Mindhunters Novellas
Christmas Stalking
Until Death
Wicked Night

The Redemption Club Series
Stacking the Deck
Sleight of Hand
Raising the Stakes

# THE MINDHUNTERS SERIES

## SEE HOW IT ALL BEGAN...

ONLY FEAR
(The Mindhunters, Book 1)

After a violent incident with a patient leaves scars on both her mind and body, psychiatrist Dr. Maggie Levine craves isolation. A radio talk show host seems to be the perfect profession, a job where she can help people from a distance while staying safe. When a strange caller begins stalking her on the air and murdering people to get her attention, Maggie realizes she can no longer close herself off from the outside world.

A personal security expert, former Secret Service Agent Ethan Townsend is no stranger to tracking down the most violent monsters of society and bringing them to justice. Still, it will take all of Ethan's skills to protect his new assignment, the irresistible Maggie, from a man intent on teaching her the ultimate lesson in fear...

Books in the Mindhunters Series:
ONLY FEAR (Book 1)

AVENGING ANGEL (Book 2)
DEADLY BONDS (Book 3)
DARK DEEDS (Book 4)
ACCEPTABLE RISK (Book 5)
END GAME (Book 6)
DEADLY HOLIDAYS (A Collection of Novellas)

# WELCOME TO THE REDEMPTION CLUB...

STACKING THE DECK (Book 1)

In a city built for sin, the Redemption Club is a secret society that exists to fulfill a person's darkest desires—including murder games —for a price.

Raised off the grid by an anti-government group, Skye Hamilton puts her resourcefulness and survival training to good use taking the dangerous tasks nobody else wants. When a job searching for a runaway teen brings Redemption Club members gunning for her, putting those she cares about in danger, she'll risk everything to fight the enemy. Including her heart.

Jared Bennigan, Las Vegas bodyguard to the elite, accepted his latest job hoping it would lead to his missing sister. All evidence points to his client as the last person to have seen her, but he's not the only one looking for a woman who disappeared. Skye's enticing blue eyes contradict her tough, distrusting exterior, revealing an intriguing combination of vulnerability and intelligence. But those eyes are watching his client—through her rifle's scope.

To find both missing women, Jared will need to convince Skye —who plays a wicked game of hard-to-get—to be his partner. And with the Redemption Club intent on making Skye the prey in a human hunting expedition, her skills, and her trust in Jared, will be put to the test. It's the ultimate game of survival of the fittest. But who will win?

AVAILABLE NOW!

The Redemption Club Trilogy:
    STACKING THE DECK
    SLEIGHT OF HAND
    RAISING THE STAKES

# ABOUT THE AUTHOR

Anne Marie has always been fascinated by people—inside and out —which led to degrees in Biology, Chemistry, Psychology, and Counseling. Her passion for understanding the human race is now satisfied by her roles as mother, wife, daughter, sister, and award-winning author of romantic suspense.

She writes to reclaim her sanity.

Find ways to connect with Anne Marie at www.AnneMarie-Becker.com. There, sign up for her newsletter to receive the latest information regarding books, appearances, and giveaways.